Lowcountry Summer

2-in-1 Edition with Sanctuary Cove and Angels Landing

Rochelle Alers

FOREVER

NEW YORK   BOSTON

Copyright © 2021 by Rochelle Alers
Sanctuary Cove copyright © 2012 by Rochelle Alers
Angels Landing copyright © 2012 by Rochelle Alers
Cover design by Daniela Medina. Cover copyright © 2021 by Hachette Book Group, Inc.

Hachette Book Group supports the right to free expression and the value of copyright. The purpose of copyright is to encourage writers and artists to produce the creative works that enrich our culture.

The scanning, uploading, and distribution of this book without permission is a theft of the author's intellectual property. If you would like permission to use material from the book (other than for review purposes), please contact permissions@hbgusa.com. Thank you for your support of the author's rights.

Forever
Hachette Book Group
1290 Avenue of the Americas, New York, NY 10104
read-forever.com
twitter.com/readforeverpub

Sanctuary Cove and *Angels Landing* originally published in 2012 by Forever.
First 2-in-1 edition: November 2021

Forever is an imprint of Grand Central Publishing. The Forever name and logo are trademarks of Hachette Book Group, Inc.

The publisher is not responsible for websites (or their content) that are not owned by the publisher.

The Hachette Speakers Bureau provides a wide range of authors for speaking events. To find out more, go to www.hachettespeakersbureau.com or call (866) 376-6591.

Library of Congress Control Number: 2021942325

ISBN: 978-1-5387-0719-7 (trade pbk. 2-in-1)

Printed in the United States of America

LSC-C

Printing 1, 2021

Also by Rochelle Alers

The Cavanaugh Island Series

Sanctuary Cove
Angels Landing
Haven Creek
Magnolia Drive
Home for the Holidays (a novella)
Cherry Lane

Sanctuary Cove

For Nancy Coffey, with sincere gratitude for the many wonderful years of friendship and wisdom.

And for Latoya Smith, who helped to make Cavanaugh Island come alive.

A time to weep, and a time to laugh; a time to mourn and a time to dance.

Ecclesiastes 3:4

Chapter One

⌒

"Barbara, are you sure you don't mind looking after Whitney and Crystal for the week? You know I can always take them with me."

"Deborah Robinson! Do you realize how many times you've asked the same question and I've given you the same answer? No, I don't mind at all. Now go before you miss your ferry. And no cell phone calls from the car."

"Thanks for everything," Deborah whispered, hugging her friend. "I'll call you from the island."

Deborah ran across the front lawn, jumped into her car, fastened the seatbelt and pulled away from the curb. Smiling at years of happy memories as she drove through the back streets of Charleston, Deborah made it to the pier before sailing time. She drove onto the ferry, turned off the car, and got out to stand at the rail, instantly refreshed by the cool breeze. This time her return to the small community of Sanctuary Cove wouldn't be for a weekend or mini-vacation, but to air out the house she'd inherited from her grandparents in order to make it her home and to look at a vacant store she'd rented where she'd open her bookstore.

Two blasts from the ferry's horn echoed it was time to sail; a man on the pier tossed the thick coil of hemp to another worker on the ferry, freeing it; below deck, engines belched, coughed, and rumbled. There came another horn blast and the ferryman deftly steered the boat through the narrow inlet until he reached open water.

Resting her elbows on the rail, Deborah watched as steeples and spires of the many churches rising above the landscape disappeared from view. As the boat headed in a southeast direction, she stared at the island shorelines of Kiawah, Seabrook and Edisto Islands before the ferryboat slowed, chugging slowly and docking at Cavanaugh Island. She was the last one off the boat, and waved to the captain as he tipped his hat.

Driving off the ferry, she felt herself blinking back tears, remembering the last time she'd come here. It had been Thanksgiving and she, Louis and their kids had decided to celebrate the holiday at the Cove rather than in Charleston. Louis never could have imagined as he'd carved turkey that a week later he would become embroiled in a scandal. That he would be seen in a compromising position with one of his female students.

Despite declaring that he was simply comforting her, and there was nothing improper going on between him and the student, Louis Robinson was suspended pending a school board hearing. Tensions and emotions were fever-pitched as Charlestonians formed opposing factions while Louis awaited his fate. Deborah blamed those who were quick to judge her husband for his death, and all of their condolences fell on deaf ears when the truth was finally revealed. The truth had come too late. She'd lost her husband of eighteen years and Whitney and Crystal their father.

Slowing and coming to a complete stop, she reached for a tissue and blotted the tears, praying for a time when the tears wouldn't come without warning, or so easily. It took several minutes, but after taking a few deep breaths, she was back in control.

Stepping on the accelerator, Deborah drove slowly along the paved road, bordered on both sides by palmetto trees and ancient oaks draped with Spanish moss.

She maneuvered onto the quaint Main Street and suddenly felt another rush of sadness, but this one was not personal. Like so many small towns across the United States she realized the Cove was slowly dying. She noticed more boarded-up storefronts; the sidewalks were cracked and even the Cove Inn, a boardinghouse and one of the grandest houses on the island, needed a new coat of white paint.

Deborah drove into the small parking lot behind Jack's Fish House. After only a cup of coffee earlier that morning, she needed to eat before throwing herself into the chore of cleaning the house. There were more than a dozen cars in the lot; some she recognized as belonging to local fishermen.

The winter temperature on Cavanaugh was at least ten degrees warmer than in Charleston, so she left her wool jacket in the car. Reaching for her purse she walked up from the lot to the entrance of the restaurant, an establishment that was known for serving some of the best seafood in the Lowcountry.

The familiar interior of Jack's Fish House hadn't

changed in decades. Tables hewn from tree trunks bore the names and initials of countless lovers, ex-lovers, and those who wanted to achieve immortality by carving their names into a piece of wood. Only the light fixtures had changed, from bulbs covered by frosted globes to hanging lamps with Tiffany-style shades. A trio of ceiling fans turned at the lowest speed to offset the buildup of heat coming from the kitchen each time the café doors swung open. The year before, the Jacksons had added a quartet of flat screen televisions, primarily for the fishermen who went out at dawn and returned midday with their nets laden with crabs, oysters, and shrimp.

Deborah walked past restaurant regulars and a few strange faces to sit at a round table for two in a far corner. The mouthwatering aromas coming from dishes carried by the waitstaff triggered a hunger she hadn't felt in weeks. She knew she'd lost too much weight, and although she had cooked for Whitney and Crystal, she would take only a few forkfuls of food before feeling full.

Suddenly, a shadow fell over the table and her head popped up. Luvina Jackson, wearing a pair of overalls and a bibbed apron, arms crossed under her ample bosom, gave Deborah a sad smile. Her gray hair was covered with a hairnet. "Stand up, baby, and let Vina hold you. I'm so sorry about Louis."

Deborah couldn't hold back tears as she sank into the comforting softness of Luvina's well-rounded figure. The smell of yeast and lily of the valley wafted in her nostrils, a fragrance Luvina had worn for as long as Deborah remembered.

"Thank you, Miss Vina."

Luvina rocked her back and forth. "You know the Cove

would have turned out for you if you hadn't had a private service."

"I know that, Miss Vina. But I would've lost it if the hypocrites who were so quick to judge Louis would've shown up to pay their so-called respects."

"All you had to do was say the word and we would've been there for you with bells on. Ain't no way we gonna let dem two-face, egg-suckin' vultures hurt one of our own. We would have turned it out."

"Then we all would've been on the front page of *The State* or *The Post and Courier*, not to mention footage on the local television news," Deborah murmured.

"I just want you to know we would have been there for you, baby. How are your kids doing?"

Easing out of her embrace, Deborah met Luvina's eyes. "They're coping as well as they can. But kids are kids and they are much more resilient than grown folks. They're spending the week with friends until school begins again."

"Thank goodness for that. Enough talk. I know you came in here to git somethin' to eat. Whatcha want?"

Deborah smiled. Even though she'd been born and raised in Charleston, coming back to the Cove and listening to the different inflections interspersed with the Gullah dialect made her feel as if she had come home. "Do you have any okra gumbo?"

Luvina's broad dark face, with features that bore her Gullah ancestry, softened as she smiled. "I jest put up a long pot earlier dis mornin'."

Deborah returned Luvina's smile. She liked Jack's okra gumbo because they fried the okra with oil to reduce the slime and added corn to the savory dish. "I'll have a bowl with a couple of buttered biscuits."

"Do you want rice?"

"No, thank you. But I'm going to order something to take home for dinner."

"Whatcha want fo' dinner?"

"Anything that's good, Miss Vina."

Eyes wide, Luvina stared at Deborah. "Now you got to know that everything we makes at Jack's is good. Have you been gone so long that you forgot that?"

"No, ma'am."

"Let me put somethin' together for you. You like oxtails?"

"I love them."

"Good. Then I'll fix you some oxtails with ham hocks. I'll also give you some rice, because you need some meat on your bones. Collards and a slice of my coconut cake should fill you right up."

"That sounds good, Miss Vina."

"Rest yourself and I'll be right back."

When Deborah sat down, closed her eyes and pressed the back of her head to the wall behind her, she realized she was hungry and unbelievably tired. Tired from stress that had worn her down like a steady rush of water over a pile of rocks.

Her parents had come up from Florida for the funeral and had all but begged her to move down there, but Deborah told them she couldn't uproot Whitney and Crystal. Whitney was in his last year of high school, and fifteen-year-old Crystal would have problems adjusting and making friends at a new school. Crystal had taken her father's death much harder than Whitney, who'd grieved in private.

Her musings were interrupted when Luvina's grand-daughter walked over to the table with a large glass of sweet tea and a plate with two biscuits. "Sorry about Mr. Robinson, Miss Deborah. All the kids cried for days when we heard he'd drowned. He was the best math teacher in the whole high school."

Deborah smiled at the girl, who lived on the island but went to high school with her children. "Thank you, Johnetta. How are you?"

"I'm good, Miss Deborah. Right now I'm applying to nursing schools up north, but my momma and daddy don't want me to leave the state, so I have to apply to one here."

"Charleston Southern University has a school of nursing. You can live here while you're taking classes. That would save you a lot of money."

Johnetta smiled, displaying the braces on her teeth. "You're right. I could take the ferry or get my father to drop me off when he goes to work."

"That sounds like a plan."

"Thank you, Miss Deborah. I'm going to go and bring out your food."

Deborah stared at the tall girl, who'd at one time admitted she liked Whitney, but he'd acted as if she didn't exist. She'd wanted to tell Johnetta that Whitney was more interested in sports than he was in a relationship with a girl. It wasn't as if he didn't like girls, but sports and academics were his priority.

Johnetta returned with a bowl of okra gumbo and after the first spoonful Deborah felt as if she'd been revived. The soup was delicious, the biscuits light and buttery and the sweet tea brewed to perfection. She'd tried over and over, but whenever she brewed tea it was either too strong or too weak. Too strong meant adding copious amounts of sugar and too weak made it taste like sugar water.

She finished her lunch and paid the check, reminding Johnetta she'd come back to pick up her takeout order. Leaving Jack's, Deborah strolled along Main Street, stopping to stare through the windows of stores and shops. Grass had sprouted up through the cracks in the sidewalk. There had been a time when there were no cracks and the only thing that had littered the sidewalks or curbs was sand and palmetto leaves. The sand-littered streets added to the charm of the town, but dead leaves and debris were swept away by shopkeepers every morning.

She continued her stroll, turning onto Moss Alley, and then came to a complete stop. Moss Alley was appropriately named because of the large oak draped in Spanish moss on the corner. Shading her eyes, Deborah peered through the glass window of a store that had once been a gift shop. The space wasn't particularly wide, but deep enough for her bookstore. And what made it even more attractive was it had a second floor—space where she could store her inventory.

A flutter of excitement raced through her. It was perfect for The Parlor. It was off the main street, but on the corner where anyone walking or driving by would notice it. With hand-painted letters on the plate-glass, a colorful awning, and furniture resembling a parlor, it would generate enough curiosity to draw in customers.

She walked down the street, stopping at the opposite end of the block. Smiling, she waved through the window of the Muffin Corner at the woman behind the counter, who beckoned her.

She opened the screen door and was met with tantalizing aromas of fruit and freshly made cakes, pies, and donuts. Lester and Mabel Kelly had opened the shop the year before. Both had worked as pastry chefs for a hotel chain, but had tired of the frantic pace of baking for catered parties and returned to the Cove to open the Muffin Corner.

Mabel Kelly flashed a gap-toothed smile when Deborah walked in. Coming from behind the counter, she hugged her. "How's it going, girl?"

Deborah returned the hug. "I'm good."

Pulling back, Mabel narrowed her eyes. She and Deborah were the same age, thirty-eight, but there was sadness in Deborah's eyes that made her appear older. "I'm sorry about Louis, Debs. It's a damn shame folks accused him of something he didn't do, and would never think of doing. I can tell you that folks here were ready to get in their cars and start some mess Charleston hasn't seen in a while."

"I know that, Mabel."

"Is that why you decided to have a private funeral?"

"It was one of the reasons."

"You know I called your house but some woman named Barbara answered. Damn, you thought I was trying to set up a lunch date with President Obama the way she interrogated me. In the end, I told her to let you know I'd called."

"She did, Mabel. And I do appreciate you calling."

"Can I get you something?"

"No thanks. I just came from Jack's."

Physically Deborah and Mabel were complete opposites. Mabel was barely five foot and had what people call birthing hips, yet she'd never had any children. She said she didn't want any because she'd helped her father raise six younger siblings after her mother got hooked on drugs. The year she'd turned fourteen her mother had taken the ferry to Charleston to score and never came back. There were reports that someone had seen her in Savannah, strung-out, but it was never confirmed.

The wind chime over the door tinkled musically. "Excuse me, Debs," Mabel whispered. "Let me take care of this customer, then we'll sit and talk." Her smile grew wider. "Afternoon, Asa. Can I get you to sample today's special along with your black coffee with a shot of espresso?"

"No thank you, Mabel. I'll just have coffee," she heard the man reply.

Deborah sat, enjoying the aromas of the shop before her gaze lingered on Mabel's customer. He was a tall, slender, middle-aged black man. Though he was dressed casually in khakis, long-sleeved light-blue button-down shirt, and black leather slip-ons, Deborah couldn't take her eyes off the handsome stranger. He didn't look familiar, so either he was a newcomer, visitor, or tourist. Cavanaugh Island didn't get many tourists during the winter months, but the balmy seventy-degree temperatures attracted a few snow-birds from the northeast and Midwest.

Without warning, he turned and caught her staring. Their gazes met and fused, and they shared a smile. He continued to stare and Deborah couldn't control the rush of heat in her face; she lowered her eyes and didn't glance up again until the wind chime tinkled when the door closed behind the very attractive man.

"I like what you've done with the shop," Deborah said to Mabel when she joined her at the table.

"We don't have a Starbucks here in the Cove, so Lester and I decided to offer something other than regular coffee to go along with the muffins. Business has really picked up since we put in the tables. We mostly get retirees who order their favorite muffin, coffee, and read the newspaper whenever it gets too hot to sit in the square, or during rainy weather. It's a big hit, especially with the snowbirds." Mabel bit her lip. "If it wasn't for the snowbirds businesses in the Cove would really have a hard time staying open."

"It's that bad?" Deborah asked.

"Just say it could be better. Most of us are hanging on by the skin of our teeth, waiting for the summer season. Take Asa Monroe, the man who just left."

"What about him?" she asked. For a reason she couldn't fathom, Deborah wanted to know more about the stranger who unknowingly intrigued her.

"He rents a suite at the Cove Inn, been here about six weeks. He eats lunch at Jack's, sends his laundry out and comes in every day for his black coffee with a shot of espresso. Multiply that by twenty or thirty snowbirds and it's enough revenue to keep small shopkeepers afloat until the summer season."

Deborah nodded. "I noticed a few more vacant stores since the last time I was here."

"The gift shop closed up last month."

"I just rented it."

A beat passed before Mabel said, "You're kidding?"

"No I'm not. I'm moving to the Cove and—"

"Permanently?"

Deborah nodded again. "Yes. I'm also moving my bookstore. I called the chamber and they gave me a listing of the vacant stores. Once I found out the gift shop had closed, I realized it would be perfect. It has more square footage than my Charleston store and having a second floor is a bonus."

Mabel leaned closer. "What about your kids?"

"Nothing's going to change, Mabel, except that they'll live here instead of in Charleston. They'll still go to the same high school and hang out with their same friends."

"What are you going to do with your house on the mainland?"

"I'm putting it up for sale. I know the real estate market is soft," Deborah said quickly when Mabel opened her mouth, "but I'm willing to accept a reasonable offer because I don't want to rent it." She glanced at her watch, then stood up, Mabel rising with her. "I have to get back to the house. I'll drop by again in a couple of days."

"How long are you staying?"

"I'm leaving New Year's Eve. I promised the kids I'd be back in time to bring in the new year with them." Extending her arms, Deborah hugged Mabel.

She left the Muffin Corner, stopping again at the vacant store on Moss Alley that was soon to be the new home of The Parlor bookstore.

Chapter Two

Asa Monroe was sitting at a bistro table outside of the Muffin Corner sipping his coffee when he saw the woman with the infectious smile walk out and head in the opposite direction. Her smile was like a ray of sunshine, spreading over her face and lighting up her eyes. And that body... Asa couldn't take his gaze off of her. She was the first woman to intrigue him since his arrival in Sanctuary Cove. As soon as she disappeared from his line of vision, he got up and walked back into the pastry shop, curiosity getting the best of him.

"Can I help you with something else?" Mabel Kelly asked when he dropped the empty cup into a plastic-lined wastebasket, a puzzled expression on her face.

"The lady that was just in here...I—"

"You must be talking about Mrs. Robinson?"

Asa nodded. Mabel referring to her as Mrs. Robinson

meant that she was married, even though he'd noticed she hadn't worn a ring. "This is the first time I've seen her. I was wondering if she lives here."

"Deborah"—she paused, amusement crossing her features—"just told me that she's moving to the Cove permanently come the first of the year. She and I were what kids nowadays call BFFs. I used to count down the days when school was out for her to come from Charleston to stay on the Cove with her grandmother. And once the summer was over and school started we would cry like we were never going to see each other again."

"Did you ever stop crying?" Asa joked.

Throwing back her head, Mabel laughed. "The year we turned twelve we decided we were too old to cry and stopped."

"Did you stay in touch after summer vacation ended?" Asa didn't know why he continued to question Mabel about Deborah Robinson, because after all she was a married woman.

Mabel nodded. "We designed our own greeting cards with peel-off stickers and mailed them to each other."

"Why didn't you call?"

"I'm one of seven, so with six other kids in the house the phone was always busy, unlike today when kids have their own cell phones."

The tinkling of the wind chime preempted Asa from asking another question. He smiled at Mabel. "Thanks, I'll see you tomorrow." Turning on his heel, he nodded to Eddie Wilkes, editor of the *Sanctuary Chronicle*, the island's biweekly newspaper.

Rather than return to the bench outside, he headed in the direction of the beach. His routine since his arrival on the island had become predictable. After lunch he came to the Muffin Corner for coffee, then spent the next hour strolling along the beach. This was nothing like his demanding life-style in Dover, Delaware. Sanctuary Cove had no fast food restaurants, malls, department stores, traffic jams, or even street lights. Life was slow, laid-back and stress-free.

When he'd come to Cavanaugh Island nearly two months ago, Asa wasn't certain what he'd been looking for until he'd checked into the Cove Inn. What he needed was peace. Staring out the window of his suite he saw palmetto trees, a stretch of beach, and the ocean—a landscape so different from the one in the Dover suburb where he'd lived and practiced medicine. Even the air smelled different.

The hardest thing for Asa to get used to was the quiet. As soon as the sun set it was as if Sanctuary Cove went to sleep. Even those who sat on the benches at the town square talked quietly to each other, as if they didn't want to disturb the stillness of the evening. He'd heard sounds that were completely foreign to his ears, and when he'd asked someone about roaring noises he was told they came from the alligators in a nearby swamp.

A friend had accused him of running away when he'd closed his medical practice and sold his house. What his friend didn't understand was that he couldn't stay there any longer, not with the memories of his family haunting him relentlessly. It was as if he could still hear his son's childish laughter through the halls, or his wife's knocking on his home office door to tell him dinner was ready. The only time they hadn't sat down to eat as a family was the one night a week when he offered evening hours. A shudder worked its way through Asa, and he shook his head trying to cleanse his mind of the past.

November made it a year since he'd lost his wife and son in a horrific automobile accident, when the car she'd been driving skidded off an icy road. A year in which he'd become a widower and a nomad, traveling from state to state, city to city while awaiting approval of his application to Doctors Without Borders.

Sanctuary Cove had become just that—a sanctuary—because it was here that he'd discovered the peace that had eluded him since that fateful day when he'd lost the two people he loved most.

Reaching into her handbag, Deborah took out the key to the vacant storefront that had been mailed to her along with the executed lease. She unlocked the front door, leaving it open, and flipped a wall switch. Track lighting cast a warm glow over the empty space with walls painted a soft, calming pistachio green.

She had lost track of the number of times she'd been inside the gift shop, and when she'd spoken to the agent handling the property she knew unequivocally that she wanted to rent the store. She'd met with the agent in Charleston, signed the necessary documents, and written checks to cover the rent for the first and last month of a two-year lease. She figured she'd know within two years if the bookstore would be a success. If not, she would go out of business and apply for a teaching position at the local school.

Deborah felt a shiver of excitement as she envisioned shelves stacked with books, tables, chairs, loveseats, and floor and table lamps that would reflect the bookstore's name. There was enough space for the concert piano that had once belonged to her maternal grandmother, and for cozy reading corners.

A door at the back led to a staircase. Deborah counted nine steps before she stood on a landing that opened out to a studio-type apartment. An antique iron bed, sans mattress, occupied one corner, a sofa and matching chair filled another; there was an efficiency kitchen with a refrigerator, stove, and sink. A table with two chairs made up the dining area, and when she opened a door she discovered a small bathroom. She touched a wall switch and light from a floor lamp cast a soft glow over the dust-covered floor. Two grimy windows faced Main Street and another two overlooked Moss Alley. The walls were off-white and like those on the first floor appeared as if they had been recently painted.

She opened one more door to a flight of stairs that led down to the rear of the store. The apartment needed a good cleaning, but with a new mattress for the bed and a wardrobe to store clothes it would be in move-in condition should she decide to rent out the space. Closing that door, she walked to the other entrance, leaving the imprint of her shoes in the dust as she descended the staircase to the first floor. Stepping outside, she locked *her* new bookstore and walked back to Jack's Fish House.

About twenty minutes later, Deborah unlocked the door to her house, shouldering it open as she cradled a large paper sack to her chest. Something told her that Luvina had added to her takeout order. The buildup of heat inside the two-story, three-bedroom house was overwhelming. Placing the bags on a table in the narrow entryway, she began opening the windows on the first floor. One window in the dining room resisted her efforts before she remembered it was the one Louis had promised to repair.

She raced up the staircase and opened windows in the

bedrooms. An ocean breeze filtered through the screens, gently lifting the sheers; within minutes the scent of salt water had dispelled the slightly musty smell. Five weeks. It'd been five weeks since she'd prepared a meal in the kitchen or slept in the queen-sized bed, but so much had changed in that time that it could have been five years.

Blowing out her breath, she retraced her steps to put away the food she'd ordered from Jack's. She was right. Luvina had added containers of shrimp, nut and apple, and potato salads.

There was also a Styrofoam container with fried chicken and Jack's celebrated poppin' fried shrimp.

"Thank you, Miss Vina," she whispered. It was obvious Luvina wasn't going to let her go hungry.

Deborah opened the refrigerator, storing the containers. Boxes of baking soda had kept it fresh smelling, although she'd also emptied it of all foodstuffs before leaving after the Thanksgiving weekend. The refrigerator had been left running because they'd planned to return to spend Christmas and the school recess on the island.

She mentally outlined what she needed to do, but first things first. She called Barbara to check on her children, and was told they had gone bowling with Barbara's son and daughter. Deborah hung up, not wanting to appear an anxious, clinging mother.

As soon as she ended the call, her cell phone rang. Deborah smiled when she recognized the number on the display. It was the real-estate broker handling the sale of her home. "Hi, Sherilee. Please give me some good news."

"I have very good news. A young couple with twin boys met your asking price. Believe it or not, I'm sitting here staring at a bank check for the full amount."

"What!"

"You heard me."

"What did they do? Rob a bank?"

"Close," Sherilee crooned. "Her father owns a bank. He wanted her to buy some monstrosity with double-digit rooms, but she'd grown up in what amounts to a mansion and she didn't want that for her children."

Deborah's smile was dazzling. "Good for her *and* good for me." Her house hadn't been on the market two weeks and she had a buyer. That also meant she had to pack up eighteen years of memories. She also had to pack up her store and make arrangements to have the books and shelves transported to Sanctuary Cove. "When do you think we'll close?"

"I'm hoping it will happen within two weeks."

"Whether it happens or not, I'm still moving."

"I understand why you're doing it, Deborah," Sherilee said sadly before continuing. "On a happier note, I also have some more good news. I just handled the sale of a house that belonged to an eighty-eight-year-old woman. Her great-grandchildren found a couple of boxes of old books in a closet, some dating back to the thirties and forties. I immediately thought of you. They were going to throw them out, but I managed to salvage them. They're here in my cubicle if you want them."

Deborah could hardly contain her excitement. "Sherilee, I love you for looking out for me."

"Come on, Deborah. We go way back, and I know you'd do the same for me."

"You know I would," she said with complete sincerity. Deborah and Sherilee had been roommates at Bennington College. Both were southern girls away from home for the first time, and during their second year they began a friendship that had lasted two decades.

"When are you coming back to Charleston?"

"I'd planned to return New Year's Eve, but it looks like I'm coming back sooner. I have to arrange to have the house and bookstore packed up."

"What are you going to do with your furniture?" Sherilee asked.

"I'm going to take mostly personal items like china, silver, crystal, and a few chairs for the bookstore, and donate the rest. I'll red tag everything I'm taking to the Cove, so if there is something you want feel free to take it."

"I have a former client who lost practically everything in a house fire. Would you mind if I picked up some things for her?" Sherilee asked. "What makes things so difficult is that she just went through a very nasty divorce and her ex won't give her one penny above what he pays for child support."

The house on the Cove was fully furnished; she'd had the plumbing and wiring updated and had replaced all the floors two years ago. The refrigerator, washer, and dryer were less than a year old and only one window in the dining room needed repair.

"As soon as I get back and inventory the house she can come over and pick out what she needs."

"God bless you, Deborah."

Again a rush of tears filled her eyes. She wiped them away with the back of her hand. "He has, Sherilee. I'll call you when I get back to Charleston." She ended the call before breaking down completely.

During the moments when she didn't wallow in self-pity, Deborah realized although she'd lost her husband she was grateful she still had her children. Her own mother had miscarried three times before she was able to carry to term, resulting in Deborah's birth. Pearl Williams had tried again to have another child, but when she miscarried a fourth time she opted for a hysterectomy.

Bringing her legs up, Deborah rested her feet on the edge of the chair, buried her head on her knees, and cried. She cried for what was and would never be again. She cried until she was spent, then got up and went into the half-bath off the kitchen to splash cold water on her face. No more crying, no more self-pity. She had to be strong for herself and her children. They were depending on her to take care of them and she would. It was something she'd promised the first time she'd held her son and daughter in her arms.

Later, lying in bed, Deborah's mind continued to wander, making her restless. Rolling over onto her belly she closed her eyes, willing sleep to claim her tired mind and exhausted body. She counted slowly, reaching one hundred sixty-three, and she was still wide awake. After tossing and turning restlessly, she got out of bed and went downstairs to make a cup of hot chocolate. The warm liquid managed to relax her enough that when she got back into bed she fell asleep within minutes of her head touching the pillow.

"What are you doing, Barbara?" Deborah asked when she was practically pushed out the door. She'd gotten up early to make the trip to Charleston and pick up the kids from Barbara's house, but barely had a chance to ring the bell before Barbara's front door flew open.

"Keep your voice down. We have to talk—at your house. Please."

She'd never known her friend to plead for anything, and there was a look in her eyes that indicated something was wrong. "Okay."

Moments later, Deborah sat opposite Barbara on matching loveseats in her family room. "You want *me* to tell *your* husband that I'm inviting you and your children to Sanctuary Cove for New Year's Eve?"

Barbara nodded, a wealth of salt-and-pepper twists moving around her round face with the motion. The registered nurse had begun graying at nineteen and now at forty was almost completely gray. "My numbskull of a husband is talking about hosting an open house get-together at our place. And, you know who he wants to invite?"

Deborah rolled her eyes upward. "Don't tell me some of the high school teachers?"

"Exactly. I don't know what Terrell was thinking about. He knows I'd invited you to spend the holiday with us."

Clasping her hands between her denim-covered knees, Deborah leaned forward. Terrell Nash was a guidance counselor and assistant football coach at the same school where Louis had taught math. "It's not the end of the world, Barbara. I can stay home."

"No!"

"Yes!"

"I'm not going to let you stay home by yourself. It's too soon."

"Too soon for what? And what are you afraid of, Barbara? That I'm going to become unhinged and harm myself because this will be the first New Year's Eve in twenty years that I'll spend alone?" Biting her lip, Barbara nodded. "Don't worry about me. I'll be all right."

"There's no way I'm going to suck up to a bunch of

fake-ass people because they just happen to work with my husband. I've been trying to change his mind. The only consolation is he still hasn't called anyone to invite them to drop in for drinks and hors d'oeuvres."

"Not dealing with Louis's former colleagues is my choice. It shouldn't be yours."

"I made it mine, Deborah, when some of them got in my face because I'd defended Louis. And now my husband wants to invite these hypocrites into my home. What the hell is he thinking?" Barbara enunciated each word. "And you know how my kids love going to Sanctuary Cove."

Deborah stared at her friend. If she'd had a sister she would've wanted her to be Barbara Nash. She didn't know what she would've done if her neighbor hadn't run interference for her when members of the press camped outside her door, seeking photographs of her and her children once the girl whom Louis was allegedly involved with had revealed she was pregnant. Barbara had called her police officer brother, who had threatened the media with trespassing if they didn't leave Deborah's property. And it was Barbara who fed Whitney and Crystal when Deborah couldn't get out of bed, and Barbara who had been with her when she went to the morgue to identify Louis's body.

"Okay. I'm officially inviting you and your family to Sanctuary Cove for the New Year's weekend. We'll take my car and Whitney's. That way you won't have to pay the outrageous parking permit fee."

Barbara's light brown eyes sparkled like newly minted copper pennies, and a smile spread across her tawny brown face. "I've already shopped for food, so I'll pack up everything in cooler chests and bring it along."

"Do you think Terrell will go along with this?"

"All he has to hear is 'Sanctuary Cove' and he's in the car ready to go."

Deborah nodded. It was Wednesday and it'd been two days since she'd spoken to Sherilee. She would've spent the week on the Cove, but had decided to come back to Charleston earlier than Friday to start packing up the house. "We'll leave Friday morning after noon."

Deborah sat staring at the photos on the fireplace mantel after she heard the door close behind her neighbor. The house was eerily silent without Crystal and Whitney. Whenever they were home the refrigerator door opened and closed like an accordion, music spilled out from ear buds and clatter filled the kitchen, since they preferred doing their homework at the dining table instead of at the desks in their bedrooms. The instant Deborah announced dinner was ready the books would disappear and together they'd wash up and set the table.

She stood up when she heard a door slam, then Whitney's voice, deep and resonant. When had it changed? "Whitney. I'm in the family room."

"Aunt Barbara told me you were back. I thought you weren't coming home until Friday." Tall and broad shouldered, seventeen-year-old Whitney had grown into a fine young man. He'd inherited his mother's fine features and hair texture. Leaning down, he kissed his mother's cheek, then folded his long frame down opposite her.

"Um, Whitney, did you actually buy jeans with ripped knees?"

"Yep. They're awesome."

"Oh . . . well."

"Is it true we're going to the Cove for New Year's?"

"Yes, Whitney. I thought it would be nice to bring in the New Year there."

He smiled and an elusive dimple showed in his right cheek. "I think it would be nice if we moved there now."

"I'm shocked you don't want to wait until the house is sold."

"Why are you so surprised, Mom? It's not as if we have to sell this house before we can move into Grandma's."

"Go get Crystal and tell her to pack enough clothes to last the weekend and all of next week. You do the same. When we drive Aunt Barbara and her family back you can bring anything you want to use on the Cove."

Whitney stood and gave his mom a firm hug and kiss. "Thanks, Mom."

Deborah pounded his hard back. "You're very welcome, Whit. Now, go and tell Crystal to come home and pack," she repeated when he finally released her.

Pushing to her feet, she walked over to the window overlooking the flower garden she'd begun the year Crystal was born. Each year for the past fourteen she had added another variety of flowers on Crystal's birthday. She sighed, realizing the ritual would end when they moved.

Celebrations would continue, but not in Charleston.

Chapter Three

"Welcome to the new Parlor Bookstore!"

Deborah opened the door, flipped the light switch, and stood aside to allow Barbara, Crystal, and thirteen-year-old Janelle Nash to enter the space that was to become her bookstore. Terrell, his son Nate, and Whitney were on their way to Jack's to reserve a table for their pre–New Year's Eve dinner. She had decided not to head over to the Abundant Life Church for the night watch service.

"What do you think?" Deborah could barely hide her excitement.

"It smells nice, Mom," Crystal said, hugging Deborah.

Deborah gave her daughter a tender smile. "Thank you."

"Can we look around, Mom?" Crystal asked.

Deborah shared a glance with Barbara, who nodded. "Yes. But be careful when you go upstairs. There's a light switch on the right wall. Make certain you turn it on before you go up."

"So, it's real," Barbara stated in a quiet tone.

Deborah nodded. "It's very real. I didn't tell you, but I have a buyer for the house. A young married couple with twin boys and they're paying cash."

"Damn! What are they into? Drugs?"

"Be nice, though I have to admit I thought they robbed a bank at first," she chided. "Her father just happens to own one."

Looping her arm through her soon-to-be ex-neighbor's arm, Deborah steered Barbara to the door that led to the upstairs apartment. Crystal and Janelle were already there peering through the windows she'd spent time cleaning.

"Oh, how charming," Barbara intoned. "Once the kids are off to college, you could certainly live up here."

"Or it could be my first apartment if I decide to go to college in Charleston," Crystal announced.

Janelle gave Crystal an incredulous stare. "Why would you need your own apartment if you already live in a house?"

Crystal returned the stare. "Once you go to college you need your own place."

"Hello!" shouted a man from the first floor.

"Wait here," Deborah told the others as she headed for the stairs. "Who is it?" she called out, walking down the staircase as quickly as she could without falling.

"Is that you, Deborah?"

Standing in the middle of the store was Jeffrey Hamilton, sheriff of Cavanaugh Island. Tall, dark, and handsome, the ex-Marine captain had managed to evade the advances of every single woman on the island since he'd returned to the Cove. He'd moved in with his grandmother, assuming the duties of sheriff after his predecessor retired.

Resting her hands at her waist, Deborah gave him a warm smile. "Hey, Jeff."

Taking a step and extending his arms, he pulled her close. "Hey yourself, beautiful." He sobered and kissed her forehead. "I'm sorry to hear about Louis. He was an incredible human being."

Deborah kissed Jeffrey's smooth cheek. "Thanks."

"How are your kids doing?"

"Coping." The single word spoke volumes.

Jeffrey released her, his dark eyes meeting hers. "I was just patrolling the area when I saw the light and open door. I thought some kids who couldn't get off the island decided to raise a little hell and break in and leave their tags."

Her eyebrows lifted a fraction. "We have a graffiti problem?"

"No. Not yet. What we're trying to do is stop it before it becomes a problem. A few of the fishermen have found tags scrawled on their boats. As soon as they paint over them the vandals strike again, then move to another location. I had the town council install cameras here on the Cove, but the folks in Angels Landing and Haven Creek claim they don't want the law monitoring their every move."

"They've always been a strange lot."

Jeffrey smiled, lines fanning out around his large, deep-set eyes. "Don't you mean *breed*?"

"Don't even go there, Jeff," Deborah admonished. "My grandmother used to give me the *look* whenever I mentioned wanting to visit the other parts of the island to see if they were the same as the Cove. I guess she got tired of me asking when she told me that some of the people who lived there had tails and cloven hooves like goats. I had nightmares for years until I saw someone from Angels Landing and the only thing I found strange was the contrast of his light-gray eyes and his very dark skin."

"What are you doing in here?" Jeffrey asked, deftly changing the topic.

"I'm renting this space. It's going to be the new location for my bookstore. And before you ask I'm going to tell you that I'm moving to the Cove!"

Jeffrey's expression was sincere as he gently patted Deborah on the back. "Good for you. How about your son and daughter? How do they feel about leaving Charleston?"

"Let's just say they're not crying about leaving."

"Good for them. I'll leave..." His words trailed off as a woman followed by two giggling teenage girls joined them. Deborah made the introductions, Jeffrey shaking each hand and wishing them health, peace, and happiness for the coming year. He touched the bill of his baseball cap, turned on his heel, and continued his patrol of the downtown district.

"We'll meet you at Jack's!" Crystal called as she and Janelle took off running.

Barbara raised her hand. "Don't—"

"It's all right," Deborah interrupted, turning off the lights and locking the front door. "Nothing's going to happen. Jeff's going that way, so I'm certain he'll keep an eye on them."

As they headed toward Jack's, Deborah nodded to long-time residents as they strolled leisurely along Main Street. They'd reached the town square with its huge fountain and statue of patriot militia General Francis Marion atop a stallion, standing more than thirty feet high. It was the tallest structure on the island. The fountain was empty, but during the summer months people threw coins into the flowing water with the hope their wishes would come true. Stone and wrought-iron benches were crowded with revelers and those taking advantage of the comfortable nighttime temperatures. There was enough space on one of the wrought-iron benches for them to sit together.

Deborah stared at the line outside of Jack's, waving to Crystal and Janelle when they turned in their direction. Janelle tugged on her father's arm, pointing. It appeared as if half of the Cove had turned out to eat at Jack's before attending the night watch service.

Barbara also waved to the girls and her husband when he raised his arm. "How long will it be before we can get a table?"

"Probably about twenty minutes, judging from the length of the line."

Deborah saw the man who had been in the Muffin Corner the first day she'd returned to the Cove. He sat a short distance away on a stone bench. Their eyes met and again they shared a smile. "Happy New Year, Mr. Monroe."

He nodded. "Happy New Year to you, too."

"Who is *that*?" Barbara asked sotto voce.

Deborah leaned closer to Barbara, while shifting her gaze to an elderly couple. "His name is Asa Monroe, and he's a snowbird."

"He's delicious," Barbara whispered again.

Deborah chanced a surreptitious glance at the man, who was sitting with one leg crossed gracefully over the other. He appeared totally relaxed, his right arm stretched out over the back of the bench he shared with a trio of teenagers.

"He is handsome," she agreed. And he was. Asa's smooth skin, even features, salt-and-pepper cropped hair made him strikingly handsome, while he possessed an elegant sophistication some men spent their entire lives striving to perfect.

"When did you meet him?" Barbara asked, continuing with her questioning.

"We were never formally introduced." Deborah told Barbara about seeing Asa when he'd walked into the Muffin Corner.

"Don't look now, but he's staring at you."

"Stop it, Babs."

Barbara smiled. "It's been a while since you've called me that."

Deborah exhaled audibly. "It's been a while since I've felt this relaxed."

"Are you relaxed enough to start over again?" Barbara asked.

"What are you talking about?"

Barbara covered Deborah's hand with hers, gently squeezing her fingers. "I know you just lost your husband, but that doesn't mean you have to stop living and loving. You're only thirty-eight and your son is seventeen. In eight months he'll be off to college. And in another three years it will be Crystal. You'll be what—forty-one or two—still a young woman who has the other half of her life in front of her. Do you plan to live it alone?"

"How can you talk about me hooking up with a man when I buried my husband exactly four weeks ago today?"

"I'm not talking about you hooking up with a man, Debs. I just want you to keep your options open. If a man shows an interest in you, I don't want you to give him a screw face.

Be nice," she continued, her voice lower, softer. "There's nothing wrong with going to dinner with him or even inviting him over for coffee."

Deborah knew Barbara was right. In another three years she would be in her early forties and alone. Both her children would be in college and she would encounter the empty-nest syndrome for the first time. "I'll think about it. But there is something I need to tell you about myself, but that will have to wait until we're alone."

Barbara nodded, then stood up. "Terrell is signaling us it's time to go in."

She also rose to her feet, and when she turned she saw that Asa was no longer there. They were ushered inside Jack's Fish House. To say the place was humming and jumping was an understatement. Every table was occupied and the noise level was ear-shattering. The muted televisions were turned to different stations, showing pre-holiday entertainment, and the platters of fried catfish, buttery, sweet cornbread, black-eyed peas, and rice made her mouth water.

Deborah did get to see Asa again, this time inside Jack's when he was seated at a table for six. She didn't recognize any of the other four men or the one woman at his table. The Cove was only three square miles with a permanent resident population of eight hundred, and that translated into everyone knew everyone—if not by name then by sight.

She thought about Mabel's statement about the monies snowbirds spent that helped to sustain the mom-and-pop businesses throughout the winter season until the horde of tourists swelled the population to more than two thousand throughout the summer. Deborah knew it was risky

opening a business in the Cove when so many were closing, but she had a slight advantage. The Parlor would be
the only bookstore on Cavanaugh Island.

What she didn't want to think about was *not* making a
go of her bookstore, and also of Asa Monroe—a stranger
who had managed to intrigue her. She knew nothing about
him other than his name, but there was something in the
way he stared that made Deborah feel slightly off-balance.
The last time that had happened was twenty years ago
when she'd met Louis Robinson.

Asa Monroe half-listened to the conversations floating
around the table as he pretended to concentrate on the food
on his plate. He sat with guests who were also living at the
Cove Inn for the winter. He hadn't wanted to join them, but
it was either share their table or wait hours until a table for
one was available.

As the diners chattered around him, Asa stole surreptitious glances at the woman he'd first seen at the Muffin
Corner, now seated a few tables away. He didn't know
anything else about her other than what Mabel had told
him, but there was something about this mystery woman
he mentally referred to as Sunshine that drew him to her
like a powerful magnet. Her smile was mesmerizing, her
sultry drawl hypnotic. Deborah Robinson was also the first
woman in the two months since he'd come to Cavanaugh
Island that piqued his interest. And in a town as small as
Sanctuary Cove, Asa loathed asking too many questions
about her. After all, he was a snowbird, a transient, and
although he'd been warmly welcomed by everyone he
didn't want to raise a red flag when he made it known he
was interested in a woman who could be married. The first

thing Asa had noticed was she wasn't wearing a ring, but neither had he when he'd been married.

Asa speared another forkful of seafood rice, enjoying the piquant blend of bacon, onion, pepper, garlic, crab-meat, oysters, and shrimp. His expression softened notice-ably when Sunshine draped an arm over a teenage girl's shoulders and then pressed a kiss to her hair.

She has to be her daughter, he mused. Asa knew the boy sitting opposite Sunshine was her son, because of their striking resemblance. He'd inherited her golden-brown coloring, the expressive black arching eyebrows, and even the shape of her eyes. He had usually never been one to engage in people-watching. But observing Sunshine was something Asa enjoyed and looked forward to doing again and again.

Reaching for his mug of beer, he held it aloft when Sunshine glanced in his direction. Holding her gaze, he winked at her then took a deep swallow. A smile crinkled the skin around Asa's eyes when Sunshine's jaw dropped. He was hard-pressed not to laugh when he noticed she had raised her glass of tea in a silent toast. He mouthed *Happy New Year*, and he wasn't disappointed when Sunshine inclined her head in acknowledgment.

Chapter Four

⌒

"Why aren't you asleep, Mom?"

"Why aren't you asleep, Whit?" Deborah asked, answering her son's question with one of her own. "It's after three."

Whitney stood by the doorway to the screened-in back porch in a tank top and pajama pants, staring at the flickering black-and-white images on the television. She'd muted the sound and closed captions appeared on the large flat-screen that sat on a stand on an oaken pedestal table.

Deborah had continued a tradition begun after her parents had introduced her to the fantasy/science fiction television show made popular in the late fifties; she'd watched six half-hour episodes of the New Year's all-day marathon of *The Twilight Zone*.

"I got up to get some water and saw that Janelle and Crystal weren't in their room."

Deborah had given Terrell and Barbara her bedroom,

while Janelle shared Crystal's bedroom and she'd paired Nate with Whitney. She'd bedded down on the queen-size convertible sofa on the back porch.

"They're under the covers." She smiled, gesturing to the bumps on the far side of the sofa bed. "They claim this episode is too scary to watch."

When Whitney entered the porch he saw what his mother was talking about. "Oh, this is the one with the talking doll." He flopped down on a cushioned rocker. One of the bumps moved under the quilt. "I loved this one, especially when Talky Tina tells the little girl's stepfather, 'My name is Talky Tina and I don't think I like you.'"

"Hush, Whit. The girls can hear you," Deborah chastised. "Why do you think I muted the sound?"

"I can't understand why they're freaking over a silly looking doll. Now, if they were afraid of the seed of Chucky I'd see why they would hide under the covers."

"That's enough talk about demonic dolls," Deborah whispered even though she'd unmuted the sound as the episode ended. "The girls don't play with dolls anymore, but they still have their collections." Placing a finger over her lips, she winked at Whitney. "Girls, it's over." Their heads emerged from under the pile of quilts. "I think it's time you go back to your bedroom."

Crystal gave her mother a sorrowful look. "Mom, please. Just until six o'clock."

"No, Crystal. You have to get enough rest because I want you and your brother to clean out the trunks in the crawl space. Something the two of you were supposed to have done over the Thanksgiving weekend."

"Can't it wait until next weekend?"

Deborah didn't want to get into a debate with her

daughter. Each and every time she asked Crystal to do something there was always a squabble because Crystal's mantra was *what you don't want to do today can be done tomorrow.* "No, it can't. You know this house is smaller than the one in Charleston, and if there is something you want and it doesn't fit in your bedroom, then it can be stored in the crawl space. If you don't clean it out and there's no room then I will donate your things to charity. Now, please get up, go to your bedroom, and go to sleep."

Crystal went still, her gaze shifting from her mother to Janelle. "Okay, Mom."

Deborah extended her arms, kissing her daughter's cheek, then Janelle's. "Sleep tight—"

"And don't let the bedbugs bite," the two girls chorused.

"I'm going back to bed, too." Whitney pushed off the rocker. Closing the distance between them, he leaned down and dropped a kiss on Deborah's hair. "Good night. Or, should I say, good morning."

"Good morning, Whit."

Waiting until she was alone, Deborah stared at the television, thinking about her new life ahead. As a widow and a single mother she would have to balance running her business with taking care of her home, because now she wouldn't have Louis to pick up the slack. He had always left home at six-thirty to work with students who needed extra help and usually returned before the bus dropped Crystal and Whitney off from school. Her Charleston-based bookstore was open Tuesday through Saturday from ten to six. Thursday was the late night when she stayed open until eight. Most days Deborah prepared dinner, set aside in oven-proof dishes with cooking instructions, and when she didn't Louis and Crystal had concocted gourmet dinners that rivaled those served in upscale restaurants.

When she opened the bookstore on Sanctuary Cove, Deborah realized she would have to hire an assistant. She was certain she would be able to get a retiree or a college student to cover the store when she had to take care of things at home. Her children didn't need a babysitter, but they did require supervision. Although she hadn't had a problem with Whitney and Crystal becoming involved with drug use or underage drinking, she didn't want to present them with the opportunity to experiment if they were left unsupervised. Deborah was a firm believer in little children, little problems. Big children, big problems. And she was firm and uncompromising when it came to no kids in the house without a parent present, and no entertaining in their bedrooms.

Her children weren't perfect, but at least she hadn't had to bail them out of jail or send them to rehab. What they hadn't known was she'd worn out her knees praying they would reach adulthood without making mistakes that would impact negatively on their futures.

She had not known when she recorded Whitney's birth in her journal that seventeen years later she and Louis would not attend his high school graduation together, or see him off to college. Over the years Deborah had recorded entries in her journal: chronicling births, deaths, earning her graduate degree, opening the bookstore, Whitney getting his driver's license, and Crystal making the cheerleading squad.

When Barbara had suggested she join her children in their grief counseling sessions, Deborah's response was she didn't need a counselor when she had her journals in which to record her innermost thoughts. However, she'd told her friend a half-truth. The last entry she'd written was on the day Louis died.

December 4th—The police came to the house today to tell me Louis had drowned. They haven't recovered his body, so there is still hope that he will be found alive.

Her journal was in the drawer of the bedside table at the house in Charleston. She made a mental note to bring it to Sanctuary Cove to record all that had happened since that tragic day in early December. She watched two more episodes of the marathon, then turned off the television and settled down on the pile of pillows cradling her shoulders. It was a new year and she'd made only one resolution, and that was to make the transition of relocating from Charleston to Sanctuary Cove as uneventful as humanly possible.

"Mom, look what we found in the last trunk!"

Crystal's strident tone shattered the quiet in the kitchen. Deborah, who'd spent the past half hour sitting at the kitchen table, drinking coffee, and flipping through the pages of magazines, stared at her daughter. The household hadn't begun to stir until noontime. Deborah had awakened as slivers of sunlight pierced the fabric of the woven blinds that covered the porch's windows and French door. Somehow she forced herself to remain in bed until ten, then showered in the bathroom off the kitchen. As she was cleaning up the family room Barbara came to tell her she was planning to prepare brunch.

Deborah hadn't wanted to think about food—not after all she'd consumed the night before. She had made certain to sample every dish, unable to believe the quality of the food hadn't diminished in all the years she'd eaten at Jack's. This morning, while everyone ate slices of sweet smoked ham, grits, eggs, and biscuits, she'd drunk two cups of coffee with a serving of soft-scrambled eggs. Another one of her resolutions should be to cut back on her coffee consumption. Lately, she'd been drinking at least four cups a day when normally one or two would suffice.

After brunch Barbara and Terrell had taken Whitney's car for a tour of Cavanaugh Island, leaving Deborah to savor a few moments of solitude. Although the island was only eight square miles, with a total population of approximately twenty-three hundred, there were unpaved roads with no markers and people had been known to get lost for hours.

"What did you find, sweetheart?"

Crystal, cradling a plastic envelope filled with letters and newspaper clippings, spilled the contents on the table. "Whitney has more."

Picking up a letter, Deborah recognized her grandmother's neatly slanting writing. She smiled. The letter was addressed to James Williams, while the return address read Sallie Ann Payne. Payne had been her grandmother's maiden name. She counted more than twenty letters. "How many does Whitney have?" she asked Crystal.

"These are journals," Whitney said as he entered the kitchen with six hard-covered books. "They belonged to Grandma Sallie."

Crystal picked up an envelope. "Can we read them? We finished emptying all the trunks," she added quickly.

Deborah knew Crystal and Whitney had spent the better part of two hours going through four steamer trunks filled with old quilts, hardcover books, and sets of dishes, and another filled with sweet-grass baskets. Everything was neatly packed and stored in plastic to ward off mildew in the tropical heat. Whitney had carried the empty trunks down the ladder that led to the crawl space and placed them on the front porch to air out, while their contents were stacked in an area off the kitchen that doubled as a pantry.

"You can read the newspaper articles," Deborah said. She didn't want her children to read their great-grandmother's letters or journals until she read them. Perhaps there was something in them that wasn't appropriate.

Whitney flopped down on a chair at the table and began unfolding the clippings. "Some of these are real old." He held up a clipping that had yellowed with age.

Deborah smiled again. "Your Grandma Sallie read everything. Remember, when she grew up the radio and newspapers were her only link with the outside world."

Crystal scrunched up her nose. "Mom, how did everyone get along without a computer and texting?"

"Quite well, thank you."

"How did you talk to your friends?" she asked.

Deborah's eyebrows lifted with her daughter's query. "I picked up the telephone and called them."

"What about Grandma Pearl?"

"She, too, picked up a phone and called her friends. However, Grandma Sallie told me she didn't get a telephone until the mid-1950s, when the island was wired for telephone service. If she had to contact someone in an emergency she would go to the store that's now the pharmacy and post office, where the telegrapher would send a telegram to someone on the mainland."

"What about television?" Whitney asked.

"My grandmother always had a television. It was

nothing like the thin flat-screen high-definition ones we have today, but I can remember watching soap operas with her during the summer months when she wasn't teaching."

Deborah watched Crystal tunnel her hands through her short hair, and then lift it with her fingertips. Crystal was a much softer feminine version of her late father, but Deborah wished she would let her hair grow out a little longer so she could style it differently.

Whitney stared at the article's headline. "This says that Grandma Sallie was the first Negro teacher to integrate the Cove's white school. She never mentioned anything to us about it."

Crystal stopped touching her hair. "You didn't have a problem when you came here as a young girl, did you, Mom?"

Reaching across the table, Deborah rested her hand atop Crystal's. "Why are you asking questions about the Cove? Are you having second thoughts about moving here permanently?"

"No. We like it here," Whitney answered, speaking for himself and his sister. "It's just that you never told us what it was like for you to spend your summers here."

"Whenever I tried talking to you about it you claimed you didn't want to hear about what I did back in the day. All you were interested in was playing with your friends and hanging out on the beach."

Crystal affected a sheepish expression. "We want to hear about it now."

Deborah leaned back in her chair. "I can remember coming to the Cove the summer I celebrated my fourth birthday. I used to get up early, put on a pair of boots, then go to gather eggs from the chicken coop for Grandpoppa's breakfast before he went out in his boat. I'd watch my grandmother make lunch for him, and then she would make breakfast for us. After that it was working in the garden before the sun got too hot."

Crystal's eyes grew larger. "How far was the coop from the house?"

"It was far enough away from the house so we didn't have to smell it," Deborah answered with a laugh. "Grandpoppa had put up a large structure made of wire like those on the window screens to keep out unwanted critters and to keep the chickens safe when they were out in their yard. Even the bugs couldn't get through. We'd had problems with snakes stealing the eggs and foxes eating the chickens."

Deborah told them about planting, weeding, and harvesting homegrown vegetables. Then the canning process began. The best part was seeing the many labeled jars lining the pantry shelves. "We had and still have a lot of fruit trees on this property and Grandmomma would gather apples, pears, cherries, and peaches to make jellies, preserves, and marmalade."

With wide eyes, Crystal clutched her mother's hand. "Mom, can I go fruit-picking and put up a garden?"

"You may, but only after I get someone to cut back the underbrush. I don't want to think of what may be hiding under a pile of leaves."

Crystal rolled her eyes upward. "I'm not afraid of snakes."

"You don't have to be afraid of them," Deborah countered, "but I still don't want you bitten by one—especially if it is venomous. You could die before we could get you to the mainland, even if you were airlifted there. I'll ask Hannah Forsyth if she knows of anyone willing to do some yard work."

"Isn't Ms. Forsyth the librarian?" Whitney questioned.

"Yes, and she's also the island historian. She knows everyone on the island, and if you want or need something she's the one to go to. I'll also let her know I want to clear some land for a garden. Just what do you intend to plant?"

Crystal pulled her lower lip between her teeth. "I don't know yet."

"You're going to have to know," Deborah said quietly, "because if you want to put in collards or watermelon you'll need to have enough room for them to grow without choking the other veggies. My grandmother divided her garden into sections for tomatoes and peppers because they grew on stakes. Another section was for leaf vegetables: collards, green and white cabbage, kale, and lettuce. Peppers and tomatoes were together as were root vegetables like carrots, beets, and turnips. That left green and wax beans, cucumbers, and melons. And you can still find the strawberries, raspberries, and blackberry bushes right before you get to the fruit trees."

"Can I put in an herb garden?"

A beat passed before Deborah said, "If you commit to putting in a garden, then I don't want you to be so consumed with it that you neglect your schoolwork. And don't forget you have cheerleading—"

"I can do it, Mama. Please say it's okay."

The last time Crystal had called her Mama was when she'd been told that her father had died. It was the only word she'd been able to utter as she cried herself to sleep, with Deborah lying beside her and comforting her whenever she woke to begin crying again. It was a full sixty seconds before Deborah said, "Okay, Crystal. But if your grades slip, then I'll pay someone to oversee the garden."

"They won't," she promised.

Whitney folded the newspaper clipping, placing it gently back into the plastic envelope and securing the clasp. "Did you make any friends?" He and Crystal were familiar with the high school students who lived on Cavanaugh Island, but didn't hang out with them.

"Yes. Mabel Davis, who lived down the road from here, and I were thick as thieves. You rarely saw one of us without the other. She's now Mabel Kelly and she and her husband own the Muffin Corner near Moss Alley. The Davises had several horses and Mabel and I would ride them down to the beach and race each other along the sand."

Whitney and Crystal shared a glance. "You never told us you could ride a horse," he said.

"You never asked, son. The highlight of my summers was when my grandfather took me with him when he went out before dawn to drop his nets and traps for shrimp, oysters, crabs, and lobsters. The first time I boarded the boat I nearly gagged from the lingering smell of fish, then after a while it was like the most expensive perfume. The only time I freaked out was when they caught a squid."

Resting her elbows on the table, Crystal leaned closer. "What did they do with it?"

"It was sold to a fish store in Charleston where it was tenderized and cut up for calamari. Most of Grandfather's catch was sold to fish stores on the mainland, and some to Jack's Fish House. The rest Grandmomma stored in the freezer. We usually had fried chicken or baked ham for Sunday dinner, and pork on special occasions. But fish played a big part in our daily diet."

Crossing his arms over his chest, Whitney leaned back on his chair. "Didn't you get tired of eating fish?"

"Never. We had fried shrimp, garlic shrimp, fried

crabs, crab cakes, broiled lobster, and shrimp and grits, Frogmore stew, shrimp and crab gumbo—and then there were the fish salads and soups. My favorite dish was jambalaya with shrimp and ham." Deborah smiled. "I have my grandmother's recipe," she said in singsong.

Crystal jumped up, nearly upsetting her chair when she raced over to a drawer under the countertop to get a pen and paper. "What ingredients do you need?" she said, her voice rising in excitement.

Deborah's expressive eyebrows lifted a fraction. "Do you intend to make it?"

"No, Mom. I want you to make it for next Sunday's dinner."

"And, what makes you think I can duplicate my grandmother's recipe?"

"Stop playing," Whitney drawled. "You know you can cook even if you don't like to."

Her son was right. She was a more than adequate cook, but had much preferred to let Louis do the cooking. "Okay. Next Sunday's dinner will be jambalaya with shrimp and ham."

Deborah didn't want to be reminded that next Sunday would be the first time since Louis's drowning they would sit down together for dinner as a family in this house. It had taken a month, and she was ready to start life anew; this time without her husband. And if she hadn't had her children Deborah knew she would've continued to wallow in a maelstrom of self-pity. She knew she had to be strong not only for herself but also for Crystal and Whitney, because they still were dependent upon her for emotional *and* physical support.

Chapter Five

"Are you certain you don't want me to drop you off?"

Deborah picked up the fob for her car. "Very certain, Whit."

"It's not going to be a problem, Mom. You can call me when the meeting is over and I'll come and pick you up."

"I'll see you later," she said over her shoulder as she walked out the front door, closing it behind her.

It had taken Deborah less than a week to figure out what her children were up to. She was certain they were attempting to keep an eye on her lest she'd undergo an emotional meltdown.

They hadn't seen her cry or get hysterical and they wouldn't. What they didn't know was that she did cry. She cried at night, in bed and in the shower, or when she locked herself in the bathroom to take a bubble bath. She cried until spent or until dry heaves made breathing difficult.

With the end of the New Year's holiday weekend, she had returned to Charleston to supervise the dismantling of her bookstore, and to confer with a moving company to pack up the contents of her household she wanted shipped to Cavanaugh Island. She'd given Sherilee a key to the house, informing her that she could take all red-tagged items and boxes.

Her grandmother's trunks yielded a treasure trove of first edition books she'd listed on The Parlor's website under rare and collectible editions and the response from various collectors was overwhelming. A new mattress, bed dressing, towels for the bathroom, and window shades were scheduled to be delivered Friday morning, and Deborah projected the bookstore would be open for business by the coming weekend.

Whitney read the many newspaper clippings and had surprised her when he announced he wanted to write articles for the *Sanctuary Chronicle*, the Cove's biweekly newspaper, about his great-grandmother's extraordinary accomplishments and contribution to the children who'd grown up on the island. He'd placed a call to the newspaper's editor to set up an appointment to meet with him to discuss his project. Deborah had no doubt the articles would be well-written because Whitney, editor of his school's newspaper, planned for a career in communications.

Touching the car's handle, she opened the door and slipped behind the wheel. Minutes later she maneuvered into a parking space behind the library. It would be the first time she would attend a monthly town council meeting. Now that she was a permanent resident and business owner she needed to know what was going on in her new hometown. There was a monthly newsletter, recapping events and activities, but Deborah wanted to see the proceedings in person.

She followed the sign directing her to the meeting room. The mayor and his town council met the second Tuesday of each month to bring residents up to date on proposed new ordinances, budget items, and reports from department heads, including but not limited to transportation, engineering, housing, fire, police, and the school board.

Walking into the brightly lit room, she took an empty chair near the front. Deborah had barely settled on the folding chair when a shadow loomed over her. Her head popped up and she stared at Asa Monroe, trying to ignore the shiver of awareness that eddied over her body. Barbara was right. Seeing him up close Deborah concluded Asa *was* truly delicious.

Her eyebrows lifted a fraction. "Are you stalking me, Mr. Monroe?"

Asa gestured to the chair beside her. "Is someone sitting here?" he asked.

"No. Please sit. You didn't answer my question," Deborah said. He sat down, looping one leg over the opposite knee. She stared at the toe of his running shoe. Tonight he wore a white cotton V-necked pullover with a pair of jeans.

"I'm not stalking you, Mrs...."

"It's Ms. Robinson."

"Does Ms. Robinson have a first name? Because it seems as if everyone in Sanctuary Cove is on a first-name basis."

Deborah stared at his distinctive profile. His strong jaw was smooth from a recent shave and the scent of his cologne was like the man—potent. "Deborah."

He extended his hand. "It's nice putting a name with a face. It's my pleasure, Deborah."

She stared at the broad palm with long, slender well-groomed fingers for several seconds before she took it. Even his hands were perfect. "Nice meeting you, Asa."

"I'm not stalking you," he said with a grin. "I was told that non-residents are welcome to attend a town council meeting and voice their opinions."

Lowering her eyes, Deborah felt properly chastised. How could she have been that self-centered? Asa had smiled at her—something men in the Cove did every day, while she'd believed he was stalking her. "I'm sorry," she apologized, withdrawing her hand from his firm grip.

"For what?"

Deborah gave him a direct stare. "For accusing you of stalking me." Asa continued to smile, attractive lines fanning out around his eyes, drawing her gaze to his straight, white teeth.

"There's no need to apologize. Sanctuary Cove is not *that* big, so there is always the possibility of running into the same people several times a day."

She nodded. "You're right. How many meetings have you attended?"

"This is my first. How many have you attended?" Asa asked.

Deborah stared straight ahead. "This is also my first."

"I thought—"

"Hey, Debs," Mabel called out as she walked into the room. "Nice seeing you, Asa," she added, giving him a friendly smile.

"Same here," Asa acknowledged.

"Was I interrupting something?" Mabel asked, her gaze shifting from Deborah to Asa.

"No," Deborah and Asa said in unison.

"Please excuse us, Asa, but I need to talk to Deborah," Mabel said, sitting on Deborah's left and patting her knee. "As soon as you're finished settling in, Les and I would like to have you and your kids over for Sunday dinner."

Deborah leaned to her left, her shoulder touching Mabel's. "There's not much I have to do at the house, but it's the bookstore that's taking up most of my time."

She'd taken out a home improvement loan to make repairs, update, expand and redecorate the house, because she and Louis had planned to use it as their permanent residence after they'd retired. All of the rooms were painted, a new roof replaced the old one, and the clapboard siding was restored with white vinyl. The navy-blue shutters, a new front porch, and the expanded back porch made the near century-old structure a standout on the Cove, especially when compared to some of the smaller homes on the island. Up until thirty years ago some of them still hadn't had indoor plumbing.

Upon the advice of the contractor, she hadn't bricked up the kitchen fireplace. It added to the character of the room with its exposed brick walls. And on the occasional cool evening she would light a fire and either roast marshmallows with her children or sit and read ghost stories to them by the light of the flames.

When her great-grandfather built the house, he'd designed it with two fireplaces: one in the kitchen and another in a separate outdoor structure as was the custom. The exterior building and fireplace had been destroyed when a hurricane swept the island in 1917.

"Do you want some help? After we close the Muffin Corner I could come over and help you unpack."

Deborah shook her head. "Thanks, but no thanks. The

shelves are up and the only thing left to do is to stack books. As soon as the piano and a few other pieces of furniture are delivered The Parlor will open for business. What I'm going to need from you is muffins."

Mabel ran a hand over her braided hair. "You need muffins?"

"Yes. I plan to set up a reading corner and I'd like to offer my customers something to munch on if they decide to browse or hang out for a while. I'm not going to serve coffee, because that would conflict with your business, but gourmet tea. If they want coffee, then they can get it at the Muffin Corner."

"That's great!" Mabel crooned. "It sounds as if you're going to bring a little class to the Cove and keep the parlor theme. That's what made your Charleston bookstore so different from the others. Do you realize what's going to happen?"

"No. What?" Deborah asked, staring at Mabel's gap-toothed grin.

"You're going to get folks who'll come in and sit so long they're going to leave a distinct imprint of their behinds on your chairs."

She smiled. "I don't mind as long as they're paying customers. I'm not going to be able to compete with the chain bookstores on the mainland, but if anyone wants a title I can call a distributor and get it within two to three days."

"Are you going..." Whatever Mabel was going to say died on her lips when the mayor and members of the town council filed in, taking seats at the table in the front of the room.

• • •

Lowering his leg, Asa settled back in his chair and crossed his arms over his chest, while cursing Mabel Kelly's timing. Just when his attempt to engage Deborah Robinson in conversation had begun, it was thwarted by the owner of the Muffin Corner. He'd been in Sanctuary Cove for a little more than two months, and Deborah Robinson was the first woman who'd made him sit up and take notice. Her face was flawless, with a light sprinkling of freckles over the bridge of her nose, high cheekbones, and a lush mouth. When she smiled it just wasn't with her mouth, but also her eyes. And they'd sparkled with laughter during the brief seconds they'd stared at each other in the Muffin Corner and again at Jack's. He glanced at her bare fingers. Deborah had introduced herself as Ms. Robinson, which probably meant she was either unmarried and/or divorced, and what he hadn't realized during those seconds in the little pastry shop was that she was someone he'd like to get to know better.

Mayor Spencer White rapped his gavel, calling the meeting to order. He had earned the distinction of becoming a third generation mayor of the Cove. His grandfather had been the Cove's first black mayor, serving six four-year terms. Spencer's father then ran for the vacated office and won. He hadn't completed his second term, when he resigned to care for his wife who'd been diagnosed with multiple sclerosis. Spencer served out his father's term, and then ran unopposed in the subsequent election. He had married a model-turned-actress, who'd spent more than half of their brief two-year marriage in Los Angeles. They'd parted amicably, and as a lawyer with movie star looks, he joined

the ranks of a small number of single men on Cavanaugh
Island who were under the age of forty.

"If I wasn't married to Lester I would definitely ask
our illustrious mayor to park his slippers under my bed,"
Mabel whispered to Deborah through clenched teeth.
"Damn! He makes Blair Underwood look ugly. And, we
both know *that* man is some kinda fine!"

Deborah pressed the back of her hand to her lips to conceal the smile tilting the corners of her mouth. She could
always count on Barbara and Mabel to make her laugh.
There had been a time growing up that she'd laughed a
lot. But that had changed once she married and became
a mother. She'd married at twenty, had become a mother
for the first time at twenty-one, and it had taken careful
planning and budgeting to stretch her husband's paycheck.
They rented movies instead of going to the theater, dele-
gated one day a month when they went out to eat, and she'd
packed home-cooked nutritional lunches for Louis to heat
up in the teachers' lounge microwave.

At twenty-three, when Deborah Robinson should have
been teaching, jetting off to exotic locales for vacations,
socializing in clubs and dating like other young women
her age, she was proficient enough to go toe-to-toe with
Martha Stewart as a goddess of homemaking.

"I think Blair is better looking," she whispered.

"I think so, too"—Mabel paused, glancing in Asa's
direction—"but you have to admit that Asa is nice on the
eyes," Mabel whispered back.

Deborah nodded. It was the second time within a week
that a woman had talked about Asa being eye candy. Yes,
she had to admit he was delicious-looking eye candy, but
also a snowbird, and that made him a transient.

Spencer straightened his tie as he cleared his throat, garnering the attention of all in the room. He was the only one sitting at the table wearing a suit and tie. Sanctuary Cove was like its residents—laidback and unpretentious.

"I'd like to thank everyone for coming out tonight. Before we start our official meeting I'd like to acknowledge a few new faces. Those who are here for the first time should know you're always welcome." He stared directly at Deborah. "Mrs. Robinson, on behalf of those on the town council and all who live in the Cove I would like to offer my condolences for your husband's accidental drowning as he tried to rescue a young man. He truly was a hero, and if there is anything you or your children need, please do not hesitate to call my office."

Deborah swallowed to relieve the constriction in her throat as a swell of emotion made it difficult for her to draw a normal breath, because she hadn't expected Spencer to put her on the spot. But she should have known he would acknowledge everyone in town, new and old. His tone and words, along with his cropped hair, tailored suit, flawless brown skin, and even features, made him the consummate politician. She wondered if he would be content to remain mayor of Sanctuary Cove, or whether he might set his sights on a position with more visibility—something loftier.

"Thank you, Mayor White."

Spencer nodded. "For those who are unfamiliar with Deborah Robinson, she is the granddaughter of our own Sallie Ann and James Williams." He paused when there was a spatter of applause. "My office also has received official notification that the Robinsons will now make Sanctuary Cove their legal residence." He flashed a toothpaste-ad smile. "Welcome home, Deborah."

Eyelids fluttering to stem the flow of tears pricking the backs of her lids, Deborah flashed a demure smile. "Thank you again."

Spencer's eyebrows lifted a fraction as he returned her smile. "Isn't there something else you'd like to tell your fellow residents?"

All eyes were trained on Deborah as she stared straight ahead. What was he talking about? Did the mayor know something she should have known? A pregnant silence ensued until it finally came to her. "Yes, there is. I'll be opening a bookstore at the corner of Main and Moss Alley." Her announcement was followed by rousing applause. "If any of you know someone looking for a part-time position, please tell them to stop by the old gift shop off Moss Alley."

"When do you expect your grand opening?" Spencer asked, flashing a practiced smile.

"I'll call your office and let you know so we can have a ribbon-cutting ceremony." Deborah almost burst out laughing when she saw his smile fade, as if someone had stuck Spencer with a sharp object. She'd usurped him, because she knew he'd wanted to mention the ribbon-cutting that had become an important component of his administration.

"Let's hope it's soon." Shifting his attention from Deborah to another, Spencer nodded to an elderly couple sitting in the front row. "Sir, madam, do you mind telling us why you've come to Sanctuary Cove?"

"I'm Shelly Miner and this is my husband Ralph. We're from Edina, Minnesota," the wife announced proudly, "and as snowbirds we usually winter in a different place every year. This year it's Sanctuary Cove." She held up a hand.

"And before you ask, Mayor White, I know I speak for Ralph as well when I say your town is wonderful." Shifting on her chair, she wagged a finger at Deborah. "And, young lady, I'll be waiting for you to open that bookstore."

Spencer laughed with the others. He gestured to Asa. "Sir, do you mind telling us what brought you to Sanctuary Cove?"

"I'm Asa Monroe. I'm a first-time snowbird, and this is my first visit to the Carolina Lowcountry and hopefully it won't be my last."

"Are you enjoying your stay, Mr. Monroe?" Spencer asked.

Asa smiled. "Most definitely."

Spencer smiled like a Cheshire cat. "Perhaps we can get you and Mr. and Mrs. Miner to consider living here year-round."

"It is something to think about," Asa said.

"Try not to think too hard, Mr. Monroe." Again, there was laughter.

There were more introductions before Spencer White rapped his gavel, officially opening the meeting. There were reports from Sheriff Jeffrey Hamilton; the commissioner of roads and transportation, who informed the assembly that Sanctuary Cove had been awarded a grant from the state to repair the sidewalks and parking lots in the business district; and a very lengthy report from the town's treasurer. Then Spencer rapped his gavel again, announcing a fifteen-minute recess.

Asa checked his watch. It was eight-fifteen. He'd come to the library to look for something to read, but when he checked the community bulletin board in the lobby and found the announcement for the open town council meeting he'd decided to stay and observe some of the proceedings.

What he hadn't expected to find was the woman who'd occupied his thoughts since the first time he saw her. Now that he knew her name and that she was opening a bookstore, there was no reason for him to stay for the remainder of the meeting.

Asa saw Deborah talking with the sheriff, the lawman tucking a curl that had escaped the elastic band on the nape of her neck behind Deborah's ear. The scene was so tender and intimate that he felt like a voyeur. Mixed feelings surged through Asa. He found himself lusting after a woman he knew nothing about, other than her name, that she was going to open a bookstore, and that she had a teenage son. He knew Jeffrey Hamilton wasn't married, so there was the remote possibility that he and Deborah were seeing each other. However, in a town as small as Sanctuary Cove it would be easy enough to find out.

He left the library and began walking back to the Cove Inn. The library was a twenty-minute brisk walk to the boardinghouse, and now he wished he'd driven. Walking allowed him time to think—something he hadn't wanted to do. At least inside his Range Rover he could turn on the radio or listen to a CD. Shoving his hands into the pockets of his jeans, Asa stared straight ahead as he made his way back to what he thought of as his temporary home.

Once he closed the door to his room, he could grieve without having to explain to anyone why he didn't want to talk. Asa knew he had to do something to keep himself busy. He was forty-six, much too young to retire, although financially he could maintain a very comfortable lifestyle well into old age. He'd closed his practice, referred his patients to another physician, put his house on the market, and submitted an application to Doctors Without Borders.

He couldn't remain in Sanctuary and continue to do the same thing every day: get up and share a buffet breakfast with the other guests, go for a walk along the beach, return to sit on the porch and read for hours, sit down to dine with the same guests, then retreat to his bedroom to watch aimless hours of television before preparing for bed.

"Mr. Monroe."

Asa turned when he heard someone call his name. Sitting on a stone bench near the fountain in the town square was Rachel Dukes's brother-in-law and the boardinghouse's handyman. It was nearly impossible to pinpoint his age despite the lines and creases in his lean jaw and forehead. The man's coloring and features reminded Asa of ebony African masks he'd seen at craft shows and museums. He wore a short-sleeved white shirt with a pair of sharply creased khakis.

Asa extended his hand. "Good evening, Mr. Walker."

"That it is," Jake Walker replied. Asa shook the proffered well-groomed hand. "Nice night for walking or sitting outside." Jake gestured to several couples sitting across the square. "They think so, too."

Since he'd moved into the boardinghouse, Asa couldn't remember hearing the taciturn man say any more than *morning* or *evening*. "That it is," he said. The square was brightly lit and nighttime temperatures were in the low seventies.

"Sit down and rest yourself, Mr. Monroe." Waiting until Asa sat facing him, Jake smiled as a network of fine lines fanned out around his raven-black eyes. "You came from the meeting?"

Asa nodded, smiling. "Yes."

"How did you like it?"

"It was interesting."

"Interesting how?"

"I would have never anticipated the mayor would ask tourists to introduce themselves."

Crossing his feet at the ankles, Jake stared at the toes of his scuffed work boots. "We do things different 'round here, 'specially now with Spencer White as the new mayor. He is a little bit of a blowhard, but we think he really wants the best for the Cove."

Asa wanted to tell Jake that the man was more pomp-ous than a blowhard, and was probably using his position as mayor as a stepping stone to advance his political career. "What about the mayors in Haven Creek and Angels Landing?"

The seconds ticked by and Jake stared at his hands sandwiched between his knees. "Folks in the Cove don't have much to do with folks in the Creek or Landing, and vice versa."

"Are you saying you don't visit the other parts of the island?"

"That's not what I'm saying. I go to Angels Landing to visit my kin, but they don't like coming here." He smiled when Asa told him about his attempt to drive to Angels Landing. "You can't drive there from here. You've got to go on foot, because it's too swampy to drive. Even with four-wheel drive you still can get stuck."

Asa gave the older man an incredulous look. "I'm not about to go walking in a swamp."

Jake grunted. "There's nothing to it, son. You just put on a pair of boots that come to the knee and head due northwest. The boots are to protect your ankles from them moccasins and copperheads. It would also help if you bring a rifle 'cause you never know what else might jump out at you."

"That's okay. The next time I'll take the causeway." Asa glanced at his watch. He wanted to return to the boarding-house and check his e-mail on his laptop. "Are you ready to go back?"

Jake had revealed that he and his wife moved into the bungalow behind the boardinghouse after their children married and moved away. He'd wanted to ask the older man about Deborah and Jeffrey, but changed his mind. That was something he would uncover himself—tomorrow.

"Yeah, I guess so." Jake rose slowly to his feet, swaying slightly until he regained his balance. "I sit out here most nights because I can't stand the chatter of the folks setting in the parlor. When you get to my age, son, you need a little peace and quiet."

Smiling, Asa slowed his stride to accommodate the much shorter man. "I know what you mean." After the evening meal, the boarders gathered in the parlor to either play cards or board games. An open bar with cordials was available for those who wanted some liquid libation. Those who imbibed too much usually fell asleep where they sat, while others became more animated. It was only when Rachel dimmed the lights at ten that they put away their games and retreated to their suites. Both men turned when they heard two short taps from a car's horn.

Jake stopped, waving to Deborah when she maneu-vered over to the curb. "Hey, Missy."

Deborah lowered the passenger-side window, leaning to her right. "Mr. Walker. Asa. Can I give you a ride back to the boardinghouse?"

"I don't mind if it won't put you out," Jake said.

"Please get in. You, too, Asa."

Asa rested a hand on Jake's shoulder. "You go. I'll walk."

The older man took a step, moving closer to Asa so Deborah couldn't overhear him. "Look, son, around here when someone offers to do you a favor you accept it. Not to is an insult. Now, please get in the car."

Knowing he'd just been chastised, Asa opened the passenger-side door, waiting until Jake was comfortably seated and belted in before he slipped onto the backseat. The subtle scent of perfume wafted in his nostrils. It was the same fragrance Deborah Robinson wore the day he saw her in the Muffin Corner.

What had shocked him was Mayor White offering his condolences on the drowning of her husband, which meant she was recently widowed. The mayor had also welcomed her home, leading Asa to surmise that she'd left Sanctuary Cove but had come back to live.

She'd lost her husband and he his wife. There were similarities yet one profound difference. He'd also lost his child, while she still had hers. Staring out the side window, Asa watched the slowly passing landscape. The bright lights from the town square disappeared, replaced by an occasional streetlight, then complete darkness as they left the downtown area.

The in-ground miniature solar lights lining the driveway led to the sprawling two-story structure that once had been the winter residence of a Charleston-based cotton planter before the Civil War. They reminded Asa of those on an airport runway. Rachel Dukes told each of her new boarders that she'd invested her blood, sweat, and tears in restoring the mansion to its original magnificence, and prided herself on offering services comparable to those found at the finest mainland-based hotels.

He could attest to that because the décor was quintessential antebellum and the cuisine classic lowcountry. At times, the charming southern hospitality generated by Rachel left Asa feeling slightly overwhelmed. The housekeeping staff moved about the eight-thousand-square-foot, twenty-two-room house silently and efficiently. At any given time a white-glove examination would not pick up a speck of dust anywhere.

He was out of the car as soon as it stopped, to assist Jake who was slower exiting. Bending lower, Asa smiled at Deborah. He extended his hand. Her bare face shimmered under the lights from the dashboard. "Thank you very much for the ride."

She returned his smile and took his hand. "It was my pleasure. Good night, Asa."

He closed the door, took a step back, and stared at the red taillights of the silver-gray sedan. Waiting until she disappeared from view, Asa turned and mounted the steps to the porch, walking around to a side door. He wanted to avoid the small crowd that had gathered in the parlor. Every time they'd asked him to join them he'd turned them down. It had reached a point where the other guests had begun avoiding him at breakfast and dinner, leaving him to sit alone while he ate in the formal dining room; he knew they thought him strange or maybe even a little crazy. He didn't want to answer their endless questions, while at the same time regurgitating his life story to strangers.

Taking a back staircase, he made it to his room without encountering anyone. He unlocked the door, reached for the Do Not Disturb placard and slipped it on the door-knob, closing and locking the door.

Walking over to the casement windows, he opened them and stepped out onto the veranda. The chaises positioned outside the other rooms were unoccupied. It wasn't often he had the veranda to himself, but tonight had to be his lucky night. Flopping down on the thick cushion, Asa ran his hand over his face, then went completely still. The lingering scent of Deborah's perfume clung to his palm. He inhaled deeply, trying to identify what made up the notes to the fragrance. He recognized musk and vanilla but there was another component that made it distinctive, memorable like its wearer.

There was something about Deborah that stirred emotions Asa did not want to feel—at least not consciously. Her beauty, smile, and feminine smell made him feel desire, something he'd sworn off after his wife was killed.

Chapter Six

Deborah sat in bed, a pile of pillows supporting her back and shoulders. A stack of her grandmother's letters and her journal lay beside her.

After the town council meeting Eddie Wilkes had approached her with the news he wanted Whitney to come to his office Saturday morning to interview for a position as a freelance reporter. The newspaper editor told her that Whitney had e-mailed him several articles he'd written for his high school newspaper. She was aware that her son was a straight-A student, but for an award-winning journalist to endorse Whitney's reporting ability filled her with pride.

Reaching for the stack of letters Sallie Ann Payne had written to James Williams, Deborah untied the ribbon she'd used to bundle the nearly two dozen envelopes. If Whitney was going to write about his great-grandmother, then she had to glean as much information about the woman who'd spent her entire life in Sanctuary Cove. Not even her father's urging could get his parents to leave once they retired. She remembered Sallie Ann declaring emphatically that if she was buried anywhere but on the Cove her soul would wander until it found its way back home. She removed the letter with the earliest postmark from its envelope.

Deborah spent the next ninety minutes reading the letters. They were erotic love letters from Sallie to James. She smiled. If she were a writer Deborah would have turned the letters into a novel. Reaching for her journal and a pen, she opened it to a blank page.

January 11th—I met a man. His name is Asa Monroe and he is spending the winter in the Cove. I don't know what it is about him, but whenever he smiles at me, something stirs my blood. He makes me feel things I've never felt with any man. Not even with Louis.

Capping the pen, Deborah stared at what she had written. *He makes me feel things I've never felt with any man.* There. She'd whispered what she had felt and had been feeling since she and Asa exchanged their first smile. Initially Deborah had been flattered that an attractive man had smiled at her, because it had been twenty years since she had returned a man's stare with a blatant one of her own. Once she had become involved with Louis she hadn't looked at another man.

Then, there was the scene in Jack's on New Year's Eve. Although there was another woman at Asa's table, he seemed intent on staring at her. It was the subtle wink that confirmed Asa Monroe was interested in her. And

Deborah wasn't so gauche that she didn't know when a man was flirting with her.

She had to ask herself whether she was willing to engage in a little harmless flirtation with a man who affected her with such intensity. Smiling, Deborah stored the journal and pen in the drawer of the bedside table, recounting her conversation with Barbara: *I know you just lost your husband, but that doesn't mean you have to stop living and loving.*

Her friend was right. She couldn't stop living or loving because of Louis's death. What Deborah had to decide was whether or not she was willing to take a chance on love again. She knew it wouldn't be with Asa, because he would leave the Cove come spring, but that didn't mean she couldn't enjoy his company in the meantime.

Slowly, methodically, Deborah stacked the letters, retied them with the ribbon and placed them in a drawer under her lingerie. Even though her grandmother hadn't left instructions, she knew the letters were for her eyes only.

Slipping back into bed, she rearranged the pillows and turned off the lamp. Within minutes of her head touching the pillow Deborah fell asleep. It was the first night since that fateful day in December that she hadn't stared at the clock waiting for sleep to overtake her, so she could forget that the man who'd lain beside her for so many years was gone and would not be coming back.

Deborah stood on the sidewalk, admiring the gold lettering on the plate-glass window: THE PARLOR BOOKSTORE. Although she hadn't yet officially opened for business just seeing the words made it all the more real. The shelves were anchored to the walls; the ladders slid easily along the rails, permitting her access to the higher rows. Half the books were stacked, and with the delivery of the piano, tables, and chairs the residents of Sanctuary Cove could avail themselves of the town's first bookstore.

Her gaze shifted to the HELP WANTED sign she'd placed in the window earlier that morning. It had taken her a while to decide on the hours of operation for the bookstore, especially now that she was solely responsible for caring for her children. She hoped that whoever filled the position would be flexible enough to allow her time to run errands and be available for meetings with her children's teachers and advisors. Deborah walked back into the store, nearly colliding with the cable technician.

"I'm going to wire upstairs, then I'll hook up your televisions. I should be out of your hair in about half an hour."

Deborah wanted to ask him if he could do it within fifteen minutes because her stomach was making gurgling noises. She'd gotten up early to make breakfast for her children, but had only drunk a cup of coffee herself. If she'd known Peter Raney was going to show up an hour later than scheduled she would've stopped at the Muffin Corner to eat something.

Picking up a box cutter off a side table, she cut through the tape on one of eight cartons labeled AFRICAN-AMERICAN. When she had dismantled her bookstore, she'd made certain the books were packed by genre. Thus far she'd shelved self-help, study guides, travel, and cookbooks. Fiction, nonfiction, mystery, teen, art, science fiction, romance, biography, literature, and African-American literature and Black Studies still needed to be dusted and alphabetized.

Deborah sat on a low stool, wiping off the covers and jackets of a carton of books featuring African-American history and literature. She flipped through the pages of *The Divine Nine—The History of African American Fraternities and Sororities* written by Lawrence C. Ross, Jr. The only thing she'd regretted when in college was that she hadn't pledged to a sorority. She'd written her grandmother asking her advice, and Sallie Ann had written back advising her to concentrate on her coursework. Now that she'd read her grandmother's letters to James Williams, Deborah regretted not saving the ones her grandmother had written to her while she'd attended college. It wasn't what she'd written, but how she'd written them, using a vintage fountain pen when most people used ballpoint pens. When she'd asked her why she still used such an antiquated writing utensil that had to be manually filled with ink, the older woman had replied that she loved seeing the flow of ink across a blank page and then waiting for it to dry.

Deborah had managed to empty one carton when a tap on the door garnered her attention. Turning, she saw Asa Monroe peering through the glass. She stared at him staring back at her, the sound of her pounding heartbeat echoing in her ears. Her feelings toward him were becoming more confusing. What, she mused, was there about Asa that made her react like an adolescent girl with her first crush? Her palms were sweating, her knees shaking, and Deborah didn't have to glance down at her chest to know her nipples were visible through her shirt.

A grin tilted the corners of her mouth, and much to her surprise Asa winked at her. Walking to the door, she unlocked and opened it a few inches. His gaze moved from her face to her white tee-shirt to her cropped jeans and ballet-type shoes.

"Good morning. We're still not open."

"I know. I came to ask you about the sign in the window."

Deborah stared up at the man, noticing for the first time he was taller than she'd expected or remembered. At five-eight, there weren't too many men who were a full head taller than she was. He looked as if he was ready to pose for an ad in a golfing magazine with his navy blue golf shirt, tan slacks, and imported slip-ons. "You...you want to work here?"

Asa smiled. "You mentioned last night that you needed a part-time employee. I just came to ask if the position has been filled."

"Oh no," she said much too quickly. "It's still available. But I just didn't expect someone like you to apply."

"May I come in?" Asa asked. He entered the shop when Deborah opened the door wider, then closed it behind him. "I don't know if you're aware of it, but it's against the law to discriminate against an employee because of age, race or gender."

Her mouth curved into an unconscious smile. Not only was Asa Monroe very attractive, but he was as equally charming. His face was the color of gold-brown autumn leaves and there was a hint of gold in his large, deep-set brown eyes. He had what Deborah thought of as balanced features: his eyes and nose making for an arresting face. She stared at his mouth, finding his lower lip a bit too sensuous for a man. But it was his voice—velvet, resonant—that unnerved her.

"I haven't discriminated against you because I haven't interviewed you."

"Will you?"

"Will I what, Asa?"

"Will you give me an interview?"

"I can't interview you now because I have someone working upstairs. As soon as he's finished we'll talk."

An expression of bewilderment crossed Asa's face when he heard the sound of Deborah's hunger. "Is that your stomach growling?"

A rush of heat that began in Deborah's chest moved upward, stinging her cheeks. "I'm afraid it is," she admitted. "I'm waiting for the technician to finish up, then I'm going to get lunch."

Crossing his arms over his chest, Asa angled his head. "Would you mind sharing lunch with me over at Jack's? You can interview me while we eat," he added quickly.

The sweep hand on Deborah's watch made a full revolution before she spoke again. "Okay. But I'm picking up the tab, because it will be a business expense."

Asa smiled again. "Okay. While you wait for the technician to finish, I'll help you shelve books."

Deborah's eyebrows lifted a fraction. Either Asa Monroe really did want a job, or he was trying to impress her. She hoped it wasn't the former reason because she could only pay him a little more than minimum wage. The woman who'd worked for her in the Charleston location was an independently wealthy, retired school librarian. Books had become her life and she couldn't bear not to be involved with them. When the discussion of a salary was broached, she'd quickly agreed to accept the lowest hourly wage mandated by law.

"Asa, I don't know what you're looking for when it comes to a salary, but I can't afford to pay much more than the minimum wage. If business is good the first three months, then I'll give you a raise."

"Are you saying I'm hired?"

Resting her hands at her hips, Deborah exhaled an audible sigh.

"I'll need someone to unpack and shelve new stock. I'll also need that person to cover the front desk when I have to run errands or look in on my children."

"How old are your children?" he asked.

"Seventeen and fifteen. They're not babies, but they still need my supervision."

"How many hours would you need me?"

"Probably between ten and fifteen hours a week."

"How many days a week?"

"No more than three or four days. The bookstore will open from Tuesday through Saturday, nine-thirty to six."

"Will you have a late night?" Asa questioned.

"Thursdays. I'll stay open until eight. May I ask you a question?"

"Of course, Deborah." She loved the way he said her name. It came out in three distinct syllables, like *De-boar-rah*, stressing the middle syllable.

"Why are you looking for work? And why a bookstore?"

Asa flashed a sheepish grin. "Becoming a snowbird isn't what I'd envisioned it to be. Most times I'm so bored I begin talking to myself just to hear my own voice. Now I know what prisoners in solitary confinement experience."

"How can it be quiet when you're staying at the boardinghouse? This time of year it's nearly filled to capacity."

"I usually keep to myself. I'm not much for board games and discussions that involve grandchildren. And, why not a bookstore? It's the perfect place to work for a bibliophile."

Deborah felt a shiver of excitement. It was apparent Asa Monroe was also an avid reader. "Who are some of your favorite authors?"

"American or across the pond?"

"Across the pond," she said in a clipped British accent.

"Is this a test?" Asa asked, smiling.

"It could be," Deborah teased.

"Coleridge, Sir Thomas More, Milton, Ben Johnson, James Joyce, E. M. Forster, and Chaucer. Did I pass?"

"Give me a few Americans and I'll let you know."

She watched as Asa seemed to search his memory for American writers. "Hannah Webster Foster—"

"You've read *The Coquette*?" Deborah asked, cutting him off.

"Not the book itself, but a photocopy. Do I pass?" he asked again.

"Give me three more."

"Charles Chesnutt, Henry James, and Sinclair Lewis."

Pressing her palms together in a prayerful gesture, Deborah pressed her fingers to her mouth. It was more than apparent Asa Monroe was an intellectual and he had no interest in board games. He was also knowledgeable enough to answer questions from customers inquiring about her rare and first edition titles.

"You pass."

Crossing his hands over his heart, Asa bowed his head. "Thank you."

Amusement danced in his eyes as they met Deborah's. She realized the man standing in her store was no ordinary clerk, and she knew she had to even the odds. Her gaze lingered on his hands. They were as exquisite as the rest of Asa Monroe. Again, she thought them beautifully formed with long tapered fingers, well-groomed with square-cut nails. She closed her eyes, fantasizing about how they would feel against her skin. Her eyes flew open as a rush of heat flooded Deborah's face when she realized the direction her thoughts had taken.

"How would you like a change of residence?" she asked, much too quickly.

Asa's smile vanished, replaced by an expression mirroring confusion. "Where would I live?"

"Upstairs, there's a furnished apartment and you can live there rent-free. It's the least I can offer to offset the low salary. I've ordered a new mattress, wardrobe, and blinds, which are scheduled to be delivered on Friday. I'm also waiting for a few other pieces, so by the time we open for business your apartment should be ready." Her cell phone chimed. "Please excuse me," Deborah said, reaching into the pocket of her jeans and walking away from Asa to answer the call.

Pushing his hands into the pockets of his slacks, Asa seemed to be deep in thought about Deborah's offer.

"Do you mind if I see the apartment before I give you my answer?" he asked when she returned after finishing her call.

"Not at all." She pointed to the back of the store. "There's a staircase behind the second door on the left that leads upstairs."

Deborah went back to unpacking books. She'd managed to shelve half the titles in the African-American Literature and Black Studies section when she heard two pairs of footsteps descending the staircase. Asa and Peter Raney, dressed in a pair of coveralls with his name and company's logo stitched over his heart, were talking about football.

"Mrs. Robinson, where is the other television, and where do you want it hooked up?"

Deborah had had the moving company bring the thirty-six-inch flat-screen television she had mounted on the wall of her Charleston store to the one at the Cove. "It's in a box against the wall. I'd appreciate it if you would also connect the DVD and tuner." She'd placed a call to a local electrician to mount the TV on the wall once the cable connection was installed.

"Do you have your audio speakers?" Peter asked.

"They are also in the box." Peter had done all the electrical work on her house when she'd had it renovated.

Asa moved closer to Deborah. "It looks as if he's going to be a while. Tell me what you want from Jack's and I'll go and pick it up."

Deborah was so grateful for his suggestion that she wanted to kiss Asa. "I'd like an order of shrimp and grits."

"You want grits for lunch?"

"What's wrong with grits for lunch?" she asked.

"I thought people usually ate grits for breakfast."

She smiled. "Down here we eat grits for breakfast, lunch, *and* dinner."

"Anything else?"

"A large sweet tea."

"How about dessert?"

Deborah shook her head. "I'll pass on dessert."

What she needed was comfort food. For some people it was mashed potatoes but for her it was grits. Reaching into his shirt pocket, Asa took out his BlackBerry, calling in the order to Jack's Fish House as he walked out the door. Walking behind him, she locked it, then took the HELP WANTED sign out of the window.

She couldn't believe her string of good luck. First she'd found an empty store in a prime location in move-in condition, and she'd just hired someone who was more than a clerk. He would become her assistant. And it was obvious he was either well-educated and/or an avid reader, and that gave him a distinct advantage when interacting with readers who preferred literature to popular fiction. The furnished apartment would become a perk for Asa—that is, if he decided to move out of the boardinghouse.

Peter programmed the television, resting on its stand on a drop-leaf table that she'd used in the other store for a collection of potted plants. The plants were now in the back porch and she would transport them to the shop for the grand opening. Deborah watched as he worked quickly to hook up the tuner, speakers, and the DVD player. Using the remote device, he turned on the television, smiling.

"Nice picture," he crooned.

Deborah nodded, smiling. "Thank you."

"Do you leave it on during the day?"

"I turn it on early in the mornings when there's not much activity, but once the regulars come to sit and read I'll turn it off and put in an MP3 with a collection of soft music. For those who just want to watch television I mute the sound and turn on the closed captions."

Peter adjusted his Atlanta Braves baseball cap. "It sounds as if you're going to have a nice place here."

"It is going to be nice," Deborah said with a modicum of pride. With the delivery of the concert piano, and once she positioned tables and chairs, hung framed prints of classic book jackets, and added the homey touches with plants, a refreshment table with Muffin Corner sweet breads, and an urn with hot water for tea, The Parlor would provide a place for residents and tourists to come, browse, and sit a while.

"I'm done here. If there's anything else you need, just call me," Peter said, smiling.

Deborah reached into a pocket of her jeans and took out a check, handing it to him. "I want to put in track lighting and a couple of ceiling fans."

The electrician pocketed the check without looking at it. "Do you want me to pick up the fans and the lights?"

"Yes. I want fans similar to those upstairs."

"I'll pick them up today and install them before the end of the week. Thank you again, Mrs. Robinson."

Deborah nodded. "Thank you."

He left through the rear door, and a minute later she opened the front door for Asa, who cradled a shopping bag to his chest.

Chapter Seven

Deborah closed and locked The Parlor door behind Asa. "Something smells delicious."

Asa peered into the bag. "That's either your shrimp and grits or my crab patties and black-eyed pea soup."

"I'm so hungry that I could eat a whole pig in one sitting. Come on. We'll eat upstairs."

He followed Deborah to the back of the store, his gaze following the gentle sway of her slim hips in her fitted jeans. There was something very sexy about the young widow. Asa hadn't wanted to believe she had a seventeen-year-old child, wondering if perhaps she had been a teenage mother. A very young teenage mother.

There were things he wanted to know about this woman. What made her laugh, what she liked to do when she wasn't at work or caring for her children. During the walk between the bookstore and the restaurant Asa couldn't steer his thoughts away from Deborah Robinson. There was something about her that he found disturbing. Not disturbing like ominous or unsettling, but a welcome distraction from what had become his daily routine.

He hadn't come to Sanctuary Cove to get involved with a woman but to heal and wait. And he was still waiting—the last time he'd e-mailed the contact person at DWB as to a potential date for his application's approval the reply had been his application was still pending. Asa had thought about checking out of the Cove Inn and driving north to Myrtle Beach, but that had been before he'd seen Deborah. He'd changed his mind because there was something about the beautiful widow that rekindled feelings he believed had died when he'd buried his wife and son.

Deborah opened the door at the top of the staircase. When Asa had come in before, the heat on the second floor was unbearable. She'd since opened all the windows and turned on the ceiling fans, and now it was cooler, more comfortable. The fans were noisy, but functional.

"I'm going to have my son put an air-conditioner in the window later this afternoon," she told Asa.

"Where is the unit?"

"It's at my house."

"I can install it," Asa volunteered. He placed the shopping bag on the kitchen countertop.

Pressing her back against the refrigerator, Deborah gave Asa a long, penetrating look. "So, you'll stay?"

He nodded. "Only if you intend to hire me."

She stood up straighter. "I thought we already assumed that you were hired."

"I never deal with assumptions."

"Do you want it in writing, or will a verbal confirmation suffice?" she asked, smiling.

He angled his head. "I wouldn't mind a verbal confirmation."

Her smile grew wider. "You're hired."

"Thank you, boss."

Deborah narrowed her eyes. "That will be the first and last time you'll refer to me as your boss. It's Deborah."

He nodded. "Yes, Miss Deborah."

"You just won't quit, will you?"

"No, Miss Deborah."

She rolled her eyes upward, then turned before Asa could see her smile. Instinct told her he was going to be good for The Parlor and good for her. He was an interesting man with above average intelligence. She didn't know why he'd come to the Cove, and it didn't much matter. Outsiders who came to the Cove were welcomed and treated with respect, and when they prepared to leave it was always with an open Lowcountry invitation to *come back real soon.*

She turned on the water in the sink, letting it run until it was clear, then reached for a sponge and a bottle of dishwashing liquid. She wiped down the countertop, then the table in the dining area. "You can wash up in the bathroom while I set the table."

The day before she'd filled the cabinets with plates, cups and glasses from an old set she'd put aside for Whitney *if* he decided to live off campus. She had just finished setting out plates for two when Asa returned. Whitney still hadn't told her whether he wanted to attend Howard University in Washington, D.C., or Bennett College in Columbia. Although he'd been leaning toward Howard Deborah knew his ambivalence had come from losing his father. When Whitney mentioned that he'd promised Louis that he would take care of his girls if anything happened to him, she knew he was wrestling with his conscience, that he didn't want to leave the state because he felt he had to protect his mother and sister.

What her son hadn't realized was that she didn't need as much protection as he did. Even if he chose Bennett he would be leaving home for the first time in his life. Her children had never gone to summer camp like some of their friends and classmates, and whenever they did leave the state it was to go to Florida to visit their grandparents. Pearl McLeary-Williams's sister had moved to Florida to be close to her grandchildren, and whenever Crystal and Whitney went to visit they had children their own age with which to interact.

"I like the colors in the bathroom."

Deborah's head popped up when Asa joined her in the kitchen. "I decided on brown and green because I like chocolate-mint ice cream." The bathroom resembled a tropical oasis with dramatic browns contrasting with cool greens. There were chocolate towels, a jade-green chenille rug, a citrus-scented diffuser, votive candles, and a quartet of small framed prints of Chinese characters symbolizing health, love, luck, and long life, all selected with a discerning eye.

"Is that why you painted the walls in the bookstore green?"

Folding paper napkins, she placed them at the place settings. "I can't take credit for that. The walls were painted by the former owner. However, I did order two area rugs in a tartan plaid with browns and greens."

Reaching into the shopping bag, Asa removed takeout

Styrofoam containers and two oversized foam cups filled with iced tea, watching as Deborah put serving pieces, flatware, white dinner plates with a cobalt-blue trim, and tall ice tea glasses on the table.

"I think I'm going to like hanging out here. There's a lot more space than in my suite at the boardinghouse." The apartment was one continuous space without walls. There were three doors: the one leading into the apartment from the bookstore, another leading out to a staircase to the parking lot, and the one to the bathroom. There were two ceiling fans with blades that resembled large brown banana leaves.

Deborah's hands stilled. "Too bad it holds heat. It's probably brutal up here in the summertime."

"It shouldn't be too bad with the fans and air conditioner," Asa said. "I meant what I said about going home with you to get the air-conditioner. After I put it in the window, I'm going back to the boardinghouse to change. If we work together we should be able to finish shelving the books by tomorrow."

"You don't have..." The ringing of her cell preempted whatever she was going to tell Asa. "Excuse me." Reaching into her back pocket, she retrieved the tiny instrument. It was the moving company. "Hello."

"Mrs. Robinson?"

"This is she."

"This is Bobby from shipping, and I'm calling to let you know we have a cancellation, so if it's all right with you we'd like to pick up the stuff from your house and deliver it to Sanctuary Cove tomorrow morning."

Deborah squeezed her eyes shut and rubbed her temple. "May I call you back, Bobby?"

"Of course, Mrs. Robinson. When do you think you'll get back to me?"

"I have to call someone to see if they can be at my house to let in your men."

Deborah ended the call, then scrolled through her cell directory for Sherilee's number. Closing her eyes again, she groaned when it went directly to voicemail.

"Sherilee, this is Debs. Please call me as soon as you get this message. The movers are coming tomorrow instead of Friday. Let me know if you'll be available to let them in." Hanging up, she began gnawing her lip between her teeth.

"Is there something wrong?" Asa asked when Deborah continued to bite on her lip.

Blinking as if coming out of a trance, she shook her head. "It's nothing that can't be resolved."

"Are you sure?"

"Very sure."

"You don't look very sure," Asa countered.

Deborah forced a smile. "How do I look?"

"Like a woman with a dilemma. It's obvious you can't be in two places at the same time."

She nodded. "I'll figure something out."

Asa pulled out one of the chairs at the table. "Please sit down and eat."

She sat, staring up at him over her shoulder. "Thank you."

Rounding the table, he sat opposite her, watching as she removed the top from an aluminum dish and ladled a portion of creamy grits topped with large pink shrimp, crumbled bacon, chopped scallions, and melted cheese onto her plate.

"Is that all you're going to eat?"

Deborah stared at the food, then at the man sitting across from her. "Do you realize there's enough here for two people?"

"What if we share?" he suggested. "I'll give you half my soup and a crab cake and I'll take half your shrimp and grits."

Her expression brightened. "Okay." Pushing back her chair, she stood up, Asa rising with her. She took another bowl from the overhead cabinet and a spoon from the cutlery drawer. "Please sit down, Asa. You don't have to stand."

"Sorry, old habit." Deborah could tell Asa was old school, rising when women entered the room, or stood up. He opened doors for them and seated them. He had impeccable manners, something missing in a lot of men nowadays.

Asa ladled soup into the bowl, handing it to Deborah. "I've eaten in a lot of places, but the food from Jack's should definitely be Zagat rated."

"I don't think Otis and Luvina would welcome that kind of attention."

"Why not?"

"Folks here are humble and live very simple lives. The last census documented that about eight hundred people live in Sanctuary Cove. Eight hundred residents who don't want their Main Street changed, or an influx of outsiders impacting their quality of life. We tolerate tourists who come here in droves during the summer because the tourist dollars keep us afloat. Everyone knows everyone else; we have little or no crime and it's not unique for people to leave their doors or cars unlocked. A Zagat rating would bring people to Jack's year-round, shutting out the locals.

"The Cove Inn is our Four Seasons and the Waldorf-Astoria all rolled into one, and Jack's is our award-winning

LeBernardin and Brasserie. The dishes at Jack's haven't changed despite the talk about black cuisine being viewed as being out of sync with what now defines healthy eating. All you have to do is look around the Cove and I doubt you'll find more than a dozen overweight people. We also have the distinction of living well into our late eighties and nineties. Do you want to know why?"

Asa nodded. The look on his face told Deborah he was quite pleased with the delicious shrimp and grits that made Jack's famous. "Tell me why," he said after swallowing.

"Because a lot of the food we prepare, especially the vegetables, is grown locally, without the harmful chemicals and pesticides that poison our bodies. The chickens come from a farm in Haven Creek and the pigs, too. Most residents have gardens and sell their surplus to restaurants and all the seafood comes from local fishermen." She flashed a winning smile. "Fresh air, fresh food, no industry polluting our air and the ocean as our playground. Life couldn't be better."

"You sound like a spokesperson for the Lowcountry tourist bureau."

Picking up her glass of tea, Deborah took a sip while staring at Asa over the rim. "If I sound a little passionate it is because I loved spending summers here."

"Where did you grow up?"

"Charleston. My father was born here, as were his parents, grandparents, and as far back as we can document."

"So, you're Gullah."

Her smile grew wider. "Down to the marrow in my bones."

"But, you don't sound like some of the people I've met."

"A lot of the older folks still speak the dialect."

"Do you?" Asa asked.

"No, but I understand it."

"How about your children? Do they understand it?"

"Yes," Deborah admitted. "They have friends in school who live on the island. They speak it when they don't want other kids who don't understand the dialect to know what they're talking about."

"I guess you can say it's like a foreign language."

Deborah nodded. "It is to those who don't understand it. The elementary schools on Cavanaugh Island are grades one through eight. All of the students are bussed into Charleston for high school, finally giving the island children a chance to mingle with each other and the city kids. Those who live in the Cove and who've never been to Haven Creek or Angels Landing meet those children for the first time in high school and usually form lifelong friendships."

"Do they marry one another?"

"I don't know."

Asa told Deborah about his attempt to tour the island, but how he'd had to turn back because he feared getting lost. "All I thought about was being forced to sleep in my truck with the windows rolled up, while praying some wild animal wouldn't get to me."

Throwing back her head, Deborah laughed until her sides hurt. "Don't you have GPS navigation in your car?"

"Yes. And what does that have to do with getting lost in the forest? Or should I say jungle? It doesn't work when there are no roads or streets. The next time I go sightseeing I'll take the causeway."

Deborah wanted to tell Asa that she'd never been to the Creek or Landing because of what her grandmother had told her about the people having tails and hooves. Once she was an adult she understood it was Sallie Ann's way of frightening her enough so she wouldn't go exploring and either get lost or bitten by some venomous reptile or insect. The causeway, which ran the length of the island, would take her past Haven Creek and Angels Landing before ending at the Cove. And she believed that was the reason why she'd continued to take the ferry instead of the causeway, which led directly to Angels Landing or Haven Creek.

Her phone rang and she answered it on the first ring. It was Sherilee returning her call. "Thanks for calling me back—oh no, don't apologize, Sherilee. It's not the end of the world. Thanks, again." Punching a button, she ended the call.

"Is everything all right?" Asa asked.

Deborah met Asa's eyes, aware for the first time they'd changed color. Pinpoints of gold had been replaced with a deep chocolate brown. "There's been a change in plans. The movers are coming tomorrow instead of Friday, and that means I'm going to have to stay at the store to try and get as many books shelved to make room for the chairs, tables, and piano."

Asa leaned forward. "You're going to put a piano in the bookstore?"

"My maternal grandmother was a concert pianist. My mother inherited it, but when she and my father moved into a condo in Florida they gave it to me. It took up a lot of space in my living room, and there's no way it could fit in my house here, so I decided it would go nicely in the bookstore in keeping with the overall parlor design." She smiled. "And before you ask, I do play."

"What do you need me to do?"

Lines of confusion appeared between her eyes. "What are you talking about, Asa?"

"Judging from your conversation you can't be at two places at the same time. So tell me what you want me to do."

Deborah knew she couldn't afford to look a gift horse in the mouth. Asa had come along at a time when she truly needed someone to help her. "Can you begin working this afternoon? I'm going to have to try and put away as many books as I can before the movers arrive tomorrow. I can't see myself moving and stacking cartons in corners just to have to move them later."

Asa nodded. "What else do you need?"

The timbre of his mellifluent voice changed, seemingly caressing her like a feather on bare skin, and Deborah couldn't stop the shudder that eddied over her body. "I'll need you to be here when the movers arrive and show them where they should position everything."

"You're going to have to let me know where you want the piano. I'm certain the tables and chairs can be rear-ranged if you decide later on that you want to move them."

Relief swept through her as if she'd been denied air but could now breathe. "I'll pay you extra for—"

"I don't want or need your money, Deborah."

"But you can't work for nothing, Asa."

"Living rent-free in this apartment is payment enough. The Cove Inn isn't the Waldorf, but the prices can get steep for the suites, two meals a day, and room service. So, I'm willing to barter working in the bookstore with free rent."

Deborah knew he was right about the rates at the mansion-turned-boardinghouse, but she felt uncomfortable not paying him for the hours he would put in at the bookstore. "I'll agree, but only if you let me pay you for your meals."

"No." Asa's face was a mask of stone.

"You can't work for free," Deborah insisted.

"I won't be working for free. How much would you charge someone if you were to rent this apartment?"

The question caught her off-guard. "I don't know," she answered truthfully. "I've never been a landlord."

"Neither have I," Asa replied, "but I know people who rent summer homes on Southampton, Long Island, starting at two thousand dollars a week. And don't forget the summer season begins with the Memorial Day weekend and runs through the Labor Day weekend. That's nice money if you can get it. Now, think of what you can charge tourists who come to the Lowcountry for the summer."

"I'd never charge someone a thousand a week for this place."

"What you could charge is a lot more than you'd be paying me. Now, may I make a suggestion?"

Deborah paused, her gaze meeting and fusing with Asa's. There was just a hint of arrogance in his query. "Of course you may."

"We drop the subject. Let's finish our lunch, go pick up the air-conditioner, and I'll put it in the window. Then I'm going back to change my clothes and we'll see how many books we can shelve before it gets too late."

"I'll drop it, Asa, but only if we can agree to the terms of your employment." His eyes narrowed suspiciously. "Please don't look at me like that."

"Like what?" he shot back.

"Like I'm going to pronounce a death sentence. I'm

willing to agree not to pay you a salary in lieu of free lodging, but..."

"But what, Deborah?" Asa questioned when she didn't complete her statement.

"I'd like to give you a hundred dollars a week for your meals."

"Damn, woman. You're like a dog with a bone. You just won't let it go."

She successfully hid a smile, picking up a napkin to wipe the corners of her mouth. Deborah knew she'd rattled Asa Monroe. Something told her the man was used to giving orders and having them followed without question.

"What is it going to be, Asa?"

"Make it fifty a week and you have a deal."

Deborah angled her head. "What's with you and money?"

"I don't need it as much as you're going to need it."

"What's that supposed to mean?"

"You're setting up a small business when there's no guarantee that it will remain viable. And that means you're going to need to save every dollar, not give it away. I don't need your money, Deborah. I love being around books so much that I'd be willing to work for free *and* pay rent for this apartment. I'll agree to accept fifty dollars a week just so we can end what has become very tiresome to me."

She extended her hand, excitement showing on her face. "Deal."

Asa took her hand, his thumb caressing her smooth knuckles. "Deal."

Believing she'd scaled a small hurdle, Deborah concentrated on finishing her lunch. She may not have been the traditional employer, but there was no way she was going to permit someone to work for free. And she knew instinctually Asa Monroe was worth more than fifty dollars a week, perhaps even ten times that amount. His intelligence, take charge approach, and the fact that he was a very attractive man was certain to bring customers into The Parlor—female customers in particular.

"Are you always this trusting?" Asa asked, breaking the comfortable silence. "Hiring someone without references?"

Propping her elbow on the table, Deborah rested her chin on the back of her fist. "I know you don't have any outstanding warrants because our sheriff runs the license plates of every outsider through a national criminal justice database. Don't forget there are only two ways off the island. And if you decided to break the law, I doubt you would get very far with Sheriff Hamilton waiting for you at the pier. If he doesn't catch you then you'd have to try and get past the roadblock on the causeway set up by the Charleston police."

"You can't tell me there's no crime on the island."

"There is. That's why we have a sheriff and several deputies. There are domestic disputes, problems with graffiti, an occasional drunk driver, and I'd heard there were a rash of burglaries over on Haven Creek before they discovered it was a cousin of one of the residents who had a serious drug problem. The man who caught the guy in his house beat him so severely that he had to be airlifted to the hospital. Unfortunately for the victim the man whose house he broke into was a former Vietnam vet suffering from PTSD. If he'd killed him it would've been the first murder on Cavanaugh Island in over thirty years."

"Why isn't the island listed on any 'best place to live and raise children' lists?"

"It isn't for the same reason why we don't have a Zagat-rated restaurant." Pushing back her chair, Deborah stood up and began clearing the table. She hadn't taken more than a step when she found her wrist trapped in Asa's strong grip. As he towered above her, the heat from his body added to her own. "What are you doing?"

"I'll clean up."

"You don't have to, Asa."

He gently tightened his hold on her arm. "Yes, I do. This is my place; therefore I'll clean up."

Tilting her chin, Deborah flashed a sensual smile. "Slow down, Asa. You won't be able to lay claim to this palatial estate until I give you a set of keys."

"Do you have an extra set?"

She nodded. "Yes. They're at my house. Let's clean up together, then we'll leave."

Working in tandem, Deborah washing and Asa drying, they were able to put the kitchen in order within five minutes. They took the back staircase to the parking lot where Asa had parked his vehicle under the shade of a palmetto tree. Opening the passenger-side door, he helped her up, waiting until she was seated and belted in before he sat beside her.

Chapter Eight

Asa started up the Range Rover, backing out of the space. "You're going to have to tell me how to get to your house."

"Once you pass the Cove Inn I'll tell you where to turn off." Deborah stared out the side window rather than look at him. "Slow down, Asa, before you're stopped for speeding."

"I'm going thirty miles an hour."

He could see her staring at him from his peripheral view. If he didn't have to keep his eyes on the road, he'd focus all his attention on her lovely face. "That's ten miles too fast."

Easing off the accelerator, Asa gave Deborah a quick glance. "If I go any slower I'll be standing still."

"There are no stop signs on the island, and you never know if a dog, cow, pig, or even a chicken will dart out across the road. If you hit and kill someone's pet or live-stock you'll have to make restitution to the owner."

Asa slowed even more. "You're kidding. How can someone identify their chicken from someone else's?"

"I knew all of my grandmother's yard birds. Whenever I called them by name, they'd come running."

Asa's laughter reverberated inside the Range Rover. "Next you'll tell me you had to get up before dawn to milk the cow."

"I did."

"Seriously?" he asked.

Deborah laughed when she saw his shocked expression. "Why do you find that so hard to believe? There was a time when most people living in rural areas owned livestock. I didn't start milking the cow until I was around ten or eleven. My grandma would skim off the cream to make butter and buttermilk, then boil and strain the milk before letting it cool enough to store in the refrigerator. I don't know whether it was actually the milk, but everything on the Cove seemed to taste better, especially Grandmomma's buttermilk fried chicken."

"Ah, youthful innocence," Asa drawled.

"Why are you so cynical?"

"Am I being cynical or honest, Deborah?"

"Cynical, Asa. Make a right turn when you see the red barn. My house is at the end of the road on the left."

"To be continued," Asa said under his breath, as he maneuvered into the driveway of the large, white, two-story house with navy blue shutters. It was larger than the house he'd pictured and wholly Southern in design, from the distinctive front porch to the white wicker chairs, rocker, and swing covered with floral-print cushions. There was even a colorful patchwork quilt draped over the back of a wicker loveseat positioned near a matching low table so that it made for the perfect place to begin or end the day.

Shifting into park, Asa left the engine running and came around to help Deborah down. His two hands spanned her waist and he held her longer than necessary. Feeling her fingertips on his shoulders, he tightened his hold, enjoying the softness of her body, the subtle fragrance clinging to her skin that he'd been unable to identify or forget.

"Please put me down, Asa."

He complied even though he had wanted to crush her to his body as a reminder of what he'd had and continued to miss: the warmth and smell of a woman's body. Asa wanted to tell Deborah he was sorry when he wasn't, so he decided not to say anything. He followed her to a side entrance. The air-conditioning unit outside the house indicated a central cooling system.

"How old is this house?" he asked as Deborah unlocked the door.

"The original deed documented it was built in 1909, but it was expanded many times over the years. I was told that my great-grandfather added the second floor a few years after he'd married my great-grandmother. It took him about four years to complete the project, because as a master carpenter and furniture-maker his skills were in demand here and on the mainland. I had to update the electrical system to accommodate several computers, and then decided to renovate the entire house. My husband and I had planned to use it for our permanent residence once we retired, but my children, who loved vacationing on the Cove, prefer living here to Charleston."

It was the first time Deborah had mentioned her late husband and Asa wondered if it had been as traumatic for her to lose her spouse as it was for him to lose his. If it had been, then she appeared to have adjusted well to being widowed. She'd relocated from Charleston to Sanctuary Cove, while he'd left all that was familiar, traveling from place to place as he waited for approval from DWB.

"How does your daughter feel about making the Cove her home?"

"She loves it here." Pushing open the door that led into the mud/laundry room, Deborah told Asa about Crystal wanting to put in a vegetable garden. "I'm certain she would've done quite well growing up on a farm."

"Do you plan to get a cow and chickens?"

Deborah gave him a sardonic smile. "Very funny," she drawled. "Here are the units. Do you think you're going to need both?"

Asa stared at two cartons labeled *air-conditioner* in a bold black marker, sitting on the floor in a brick-walled pantry. Mason jars filled with labeled fruits, vegetables, relishes, jams, and preserves lined the many shelves. The pantry was cool, much cooler that the outdoor temperature.

"I think one will do. Two air-conditioners going at the same time may blow the fuse. And, don't forget you have one in the shop."

"I'm going to put in some ceiling fans. I doubt I'll have to use the air until early May. Even though we don't officially have winter, sometimes it gets a little cool."

"What do you call cool, Deborah?"

Crossing her arms under her breasts, she smiled up at Asa. "Low sixties."

"That's short-sleeve and shorts weather."

Her smile grew wider. "Maybe for someone in New

York or Boston, but any time the temperature drops below seventy folks start complaining."

Bending from his knees, Asa picked up the carton, shifting the weight until he could carry it without putting a strain on his back. "After I put this in, we should turn on both units to see if the electrical system can support them."

"Let's go before you throw your back out carrying that thing."

Asa and Deborah retraced their steps and the route, returning to the bookstore. He spent a quarter of an hour putting the unit in the window, making certain it was secured, then used the remote device to turn it on and program it to shut off in half an hour.

Both units were humming when he returned to the parking lot to drive back to the boardinghouse. Impulse and curiosity had gotten him a position in a Lowcountry bookstore and a different place to live while he bided his time on the island.

In just a short time his life had changed again—this time it promised a respite from the grief and guilt that had become so much a part of his day-to-day existence. Not only could he lose himself in the many titles that lined the shelves in The Parlor, but he could also interact with the customers who would come in to either browse or buy. Working the part-time, temporary position was certain to make his wait on the island a lot more gratifying.

And having Deborah Robinson as his employer was something he looked forward to. She was gorgeous, very smart, and a bit feisty, and claimed a strength that did not diminish her femininity. Yes, he mused, working at The Parlor was certain to become a pleasant and unexpected diversion.

• • •

Deborah sat on the floor in the bookstore, texting her son: Working late. Have Crystal reheat leftovers & make salad 4 dinner. Luv Mom.

Crystal had given her a crash course in texting, claiming she didn't have to type out every word and letter. As a former English teacher she still didn't use all the abbreviations and symbols that had become a language so inherent to the adolescent lexicon, but she had to admit texting was faster.

She'd lowered and closed the wooden blinds over the bookstore's plate glass window and had emptied three more cartons, flattening and stacking them in a pile where they would be picked up for recycling, when Asa tapped on the door. Pushing to her feet, she walked over and opened it. He'd changed into a black tee, jeans, and running shoes. The muscles and tendons in his arms and biceps bulged under the weight of a carton of bottled water.

"Can you take the shopping bag please, Deborah?"

She took the plastic bag from his fingers, peering inside to find another bag, this one also in plastic. "What did you buy?"

He smiled. "Dinner. I stopped at the supermarket and picked up a couple of salads from the deli section. I bought a Caesar with shrimp and a Thai salad with steak. I had them put the dressing on the side. I'm going to put a few bottles of water in the refrigerator."

"My, my, my. You've thought of everything."

"My motto is always plan ahead."

Deborah realized her instincts were right when she'd hired Asa. He was always just one step ahead of her, because she'd planned to call and have dinner delivered. "I'll bring up the salads."

"That's all right. I'll come back for them," Asa said.

"I'll leave them on the table." Picking up her MP3 player, she inserted the wire into a port in the tuner, then punched a button and the melodious voice of Anthony Hamilton singing "Ain't Nobody Worryin'" filled the space. She was swaying and singing along with the Commodores' "Three Times a Lady" when Asa returned for the salads.

"You like dancing?" he asked.

"I do, but I haven't danced much since my kids were born. As a working mom I never seemed to find the time to go out dancing."

"Although you're still a working mom, would you dance with me?" Asa asked, smiling and extending his hand.

Deborah hesitated, then placed her hand on his outstretched palm. "Yes, I would." Her voice was low, calm. Asa's arm went around her waist and he swung her around in an intricate dance step. He'd tightened his hold on her when she tried extricating herself from his firm grip.

"Asa!"

He smiled. "Yes, Deborah."

"Please let me go."

"Why? I love this song."

The heat in her face had nothing to do with the exertion, but from embarrassment. Suddenly Deborah realized anyone walking by the shop could see them. "Someone will see us."

Asa pulled Deborah closer. "Unless they have x-ray vision, they won't be able to see through the blinds." He chuckled softly. "If they're that nosey, then they'll get an eyeful. Relax. We're only dancing, and the song will be over soon."

She wanted to relax, but it wasn't easy. Not with his hard body pressed to hers. Not when the man holding her to his heart was a stranger. Not when he reminded her that the man she'd loved beyond description was gone and would never return. Yet, what bothered her most was she couldn't remember the last time she'd danced with Louis.

Resting her forehead on Asa's shoulder, she closed her eyes. The selection ended, segueing into the Marvin Gaye classic "What's Going On?"

"Thank you for the dance," Asa said in her ear.

Pulling back, Deborah stared up at him, meeting his amused gaze. "You're welcome."

He released her, breaking the spell. The next two hours were spent unpacking and shelving books as music flowed throughout the store.

Her cell phone rang and she scrambled off the floor to retrieve it. It was her daughter. "Hi, Crystal. What's up?"

"Whitney and I are just leaving school. He waited for me because I had cheerleading practice. He told me you texted him about heating up leftovers."

"Yes I did."

"Can we eat at Perry's before we come home?"

Deborah knew Perry's was a hangout hamburger spot for high school students. She took a glance at her watch. It was after four, and she knew it would be dark before her son and daughter returned to the Cove. It wouldn't be the first time they would stop off to eat before coming home, but they no longer lived in Charleston.

"Not tonight, baby."

"Why not, Mom?"

Crystal's whining grated on her nerves. "Please put Whitney on the phone."

"What's up, Mom?" Her son's deep voice came through the earpiece.

"I want you to come home now."

"Chrissie wants to eat with her friends."

"Chrissie can eat with her friends when she doesn't have to go to school the next day. I want you home before it gets too dark."

He sighed heavily. "Okay, but Crystal's about to catch an attitude."

"What she shouldn't want is for me to catch one. Call me from the house phone once you get there. Good-bye."

Deborah ended the call and placed the phone on a padded folding chair. She could always count on her daughter to try and push the envelope. She knew the rules: no socializing on school nights. If it had been a Friday night, Deborah might have considered letting her hang out with her friends. But not when she had to get up even earlier now that they lived on the island to make it to school on time. And Crystal always had a problem waking up—even with an alarm clock.

Brushing off the seat of her jeans, she walked into the bathroom and washed her hands. She stared at her reflection in the mirror over the vanity and the face that stared back at her was that of a stranger. It had been weeks since she'd gone to the salon to have her hair trimmed and styled; she needed a mani/pedi and a hydrating facial. In other words she needed a beauty makeover. The Beauty Box was several doors from the Muffin Corner and Deborah knew she had to make an appointment before her grand opening.

Drying her hands on a decorative guest towel, she left the bathroom. With Asa's assistance, they'd shelved most of the books. Only six cartons remained. "I'm going out for a few minutes to stretch my legs. Do you want me to bring you something from the Muffin Corner?"

Reaching into the pocket of his jeans, Asa took out a money clip. "I'll have large black coffee with a shot of espresso."

Deborah waved her hand. "Put your money away. I still owe you for lunch and dinner."

"I'm sorry, boss—I mean, Miss Deborah."

Deborah narrowed her eyes, then smiled. "Don't give away the store."

It had been after eight when Deborah turned off the lights, locked up The Parlor, gave Asa her set of keys, and selected a spot for the piano for when the movers arrived. Miraculously she and Asa had finished shelving all the books. She'd gone home to take a leisurely bubble bath. Deborah hadn't realized how tired she was until she lay in bed. She remembered Crystal coming into her room, but could not remember what they'd talked about.

Today was to become as hectic as the day before. She'd gotten up early to go into Charleston to supervise the movers as to what she wanted delivered to the bookstore. She was also expecting the delivery of the mattress and other furnishings for the second floor apartment. The receptionist at the Beauty Box had managed to squeeze her in, but she had to be there at four, or she would have to wait until Saturday for her favorite stylist to fit her in.

Her cell phone rang, and she answered it before it rang again. "Hello."

"Good morning, Deborah."

A smile tilted the corners of her mouth. "Good morning, Asa. How are you?"

"Good."

"Where are you?"

"I'm at the store."

"I'm leaving Charleston now, and I'm going to try and make the next sailing." Taking the ferry would get her there faster than taking the causeway, because it was a direct route.

"I'll see you when you get here."

Deborah ended the call; walking in and out of the rooms she checked to make certain the movers hadn't forgotten anything. The linen closet was empty, as were the closets in all the bedrooms. She and Whitney had loaded up the trunks of their cars with clothing they would take with them. Every year she would go through her children's closets and drawers to pack up what they'd outgrown or no longer wore, donating used and gently used clothes. Unnecessary clutter had become her pet peeve. Deborah had also packed up pots and pans, linens, and cleaning supplies for Asa's apartment.

She lingered when she should've been in her car driving for the pier, her fingertips caressing the backs of chairs, the surfaces of tables, lamps she'd waxed and dusted for as long as she could remember. The bed where she'd lain and made love with Louis would go to a single mother who'd lost everything. The furniture in her son's and daughter's rooms would go to other children whose need was much greater than any Crystal or Whitney had experienced in their young lives.

Let it go, Deborah. It's time to say good-bye, her silent voice taunted. Deborah took a final look around, and then walked out of the bedroom, down the hallway and the staircase to the first floor. Reaching for her handbag, she went to the door, opened it, then closed and locked it for the last time.

"Deborah!"

She turned around to find Barbara in a bathrobe, standing on her porch and sipping from a large mug. "Hey you."

Barbara came down off the porch. Tears shimmered in her eyes. "I guess this is it."

"No, it's not," Deborah countered. "You know you and your family are welcome to come to the Cove anytime you want. And I hope you're coming to my grand opening tomorrow. I'm getting my hair done this afternoon," she added when Barbara stared at the hair she'd pulled into a ponytail.

"Of course, Deborah. I wouldn't miss it for the world. I changed my shift just so I could be off. What time should I get there?"

"I'm opening at noon, and the ribbon-cutting will be at one."

"Will you need help setting up?"

Deborah smiled and shook her head. "No. I hired someone to assist me in the store."

"Good for you." Barbara hugged Deborah, taking care not to slosh coffee on her white cotton pullover. "I'll see you tomorrow."

Deborah returned the hug, kissing her now ex-neighbor's cheek. "Tomorrow. Got to go, because I want to get to the Cove before the movers."

"Can I bring Nate and Janelle?"

"Of course. Maybe they can stay over to give you and Terrell a night to yourselves."

"I'd love that, but I promised my mother-in-law we would take her out to dinner."

"Perhaps another time then." Deborah glanced at her watch. She had thirty-five minutes before the next sailing. She looked up at the overcast sky. It was cool, but felt warmer because of the near one hundred percent humidity. If it was going to rain, then she hoped it would hold off until she reached the island.

An hour later, Deborah maneuvered into her parking space as the movers' van pulled up next to her. They'd arrived at the same time. Her stomach did a flip-flop when she saw Asa standing in the doorway dressed entirely in black: golf shirt, slacks, and slip-ons. There was something about his standing there, arms crossed over his chest, that was so male and virile. It took her breath away. He glanced her way and smiled. She returned it with one of her own. She didn't know what she would've done if he hadn't been there to help her. He was more than an employee. He was a godsend.

Stepping aside, Asa winked at Deborah when she walked in through the back door. "Mabel dropped off the muffins and coffee. Today's special is carrot-molasses."

She saw a tray of assorted muffins covered with cellophane and an urn of coffee on the table, along with hot/cold paper cups, small paper plates, and a dish filled with packets of sugar and sugar substitutes and a bowl filled with ice and prepackaged milk and half-and-half. Deborah had stopped at the Muffin Corner the night before and arranged to have the sweet breads delivered to the store to offer the workmen who would be coming and going throughout the morning. The smell of the brewing coffee was intoxicating.

"As soon as the coffee finishes brewing I'm going to get a cup."

"How do you take yours?" Asa asked Deborah.

"Very light with half-and-half."

"Sugar?"

"Yes please. Two."

"Mrs. Robinson."

Deborah turned to find the foreman of the work crew striding into the store. "Yes."

"We're going to either have to take off the door and the frame to get the piano inside or remove your plate glass window."

Deborah shuddered to think what would happen if they broke or cracked her window. "What is easier for you?"

"Take off the door and the frame," Asa said before the man could respond. "The window might be easier, but if there's any trouble replacing it, we could end up with leaks whenever it rains."

"Bring it through the back door," she said, confirming Asa's directive. "You and your men are welcome to coffee, muffins, and breakfast breads."

"Much appreciate the offer, ma'am."

One man in the three-man team quickly took the door off the hinges, then the frame, as the other two lowered the piano on a hydraulic lift and wheeled the dolly into the shop with relative ease. "Where do you want this, ma'am?"

"Position it in front of the window." Deborah had decided she wanted the piano near the front of the store, where passersby would be intrigued enough to want to come in and browse. Before leaving the night before, she'd had Asa tape newspaper over the front door to conceal the interior from onlookers.

The men replaced the legs on the magnificent concert piano, positioning it perfectly. Thankfully it came with casters, which made moving it around easy. Cordovan-brown club chairs with footstools and loveseats were set up to form a reading corner where customers could read or watch television. A generous supply of glass coasters were stacked on the coffee and side tables.

Deborah picked up an all-in-one computer and cash register off the floor, placing them on a mahogany writing table. She set a landline telephone on a matching desk, the file drawers filled with orders and receipts. Another mahogany piece—this one a buffet server that would provide a surface for the urn of hot water and packets of tea and condiments—faced the desk and writing table against the opposite wall. Once the rug was down, the ceiling fans installed, and the hand-painted pots with live green plants in place, The Parlor would resemble an actual parlor.

Asa stood with his back to the front door, surveying the bookstore as if it were his first time. The reading area was inviting, with twin floor and table lamps with Tiffany-style shades. He had visited countless bookstores—small and large—but none had the warmth and homey charm of The Parlor. Setting up the tea bar was an ingenious idea, because Deborah had mentioned she wanted to revive the ritual of afternoon tea with pretty tablecloths and china cups with matching saucers. The bar would be reserved for a small gathering of eight with tiny cakes, cookies, and tarts to accompany the various blends of tea.

"What do you think, Asa?"

"It's wonderful. Once people come in they're not going to want to leave. You have a nice selection of titles, so you should do okay."

"I have to do more than okay."

"What are you concerned about, Deborah? It's everything that you want and need."

"The Parlor has to be more than a bookstore, Asa. I have to come up with something to keep the customers coming back again and again. And it can't only be because of three o'clock afternoon tea."

Unconsciously, Asa's brow furrowed. "Why are you serving tea at three?"

"Haven't you noticed, with the exception of a few businesses, most places close between the hours of twelve and two?"

"Yes, I did. Why's that?"

"It's an island tradition that goes back about three hundred years. The summer sun is so brutal that it is dangerous to stay outdoors during that time of the day, so everyone and everything stops. The custom isn't adhered to as much during the winter months, but during the summer all businesses close down—even the restaurants, post office, and supermarket. Some people who've been to Europe refer to it as siesta, so when you hear folks talk about taking siesta you'll know what they mean."

"Are you going to observe the ritual now or during the summer months?" Asa asked.

"I'll keep the tradition year-round. It will give us a chance to put everything in order. It will also give us time to relax with a midday snack and set up for tea."

Lowering his arms, Asa rested a hand on Deborah's back. She stiffened, then relaxed against his outstretched fingers. "I just thought of something."

Shifting slightly, she met his eyes. "What?"

"Did you have a book discussion group in your Charleston bookstore?"

Deborah shook her head. "No. I'd tried setting one up, but most of my customers were too busy to commit."

"I think it would work well here," Asa said, "because there are a lot retirees and snowbirds. You can hold it every two weeks, which means they would have to buy at least two books a month. That would definitely guarantee sales."

"Are you certain you never ran a bookstore before?" she joked.

He smiled, attractive lines fanning out around his eyes. "Very certain."

"What did you do before you retired?"

"I worked in a hospital."

"Were you a doctor?"

Asa's chest tightened. "Yes." He quickly changed the subject before she could probe further. "So, how are you going to run this book club of yours?"

"Well, if I'm going to moderate the discussions, then I'll have to read the books, too."

"You're a former English literature instructor. Select something you've already read."

Deborah froze. "Who told you I was a teacher?"

"Mabel did when she dropped off the muffins and coffee. She said she'd expected you to become a librarian because you were always obsessed with books."

Deborah paled for a moment, but shrugged it off quickly. "And I'd predicted that she would become a pastry chef. Whenever there was a cooking contest Mabel always came in first place. She's established a reputation for making the best piecrusts in the Lowcountry."

"Does she ever sell pies in her shop?"

"Pies and cakes are special orders. Her husband Lester is the cake man."

"Are you going to get them to provide the tea cakes? And will the ladies be required to wear fancy hats whenever they come for high tea?" Lifting his chin, he peered down his nose as if he'd detected something malodorous.

Deborah gave him a soft punch to his shoulder. "Stop it! It's not nice to begrudge our genteel Sanctuary Cove ladies."

Asa rested his hands on her shoulders. "I wouldn't dare. After all, you just happen to be one of those genteel ladies."

"You think?"

He nodded. "I know. You are incredible."

Asa fought against the tumult of emotions that left him feeling off-balance. It was as if he was metal and she was a powerful magnet, drawing him in, holding him captive. With each encounter he found it more and more difficult to relate to her not as an employer but as a woman.

She looked up at him, an unsure expression on her face. "Please, Asa…"

His hands fell away. "I'm not coming onto you, Deborah."

She took a step back, putting some distance between them. "Did I imply you were?"

He angled his head, giving her a long, penetrating stare. "No. But, if it makes you uncomfortable, then I won't touch you again."

"Did I say it made me uncomfortable?" she replied smoothly.

Asa crossed his arms over his chest in a gesture that had become very familiar to Deborah. "You don't have to say it. You freeze up even if I inadvertently brush against you. I'm not a sexual predator, so put your mind at ease that you're not going to be attacked when you least expect it. I'm forty-six years old and I've never had to force my attentions on any woman, and I'm not about to do it now."

Deborah watched him walk to the back of the book-store. "Where are you going?"

He stopped but didn't turn around. "Out for a smoke."

Her eyelids fluttered. "But you don't smoke."

Asa turned, glaring at her. "Maybe it's time I start."

The seconds ticked as they continued to stare at each other. "My husband wasn't a touchy-feely person," she finally admitted.

Asa nodded. "Well, maybe what you need after a stress-ful few days is a friend who is."

He extended his arms, beckoning her closer.

She took a step, anchoring her arms under his shoul-ders, and found herself enveloped in his embrace, making Asa feel things he didn't want to feel. The runaway beating of her heart slowed until it resumed a normal rhythm.

"I'm sorry I snapped at you," Deborah said, burying her face in the crux of his shoulder.

Asa pressed his mouth to her hair, the curls piled atop her head tickling his nose. "I think we've done enough apologizing for one day, and definitely no pity parties."

Asa heard Deborah's audible sigh before she pulled out of his embrace. A tap sounded at the front door. "You're right. That's either the electrician or the furniture deliv-ery." As she walked away, Asa realized how much he already missed having his arms around her.

Chapter Nine

Whoever it was, Asa cursed their timing. Holding Deborah, burying his face in her hair, felt so natural, as if he'd executed the motion countless times. She looked nothing like Claire, but holding Deborah had reminded him of what he missed.

Asa *was* a touchy-feely person, and touching Deborah made him feel more alive than he'd been in over a year. She had become a constant reminder that he was a man with physical urges he had managed to repress. Women had come on to him at the boardinghouse, but with them he'd felt nothing.

However, it was different with Deborah. Asa didn't know whether it was because they'd lost their spouses, or if it was glimpses of vulnerability he saw in Deborah that appealed to his protective instincts, but he knew that he wanted her for more than friendship.

Snapping out of his thoughts, Asa realized it hadn't been the furniture delivery, but the electrician, who'd arrived carrying an oversized sailcloth satchel containing his tools. Peter Raney returned to his van and brought in cartons filled with the ceiling fans and track lighting Deborah had requested.

"Where do you want the fans, Mrs. Robinson?"

"I'd like you to replace the light fixture in the front and the one behind the loveseat with the fans. I have Tiffany-style globes to cover the other naked bulbs. But, there is one more thing I'd like you to do." The slightly built, pale man had a sparse graying pate and watery blue eyes that looked like they belonged on a heavy-lidded owl, and the bored expression on his face did not change.

"What's that?"

"I need a doorbell."

Peter squinted. "I just may have one in my bag. May I suggest something, Mrs. Robinson?" Deborah nodded. "I think you should replace your front door with a decorative one with beveled glass. It would let in light while still providing some privacy."

A blush made its way across her cheeks. There was no doubt the electrician was referring to the newspaper taped to the door to keep out prying eyes. "I'm planning on hosting my grand opening tomorrow."

"I can have it installed today," Peter said. "I'll measure the doorframe, then call my son and have him pick up one on the mainland. I'm not certain how much you want to spend, but a nice fiberglass door will probably run you, including installation, around seven-fifty. You'd want a storm-type door that will convert from glass to a screen to protect it from the saltwater. That's probably another three hundred. Both doors are a nice investment that will enhance the look of your store. What else do you need?"

"There are two ceiling fans in the upstairs apartment that work but make a lot of noise."

He gave her a rare smile. "I'll check them first. If they're bad, then I'll have my boy pick up a couple for you when he goes to get the doors. By the way, it looks real nice in here."

"Thank you. I know every dollar spent in the bookstore is a needed business expense." She paused before turning back to Peter. "You can put in the doors."

Asa came up behind Deborah when the electrician went to measure the door. "He's right about replacing the front door."

She glanced up at him over her shoulder. "What about the back door?"

"There's no need to replace it because it's made with reinforced steel. Are you going to install a security system?"

Deborah shook her head. "No. Only the bank and the pharmacy have security systems that are connected to the sheriff's office. The pharmacy has to have one because of the drugs and because it also houses the post office. In case you haven't noticed, all of Main Street, including the business district and waterfront, is monitored by cameras. Unfortunately some kids decided it was fun to leave their tags around the Cove. Though not a serious problem yet, the town council voted to install them. As soon as they went up the vandalism stopped."

"The sheriff looks like he's no-nonsense." When Asa had sat in at the town meeting he'd noticed that Jeffrey Hamilton hadn't smiled once.

"He gave the Marine Corps twenty years before

becoming sheriff. Jeff would lock up his grandmother if she spat on the sidewalk. He grew up on the Cove, but has relatives in Angels Landing and Haven Creek. Folks called him Sheriff Buford Pusser from the *Walking Tall* movie after he caught some kids who'd come over from the mainland shooting up drugs in the schoolyard late one night. One came at him with a baseball bat, while another pulled a gun. He managed to get the bat and that was all she wrote. The boy with the gun ended up with two broken arms and the other was so lumped up that he couldn't see out both eyes for at least a week."

"Damn," Asa drawled.

"That's what I said when I heard the story. He's the sheriff for the entire island. He also supervises part-time deputies in the other towns."

"Why don't they have their own sheriffs?"

"They did at one time, but when they restructured their budget the mayors decided to pay Jeff to police their towns, too. The deputies are retired police, probation, and corrections officers who accepted the positions to supplement their pensions." Knocking interrupted their conversation, this time on the back door. Deborah smiled at Asa. "That must be the furniture delivery." She walked to the door, Asa following close behind.

He opened the door for her. "Yes?"

A burly man in a pair of overalls touched the brim of his oversized cap. "I have a furniture delivery for..." He squinted at his work order. "It looks like D. Robinson."

"You can bring it in." Waiting until the man went back to his truck, Asa turned to Deborah. "You can show them where you want them to put the furniture, while I'll hang out down here."

"You'll have to move the piano to put down one rug, and the other will go in the sitting area."

"Don't stress yourself, Debs. I'll take care of whatever it is you need."

"No, you didn't call me Debs."

Asa winked at her. "Yes I did. Don't you call yourself that?"

Her dark eyes sparkling in amusement, Deborah stared at Asa's smiling mouth. "Yes, but only my good friends call me Debs."

Asa leaned closer. "What about me, Debs? Am I not your good friend?"

He held his breath, hoping that she considered him a friend, wanting to become so much more. He was friend, protector, and guardian angel. "Yes. Right now you're my best friend."

He winked at her. "I like that. I've known a few girls who were called Debbie, but not Debs."

"Mabel shortened my name to Debs and it stuck. Very few folks on the Cove call me Deborah. My mother named me after her mother, who thought I was the best thing to come along since sliced bread because I was her first grandchild."

"Is she still alive?"

"No. She died two years ago. She'd moved to Florida because she couldn't take the cold weather, but when she was diagnosed with dementia my parents relocated to be close to her. When she began going outdoors alone and the police would bring her home dehydrated with second and occasionally third degree burns, Mom knew she had to put her in a skilled nursing facility. Once there she declined rapidly, losing control of her bodily functions. I flew down to see her and the doctor had to sedate me. I lost it when I saw her strapped to her bed. But I understood why they had to do it. She'd begun hallucinating and calling for my grandfather who'd died many years before. I was in the airport on my way back to South Carolina when my dad called to tell me that my grandmother had passed away. She was lucid for the first time in years and had told him that she wanted to see me. That was a dark period in my life because I'd lost three grandparents within the span of five years. I guess that's why I tell my children every day that I love them."

"I know you're a widow, but you're lucky to have your children."

Deborah pulled her lips between her teeth. "I'm more than lucky. I'm blessed. Do you have any, Asa?"

A beat passed. "No, I don't." He was saved from having to explain how he'd lost his only child when one of the delivery men, balancing a box spring on his shoulder, came through the door.

Deborah nodded to the man. "Please follow me. It goes upstairs."

She preceded him up the staircase, standing aside while he placed it on the springs of the massive antique iron bed. It had taken a lot of straining, but Asa soon appeared to help and together, they'd managed to pull the bed from the corner to the middle of the room. With the bed dressing, shades, wardrobe, and other accessories the apartment began to take on a homey atmosphere.

Peter, who'd taken the cover off the wall switch, flipped it several times and the blades to the fans turned slowly until they were whirling on the fastest speed. "The noise was because they were off-kilter."

Deborah smiled, causing Asa's heart to skip a beat. "Thank goodness for that."

"I'll replace the wires because they look a little frayed."

"Thank you, Peter."

Deborah stored the rest of the linens in the drawers at the bottom of the wardrobe after she made up the bed. When she'd ordered it she thought of what Crystal had said about moving into the apartment once she attended college. There had to be enough space for her to hang her clothes and drawers to store her lingerie, tees, and whatever else she needed to wear. There was still another three years before her daughter would graduate high school, and that was enough time for her to decide whether she would attend a local or out-of-town college. Or maybe Whitney would make use of the apartment should he decide to attend college in Charleston, rather than going away to Howard.

She overheard Peter, who'd replaced the cover to the wall switch, call his son and tell him what he needed, while she tore open the package to the slipcovers. Cursing under her breath, Deborah saw that she had to steam the wrinkles and creases.

"What's the matter?" Asa asked when she returned to the bookstore and opened the desk drawer, reaching for her key fob.

"I have to go home and get my steamer."

"For what?"

"I bought slipcovers for the chair and sofa, but they're wrinkled."

Asa took the key fob from her loose grip, pushing it into the pocket of his slacks. "No, Deborah. I'm not moving in tonight, so the wrinkles can wait. They'll probably fall out over time, so don't stress yourself out about it."

"When are you moving in?"

"Probably not until Monday or Tuesday. And I'm certain when I do move in the apartment will be lovely."

A smile like sunshine brightened her face. "The ceiling fans are quieter now."

Deborah didn't know why, but she wanted Asa to lower his head and kiss her. Not a passionate openmouthed kiss, but one that would allow her to see if he was as sweet as he looked. He stared at her under lowered lids. "Good."

"And I made up your bed."

"Thank you."

Deborah's eyebrows lifted slightly. "I hope Peter will be finished by four, but if he isn't can you hang out here until he is? I have a hair appointment and probably won't be finished until six."

Asa nodded. "No problem."

Pushing her hands in the back pockets of her jeans, Deborah pulled the denim taut over her hips as she stared at the rug under the piano. "Did you have a problem moving the piano?"

"Piece of cake," Asa crooned, walking over to the piano and sitting on the bench. Resting his hands on the keys he began to play, his fingers caressing the ivory.

Deborah felt her pulse quicken. She played piano, but even after years of lessons and recitals her skill wouldn't begin to match Asa's. Closing her eyes, she swayed gently. She opened them when Peter walked over to listen and they shared a knowing smile. No words were needed.

"That was real pretty," Peter said when the last note faded. Asa nodded. "Excuse me, but I'd better get to work."

Sitting on the bench beside Asa, Deborah leaned into him. "Where did you learn to play like that?"

He stared at his hands resting in his lap. "Practice, practice, and more practice."

"I practiced until my fingers bled, and I still couldn't play 'Bella's Lullaby' like you just did."

A hint of a smile tilted the corners of Asa's mouth. "So you recognized it?"

"There's no way I wouldn't. My daughter is obsessed with the Twilight Saga. She's read the four books at least twice and I've lost count how many times she's watched the DVDs."

"These young girls seem to be fascinated with vampires."

"Well, you have to admit that Edward is somewhat of a sexy vampire."

"Please don't tell me that you were one of those mothers who stood in line with their daughters to catch the midnight premiere."

Deborah folded her hands at her waist. "I was. There was no way I was going to let my child go to a movie theater that time of night without my supervision." She flashed a sheepish grin. "I think I would've enjoyed the film more if I hadn't had to deal with a theater filled with teenage girls screaming hysterically whenever Edward kissed Bella."

"I can't believe you bought into the hype."

"Why?"

"I don't know. I just wouldn't take you for someone who would go for a vampire flick."

"It was a paranormal romance film."

"And that makes it different?"

"Of course it does," she argued softly.

Asa reached for her left hand. "Play something for me."

"What?"

"Anything, Deborah."

She searched her memory for a piece she could play without music, deciding on a Chopin nocturne. She hadn't played more than a dozen notes when Asa began playing with her. They shared a grin, he winking at her as their fingers flew over the keys as if they'd practiced together in the past. Deborah knew playing with Asa made her step up her game, and she lost herself in the music.

They segued from classical music to the show tunes from Andrew Lloyd Webber's stage productions: "All I Ask of You," "Don't Cry for Me Argentina," and "I Don't Know How to Love Him." Overcome with emotion, Deborah collapsed against Asa. Playing with him had been a way for her to open up herself to release the grief that had hung over her like a shroud. The songs he'd selected were sadly haunting and evocative. It was as if he, too, was in pain and needed to surface from a dark place filled with sadness and melancholy.

Covering her mouth with her hand, she cried silently. "I'm sorry," she sobbed, sliding off the bench. She hadn't taken more than three steps when he caught her wrist, spinning her around to face him.

Cradling her face between his hands, Asa stared at Deborah's tear-stained face. "I'm sorry." Reaching into a pocket of his slacks, he took out a handkerchief and gently blotted her face.

She managed a half-smile. "There's no need to apologize. I get a little sentimental when I hear certain songs."

Asa put the handkerchief back in his pocket. "You're not a very good liar, Deborah."

Deborah's temper flared, but she managed at the last possible second to clamp her teeth together to keep from spewing curses. She was upset because Asa had made her feel vulnerable, and after only two days he'd come to know whether she was lying or telling the truth. Was she that transparent, or was he just perceptive? She'd told him about her family, but little about herself. He knew she'd been a teacher, had owned a bookstore in Charleston, and was widowed with two teenaged children, but not much else. She hadn't told him her age, where she'd attended college or what she'd planned for her future. "Excuse me, but I'm going out for a smoke."

"But you don't smoke." He'd repeated what she'd said to him earlier that morning.

"Maybe I do. Maybe I don't. I'll right be back," she replied with a sad smile.

As Deborah opened the door and walked out into a light drizzle, she could hear the sounds of Andrew Lloyd Webber music being played on the piano. She stood still for a moment, allowing the melody to envelop her, before heading to the parking lot.

Deborah walked into the Muffin Corner, the wind chime affixed to the door jangling musically. She folded her body down on a chair at the only unoccupied table, waving to Mabel who'd come from the rear of the shop.

"What's up, Debs?"

She pulled her wet blouse away from her skin. "I'll have your largest cappuccino with plenty of sugar and whipped cream."

Mabel made Deborah's coffee, adding a generous amount of whipped cream, and then came over to sit down opposite her. "What in the world set you off? You look like a ruffled cat."

Taking a sip of the hot liquid, Deborah moaned softly as the perfectly made coffee warmed her throat and chest. "Thanks for the compliment," she said facetiously. She immediately apologized when Mabel's face fell. "I guess I'm a little stressed out trying to get the store ready for tomorrow."

"When I dropped off the muffins I noticed that you'd shelved all the books."

Deborah took another sip, licking the cream off her lips. "I couldn't have done it without Asa Monroe."

Mabel gave her a mischievous smirk.

"Don't look at me like that, Mabel."

"Like what, Debs?"

"Like the cat that just licked the cream off Sunday dinner's dessert."

Mabel affected an impassive expression. "Is this better?"

Deborah laughed when she felt like crying again. She could not have found better friends in Mabel and Barbara. They always knew what to do to make her laugh. She told her friend how she'd come to hire Asa.

"I still would have been unpacking books if it wasn't for him," Deborah concluded.

"The man is smooth as creamy peanut butter."

"What are you talking about?"

"Breeding and elegance, Debs. That's something you're born with, and the man definitely has a monopoly on both."

Cradling the mug in her hands, testing its warmth against her palms, Deborah had to agree. "He's very intelligent and extremely talented."

"Could it be that you like him?"

"No! No," Deborah repeated in a softer tone. "How can you say that when I just lost my husband?"

"Losing your husband has nothing to do with finding yourself attracted to a man. What if Louis were alive? Would you still think your Mr. Monroe intelligent and creative?"

"He is *not* my Mr. Monroe, Mabel. He happens to be someone who is vacationing on the Cove for the winter, and come spring he'll be gone like so many of the other snowbirds. He wants to work and I need someone to help me manage the bookstore. End of story."

Mabel applauded slowly. "Bravo, Debs. Nice speech."

Deborah's hands fell away from the mug as she began to massage her temples. "I came here to de-stress, Mabel. I don't want to talk about Asa. What I do want to discuss with you is afternoon tea."

"Afternoon tea?" Mabel repeated.

Deborah nodded. "Yes." Throwing back her head, Mabel laughed. The sound was so infectious that Deborah laughed with her. "What's so funny?"

"Are you talking about tea time when ladies put on their fancy hats and lace gloves and nibble on cucumber sandwiches?"

"Yes." Deborah revealed to the pastry chef what she'd planned for weekday afternoons at The Parlor. Deborah also told her about the book club, leaving out the fact that Asa had given her the idea. The less she mentioned his name the easier it would be for her to dismiss the strange sensations that he made her feel, which were far more frightening than the tales her grandmother had told her about the people on the north side of the island.

Mabel flashed her trademark gap-toothed grin. "I like it, Debs. I remember hearing my great-grandmomma talk about the rich ladies who'd lived in the big houses. Their so-called grand mansions were falling down around them, yet they still managed to get together most afternoons for tea."

"Bless you, Mabel Davis-Kelly. You just gave me my first title for the book club discussion: Kathryn Stockett's *The Help*. And I'm going to place an ad in the *Chronicle* advertising the book club. I have to make certain to emphasize that we will be reading and discussing literary and popular fiction. Those who want to read literature will be in one group, and those who prefer popular fiction will be in another. Each group will be required to read two titles each month and every two weeks we'll have the discussion. The highbrow ladies will meet every other Tuesday, and the ordinary folk every other Wednesday."

"I know what you're up to, Debs."

"What's that?" she asked, grinning from ear to ear.

"I bet those snooty heifers will want to read the literary stuff, and us regular people will go for the popular stuff."

"You know you ain't right," Deborah drawled.

Mabel sucked her teeth loudly. "I'm as right as rain and you know it. What if they buy their books on those electronic readers, then join the group?"

"The criteria for joining will be that they have to buy the book from The Parlor."

The wind chime jangled again, and Mabel stood up. "I'll have Lester make a few cakes for your grand opening. It will be our homecoming gift."

"Thanks, friend. We'll talk later about what I'll need for my afternoon tea."

"It's not going to be that complicated, Debs. Whatever muffin is the special for that day I'll make into loaves and cut them into little squares. And for those who have a nut allergy I'll make shortbread cookies." She waved her hand. "Don't worry. I'll hook you up real nice."

Deborah squeezed Mabel's hand. "I don't know what I'd do without you."

"Yeah, you would. You'd look for another gap-toothed gal to make you laugh."

"You know you're crazy, Mabel."

"Yeah, I know. Crazy like a fox. Let me go and take care of this customer before she starts spreading gossip that I ignored her even though I can't stand her old ass," she said sotto voce.

Deborah watched in awe as Mabel interacted with Hannah Forsyth. Hannah had been the librarian when Deborah was a teenager, and nearly three decades later the woman was still in the position. She was also the Cove's historian and a notorious gossip. If she'd been a Hollywood gossip columnist, she would've become wealthy selling information about the residents of the island.

Deborah finished her coffee, pulled a bill out of the pocket of her jeans, left it on the counter, and walked out. The drizzle was now a heavy steady rain. Sprinting out the door, she ran through Moss Alley and around the back to The Parlor. By the time she made it into the store she was soaked through.

She stopped short when she saw Asa staring at her as if she were an apparition. "What's the matter?" When he didn't answer she looked down to see what he'd been staring at. Her white blouse was pasted to her chest and the outline of her breasts was clearly visible through her sheer white bra. Curbing the urge to cover her chest, she hunched her shoulders.

"Why don't you go upstairs and dry off?" Asa suggested.

Deborah nodded only because she couldn't speak. It was as if her voice had been locked in her throat, rendering her completely mute. Turning on her heels, she raced up the staircase. Peter was nowhere to be seen and for that she was thankful. Walking into the bathroom, she stripped off her blouse and bra, spreading both over the shower door. Reaching for a towel under the vanity, she blotted the moisture from her arms and chest.

Deborah stared at her reflection in the mirror over the vanity and then closed her eyes as the area between her thighs throbbed when she recalled the naked hungry lust in Asa's eyes. Moaning softly, she bit her lip when the throbbing increased until she felt as if she were coming out of her skin.

I need him. A rush of guilt assailed Deborah's traitorous thoughts. She'd buried her husband six weeks ago and now she found herself lusting after a man—a stranger who made her feel something she did not want to feel: desire. Pressing her fist to her mouth, she waited until the throbbing eased, then wrapped the towel around her body, tucking the ends together over her breasts. Her jeans were damp, but tolerable.

Deciding on a bit of ingenuity, Deborah draped her blouse and bra over the back of the dining area chair. Bringing it within a foot of the stove, she turned on the oven, waited for it to heat up, and then opened the oven door. She'd read stories about people using their oven to heat their homes, but she didn't think it would take that long for her clothes to dry and she'd installed carbon monoxide detectors on both levels. Her drying method may have been a little primitive, but the result would be the same if she'd used her programmable dryer at home.

Settling down to the chair, she picked up the remote

and turned on the flat-screen TV resting on the table across from the bed and seating area. She was so engrossed in a Victorian-period drama that she almost didn't hear the soft rapping on the closed door.

Sitting up straight, she pressed a hand over the towel. "Yes?"

"It's Asa. May I come in?"

Though her head said no, her unsteady voice replied, "Yes."

Chapter Ten

Asa held the doorknob for a full minute before deciding to enter the room. Slowly, he closed the distance between them and sat on the sofa. He tried swallowing the lump that had risen in his throat when he found that he couldn't pull his gaze away from the erotic sight of the soft swell of Deborah's breasts rising and falling under the towel. Asa also couldn't get the image of her erect nipples showing through her wet blouse out of his head. It hadn't mattered that he was a doctor and seeing a naked human body held as much appeal as a dead bug on his windshield. But it was different with Deborah Robinson. She was a very special woman who reminded him that he was a man whose physical urges hadn't died when he'd buried his wife.

Sandwiching his hands between his knees, Asa stared at the pattern on the rug under his feet. The chocolate-brown comforter with its large green leaves, the pile of bed pillows, the white window blinds, off-white slipcovers, and the oak wardrobe in an alcove had turned what had been a cold, empty space into an inviting apartment where he hoped to spend many relaxing hours.

"I like your dryer." His head came up when Deborah laughed; the sound was like music to his ears. He liked her best when she was laughing.

"It's said that necessity is the mother of invention. Maybe I should put in a stackable washer/dryer."

"Don't bother, Debs. I send my clothes out to be cleaned and laundered."

"Doesn't the boardinghouse have laundry service?"

He nodded slowly. "The first time they did my laundry I got someone else's underwear. And that told me either they wash everyone's clothes together, or they got mixed up in the folding phase." He stood up. "I came up to check on you."

"I'm going to give my very unique dryer another half an hour, then I'll be down."

"Take your time, Debs. Peter put up the track lights. He's now working on installing the fans."

Asa wished there was more information he could give her, if only to be in her presence a second longer. When he could think of nothing else to add, he turned and walked away, her image emblazoned in his mind.

"Look at you!" Crystal squealed when she saw her mother walk in through the side door. She'd just finished taking clothes out of the dryer. "Oh, Mom, you look *faboolicious.*"

"I decided it was time to get my hair done."

Crystal reached for her mother's hand. "You also got a mani."

Deborah wiggled her toes, painted a soft raspberry color in a pair of flip-flops. "And a pedi, and my eyebrows plucked," she added.

"Can I get my hair and nails done?" Crystal asked.

"Sure. But what's the occasion?" Her daughter only visited the salon when she wanted her hair cut. And she claimed she couldn't sit still long enough for a manicure and pedicure.

"I want to go to the school's Valentine's Day dance next month. Whitney's going, so I'll be with him. Please, Mom."

Wrapping an arm around Crystal's waist, Deborah led her into the kitchen. "Is there someone special that's going to be at this dance?" She dropped her handbag on a stool near the wall phone and sat at the table with her daughter.

Crystal affected a bored expression. "He's not special."

"What is he?"

"He's just a friend. He lives in Charleston. He asked me to go to the dance with him, but I told him I'm not allowed to date, so we're going to meet at the school."

Reaching across the space separating them, Deborah reached for Crystal, holding her hand gently. "It's not that you're not allowed to date. It's just that I think you're too young to get involved with a boy."

"You were twenty—only five years older than me when you married Dad."

"That's true, but I'd graduated high school and was close to finishing college. Remember, your father had finished and he was teaching. That meant he could support a family. If you get too involved with this boy and heaven forbid you get pregnant, where do you think you'll end up? By the way, how old is he?"

"Sixteen."

Deborah shook her head. "Fifteen and sixteen. Even if you got a job flipping burgers you can't work full-time, and that means how are you going to pay rent, buy food, and take care of a baby?"

Crystal rolled her eyes. "I'm not going to get pregnant."

"And why not, Crystal?"

"Because I'm not going to have sex."

"You say that now, but what if you get caught up in the moment and it happens? I've always been open with you when it comes to sex and birth control. After your dad and I were married we decided we would wait five years before we would start a family. It didn't happen because one night we got caught up in the moment and I found myself pregnant with Whitney. Two years later you came along."

"Was I a 'caught up in the moment' baby?"

Deborah tunneled her fingers through her now bone-straight tresses. Whenever she wore her hair straight, she was reminded of photos of her mother, who had been the consummate hippie with long, curly auburn hair, bell-bottom pants, sandals, colorful dashiki, and love beads.

"No, baby. We planned to have you."

"That's nice to know. Back to the dance, Mom. I want a dress and heels."

This boy must really be something if my daughter wants to put on a pair of high heels, Deborah mused. "Do you know what type of dress and heels you want?"

"Not yet. I've been going through magazines looking for one. Shoes aren't as important."

"That's where you're wrong, Crystal. Accessories can make or break an outfit. You can look through my closet and try on a few of my shoes and see what style you like."

She and her daughter had the same size foot, and Deborah's weakness had always been shoes and handbags.

"Can I wear the pair with the black silk bow?"

"Don't even try and go there, Crystal Robinson. I'm going to let you try my shoes on, but you're not going to wear them. Besides, those heels are four inches, and I doubt whether you'd be able to walk in heels that high."

"I have almost a month to practice."

"How tall is this boy?"

"He's taller than me."

"Will he be taller than you when you put on four-inch heels?" Deborah questioned.

Crystal scrunched up her face. "I don't know."

"Find out how tall he is before we buy your shoes. At sixteen boys don't like it too much when a girl is taller than them."

"I don't like being tall."

"I'm tall, Crystal, and so is your grandmother. Learn to accept it." Pearl Williams was five-ten, Deborah five-eight and Crystal was five-nine—and still growing. She glanced at the clock on the microwave. It was after seven. "Where's Whitney?"

"He's in his room typing a sample article for his meeting with Mr. Wilkes tomorrow. I should let you know that there's talk going around the school about Whitney."

Deborah closed her eyes. What she didn't want was a repeat of what had happened to Louis. "What kind of talk?" she asked, opening her eyes.

"Some kids are saying he's gay. That he doesn't like girls."

"What does Whitney say?"

"He doesn't say anything. I know he likes girls, because

he's been talking and texting one who lives in Haven Creek."

"I take it the other kids don't know this?"

"He says it's none of their business."

Deborah smiled. "Good for him. I'm not going to say anything to him about what you just told me, but I hope she's at least a nice girl."

"I don't think she's a ho, but I don't know her like that."

"I hope you don't talk like this around that boy you like."

"I don't," Crystal confirmed.

"Then why me, Crystal?"

"Because you're cool like that, Mom."

Smiling, Deborah ruffled her daughter's hair. "Yeah. I guess I am cool like that. I'm glad you found a boy you like."

"He's nice, Mom."

"That's even better. Where does he live again?"

"Charleston."

"I'd like to meet him," Deborah said.

Crystal's eyebrows lifted. "Really?"

"Yes, really."

"Can he come tomorrow for the grand opening?"

Deborah nodded. It had been a while since Crystal seemed so upbeat about someone or something. "Of course. After dinner I want you to call his mother and I'll talk to her."

Crystal's expression changed, the excitement in her eyes fading quickly. "How is he going to get here, Mom? Darius doesn't drive. That's his name. Darius."

Deborah knew her daughter was flustered because her words came out choppy. "Don't worry about him getting here, baby. If his mother says he can come, then she can drop him off at the ferry and I'll have Whitney meet him at the pier."

Springing up from her chair like a jack-in-the-box, Crystal wrapped her arms around her mother's neck and kissed her cheek. "You're the best, Mom."

Deborah hugged her back. "I thought I was cool."

Crystal kissed her again. "That, too."

"What are we going to make for dinner?"

Crystal jumped and ran over to the refrigerator, holding the door open while she peered inside. "I defrosted some ground beef yesterday because I wanted burgers. But we can always use it for chili."

Deborah rose to her feet. "Chili sounds good. There should be some kidney beans in the pantry," she said as she walked to the half-bath to wash up. "See if the lettuce is still good. I'll put together a salad."

"How about garlic bread, Mom?"

"That sounds good," she called out from the bathroom.

She returned to the kitchen to find Whitney standing there in bare feet, holding several printed pages. He wore a white tee and jeans. She could never understand his aversion to wearing shoes.

"Hey, you look nice."

"Thank you, Whit." It had been weeks since her children had seen her made over, and having them compliment her buoyed her spirits.

"Mom, can you look these over when you get a chance?"

Deborah tossed the paper towel on which she had dried her hands into the wastebasket under the countertop. "Are you sure you want me to see them before they're published in the *Chronicle*?"

"What makes you so sure that Mr. Wilkes is going to hire me?"

"The news he prints is old and tired, Whit. Hannah Forsyth's column about the history of the island is repetitious. People only buy the paper because they're hoping for something new. I've read the articles you've published in your school paper, and they are a lot better than what's in the *Chronicle*. If it wasn't for the ads, Eddie would've closed up shop a long time ago."

"Let's hope he doesn't close down until I get some articles in print. These are about Grandma Sallie Ann. I need you to tell me if I got the facts straight."

Deborah nodded. "Okay. I'll look at them after dinner. Leave them on the table in the back porch. And I promise not to take out my red pencil."

Whitney cut his eyes at his mother. "Real funny, Mom. I meant to ask you if you've read Grandma's letters."

"Yes, and burned them."

"Why?"

"What's in them was for my eyes only."

"Were they X-rated?"

"No, Whit. They were very personal. Things that happened before she married my grandfather. I plan to start reading her journals tonight. I'm willing to bet they'll be less personal. And if they are, then I'll let you read them for yourself. Maybe one of these days you'll write a book about her."

"Why haven't you written a book?" Whitney asked his mother.

"What would I write about? My life hasn't been that exciting that someone would want to read about it."

"It doesn't have to be nonfiction."

Deborah opened a cabinet and took out the pressure cooker. "I'd rather read books than try to write one."

"If I do write one, will you edit it for me?" Whitney asked.

"Yes, I will. Remember, I want you and Crystal to come to the grand opening tomorrow. In fact, you should write about it. I know it smacks of nepotism, but who cares."

"What are you wearing, Mom?" Crystal asked as she cradled two large cans of beans to her chest.

"Probably a blouse and dress slacks."

She set down the cans. "Can I pick out your shoes?"

"Don't pick out anything that will make her look like a hoochie, because you know there will be photos," Whitney warned his sister.

Deborah gasped. "I beg your pardon, young man. For your information none of my shoes come even close to hoochie status. So, mind your mouth."

"I guess I'd better take my foot out my mouth and get out of here while I can still walk," Whitney whispered under his breath.

"Good advice, brother love," Crystal drawled face-tiously, laughing when her brother left the kitchen. "What if we have chili burgers instead of chili con carne?"

"You're the chef tonight and I'm the sous chef. It's whatever you decide. What do you want me to do?" Deborah asked.

"I need you to cut up several onions, garlic, bell pepper, and a few jalapeños."

"How much is a few, Crystal?"

"Three, four."

"No pepper mouth. I'm not going to eat food so spicy that I'm reliving it days later."

"Okay, Mom. Two jalapeños."

. . .

Deborah sat up in bed, her journal on her lap. Crystal had outdone herself when she added cubes of pepper jack cheese and finely chopped jalapeños to the ground beef patties, cooking them on the stovetop grill until they were tender and juicy with just enough heat to tantalize the palate. The garlic butter slathered on toasted hamburger buns and covered with a thick piquant chili along with an accompanying Greek salad had surpassed what they would've eaten at their favorite restaurant. She could see Crystal growing her own vegetables and serving them for dinner.

Reaching for a pen, she opened the cloth-covered book.

January 14th—I don't know what's happening to me. I find myself thinking about Asa when I least expect it. And I find myself wanting him when I don't want to. I say *want* because I don't want to need him. Needing Asa would make me dependent upon him, and that would prove disastrous when it comes time for him to leave the Cove. However, whenever I am around him I feel good—very good.

He's been a perfect gentleman, not giving me any indication that he wants more than friendship. But, I have to be honest when I say I don't know what I would do if he did. I'm still in love with Louis. I will always love Louis, and right now there is no room in my life for romance or another man.

Deborah closed the journal, placed it in the drawer, and turned off the bedside lamp. As she lay down to fall asleep her mind was flooded with images of Asa. His face, his smile, his tall, strong body, his hands. She loved his hands and the way they felt when he touched her. She thought about the way they skimmed the keys when he'd played the piano, envisioning his fingers caressing her naked body as they had the ivory. She imagined what it would feel like to have him stroke her most intimate places, bringing herself to climax before she realized what she'd been doing. Exhausted, she finally fell asleep, but not before trying to convince her heart that she was *not* falling in love with Asa Monroe.

Chapter Eleven

⁓

As Deborah maneuvered her car into the lot behind Moss Alley, she spotted Asa's truck. She shut off the engine and exited her car, but instead of entering the bookstore from the back door, she came around to the front. She wanted to see the new door in the bright daylight. The rain had stopped at dawn and the heat had returned with the rising sun. The weather was perfect for a grand opening. It was Saturday, the weekend, and a time when tourists came to the Sea Islands to shop.

Deborah had a sudden memory of years before. When she'd first told Louis her intent to stop teaching and open a store, he'd looked at her as if she had taken leave of her senses. Although in the end he'd given her his support Deborah knew he'd believed she would fail. However, she proved him and the other skeptics wrong because The Parlor offered the public what other bookstores hadn't—a nostalgic down-home, small-town charm that was wholly Americana. Those were past times when life was hard, but simple. Most people didn't have much, but they were content with their existence. Sunday dinners were family-oriented and national holidays meant fireworks, picnics, and county fairs. When her customers walked into The Parlor they felt that and more. Most were repeat customers, some who sat and talked long enough to form friendships. The homey atmosphere was what she'd tried to evoke, and had with much success.

This was what she'd duplicated with the Cove's bookstore. The piano was certain to garner a lot of interest, and the fact that she *and* Asa could play the magnificent instrument—he a lot better than she—was a double asset. There had been a time when she'd played for her children every night before putting them to bed. She'd gone from playing nursery rhymes to pop and show tunes to classical compositions once they'd begun taking lessons.

She still played duets with Crystal, who'd taken to the instrument like a duck to water, and Deborah attended her many recitals. Whitney, who'd hated to practice, stopped playing altogether when he turned ten. Crystal had continued taking lessons until she was thirteen. Deborah knew that Deborah McLeary would be proud to know that her precious piano hadn't been sold or left to gather dust in some warehouse, and that her namesake had kept it in concert-ready condition.

Standing outside the bookstore, she stared at the newly installed doors. The glass on the outer door was spotless. Moving closer she peered at the designer door, with its pattern reminiscent of those designed by Frank Lloyd Wright. Peter Raney was right. The beveled glass distorted objects inside the store, while the blinds covering the plate glass window concealed the piano and everything beyond it from view.

The day before, Deborah had set up her computer and printed a sign with the store's hours of operation, and set it in a silver frame that she placed in the window for all to see. Whitney had been given the task of designing a business card and the result was in keeping with the locale. Green lettering on buff-colored parchment with the image of a palmetto tree advertised the Cove's first and only bookstore.

Returning to her car, she opened the trunk and retrieved the hand-quilted runner for the table where she would place the live plants. She'd just put the key in the lock when the door opened and Asa stood, gaze fixated on her.

"Welcome to The Parlor." He bowed low as if she were royalty.

Deborah was too stunned to react, her breath catching in her throat. Asa had exchanged his casual attire for a white shirt, dark-gray silk tie, and a pair of charcoal gray suit trousers with a faint pinstripe. His footwear was a pair of Stacey Adams black leather slip-ons. He looked and smelled incredible.

She recovered quickly, giving him a modified curtsey. "Thank you, sir. You're here early," she said when he stepped aside to let her in.

"I decided not to wait and moved in earlier this morning."

Deborah smiled. "Good for you."

"You look beautiful."

Deborah froze, her eyes meeting Asa's. She'd wanted to tell him how handsome he looked, but he had complimented her first. A swath of heat swept over her, settling in her chest before moving lower. When she'd gotten up that morning she'd wondered about his reaction to seeing her with makeup, heels, and a different hairstyle. What she hadn't understood was why she was concerned about his reaction to her appearance, but seeing the way he was looking at her made it all the more clear. She wanted him to think her pretty, because she liked Asa Monroe.

Lowering her eyes and giving him a demure smile, Deborah said, "Thank you." As she turned to put the finishing touches on the store's appearance, she could feel the heat from Asa's gaze on her back.

Asa stared at the woman he'd grown to care for during his stay on the island. The electrician and his son had installed the doors before Deborah was to leave for her hair appointment, so he left after they did to return to the boardinghouse to pack. When he'd sat down to eat with the other guests he realized it would be the last time he would dine with them. Just knowing he would have a place to eat, sleep, and read in peace had made it difficult for him to contain his excitement. And for the first time, he'd joined the others in the parlor for cordials. That night when he went to bed, there was luggage sitting by the door. And when he finally fell asleep he'd dreamed of a beautiful woman with curly hair and a face like the angels in Renaissance paintings.

But the Deborah Robinson he knew had morphed into a sophisticate who belonged on the slick pages of *Town and Country*. The curls were missing and in their place was a sleek coif that swayed around her face and neck whenever she moved her head. Parted off-center, the smooth dark-brown strands with streaks of gold looked like threads of liquid silk. A light covering of makeup enhanced her dark eyes and full mouth.

How, he mused, could a woman look so utterly sexy in a tailored white blouse and black slacks? Some men liked their women in a state of undress, while he preferred his women clothed so he could imagine what they looked like without them. And right now his imagination had gone into overdrive. A single strand of large pearls, matching studs in her ears, and a pair of black cloth-covered pumps with decorative silk bows complemented her incredible look.

"What are you going to put on the table?" Asa asked.

"I have potted plants in the trunk of my car. I thought having live green plants would add a nice touch."

"I'll bring them in. What else do you need me to do?"

Deborah turned and patted his chest. "Nothing. Just look gorgeous for the ladies."

"So, I'm going to be your piece of meat."

Deborah ran her hands along his solid shoulders, smoothing the pristine shirt. "You're more than just meat. You're filet mignon."

Asa shook his head, smiling. "I prefer well-done rib eye with garlic butter or prime rib with horseradish."

Her smile matched his. "I'll keep that in mind when I treat you to dinner."

"Let me go and get those plants."

Deborah glanced at the time on the cable box. She had twenty minutes before The Parlor would open for business. She turned on the fans to circulate the warm air and lit scented candles, and the glow from track lighting and the sound of soft music set the stage for when she would finally open the door to welcome her first customer.

Asa came through the back door, kicking it closed behind him while carrying a plastic crate overflowing with greenery. "I'll leave you to arrange them however you want."

"Put the crate on the floor and I'll take care of them," Deborah called out. "Can you come over here for a minute?" She waited for Asa to come to where she sat at the desk, opening the top drawer and handing him a key on a black elastic band. "That's the key to the drawer in the writing table. Please open it."

Asa sat down at the table and opened the drawer, revealing the built-in compartment with stacks of bills in denominations from twenties to singles. There were also compartments for coins. "Nice."

"We need enough cash on hand to make change for customers." She punched several buttons on the cash register and the drawer opened. "You'll have to put in a pin number to open the register."

"A little security to keep someone from reaching over and dipping in the till," Asa said, nodding.

Deborah nodded. "I had to learn that the hard way. One time when I'd stepped away from the front someone walked in, opened the cash register, and scooped up whatever money was there before I realized what was happening. That's why I bought this one and I don't leave much cash in it. The credit card machine is connected to the landline telephone." She'd plugged in a cordless phone extension in the apartment and had an additional handset on the writing table. "All daily receipts will go here, orders in this one," she said opening and closing drawers in the desk. "I keep thinking I'm forgetting something."

"Stop worrying, Debs. Everything is perfect."

She smiled up at him. "I couldn't have done it without you."

"Yes, you would have. It may have taken a bit longer, but you would've done just fine."

Deborah stared at Asa's delectable mouth inches from her own, willing him to kiss her. Kiss her and remind her that she was a woman who'd realized she still had needs—sexual needs that had to be assuaged. Her gaze did not falter as she inhaled the citrus-blended fragrance that made up Asa's cologne and aftershave. She felt unable to move or speak as Asa came closer.

Her breasts felt heavy, nipples tightening in arousal as her chest touched his. Deborah's eyes closed; her heart stopped when his mouth brushed over hers. Asa's kiss was gentle, yet persuasive and she kissed him with a hunger that belied her noticeable calm.

"Deborah," Asa whispered, his heavy breathing echoing in her ear.

"Asa, I..."

His mouth moved over hers again, swallowing her words, while devouring her softness. "Don't talk, baby," Asa pleaded. "Please don't say anything." His lips left hers, trailing feathery kisses under her ear, along the column of her neck. "You smell delicious."

"Thank you," Deborah mumbled dreamily.

Asa kissed her again. "You taste delicious." Both were breathing heavily when the kiss ended. "That was for good luck, Debs."

"Thank you," Deborah said again in a husky whisper. The breathlessness of her own voice made her blush.

His smile was as tender as a caress. "As soon as you arrange the plants we can open the door."

Deborah didn't want to believe Asa could appear so calm when her insides were quivering like gelatin. Her mouth was tingling from his kisses. Asa had stoked a fire that grew hotter every time they were together.

Deborah set out hand-painted ceramic pots on the quilted table runner stitched with irregular shapes and various fabrics that her great-grandmother had pieced together. When her grandmother had shown Deborah her collection of quilts she had a story to tell about each of them. There were pieces that had come from a tattered apron, a worn tie, dress, work pants, shirt or jacket. The quilts were a textile history of her family and the time in which they'd lived.

Taking a step backward, she surveyed her handiwork before glancing over at Asa. She watched as he slipped his muscular frame into the suit jacket before adjusting his shirt cuffs and tie. He looked up at her then, their gazes locking before he walked over to meet her by the counter. Her shoes added at least three inches to her slender height, putting the top of her head at his nose. Deborah's chest fluttered at the thought of being this close to him, reminding her of the kiss they'd shared. She shook her head free of the thoughts and instinctively reached up to adjust his tie.

Raising his left arm, Asa stared at his watch. "It's ten." Reaching for her hand, he tucked it into the bend of his arm. "Are you ready?"

Deborah's eyes moved slowly over his face. "I was born ready."

Throwing back his head, Asa laughed loudly. Walking to the door, he propped it open to allow for The Parlor's first customers to come through. Deborah stood at the counter, staring out at the clear glass, while Asa opened and raised the blinds over the plate glass. The bookstore was situated on the west side of Main Street, and that meant the sun would not reach them until late morning.

Within fifteen minutes of opening a young man from the local florist walked in carrying a large potted plant wrapped in shiny green paper tied with a bright red bow. Deborah indicated where he could set the plant, signed the receipt, and gave him a tip. She plucked off the attached card. "It's from Lester and Mabel Kelly."

Asa ran a forefinger over the large green waxy leaves. "It probably will be the first of many you'll receive today."

The words were barely out of his mouth when Eddie Wilkes walked in with a large vase of long-stemmed roses in hues ranging from pure white to near purple. "Congratulations, Debs. The place looks fantastic. Where should I put this?"

Asa came over and took the vase. "I'll take it."

Eddie stared up at Asa. "Mr. Monroe, isn't it?"

"Just Asa is fine."

Eddie nodded. "Asa it is." Shifting his attention, he took a step closer to Deborah. "You did good, girl." He leaned in to kiss her, but she turned her head at the last possible moment, his mouth connecting with her jaw. "If I'd known twenty years ago that you were going to look like this I never would've let you go."

"Shame on you, Eddie," she chided. "You're lucky Asa doesn't know your wife, or he would be forced to repeat gossip. And you should know how fast gossip spreads in the Cove."

"Kitty knows all about you."

"She knows what, Eddie?" Deborah asked. They'd gone out twice. The first time was their senior prom and the second time it was to hang out on the beach with a group of kids in their graduating class.

"That we're old friends."

She smiled. "You're right. But I don't want your wife to get the wrong idea and come after me with something. I heard through the rumor mill that not only is she jealous, but has a hair-trigger temper."

A rush of color darkened Eddie's face. "She does go off every once in a while. I just came to drop off the flowers," he continued without taking a breath. "I have to get back because I have an interview with your son. The boy has a lot of talent, Debs. It's not often I meet someone whose writing is equal to their verbal ability. Kudos to you and Louis for producing a fine young man."

Deborah forced a smile she didn't feel. Every time someone mentioned Louis's name she felt as if she'd been stabbed. She didn't want to play the grieving widow, but she also didn't want to be reminded that she'd lost her husband whenever someone offered their condolence. What she wanted was to heal and move on. Her sole focus was to take care of her children and to make certain her business remained solvent.

"Thank you, Eddie."

"I'll see you later when I cover the grand opening ceremonies."

Seconds later, Asa, who'd overheard the conversation, placed a gentle hand on Deborah's shoulder. "You okay?"

"Of course. Why wouldn't I be?" She started to move away from his touch, but he squeezed her softly.

"How long were you married?"

A beat passed. "Eighteen years."

"I have to assume that you went to bed and woke up with your husband for most of those years."

"The only time we were separated was when he had to attend a conference or if I took my kids on vacation without him."

"The most difficult thing to adjust to now that he's gone is sleeping alone, right?" He didn't wait for her to answer. "You get into bed expecting him to be there, but he's not." Asa removed his hand and chuckled. "Lucky for you, your old friend Eddie seems more than willing to warm your bed. Not that I'd let a man like that near you…"

"So, what are you going to do, Asa? Become my protector?" Deborah rolled her eyes at Asa's macho talk, but she had to admit his protectiveness was flattering.

He grinned. "I will if I have to."

"There are quite a few single men on the island you may have to fight off," she teased.

"Don't worry, Debs. I'm up for the task."

Deborah sobered quickly. "I'm honored and appreciate your willingness to protect me, but at this time in my life I'm not interested in hooking up with a man. I don't care who or what he is. My first priority is my children."

Before Asa could respond, the door opened and two women walked in. One zeroed in on him like a heat-seeking missile. "Mr. Monroe. Fancy meeting you here," she crooned, "and how nice you look."

Deborah lowered her arms. She estimated both women were between forty and fifty, and it was obvious they were sisters. Both had the same platinum blond hair color, sea-green eyes, and coloring as translucent as fine bone china. They wore white camp shirts, and black cropped pants and black-and-white striped espadrilles. They were tall and much too thin.

"Welcome, ladies. I'm Deborah and Asa is the bookstore's manager." She extended her hand, smiling as each one shook it.

"I'm Dora Levin and this is my twin sister Cora Varney."

Deborah angled her head. "Do I detect a New England accent?"

"We're from Massachusetts," Dora confirmed. "We plan to stay in Sanctuary Cove until mid-April. We've been at the boardinghouse," she finished, sliding her gaze back to Asa.

"You have a very good ear," Cora crooned.

"I spent four years at Bennington College," Deborah added.

Dora's eyes brightened like spotlights. "We went there, too. But, of course we're a little older than you. Did you like it?"

"I loved it," Deborah replied. "My first winter I felt as if I'd never get warm, but by the time I was a sophomore you wouldn't have known I was born in the South if I didn't open my mouth to speak. You're welcome to browse, and hopefully you find something you'd like to read. I also want to let you know that we're having a ribbon-cutting ceremony at one. This will be followed by an open house with refreshments."

Cora, the less dominant twin, spoke up. "We must get together and reminisce. I wonder if the same professors we had were still there when you attended."

"But, of course," Deborah agreed, smiling. "If you're going to be here until April, then I think you might be interested in several activities we are hosting here at the store." She raised her brow, a playful smirk crossing her lips. "I'm certain Mr. Monroe will be more than happy to tell you about them."

Chapter Twelve

Asa cut his eyes at Deborah. He wanted to tell her that the sisters weren't as benign as they appeared. One was widowed and the other had never married and both were barracudas. No man, married or single, was exempt when they decided to target one. Dora had even attempted to compromise Jake Walker, who'd pretended he was hard of hearing.

You owe me, he mouthed to Deborah as he led the sisters to the seating area. She responded by blowing him a kiss.

It had to be word of mouth that brought a steady stream of people into the bookstore. Those who'd come to browse claimed seats when Asa sat down at the piano and began to play a medley of show tunes and movie soundtracks.

Mabel arrived, pushing a trolley with covered trays of cookies and tarts, as well as a sheet cake. Her husband carried in a large coffee urn, while Deborah set up another one filled with hot water for tea. The Kellys provided sugar, sweeteners, milk, cream, fresh lemon slices, plates, forks, and spoons.

There was another delivery, this one from Jack's Fish House. Otis set out platters of catfish fritters, shrimp with dipping sauces, and a seafood salad. He kissed Deborah, wishing her the best, stating he had to get back to the restaurant because he had to cater a party later that evening.

She was pleasantly surprised when a clerk from the local wine and liquor store walked in with a case of assorted wines and packages of colorful plastic cups. "I didn't order wine."

He smiled. "Mr. Monroe did." Reaching into the pocket of her slacks, she took out a bill, but he backed away. "I can't take that, Mrs. Robinson. Mr. Monroe took care of the tip. Good luck with the bookstore."

"Thank you." Walking over to the piano, Deborah rested a hand on Asa's back and put her mouth to his ear. "You're going to have to set up the bar."

Smiling, he continued to play. "Where?"

"Where I have the plants. You can put them on the floor under the table."

Glancing up at her over his shoulder, Asa met her eyes. They were dancing with excitement. "As soon as you turn on the music I'll stop playing."

Murmurs and groans went up when Asa slipped off the bench, while Deborah called the mayor's office, asking if he could stop by earlier than one for his photo-op. Ten minutes later Spencer White strolled in with his official photographer and members of the town council, amid a smattering of applause. Crystal and Whitney came in behind them. Deborah hugged and kissed her children, and the photographer captured the tender moment. Crystal's friend Darius couldn't attend because he'd had an appointment with his orthodontist.

"Oh, Mom, everything looks so beautiful," Crystal whispered.

"Thank you, baby." Deborah thought her daughter looked very pretty with a long-sleeved black tee, short, flaring pink-and-black striped skirt, pink leggings, and black ballet-type flats. "You look so cute."

"Thanks, Mom."

Deborah looped her arm through her son's. "How was the interview?"

The dimple in Whitney's right cheek winked attractively when he smiled. "I got the job. My first assignment is to cover your grand opening."

"But isn't that a conflict of interest?" Deborah whispered.

"No it's not, Mom. It's a test to see if I can be an impartial journalist."

Deborah was filled with an overwhelming surge of pride when she stared at her son. "Do you want to interview me now, or later?"

Whitney pulled a small handheld tape recorder from the pocket of his jeans. "Let's see how much we can get in before Mayor White gets started."

Deborah answered all of Whitney's questions, outlining the details for the book club discussions and afternoon tea, while Spencer strutted around the store pressing the flesh like a candidate on the campaign trail. She noticed the number of women crowding around Asa, grinning and touching his arm to get his attention.

"Who is the man in the suit?" Whitney asked when he saw the direction of his mother's gaze.

"Asa Monroe. I hired him to manage the store. If it hadn't been for him I doubt whether I would've opened today."

"I'm glad you decided to reopen the bookstore. And, it's good that you found someone to help you run it."

"Yes it is."

Glancing around, Deborah attempted to count the number of people who'd come to The Parlor and lost count at twenty-seven. Most were eating and drinking, but there were a few who'd taken books off the shelves and were either sitting or standing around reading.

Dora and Cora had their arms full of paperback novels. Deborah excused herself and went over to help them. "Please, let me take your books to the front and I'll put them aside for you." She had to get Asa to bring down a carton with reinforced paper shopping bags stamped with The Parlor Bookstore logo and website.

Deborah had placed the twins' books in a large sweet-grass basket under the writing table when Rose Dukes-Walker, the woman who had woven the basket, entered with her husband Jake. Rose was the local artisan and Rachel's sister. Many of Rose's sweet-grass baskets and quilts were in private collections throughout the country. She'd begun giving private lessons to those who wanted to learn the craft, which had come to the American South with enslaved Africans.

Rose handed Deborah a large hat box. "There's a little something in here for your bookstore."

Leaning down, she kissed the petite woman's silken cheek. "Thank you so much, Miss Rose. Whatever it is I know I will treasure it."

Rose patted Deborah's arm. "I'm just glad you decided to come home. You're going to have to excuse me, but I'm going to rescue my husband from these hungry women. I don't know what it is about these women who come to the Cove. They think every man, whether single or married, is fair game. Rachel told me they were all over Mr. Monroe like white on rice. It's a crying shame that the poor man had to move out to get away from them."

Deborah didn't tell Rose that Asa had moved in over the store. It was only a matter of time before everyone would know. There were very few secrets in Sanctuary Cove. There was a running joke that if you wanted to keep a secret, then never tell it.

She caught Spencer's attention, and he motioned for her to join him outside. It took an interminable amount of time for the photographer to position everyone so he could get them in the photo. Deborah stood next to Spencer. Three of the four members of the town council flanked his left, while Whitney, Crystal, and Asa stood on Deborah's right. Asa and the head of transportation held the length of wide red ribbon while the mayor gave Deborah an oversized pair of scissors. At the exact moment she cut the ribbon several flashbulbs went off, followed by applause. The Parlor Bookstore was officially open for business.

Deborah flopped down on the loveseat, kicked off her heels, and rested her head on the arm. She was exhausted. When she'd opened the Charleston store it had been without fanfare. However, on the Cove it was as if everyone had turned out to browse, buy, and eat and drink their fill. Unfortunately Barbara had called to say she couldn't make it because of a multiple-vehicle accident on the interstate; many of the patients were taken to her hospital and as an on-call nurse she had to report for duty.

The last customer had filed out minutes before six, and she and Asa closed and locked doors and pulled the blinds. Large plastic bags filled with the remnants of uneaten food and trash were deposited in a Dumpster in a corner of the parking lot.

Now, a smile parted her lips when she felt the heat from Asa's body as he leaned over her. "Wake up, Sleeping Beauty."

She smiled up at him. "I was just resting my eyes." He'd dimmed the track lights but hadn't turned off the ceiling fans. She saw that he'd taken off his suit jacket and tie and had undone several buttons on his shirt.

Cupping her ankles, Asa lifted her legs, sat down, and rested her bare feet on his thigh.

He stared at the slender groomed feet with the red polish on toes that were much lighter-skinned than her face. "You need a little sun on your feet."

"My feet are always pale."

"Even in the summer?"

Deborah nodded. "They don't tan. I guess I get that from my mother. When she was growing up her friends used to call her Casper because of her pale skin. As a redhead she had to stay out of the sun or burn to a crisp."

"Your mother is white." The question was a statement.

Deborah nodded again. "Yes. She and my father met when they were Civil Rights attorneys."

"Are you an only child?"

"Yes. My mother had had three miscarriages before she had me. I always wanted a brother or sister, but when my parents didn't have any more children I told them to adopt a baby. By then Mom had gone back to work part-time and she didn't want to start over with diapers, colic, and teething. What about you, Asa? Do you have any brothers or sisters?"

"Siblings aren't always so great."

"What do you mean?" Deborah asked.

"I haven't seen my brother Jesse in years. He always had a weakness for women, gambling, and drugs. I don't know if he's dead or alive." Exhaling audibly, Asa shook his head as if to push all thoughts of his estranged brother to the furthest recesses of his mind. Grasping Deborah's feet, he pressed his thumb to her instep. "Your grand opening was a rip-roaring success."

Deborah recognized he wanted to change the subject and was happy to oblige. "It was better than I could have ever imagined. I sold a lot of romances."

"That's because women love reading about love, and are also in love with love."

"Why are you always so cynical?"

"I'm not cynical, Debs. It's called being realistic."

"I had a few male customers who bought romance novels for their wives." Deborah smothered a moan when Asa massaged her feet. It was as if he had magical fingers. "That feels wonderful."

Asa applied more pressure. "I also give body massages."

"How much do you charge?"

"I offer reduced rates for my good friends."

"Oh!" she gasped. "That feels good." Asa's hands had moved from her feet up to her legs and calves.

"Why do you torture yourself walking in those stilts?"

Pushing up on an elbow, Deborah rolled her eyes at Asa. "They are not stilts."

"Aren't they called stilettos?"

"Stilettos are skinny heels that are at least four inches or higher. Mine are thicker and only three."

Lifting her legs, Asa slid them off his lap and stood up. "Don't move. I'll be right back."

Deborah sat up. "Where are you going?"

"Upstairs to change into something more comfortable," he said over his shoulder.

She lay back down, sinking into the butter-soft leather. Asa was right. The grand opening was more than a success. It was spectacular, the day's total sales exceeding her expectations. Asa had gotten customers to sign up for both book discussions, and she had spoken to Eddie Wilkes about advertising store specials and promotions in the *Chronicle*.

Deborah hadn't known what to expect when she'd introduced Crystal and Whitney to Asa, but both were friendly and respectful, and Whitney thanked him profusely for helping out his mother. Some women didn't have protective men they could rely on, but it was different with her. Her son and her store manager were there for her. It felt good, even safe, knowing they were around.

She knew she should get up and go home, but her body refused to obey the dictates of her brain. *I'll take a power nap.* It was the last thought she remembered before Morpheus claimed her.

It was only minutes, though it could have been hours, when she felt someone gently shaking her. "Wake up, Deborah."

Eyelids fluttering wildly, Deborah sat up as if she'd been impaled with a sharp object. "What-what?"

Hunkering down in front of her, Asa rested his hand on the side of her face. "It's all right, Debs. I'm sorry if I frightened you."

Swinging her legs over the side of the loveseat, she dug her bare toes into the pile on the area rug. "I must have fallen asleep again." He'd changed into a tee-shirt with a faded Virginia Beach logo, jeans, and thick black socks.

Asa leaned in and pressed a kiss to her forehead. "You did. I thought we'd celebrate before you go home."

"Celebrate . . . celebrate how?" It was hard for Deborah to sound coherent when Asa was so close. In fact he was much too close.

Wrapping an arm around her waist, Asa eased Deborah off the loveseat. "Come with me."

"Wait! I have to put my shoes on."

Bending slightly, he scooped her up in his arms. "You don't need shoes."

She looped her arms around his neck to keep her balance. "Where are you taking me?"

Asa smiled down at her. "Do you always have to ask so many questions?"

"Yes. Especially when you play caveman."

"Superhero, Debs."

"Which one?"

Asa carried Deborah up the staircase to his apartment. "Batman. I've been told women like men in black leather."

Laughing, she shook her head, her hair swaying sensuously around her face and neck. "Don't tell me you're a freak."

"I plead the Fifth."

"You *are* a freak, Asa Monroe."

Asa carried Deborah into his apartment, placing her on the sofa and dropping down beside her. "I thought we would have our own private celebration," he said when she stared at the bottle of chilled champagne, two flutes, and an antipasto salad.

"You are just full of surprises."

He stared at her delicate profile. "Do you like it?"

Shifting slightly, Deborah gave him a long, penetrating stare. "Very much." Leaning forward, she pressed her mouth to his. "Thank you."

"You're welcome. Shall I serve you?"

She nodded. "Please." Deborah watched intently as Asa filled a plate with salad before expertly uncorking the bottle of champagne, muscles flexing as he filled the flutes. He handed her one, his fingers brushing against hers.

Raising his flute, he extended it to Deborah. "To The Parlor and beyond," Asa barked out like an announcer.

"You are so silly."

Asa winked at her as he took a sip of the bubbling wine. "Not bad."

Deborah put the flute to her mouth and took a swallow, holding it for several seconds before letting it slide down the back of her throat. First there was cold, then a slow building heat. Pressing a hand to her chest, she blew out her breath. "I'd better eat before I take another sip." Reaching for a napkin, she spread it over her lap, and then picked up a fork and speared a portion of the salad.

"You don't drink?" Asa asked when she set down her flute.

"Not on an empty stomach, and especially not when drinking champagne."

"I didn't know you'd be a cheap date," he teased.

She ate slowly. The spicy salad had triggered an unnatural thirst and Deborah drank two glasses of champagne when she normally wouldn't drink more than one. Setting down the flute, she slumped back and closed her eyes. "I think I'm under the influence."

"How can you say that when you've only had two glasses?"

"Like you said. I'm a cheap date." Raising her arm, she peered at her watch. "I'm going to have to get home."

Lowering his head, Asa buried his face in her hair. He knew he had to move, but didn't want to. They shared the sofa, her soft curves molded to his body. It was pleasurable, sat-isfying. What he felt wasn't much different than the after-math of lovemaking.

He shifted, wrapping an arm around Deborah's waist until she was sitting between his outstretched legs. They lay together, her back pressed against him, their chests rising and falling in unison. "You can't drive home now if you think you're impaired. Why don't you wait until your head clears?"

"I have to call my children to let them know I'm going to be late."

"I'll get the phone." Deborah leaned forward while he slid out from behind her and went to retrieve the cordless receiver from the handset on the kitchen countertop.

She took the phone, punching in the numbers to her home. It rang three times before there was a break in the connection. "Whit, this is Mom."

"Hi, Mom. What's up?"

"I'm still at the store. I'll be home later."

"Shall I leave the porch lights on?"

"Yes, please. Where's Crystal?"

"She's in her bedroom. Either she's on the phone or the computer."

"Tell her not to stay up too late, because we're going to the early service tomorrow."

"Okay, Mom. Is there anything else?"

"No. See you later."

"Later."

Deborah hung up, handing Asa the phone. Their eyes met. "I'm going to give myself an hour to sober up, and then I'm going home."

"Why don't you lie down on the bed, while I put every-thing away?"

She affected a lopsided smile. "I'm good here."

"The bed is a lot more comfortable than the sofa."

"That would pose a problem. If I get into that bed I won't get out until tomorrow morning."

"Go lie down, Deborah. I'll wake you in an hour."

"I'll lie down, but only if you promise you'll wake me in an hour. I've never left my children home alone here in the Cove. It was different in Charleston because I had my neighbor look in on them."

"I promise to wake you. And, when you leave I'll follow you to make certain you get home safely. I can't have my boss charged with DUI."

Asa didn't know whether to stay where he sat or go to her. He knew if he joined Deborah on the bed it would shatter their already fragile friendship. It hadn't been easy working with her, and he had had to call on all of his self-control not to take her into his arms and do more than kiss her. For now, he thought about how it would feel to really kiss her with a repressed passion that would communicate without words how much he'd come to like and want her. But he knew one kiss would lead to a caress and still further. He didn't want so much to be inside her as much as he wanted to feel her naked skin against his.

Deborah moved off the sofa and over to the bed. Turning back the comforter, she lay on the crisp cool sheets and closed her eyes. She didn't fall asleep. Her mind was a tumult of images like frames of film. She recalled the first time she saw Louis, the sound of his voice when he'd introduced himself to her. The next frame was her waking up in bed—naked with a naked man beside her. At first she panicked, and then she'd remembered where she was and who the man was. She hadn't recognized him without his glasses.

Her mind fast-forwarded to her wedding day. Her hands had shaken uncontrollably throughout the ceremony, especially when it came time to exchange rings. She'd worn her wedding band for all of four hours. Once she got back to her dorm, she'd taken it off and put it on a chain around her neck.

There came another frame, the images moving so fast she could hardly recognize the couple writhing on twisted sheets. Stop moving! the silent voice in her head shouted. The man and woman did stop, and a gasp escaped Deborah when she saw herself and Asa locked in a passionate embrace.

Deborah must have drifted off before she was jolted awake. Asa had turned off all the lights except the one on the range hood. She sat up. "Asa?"

"It's all right, baby."

His disembodied voice came from somewhere in the room. "Where are you?" He sat up and she could make out the outline of his body. He had been reclining on the sofa. "What time is it?"

"It's seven-forty. Go back to sleep, Deborah."

She tucked her hair behind her ears. "I can't. I've been thinking too much."

"What are you thinking about?" Asa asked, the soft tone of his voice soothing.

"My life."

"All thirty-eight years?"

"Very funny, Asa."

"Well, you sound as if you're eighty and you're reminiscing about what happened back in the day."

Deborah lay down again, cradling her head on folded arms. "Do you ever reminisce?"

"I try not to."

"Why not?" she asked.

"I plan ahead and try to look ahead."

"You make it sound so easy. Forget the past and only concentrate on the future."

"It works for me, Deborah."

"Hopefully one day it will work for me." She sat up and swung her legs over the side of the bed. "My head feels better. I'm going home."

Asa popped up, walking to the bed on sock-covered feet. "Are you sure?"

Deborah stood up. "I'm good."

Reaching for her hand, Asa laced their fingers together. "I'll follow to make certain you get there okay."

Leaning into him, Deborah anchored one arm under his shoulder. "Do you know what?"

"What, Debs?"

"You're the first male friend I've ever had since my husband. I met Louis at eighteen and married him at twenty. We..."

Asa waited for her to complete her statement, seemingly wanting to know something about the man she had married. When she appeared reluctant to talk, he eased her arm down, pausing long enough to put on a pair of running shoes. Then he got the key to his truck and a small leather case containing his driver's license, and then led her out of the bedroom and down to the bookstore. She slipped into her heels and retrieved her handbag.

Asa then locked the rear door to the store, before catching up with Deborah as she walked to the Audi. The parking lot was unlit. If it weren't for the lights over the rear doors of the various businesses and the glow from a half-moon it would have been pitch black.

"There is one thing you should know, Deborah."

She blinked slowly. "What's that?"

"I'm willing to lend an ear or a shoulder if you feel the need to talk about your husband."

She managed a smile, but it looked more like a grimace. "Thank you, Asa."

He dipped his head and kissed her cheek. "Get in. I'll be right behind you."

Deborah slipped in behind the wheel, pushing the Start Engine button. The soft purr of the engine sounded unusually loud in the stillness of the night as she maneuvered out of the parking lot. It was just a few minutes to eight o'clock yet most of Sanctuary Cove's businesses were closed. In Charleston, most restaurants and clubs would be crowded with college students, tourists, or local residents going out for a night on the town.

It was different in the Cove because there were only a few eating places and the single-screen movie theater showed new movies several months after they'd premiered in other major cities. Occasionally an out-of-town theater group used a converted warehouse to put on their productions.

She turned onto the road leading to her house. Peering up in her rearview mirror, she saw Asa following at a safe distance. A tender smile parted her lips. Not only was Asa her friend, but he had also become her guardian angel. A most winning combination. Deborah still hadn't figured out why she felt so relaxed around him, even more relaxed than she had when she'd met Louis for the first time. Perhaps it had something to do with them not sleeping together. It wasn't that she wasn't physically attracted to Asa, because she was, but there was so much more to him and she was determined to find out what it was. The erotic images of them had left Deborah more shaken than she wanted to acknowledge, and she found the notion of sleeping with Asa intimidating because she was newly widowed.

Her smile faded as if someone had pulled down a shade, shutting out the light behind her eyes. A flicker of apprehension coursed through her when she thought about him leaving the Cove. And it was going to happen. Come spring he would get into his car like so many of the other snowbirds and return to his northern climes.

Following the sweep of her headlights, Deborah decelerated and then pulled into the driveway alongside Whitney's Corolla. Getting out of the car, her eyebrows lifted a fraction when she saw that not only had her son left the lights lit on the porch, but in every room.

Deborah waved to Asa, turned on her heel, and mounted the porch steps. She unlocked the front door, walked in, closed it behind her, and slipped out of her shoes. Tossing her keys in a small sweet-grass basket, she went about the task of turning off lights, leaving on the lamp in the entryway and the high-hat between the kitchen and pantry.

She climbed the staircase to the second floor, holding tightly to the banister in order to keep her balance. Her head was still a little fuzzy from the champagne. The door to Whitney's bedroom was closed, as was Crystal's. Carefully placing one foot in front of the other, she made it to her bedroom, closed the door, and fell across the bed—fully clothed. *I'll get up in fifteen minutes, and then take a bath*, Deborah told herself. Fifteen minutes became an hour, then two.

Chapter Thirteen

⁓

Light had brightened the sky, heralding the dawn of a new day. Deborah woke to the sound of knocking and someone calling her name. It sounded as if they were in a tunnel.

"Mom, may I come in?"

Rolling over, Deborah sat up. Not only was she incredibly thirsty, but her mouth felt as if it was filled with cotton.

"Oh!" she moaned. She'd slept in her clothes—something she'd never done.

"Mom, open the door."

"Hold on. I'm coming." Sliding off the bed, Deborah shuffled over to the door and opened it. The look on her daughter's face was something she would take to her grave. It was etched with fear as tears trickled down Crystal's face. "What's the matter, baby?"

Crystal fell against her mother, nearly making her lose

her footing. "I've been banging on the door and calling you for almost five minutes."

Deborah, rubbing Crystal's back in an attempt to console her, kissed her daughter's cheek. "I was asleep."

"Why . . . why did you lock your door?"

Blinking, Deborah tried remembering when she'd locked the door. She couldn't. "I don't know," she answered truthfully. "Why are you crying?"

Crystal sniffled, wiping the back of her hand over her face. "I thought you'd hurt yourself."

Lowering her arms, Deborah made her way toward the en suite bath. "Come and talk to me while I wash my face and brush my teeth."

"I have to wash my face, too."

Deborah stood at the double-sink, staring at her reflection in the mirror. She looked a hot mess! If she'd been Sallie Ann Williams she would've said she looked a *"dog's mess."* When she'd asked her grandmother what she meant by a dog's mess, her response had been she didn't know, but had grown up hearing people on the island mutter it whenever they disapproved of what someone looked like or wore.

Smudged mascara, eyeliner, and what had been a smoky shadow now made her look like a raccoon. Her eyes were a little red and her bed hair looked as if she'd been made love to. A blush darkened her cheeks when she thought of waking up in bed beside Asa. No doubt if she had, she wouldn't be in her clothes. She didn't want to think about her clothes: Her blouse was a mass of wrinkles and creases and the wool gabardine slacks Deborah had just picked up from the drycleaner would have to go back again.

Reaching for her toothbrush, she squeezed a glob of

toothpaste on the bristles. With the flick of a switch the vibrating bristles spread the foaming paste over her teeth and gums. Deborah winked at Crystal, who after splashing water on her face had blotted it with a towel from an ample supply stacked on a low table. She swished a cupful of minty mouthwash around in her mouth, depositing it in the sink before applying a thick layer of cold cream around her eyes and over her face, gently wiping away the makeup with a soft, moist cloth.

Meeting Crystal's puffy eyes in the mirror, she drew a wide-tooth comb through her hair. "Why are you up so early?"

Crystal dropped her gaze. "I bet Whitney ten dollars that I'd get up before him, so I set my clock for five instead of six."

"I give you an allowance, so why would you need more money?"

"I need enough money to buy a crate and dog food."

Deborah shook her head, unable to believe what she'd just heard. "Did you just say 'dog' as in a canine pet?"

"Yes! Please, Mom, can I have a puppy?"

"First you want to put down a vegetable garden, and now you want a dog." She'd asked Hannah Forsyth for the name of a local landscaper willing to clear enough land for her daughter to start a vegetable garden and the man was scheduled to come the following morning to survey the area and give her an estimate of the cost.

"I want both."

"Do you realize the enormity of taking care of a garden? It has to be weeded and watered, and you have to stay one step ahead of the critters who decide it's easier to eat your vegetables than go foraging for food. Then there is the responsibility of taking care of a dog."

"I can do both, Mom. Please, Mom."

Deborah stared at Crystal. This wasn't the first time her daughter had talked about a dog, but Deborah hadn't warmed to the idea because she felt Crystal wasn't responsible enough to take care of it. Extending her arms, she wasn't disappointed when Crystal hugged her.

"What if we talk about this later?"

Pulling back, Crystal gave her mother an expectant look. "How much later, Mom?"

Deborah smiled. "Tonight. Now, what was up with all the crying?"

"I thought that something had happened to you."

"Happened how?"

Crystal worried her lower lip, as if carefully composing her thoughts so the words would come out right. "Remember my friend Roxanna?"

Deborah met her daughter's eyes. "Yes I do. What about her?"

"Remember after her father died in Iraq and her mother was sent away?"

Suddenly Crystal's histrionics made sense to her. She tightened her hold on her child. Roxanna's mother had tried to take her life when she'd lost her husband. After swallowing more than two dozen sleeping pills washed down with a bottle of whiskey, she was now in a vegetative state. The girl's grandparents had had to sell their Ohio home to move to Charleston to take care of their grandchildren, or they would have become wards of the state.

"What makes you think I would ever take my life and

leave you and Whitney without a father *and* mother? Baby, I love you and your brother, and all I want is for you to grow up and become the best you can be. Things happen in life, things over which we have no control, but unless I was certifiably insane I would never think of taking my life." She kissed Crystal's short hair. "I want to live long enough to become a grandmother and spoil my grandchildren like my mother does."

Easing back, Crystal smiled. "You think Grandma spoils us?"

"Please, Crystal. You should know better than to ask me that."

"Do you think she likes Whitney more than me?"

Deborah's eyes narrowed. "Where did you get that idea?"

"She gives him money, but buys me whatever I want."

She had never noticed any sibling rivalry between her children, and loathed thinking Crystal harbored resentment of her brother. "Whitney is seventeen and will soon be eighteen. Come August he'll be off to college, and that means he's going to need money to put gas in his car or do his laundry, while you'll be here having all of your needs met. I give you an allowance so you can buy what I call incidentals. Other than that, what would you need money for? You're not starting any habits I should know about, are you?" Deborah gave her daughter a playful, yet stern look.

"Mama!"

"Don't 'Mama' me, Crystal! Why would you need more than what I'm giving you?"

"Like for a dog."

"Like I said, we'll talk about this tonight."

"I want a Bichon or a Yorkshire Terrier."

Deborah rolled her eyes. "What you want is a lot of noise."

Crystal affected a smile just like her late father, with her eyes but not her mouth. At times it appeared to be more of a smirk. "They are good watchdogs."

"Where are you going to get your dog?"

"Grandma says she has a friend who lives on Isle of Palms who breeds small purebred dogs. Whenever I'm ready she will call her for me."

"Let me talk to your grandmother before the two of you make any more plans about bringing an animal into this house. Now, scoot while I take a shower."

"I'm making pancakes for breakfast. How many do you want?"

"One."

"One big one?"

"No. One medium."

"You want it with strawberries and cream?"

Deborah began unbuttoning her blouse. "That sounds good."

She waited until Crystal left, then closed the door behind her. Her daughter's head was all over the place. When asked what she wanted to be when she grew up Crystal didn't have a clue. But she refused to acknowledge the obvious: she was an incredible cook. Deborah could envision her daughter owning and operating a restaurant, serving homegrown vegetables. She also had a green thumb and a magic when it came to bringing plants back from the dead. Deborah called her the Plant Whisperer.

Stripping off her clothes, she ran a wide-tooth comb through her tangled strands, covered her hair with a bouffant shower cap, and stepped into the shower stall. Within minutes she felt revived and energized enough to face the day.

Deborah sat in the pew between Whitney and Crystal, listening to Reverend Malcolm Crawford read announcements before the closing hymn. His sermon, taken from the book of Ecclesiastes, chapter one, verse four, spoke directly to her: A time to weep and a time to laugh; a time to mourn and a time to dance.

She'd wept, mourned, laughed, and danced. And she had to thank Asa for the laughing and dancing part. Before he'd walked into The Parlor asking to be hired she'd hadn't laughed—really laughed—in weeks. And before she'd danced with him she hadn't been able to remember the last time she had with Louis. Perhaps it was because Louis hadn't liked to dance, claiming he'd been born with two left feet.

The image of Louis in her mind made Deborah think of Crystal. Her daughter's crying jag earlier that morning reinforced the idea that her children still needed her and she needed them to help her to stay strong. Asa Monroe had been doing the same thing without trying. His continuous displays of affection seemed effortless.

"My brothers and sisters, we have several new faces with us this fine Sunday morning. Some of you may recognize his face from television news footage, but I would like newly elected U.S. Representative Jason Parker, his lovely wife Alice, and their two beautiful children to stand up. Representative Parker, whose election district includes Cavanaugh Island, has decided to make Sanctuary Cove his legal residence. The Parker name isn't new on the island. In fact they go back more than two hundred years, when Cyrus Parker established a rice plantation on Haven Creek. On behalf of all the members of Abundant Life Christian Church, we welcome you home."

Deborah applauded with the other hundred-plus people sitting in the small, homey church. She'd recognized Jason Parker because he'd campaigned on the corner only steps from the Charleston store, shaking hands while a worker handed out campaign literature extolling his accomplishments. He and Alice were both tall and very blond, and their adorable children had inherited their parents' flaxen hair.

"We also want to say a prayer for Sergeant Nelson Lambert who has been deployed to the Middle East. Let us bow our heads and pray for Sergeant Lambert's safe return and for his wife, Samara, and their children to stay strong during his absence."

Deborah grasped Whitney and Crystal's hands, giving their fingers a gentle squeeze as she whispered a silent prayer. She prayed for the young soldier and his family; she prayed for her children; she prayed for her parents; she prayed for everyone but herself.

"Everyone please stand for our closing song, number one twenty-two in the hymnal, 'We Are Marching to Zion.'" There came a rustling and flipping of pages as the organist played the opening chords to the upbeat hymn. The choral group began the first verse, then the congregation joined in, voices blending in sweet, rich harmony. The last note faded and Reverend Crawford raised his hands in a farewell blessing as congregants turned and filed out, hugging and kissing as if they hadn't seen one another in months when it had only been the week before.

Malcolm Crawford stood on the church steps, shaking

hands with each and every member of his congregation. Not even infants were exempt from his greetings. He shook Deborah's hand, flashing his straight, white teeth. "I was thinking of you when I sat down to write my sermon for today."

She nodded, returning his warm smile with one of her own. "Thank you."

"It's good to see you and your children in church. Nowadays too many young folks stray from the Lord. It's only when something drastic happens that they seem to look for Him."

"Lambs will stray, Reverend Crawford," Deborah said.

"I'm certain you've heard of the parable about the shepherd who left ninety-nine sheep to look for one that had been lost."

"I remember it well."

Deborah thanked the minister again and then descended the stairs. She had understood the meaning of his sermon—loud and very clear. She had wept, and continued to weep because she missed Louis. And his loss was never more profound than when she woke in the morning expecting to feel the warmth of her husband's body next to hers.

She had mourned—mourned the loss of her life partner and the father of her children. But lately she had begun to enjoy living—with her children, with her friends, with the residents of the Cove and with Asa. Excitement filled her chest as she remembered dancing with him.

Deborah knew it would take time to heal, but with each passing day she was beginning to feel stronger, more in control. Asa had told her everything would get better with time. Time—a moment, instance, and interval measuring the number of breaths she took. Grinning, she walked to the church's parking area with an extra pep in her step.

Whitney would drop her back at the house before driving into Charleston for basketball practice. Crystal had asked to go with him, and after she pouted for a full two minutes he'd agreed to take her. Whitney had suggested Deborah not cook for them because they would stop at Perry's to eat with the other kids. That left her all the time in the world to sit back and fantasize about the man who'd been occupying her thoughts since the day they'd met.

As soon as she arrived home, she dropped her things in the living room, grabbed her journal and headed out onto the front porch. Opening the book, she stared at her latest entry:

January 16th—Well I think I'm going out of my head. Yes I think I'm going out of my head over you, over you. The first three lines of the Luther Vandross classic "Goin' Out of My Head" keeps echoing in my mind, and I know it's because of my feelings for Asa. I still don't know whether I made a mistake to let him kiss me, and for me to kiss him back. I also know anything other than friendship between us would spell certain disaster—at least for me emotionally. I'm not ready to become involved with a man, at least I don't think I am, but try telling that to my traitorous body. However, I'm honest enough with myself to now admit that I need Asa— if only to assuage a sexual frustration that is triggering erotic dreams.

Deborah closed the cloth-covered book and her eyes, willing her mind blank. However, she was unsuccessful when images of the intimacy they'd shared at her grand opening came flooding back. Trying to draw her attention away from naughty fantasies of Asa, she reveled at his ability to sign up twelve women for two book discussion groups, leaving it to her to select the titles. The novels were what she'd considered modern day classics, with a cross section of time periods and cultures: *The Help*, *Like Water for Chocolate*, *The Alienist*, *This Side of Brightness*, *Memoirs of a Geisha*, and *Water for Elephants*. She was certain some of the women had read the titles on the reading list, but it was very different to get another perspective during an active and in-depth discussion.

Her decision to close Mondays allowed her time to do housework, shop for groceries, do her banking, and visit the Charleston book distributor to restock her shelves. She added another item to her to-do list: shop for tea. Two hand-painted porcelain teapots, eight china cups, saucers, and dessert plates, encased in bubble wrap, were packed in a crate she would take to the store for her afternoon teas.

The phone resting on the cushion rang and Deborah opened her eyes and picked it up without looking at the display. "Hello."

"Good afternoon, darling."

She smiled. "Hello, Mama. How are you?"

"Sweating. These hot flashes are driving me crazy."

"What happened to your central air?"

"I have it cranked up to the highest setting, but Herman keeps turning it down because he said he's freezing. Enough about me. How are you, darling?"

Deborah told Pearl Williams about the conversation she'd had with Crystal earlier that morning. "Mama, you can't promise her something without talking to me first."

"I told her not to say anything until I spoke to you."

Deborah smiled. "Well, apparently your granddaughter didn't listen to you. I told her we would talk about it tonight."

"Are you going to let her get one?" Pearl asked. "Every child should have a pet. You had your cat."

"Muffin wouldn't let me hold her, but would invariably jump on the bed and sit on my face every morning at six o'clock. She wasn't a pet. She was possessed with an evil spirit."

"Deborah, you know I don't like it when you talk about those ignorant Gullah superstitions."

"I don't understand you, Mama."

"What don't you understand?"

"You've been married to a Gullah for more than forty years, and you've spent time on Cavanaugh Island, yet you still view *us* as ignorant."

"Not you, darling. And I resent your implication that I believe people are ignorant. It's the superstitions that are ignorant."

Deborah knew arguing with her mother would end in a stalemate. "What do you have planned for Whitney and Crystal when they come down at the end of February?" she asked, deliberately changing the topic of conversation.

"We're going to meet up with my sister and her grandchildren in Key West. Patricia is renting a bungalow and we're all going out on a charter boat to do some fishing. And of course Crystal and I will do a little shopping."

A little shopping, Deborah mused. Her mother was totally unfamiliar with the phrase. Pearl McLeary-Williams, who had grown up with a silver spoon in her mouth, had never had to struggle for anything. She had come into her trust at twenty-three, due to the death of her parents, and she and her sister had inherited equal shares to a multimillion dollar estate.

"You didn't answer my question about Crystal getting a dog."

"Yes, I'm going to let Crystal get a dog. It hasn't been easy for her, Mama, so right now I'm willing to give her whatever she wants—within reason, of course. But she can't get one until after she comes back from her *little* shopping spree with you."

Pearl's soft laughter came through the earpiece. "Whenever you're ready, I'll call my friend on Isle of Palms to let her know you're coming to look at her puppies. I'd have one right now if we were allowed to have pets. A house is not a home without pets and children underfoot."

Deborah chatted with her mother for another ten minutes, before ending the call. She didn't ask to speak to her father because her father was usually off fishing or golfing with a trio of retired businessmen.

Reaching for her laptop, she tapped a key and turned it on. Waiting for it to boot up, she went into teacher mode. Teachers in the lower grades usually put up colorful decorations celebrating the seasons or important holidays. As the owner and operator of an independent bookstore Deborah had to come up with a theme or promotion for each month. Luckily, she didn't have to concern herself with January because of the grand opening.

February was designated as Black History Month and of course there was Valentine's Day. Resting her fingers on the keys, she began typing. The Parlor would offer a fifteen percent discount for all books in the Black Studies and African-American Literature section. Romance, her bestselling genre, would be given ten percent off, but she also had to come up with something with a romance theme.

Her phone rang again, and Deborah picked it up, staring at the strange number with the 302 area code. "Hello."

"Deborah, Asa."

Her pulse quickened when his distinctive baritone voice caressed her ear. But her joy at hearing his voice quickly faded, replaced by concern. Why was he calling her when the store was closed? "What's wrong?"

He chuckled softly. "Nothing's wrong. It's just that I came downstairs to look for something to read when I found the envelope with your receipts on the desk. I didn't know if you'd thought you had taken it with you."

Deborah smothered a groan. She knew she would've freaked out when she arrived at the bank the next day with the anticipation of making a deposit. "I thought I had taken it with me."

"Do you want me to drop it off to you?"

"No, please don't bother, Asa. I'll come and pick it up. Besides, I have to drop off a box of things I'll need for tea."

"I'll be here."

She smiled. "I'll see you later."

Deborah went back to filling in her promotional event calendar. March was the month for spring and also St. Patrick's Day. She could feature the works of celebrated Irish writers, poets, and playwrights, many of whom were on her list of favorites: Oscar Wilde, W.B. Yeats, George Bernard Shaw, James Joyce, and Samuel Beckett. She didn't have much for April. That meant she would have to search the Internet for writers born in that month. May was Mother's Day and graduations. The list continued until she reached December. Saving what she'd typed on a flash drive, she dropped it into her handbag, pushed her bare feet into leather mules, and picked up the crate with the tea set. After locking up the house, she drove to the bookstore.

After a short drive, she turned down a narrow street and into the parking lot behind a row of stores. Twenty minutes later she emerged from De Fountain with a half-pint of chocolate mint ice cream and a pint of peach and strawberry gelato. Minutes later, when she maneuvered into her space at the rear of the bookstore, Asa was standing in the doorway.

A bright smile flitted across her features when she saw his legs for the first time under a pair of khaki walking shorts. A matching short-sleeve shirt and leather woven sandals completed his casual look. His five o'clock shadow told her he hadn't shaved.

Deborah handed him a small shopping bag with the ice cream. "Can you please put this in the freezer before it melts?"

Asa lifted his eyebrows when he peered into the bag. "What's the occasion?"

"There is no occasion. You've been feeding me, so I thought I'd return the favor and bring dessert."

He smiled. "Thanks. Where are you going?" Asa asked when Deborah headed back to her car.

"I have to get something out of the trunk."

"Is it heavy?"

"Not too heavy."

Reaching for her hand, Asa transferred the shopping bag from his to hers. "You take this upstairs and I'll get the stuff from your car."

"The trunk is open. You can bring in the orange crate, a box labeled 'paper,' and a canvas bag with the plant light." She made her way to the staircase while Asa went to unload her car.

The door at the top of the staircase was ajar, and when she walked in she was shocked to find it immaculate. The bed was made, there were no dishes in the sink, and not one article of clothing was on display. It was as neat as it had been before Asa had moved in. He was either an obsessive-compulsive or a neat freak.

When she returned to the bookstore she found Asa reclining on one of the club chairs, his feet resting on the matching footstool, reading *A Heartbeat Away*, a mystery thriller by Michael Palmer. He'd tuned the radio to a station featuring soft music and the overhead track lighting cast a golden glow on his salt-and-pepper head. The bag with the plant light was near the table with the plants, the crate with the tea set sat on the floor by the buffet server, and the box with the printer on the writing desk. Her handbag was on the desk chair. She placed the envelope with the cash and credit card receipts in her handbag.

Deborah busied herself with unwrapping the cups, saucers, plates, and tea pots, then storing them in the buffet before connecting the printer to the computer. Retrieving her flash drive, she pulled up what she'd stored. She was so engrossed in editing and tweaking what she'd typed that she hadn't realized Asa had put aside his book and stood over her until his intoxicating scent filtered into her nostrils. She could always tell when he was near by the cologne he wore.

She patted the desk chair. "Please sit down. I want to show you what I've been working on." With a click of the mouse, Deborah printed out the reading list and templates for the calendar, handing it over to him.

Asa studied the book titles. "I've read them all except *The Alienist.*"

Deborah smiled. "It's one of my personal favorites, and I'm certain you would enjoy it, too. It's a mystery/thriller set in New York City in 1896. During that time people who studied abnormal psychology were called alienists. In the story, Teddy Roosevelt, a reform police commissioner, recruits an alienist to track down a serial killer who is slaughtering boy prostitutes."

"Don't tell me any more. I want to read it," he said. He noted Deborah had chosen an interesting and eclectic mix.

"I may have a few copies on the shelf. I've e-mailed my distributor in Charleston, asking him to set aside copies of these titles. I'll know by tomorrow if he has them in stock, and if not how soon he'll be able to get them."

Asa perused the calendars, noting the various holidays and other observances. "Where did you find these observances?" he asked, staring at the calendar for the month of July. "July sixth is fried chicken day and the thirteenth is beans and franks day."

Leaning to her left, she stared at the page. "I like ugly truck day on the twentieth. I thought we could tie some of these holidays and observances into store promotions. What do you think?"

"I think you're bright *and* beautiful."

Asa had finally said what he'd thought when he first saw Deborah walk into the town hall meeting. He had thought her stunning with her golden brown skin and curly hair with glints of red and gold. At first he'd wanted to categorize her as exotic, but that was a word used too loosely whenever the media described an exceptional looking woman of color. To him "exotic" meant foreign or alien and there was nothing about Deborah Robinson that was strange or odd.

Initially he'd believed she was too thin, but after working closely with her he realized she wasn't. She was slender with enough curves to make a man crazy. Her fitted jeans displayed long legs and blatantly curvy womanly hips. And she'd become a chameleon when she'd transformed from the girl-next-door into a genteel lady with her coiffed hair and chic blouse, slacks, makeup, and jewelry.

It had taken a night of soul-searching, tossing and turning in the antique iron bed in the apartment above the bookstore, for Asa to admit to himself that he was entranced with Deborah. It had begun at the meeting, continued when she'd offered to give him and Jake Walker a ride back to the Cove Inn, and did not abate when he'd peered through the plate glass window of The Parlor and spied the HELP WANTED sign. And God help him when he'd caught sight of her rain-soaked top...the things he had envisioned. He'd believed that he hadn't had an impulsive bone in his body, yet Asa had proven himself wrong when he'd walked in and asked to be hired. What he couldn't understand was his reaction to the newspaper editor flirting with her and his wanting to punch out the insipid little man.

Had he become bored living at the boardinghouse? Yes.

Had the other guests begun to annoy him? The answer was yes.

Did he want to remain in Sanctuary Cove until he received notification that his application to DWB was approved? Again, the answer was yes, but only because he'd grown tired of driving aimlessly from state to state, city to city, and town to town. Sleeping in a strange bed that he didn't have to change or make up had lost its appeal. Cavanaugh Island had become somewhat of a refuge, a place he could stay until he began the next phase of his life. Even the names of the towns on the island denoted shelter and protection: Haven, Sanctuary, Angels. Fate had brought him to Sanctuary Cove and some strange and unknown force had brought Deborah into his life. He knew their time together would be short, but he'd promised himself he would make it into something he would remember for much longer.

Asa wanted to take more than the memory of his deceased wife and son with him when he retired to his future lodgings, after treating people who lacked even the most basic medical care.

"Now I know why the ladies like you, Asa." Deborah's voice broke into his thoughts.

"What did you say?"

"I said I know why the ladies are drawn to you."

A frown of confusion appeared between his eyes. "I don't understand what you're talking about."

"You're quite the silver-tongued devil. You know exactly what to say to make a woman feel good about herself."

Realization dawned when Asa stared at Deborah as if he'd never seen her before. "You don't believe you're beautiful?"

"No, Asa."

"What are you then? Ugly?"

"No! At least I don't believe I am."

"How do you see yourself, Deborah?" Asa whispered.

Time seemed to stand still as Asa waited for Deborah's response. The look on her face told him she was searching for an answer that didn't come easily. Asa wanted to say so many things. He wanted to tell her that in order to move past her husband's death, she needed to deal with it; confront it head-on so that she could move past the emotions, but he was afraid of her reaction. He didn't want to push her away but he knew this was what she needed to heal. That's how he'd managed to get over his own grief.

Just as he started to say something, she cut him off.

"I guess you could say that I'm attractive."

Asa's smile and the gold in his eyes sparkled like polished amber. "You're a lot more than attractive, Deborah. You're stunning."

Lowering his gaze, Asa stared at Deborah's mouth as a warning voice whispered in his head that they were treading out onto dangerous waters. If they weren't careful they would be pulled under by strong and dangerous currents, unable to make it back to where it was safe, comfortable. That was what he felt whenever he and Deborah shared the same space. He'd become her friend, someone he hoped she could rely on, someone she believed she could go to with a problem or dilemma.

As much as he wanted Deborah to trust in him he also ran the risk of loving and losing for the second time. He'd lost his wife and son, and if he fell in love with Deborah he would lose her also, when he eventually left the Cove at the end of the winter season. Asa's heart sank with that notion and he found himself wanting to pull her close. He leaned toward her, his breath feathering over her mouth.

"I feel beautiful when I'm with you," she whispered.

Asa stared at the length of lashes touching the top of Deborah's high cheekbones. "You should feel beautiful even when you're not with me, because you are. Inside and out."

Awkwardly, she cleared her throat and looked away from him.

"Thank you, Asa."

"Is that all I get? A thank you."

Shifting slightly, Deborah gave him a long stare. "What else do you want?"

The query was a hushed whisper as Asa's expression changed.

"At this very moment I don't know what I want," he said after an interminable silence. "I suppose 'thank you' will have to suffice. Let's get back to your monthly store promotions," Asa said, as if what had just occurred between him and Deborah had never happened. "What do you plan to do with the calendars?"

"I think I'll print out a stack and leave them around the bookstore for customers to pick up. The observances and holidays tied to store promotions will be highlighted in color. We can't highlight all of February because it's National Black History Month, but we can highlight Valentine's Day. I've been trying to come up with something other than featuring popular romance authors or collections of poems dedicated to romance."

"Turn off your computer, and let's go for a walk."

Deborah gave him a puzzled look. "A walk?"

Asa smiled. "I think a lot better when I'm walking."

She shut down the computer and within minutes she and Asa were strolling along Main Street.

Chapter Fourteen

Deborah went completely still, then managed to relax when Asa reached for her hand. She couldn't help but wonder what people were thinking when they saw them walking hand-in-hand. The day was warm and sunny and the streets were teeming with locals and sightseers.

The bank, as well as Jack's Fish House and the hardware store, were closed, as were a number of small mom-and-pop shops. The drycleaner was also closed but the adjoining Laundromat was open. De Fountain, nestled between the variety store and Rose Dukes-Walker's A Tisket A Basket—a take on Ella Fitzgerald's "A Tisket A Tasket"—was crowded. It had become a favorite with the locals because all of the ice cream, sorbet, and gelato were made on the premises. They'd begun serving exotic flavored pop with bizarre names that appealed to the island's teenagers before trying their hand at making ice cream.

The first time Deborah bought a pint of peach gelato and chocolate mint ice cream she was hooked. Now, if the ice cream did not come from De Fountain, she wouldn't eat it.

"Have you thought about a raffle?" Asa asked after a comfortable silence.

The mention of a raffle piqued Deborah's curiosity. "What type of raffle?"

"It will be up to you to determine the criteria, but I'm willing to donate a basket with champagne, a chocolate assortment, gourmet cookies, and other goodies."

"Oh my goodness! You're a genius, Asa. We can have several baskets, each with a free book and a gift certificate that will have to be redeemed within thirty days." Deborah smiled at him, brainstorming. "If I give the winners any longer I might lose the opportunity to make them repeat customers. The rule is anyone who makes a purchase between now and February fourteenth is eligible to win."

"Do you want them to purchase a minimum number of books?"

"No," she said quickly. "That would be unfair to those who don't have the money to buy more than one book at a time. Even a single purchase should have as much chance of winning as a multiple purchase. I'll pick up a roll of raffle tickets and a fishbowl tomorrow. Then I'll stop by Rose's A Tisket A Basket and pick up a few sweet-grass baskets."

"Aren't they expensive?"

"Yes. But Rose will give me a discount. Please don't repeat this, but she inflates her prices for the tourists who come here in droves during the summer months. They are worth every penny, because it takes hours for her to weave a basket and basket weaving has become a dying art."

"How much would the round tray Rose gave you as a grand opening gift go for?" Asa asked.

"Rose could easily have sold that for up to fifteen hundred dollars." Deborah still hadn't decided what she wanted to use it for.

"It's an incredible piece."

"I agree. Did you know that slaves wove baskets so tightly that they held water?"

"I didn't know," Asa admitted. "Do you know how to weave them?"

Smiling, Deborah shook her head. "No. Learning to hand quilt was enough for me."

"One of these days I'm going into Charleston to take the Gullah tour."

"It's fascinating. Put Middleton Place on your places to see. The tour of the gardens and grounds include an African American focus tour that explores the lives of slaves and freedmen at Middleton Place and other Lowcountry plantations. I took my son and daughter on the carriage tour when they were much younger and that was all they could talk about for days."

"How long has it been since you've taken the tour?" Asa asked.

Deborah counted back in her head. "At least seven or eight years ago."

"If I sign up to go will you come with me?"

"Sure," she replied offhandedly. "But it will have to be on a Sunday."

"Don't you go to church on Sundays?"

She smiled. "Yes. But I usually attend the early service, so I'm free from ten on. Why don't you come to church with me, then we can leave directly from there?"

"No."

Deborah was caught off guard by the sudden hostility in his voice. "Are you an atheist?

"No, I'm not an atheist."

"Are you agnostic?"

"My not going to church has nothing to do with being a nonbeliever. At this time in my life I'm struggling with my faith."

Asa didn't want to tell Deborah that he'd become embittered, blaming God for giving him a son, then taking him. He was no Abraham, with faith in God so strong and unwavering that he was willing to offer up his Isaac as a sacrifice.

If God had been testing Asa Monroe's faith, then his so-called faithful servant had failed, because he was still struggling with *"Why me, Lord?"* As a doctor he was more than familiar with the cycle of life and death but nothing could have prepared him for losing his wife and six-year-old son.

Deborah met his stony stare. "I'm sorry for being presumptuous."

Asa smiled, but the warmth did not reach his eyes. "There's no need to apologize."

"What would you think if I made room for a reading corner for teens and little children?" she asked, smoothly bringing them back to discussing the bookstore.

"What would you use? Little tables and chairs?"

"They would take up too much room. What if we use beanbag cushions? I bought one as a birthday gift for one of Crystal's friends. What made it special was that I had Pottery Barn Teen embroider her name on it. We can get probably about three in different sizes and colors. When we get back to the store I'll show you them online."

"You have books for teens, but not many children's books."

"You're right," Deborah said, agreeing with Asa. "A new family just moved to the Cove and they have two kids that are probably in the first and second grade. They're going to need picture and eventually chapter books. I'm also thinking about teenagers who will need another place to hang out during the summer. Why not at The Parlor for a couple of hours?"

Before he could respond, they arrived at the town square and found a bench under the sweeping branches of an antique oak tree draped in Spanish moss. Stretching out her legs and crossing her sandaled feet at the ankles, Deborah rested her head on Asa's shoulder and closed her eyes. The warmth of the sun filtering through the branches of the towering tree, the incessant buzzing of insects and the murmurs of voices lulled her into a state of total relaxation.

"Debs Robinson. Is that you?"

Deborah opened her eyes to find Hannah Forsyth standing a short distance away, hands resting at her waist. The librarian was stuck in another era, with her oversized glasses, teased champagne-pink hair, and blood-red lipstick.

A smirk parted Deborah's lips. "It sure is. How are you this fine day, Miss Hannah?"

"Fine to middling," Hannah answered. "I hadn't expected to find you out here and with Mr. Monroe at that. Shouldn't you be home taking care of your babies?"

Deborah struggled to control her rising temper. She didn't mind if folks talked about her, but she didn't want her children brought into something that had nothing to do with them. "I would if I had babies, Miss Hannah. But in case you've forgotten my children are old enough to drive.

I hope you enjoyed the grand opening," she continued, not bothering to take a breath.

Hannah smiled, her mouth a slash of red in her pale face. "It was simply charming." Her gaze shifted to Asa. "How are you?" she asked Asa, who'd stood up.

"I'm well; thank you, Miss Hannah. Would you like to sit down?"

"No thank you. I was just trying to get some walking in, because my doctor claims I need more exercise. Have a good afternoon."

"You, too," Deborah and Asa said in unison.

Deborah took a deep breath, trying to calm herself as Hannah continued walking. "She's nosey as hell," she mumbled.

Asa sat, staring at Deborah's strained expression. "What's the matter?"

Deborah focused on the vibrant color on her bare toes. "It's going to be all over the Cove that the town crier saw us together."

"It shouldn't matter, Deborah. After all we do work together." A beat passed, then Asa's expression changed. "Don't tell me you're talking about us having an affair?"

"That's exactly what I'm saying."

"Since when did sitting in public together translate into having an affair?"

"Have you ever heard of 'small towns, small minds'?" she asked.

There came another pause. "It's nobody's business what goes on between us."

Deborah laughed. "You're preaching to the choir, Asa." She stood up. "Let's head back."

They walked back to the store in no time, spending

the next few hours researching websites for the items that would go into their Valentine's Day gift baskets. In the end Deborah decided she would order an assortment of Godiva chocolates, boxes of mini Baci by Perugina, and Charleston Cookie Company double fudge cookie whoopee pies and mini chocolate chip cookies.

"I'll order chocolate-covered strawberries with sprinkles from the Muffin Corner and imported cheese from the supermarket deli. I think one basket should contain sparkling cider, fruit and cheese for those who don't want a sugar rush. The largest basket will have the champagne and the other a bottle of red and white wine. Let me know if I'm missing something."

Asa angled his head. "I think you've covered everything."

Deborah stared deeply into his eyes. "Thank you."

"For what?"

"For bringing me back to center whenever I get excited about a new project."

Running a finger down the length of her nose, Asa gave her a tender smile. "You're like a different person when you get into something. It's as if I can feel your excitement."

"This is all very new for me. The Charleston bookstore was just a store, but this place feels like a real parlor. It's like coming home."

"It could be because this is where you really belong."

Her smile faded and her eyes grew serious. "Where do you belong, Asa?"

"Go home, Deborah." Suddenly Asa's face had become a mask of stone.

She blinked. "All you had to say is that you don't want to answer the question."

"I don't want to answer the question."

"Good enough." Deborah exhaled an audible breath. She noted the time at the bottom of her computer monitor. "It's a lot later than I thought. Do you want me to leave the computer on for you?"

Asa shook his head. "No. I have a Netbook and my BlackBerry if I need to access the Internet."

Deborah gathered her papers and the receipt envelope, pushing them into her handbag that occasionally doubled as a tote. She walked to the back door, Asa following. "Thank you again for your help."

Pushing her hair behind her ear, Asa leaned over, pressing his mouth to hers. This time it wasn't a soft brushing of lips. His kiss was a slow, warm caress that left her mouth burning with fire. "I'm sorry. And you're welcome," he said, finally releasing her. "Get home safe."

She blinked as if coming out of a trance. "Thank you." Deborah was breathing heavily, like a runner who'd just finished a long grueling race. Her knees were shaking when she walked to her car and got in.

The rear door to the bookstore closed as she put the car in reverse and backed out of the space. She wanted to lick her lips and taste Asa again, but curbed the urge because her mouth was still tingling from his kiss. If he could do that to just her lips she shuddered to think of what she would do if he kissed her body.

The smile that tilted the corners of her mouth was still there when she maneuvered into the driveway to her house, coming to a stop next to Whitney's car. She found Whitney and Crystal on the back porch watching a playoff football game. In the South, it was high school football on Friday nights, college ball on Saturdays, and professional teams on Sundays.

"Who's playing?" she asked.

"The Panthers and Tampa Bay," Whitney said without taking his eyes off the screen.

"Who's winning?"

"Tampa Bay," they chorused in unison.

Deborah knew they were rooting for the Carolina Panthers, so she left, leaving them to their game. Not having to prepare dinner had freed up her time; she could put up several loads of wash and possibly dust and vacuum.

Her cell rang as she mounted the staircase. Pulling it out of her blouse pocket, she glanced at the display then answered. "How's it going, Barbara?"

"That's what I want you ask you. How was the grand opening?"

"Quite grand," Deborah confirmed. "What are you doing tomorrow?"

"Relaxing. Why?"

"Come to the Cove and hang out with me."

"What about the bookstore?"

"I close on Monday."

"What time do you want me to come?" Barbara asked.

"Any time is good for me. I'm up early to see the kids off to school. I'll make brunch."

"If that's the case, then I'll see you around ten."

Deborah stood on the porch, watching Barbara as she mounted the steps. She had covered the wicker table with a floral tablecloth, silver, china, and crystal for two. A serving cart with covered dishes was positioned next to the table.

They exchanged hugs and air kisses. "Thanks for coming."

Barbara flashed a wide grin. "Thank you for inviting

me." She dropped her tote on a cushioned rocker. "Every time I leave here and go back to Charleston I ask myself why I am still living in the city. Don't get me wrong, Deborah. I love my hometown, but there is something about this place that's like another world." She sniffed the air. "It even smells different here."

"Sit down and sniff away." Deborah uncovered dishes with sliced melon, scrambled eggs, an assortment of breakfast meats, and lemony brioche. She also set out tiny jars of apple butter, and peach and strawberry preserves.

Reaching for a carafe of chilled fresh-squeezed orange juice, Barbara filled her goblet, then Deborah's. "You look different."

Deborah's hand stopped in midair as she spooned melon into a fruit cup. "Different how?"

"You look like you did before losing Louis."

"How is that?"

"Relaxed. Content."

Deborah smiled. "I am."

"Who is he, Deborah?"

"What makes you think it's a man?"

Barbara set down the carafe. "How long have we known each other? A long time," she said, answering her own question. "You didn't ask me to come here to keep you company. You asked me because you need someone to talk to. Someone you trust."

Deborah nodded. She ladled a spoonful of eggs onto her plate. "You're right. I need your opinion on something."

"I'm all ears," Barbara said.

In between bites of food, and sips of juice and coffee, Deborah told Barbara everything about Asa: how he'd helped her get the bookstore up and running, how she had come to depend on him. "I like him, Barbara. I like him more than I should."

"What's wrong with liking him, Deborah? He's gorgeous, and from what you've told me he's intelligent *and* a gentleman. In case you haven't noticed you have wonderful hair, good skin, and an incredible body for an almost middle-aged woman with two teenage kids. And you didn't have to dip into your kids' college fund to pay a plastic surgeon to look the way you do."

"Thanks for the compliment, but that's not helping me with my dilemma."

Resting an elbow on the table, Barbara gave her former neighbor a long, penetrating stare. "You are creating a dilemma where there is none. You are a single woman, Debs, and from what you've told me your Asa Monroe is a single man." She put up a hand. "Louis is gone, Deborah, and he's not coming back. And if the situation were reversed I'm certain you wouldn't want him to spend the rest of his life alone."

"Of course not."

"Then why are we having this discussion, Debs?"

Deborah ran a hand through her hair. "Louis is the first and only man I've ever slept with." The admission was a whisper.

Barbara slumped back in her chair and gave Deborah an incredulous stare. "You're kidding?"

"No. I was in my first year at Bennington when I met Louis. He'd come up to Vermont for a holiday weekend to ski with a few of his MIT classmates. They invited a group of us to their ski lodge for a party. I was seventeen and away from home for the first time, and I was always the nice girl because my parents were well-known attorneys and heaven forbid if I did something to embarrass them. There was something about Louis's nerdy appearance that appealed to me. I'd had too much to drink and wound up in bed with him. I think he felt worse than I did because he hadn't known I was a virgin."

With wide eyes, Barbara stared. "Did he use a condom?"

"I wasn't so drunk that I would've had unprotected sex. He kept apologizing and I kept telling him it was all right. We exchanged phone numbers and I thought I'd never hear from him again."

"But you did."

Deborah nodded. "He called me every other day and whenever he had a break he'd drive up to see me. By the end of my junior year I knew I was in love with him. Instead of returning to Boston for the summer Louis took summer courses, accelerating to graduate in three years instead of four so we could marry. We got married, but decided not to tell anyone.

"He got a teaching position in Boston and I'd either take the train down or he would drive up to Bennington on weekends. I finally tired of the subterfuge and told my parents. They weren't too happy, and there was nothing they could do because I was of legal age to marry. The day before my graduation Louis's aunt and my parents sat us down and told us what they'd planned. My dad, through his connections, asked a Charleston principal to hire his son-in-law, while Louis's aunt gave us enough money for a down payment on a house as a wedding gift."

"You talk about Louis's aunt. What happened to his parents?"

"He never knew his father, and when he was nine his mother dropped him off with her sister and never returned to pick him up. His aunt, who was a schoolteacher, petitioned the court to make her his legal guardian. And because he'd been abandoned by both parents his aunt overindulged him. She was gentle, kind, and extremely generous and Louis had adopted her best qualities. He would never have hurt anyone, so for him to have been accused, later, of getting a teenage girl pregnant... it nearly destroyed him. I kept telling him we were going to beat the charge, but I don't know whether or not he believed me."

"Did you ever doubt his innocence?" Barbara asked.

"Never. Louis didn't do well with guilt. If he'd slept with another woman it would've haunted him until he had to tell me. We'd had a good sex life, so there wasn't a need for him to go looking for another woman."

Barbara exhaled an audible sigh. "I know you may not believe this, but there are men who sleep with other women even though they're sleeping with their wives."

Deborah shook her head. "As much as I enjoyed making love to my husband, that wasn't happening at the time of the accusation. About a year ago Louis was diagnosed with hypertension. One of the side effects of his medication was impotence. That's also why he couldn't have gotten Melissa Perry pregnant."

Barbara emitted an unladylike snort. "All he had to do was say he had ED and none of that crap would've happened. Why didn't you say something, Deborah?"

"I couldn't. Louis made me promise not to tell anyone. He was one of the good guys, and I'm not just saying that because he was my husband, but in the end he got a raw deal. People are so willing to believe the worst, and that's what made me so angry. If the principal and the school board hadn't been so quick to judge him I believe Louis would still be alive today." A wry smile twisted her mouth. "Now you know everything."

"I wish I would've known before," Barbara countered, "because promise be damned I would've told that school board where they could stick their bogus accusation. I don't know if I'll ever feel the same way about some of the folks Terrell works with. If things were different, then we wouldn't be talking about your Asa."

"He's not *my* Asa."

Barbara flashed a Cheshire cat grin. "You really like the man, don't you?"

Deborah nodded. "Yes. I told you I like him."

"Have your kids met him?"

She nodded again. "Yes. At the grand opening."

"Do they like him?"

"Crystal and Whitney said they did."

Barbara leaned over the table. "Invite him to Sunday dinner."

Deborah snapped her fingers. "Just like that. I invite him over to my house."

"You really are naïve when it comes to men, aren't you?"

"I'm inexperienced when it comes to dating. Remember, I had one serious boyfriend, and I married him. I never learned to flirt, because I didn't have to."

"And there's no need for you to learn. All you have to do is be Deborah. The man has danced with you, kissed you, and massaged your feet. The only thing left is his making love to you. Close your mouth, Debs," Barbara said when Deborah's jaw dropped. "I just hope you'll be able to deal with it when it happens."

Deborah thought about Barbara's prediction. She'd told

her everything except that she wanted to sleep with Asa, probably because she had trouble admitting it to herself. "I don't have a problem sleeping with a man."

"What *is* the problem?"

She stared at the salt-and-pepper twists framing her friend's face. "I don't want to get emotionally involved."

Barbara placed her hand over Deborah's. "You're no different than most women. We live for love, and once we decide to sleep with a man we not only offer them our bodies but also our hearts. But you're ahead of the game, because you know Asa isn't going to stay. If you keep reminding yourself of that, then when he does leave you will have prepared yourself for it. I've slept with guys that I never should have even said hello to, and one or two that I'd believed I couldn't live without. Then I met Terrell and I wasn't very nice to him, because I felt he had to pay for what I had to put up with all the other scrubs. When he told me he wasn't going anywhere I knew he was a keeper."

"Terrell is wonderful."

"So was Louis," Barbara countered.

"But, I still love Louis."

"And because you do it should make it easier for you not to fall in love with another man. If Asa is offering, then take it. And if he's not then I want you to take it anyway."

Throwing back her head, Deborah laughed until tears rolled down her face. Picking up a napkin, she blotted her cheeks. "You're unbelievable."

"No I'm not. I just believe in keeping it real. You've been celibate long enough, and if you don't use it you'll lose it."

"There are always—"

"Don't you dare say the 'v' word, Debs Robinson. There's nothing like the real thing."

Deborah sobered, asking, "How would you know?"

Barbara waved a hand. "Girl, please. There was a time before I married Terrell that I had so many sex toys that I had a name for each of them."

"What were their names?"

"Chocolate Thunder. White Lightning. The Stallion. And my favorite was Timex. It took a licking but kept on kicking."

"I thought it was ticking."

"That too," Barbara confirmed. "It came with a special battery that worked on solar power, and never had to be replaced."

"What did you do with them after you married Terrell?"

"I keep them in a box in the top of my closet. I never know when I might need them." She burst into laughter.

"You are crazy!"

Deborah and Barbara sat on the porch, talking and laughing as the sun reached its zenith, then they stood up together, cleared the table, put everything away, and retreated to the back porch to watch *All My Children*. When the show ended, Deborah offered Barbara the chance to see the new bookstore setup, but she refused, stating she wanted to get back to Charleston before she got caught in school bus traffic. Deborah herself left as soon as the taillights of Barbara's car disappeared, driving to the bank to deposit Saturday's receipts.

Stepping up to the teller's cage, she slid her deposit ticket, cash, and checks under the slot at the window. "Good afternoon, Jennifer."

The teller's head popped up, her blue-gray eyes sparkling in amusement. "Oh. Good afternoon, Debs. Miss

Hannah was here just before you came in and she said it's a shame you were keeping company so soon after burying your husband. I don't think she liked me telling her that I didn't appreciate her gossiping about my friend, and that I was going to tell you."

Deborah's lips parted in a smile. "Thanks for letting me know." She and Jennifer Stewart were of the same high school graduating class. When Deborah went off to college Jennifer had stayed in the Cove to marry her high school sweetheart.

Jennifer flipped a wave of highlighted hair over her shoulder, frowning. "What I can't understand is why she feels the need to get into everyone's business."

"I don't think anyone has an answer to that question. Maybe I should give her something to really talk about."

Rolling her eyes and shaking her head, Jennifer said, "It would serve her right if it came back to bite her in the butt." She processed the deposit, pushing the receipt through the opening. "Try not to let her get to you, Debs."

"I have better things to worry about than Miss Hannah's gossip."

"Good for you."

Deborah walked out of the bank, trying not to lose her composure. She had warned Asa about Hannah when she saw them together. After a while, it wouldn't matter who saw them because Deborah knew Asa wasn't going to stay in the Cove, that he was going to leave with the other snowbirds. She had at least another three months to prepare herself for the inevitable.

Chapter Fifteen

January 22nd—Yesterday Asa overheard someone in the store whispering about us having an affair and to say he was upset is putting it mildly. I told him to ignore it, let it go, and it took a while before he was calm again. When I mentioned the ditty about sticks and stones, he shocked me when he said he wanted to go to the library and openly confront Hannah Forsyth.

Talk about putting fuel on the fire. He went to the pharmacy and bought a supply of condoms, making certain Grady Forsyth saw him so he could pass the information along to his "nosey-ass wife." I actually think he got a kick out of doing that.

Hannah came into the store today to pick up a book I'd ordered for her, and Asa put on a show, calling me darling and sweetheart. I thought the poor woman was going to have a stroke when we shared a tight hug. Once she left I playfully chastised him for misbehaving, but he claimed he'd been on his best behavior. What I couldn't tell him was that I enjoyed being in his arms and having him call me *his* darling. And if I were a bolder woman I would admit to him that I want to be his sweetheart and so much more.

February 1st—When I walked into The Parlor earlier this morning Asa was at the piano playing ragtime. He winked at me, smiled, and continued to play. It wasn't his day to work, but he hung out in the store, taking personal requests from the customers. I've finally realized the days he is scheduled to work we have a lot more customers than when he isn't there. I know the women come to see him and although I've told him this, Asa says I'm imagining things. It's as if he's totally oblivious to his charm. But I'm not and sometimes I wonder if the attentions shown to him spark a bit of jealousy in me.

It was the second Tuesday in February and Mayor White had asked Deborah if she would host the monthly town hall meeting at The Parlor; meeting rooms at the library and town hall were undergoing much-needed repairs that included installing new windows and roofing. She told him he and the members of the council could use the space if he sent someone over to move the furniture, then at the conclusion of the meeting move everything back. Spencer told her his men would be over at three to set up and she was forced to cancel afternoon tea and close the store at noon.

Deborah still couldn't believe how successful her Valentine's Day promotion was until she saw the fishbowl filled with colorful red tickets. Two weeks ago the ad had appeared in the biweekly paper, outlining the rules for winning three gift baskets filled with fine wines, gourmet chocolate, cheese, and other delectable goodies. The following day a steady stream of men and women came into The Parlor to purchase books or cloth-covered journals. And to enter their raffle tickets.

Book club members had picked up their books and were scheduled to return at the end of the month for their discussion meeting, and afternoon tea had become a favorite for a group of retired women who arrived on the stroke of three every day. Deborah served hot and cold tea with butter cookies, miniature tarts, and brioche from the Muffin Corner; on several occasions she made dainty sandwiches. The women seemed to favor her spicy chicken salad made with mango chutney, mayonnaise, and curry powder. Then Asa had surprised her when he produced a platter of round avocado and bacon sandwiches on cracked wheat bread, salmon pinwheels, and date and walnut sandwiches for those without nut allergies.

Before the meeting, Deborah stood at the front door, staring at the rain sluicing down the glass. It had been raining steadily for two days now, leaving the streets empty. She had placed the CLOSED sign in the window.

"I doubt if the ladies would have come to tea today even if we hadn't closed early," Deborah said when she felt the heat from Asa's body as he came up behind her.

"Do you think the mayor will call off tonight's meeting?"

Turning, she looked up at Asa. "I doubt it. The only time he's ever canceled a meeting is when council members don't show up, and that doesn't happen too often. Spencer ran on a platform of transparency, so he wants to keep townsfolk abreast of everything that's going on in the Cove."

Pushing his hands into the pockets of his slacks, Asa angled his head. One hundred percent humidity left Deborah's hair in tiny ringlets. "Why don't you come upstairs? I'll make lunch for you." Between twelve and two he usually retreated to his apartment to eat or watch the midday news while Deborah either went home to eat or ordered takeout.

She smiled. "What's on the menu?"

"Shrimp ravioli with lobster and a garlic butter sauce."

Her eyes lit up. "You're kidding?"

"Nope. I made it last night for tonight's dinner."

"You're a man of many talents. You said you're not married, so why hasn't some woman scooped you up?" Deborah asked.

Shock crossed over Asa's handsome features as he stood momentarily speechless He continued to stare at her. "I was married once," he said, recovering his voice and changing the subject. "Are you going to join me for lunch, or would you prefer we go out?"

"If I go out, then I'm not coming back. I'm like a cat. I don't like getting wet in the rain."

"Let's go up to the penthouse," he said jokingly.

Reaching for her hand, Asa led her over to the wall switch where he turned out all the lights, plunging the bookstore in total darkness. He flipped the switch on the wall at the bottom of the staircase. Resting his hands on her waist, he guided her gently up the stairs. When he opened the door to the apartment, Deborah noticed the difference in temperature immediately. It was at least ten degrees cooler here than it was downstairs.

"The penthouse is cold," Deborah remarked, rubbing her bare arms.

Asa walked to the wardrobe and came back with a cotton pullover sweater. "I'll turn off the air, but put this on until it warms up."

She pulled the sweater over her head, adjusting the sleeves and hem. "It's a little big, but it will have to do."

Asa winked. "It's cute."

Deborah glanced around. She hadn't been in his apartment since the Sunday following the grand opening. It was clean and neat—everything in its place. "Your apartment is immaculate."

"What did you say?" Asa called out from the bathroom where he was washing his hands.

"I said your place is very neat."

He stuck out his head as he dried his hands. "I don't do well with clutter."

"I wish my son felt that way."

Asa came out of the bathroom and opened the refrigerator. "He'll grow out of it."

Deborah moved over to the table, watching as Asa removed a large plastic container from a shelf. "When?"

Smiling, Asa gave her a sidelong glance she found so endearing. "When he goes to college and lives on campus. I had a roommate that was a complete slob. I sat him down and told him either he cleaned up after himself or I was going to request a new roommate. We worked out a deal: I would clean and he would cook."

Folding her arms under her breasts, Deborah watched as he filled a large pot with water and placed it on a burner. "I didn't know there were kitchens in dorm rooms."

"Well, we found ways around that," he replied, a look of mischief crossing his face.

"Could he cook?"

" 'Cook' couldn't begin to describe what Joey Farina could do. His parents owned a restaurant and he'd begun working there when he was ten. By the time he was sixteen he was in the kitchen. In the four years we roomed together he taught me how to make pasta and tomato sauce from scratch. I didn't have a pasta machine, but a rolling pin did the trick."

"Tell me what you need and I'll bring it over for you."

"You gave me enough pots and pans, dishes, glassware, and serving utensils, so I'm good for now," he said. Deborah had even given him a small electric food processor.

"Is there something I can do besides stand around and watch you?" Deborah asked. It wasn't that she didn't like just looking at Asa because she did. He was handsome, fastidious, and claimed an incredibly conditioned physique for a man his age. There wasn't an ounce of fat on his toned body.

"Do you want me to make a salad?" Deborah asked.

"Yes."

"What kind of greens do you have?"

Asa opened the refrigerator to browse. "Red leaf, radicchio, endive, escarole, and romaine."

Deborah stood up. "I'll be right back after I wash my hands."

She returned to the sound of music filling the space. Asa had turned the television on to a station featuring cool jazz. When Deborah opened the refrigerator she found it fully stocked. This was the same with the overhead cabinets. A countertop wine rack held two bottles each of white, red, and rosé. None were opened.

"Do you make your own salad dressing?" she asked.

"Yes. What about you?"

"There hasn't been a bottle of store-bought dressing in my house in over ten years," Deborah admitted, sharing a smile with him.

"There's a tin of anchovy filets in the cabinet on your right and a fresh wedge of parmesan in the fridge if you want to make a Caesar dressing."

"How about a basic vinaigrette with minced garlic and red wine vinegar?" She planned to make a mixed green salad with a Mediterranean flavor.

"Make whatever you like. I'm certain it will be delicious."

Standing side by side Deborah and Asa worked together as if it was something they'd done many times before. She washed, dried, and tore lettuce leaves while Asa dropped half a dozen lobster tails in a pot of boiling water. Within minutes they were bright red. He drained and cooled them, then split the shells with a sharp knife, removing the meat and dividing it into equal portions. He sliced the tender chunks into pieces and minced the rest.

"I'm going to set the table," Deborah said as she placed the bowl of greens on a shelf in the refrigerator.

"Please take down soup and salad bowls. There's a container of lobster bisque in the refrigerator. I would've attempted to make it myself, but the woman where I bought the lobster said they made the best fish soups on the island."

She took out the container. Asa had bought the soup from Sanctuary Harbor's Fishery, where Elias Fletcher owned and operated a seafood clearinghouse. Elias purchased the catch of the local fisherman and then sold it to mainland restaurants. "She's right, Asa. You have to try their conch soup."

"I ate conch soup once, and I didn't like it. They were too chewy."

"They probably weren't cooked long enough. Try the Fishery's and you'll change your mind," Deborah suggested.

She watched mutely as Asa opened a drawer in the refrigerator and removed a bottle of chilled rosé, recalling the last time she'd shared a glass of wine with him. Today would be different because she would eat first, then drink. And she wasn't going home until after the meeting; she'd gotten up early to roast a chicken with herb stuffing and new potatoes for the children. There was a note on the refrigerator telling Crystal to make a salad to accompany their dinner.

A delicious mouth-watering aroma permeated the kitchen as Asa filled bowls with the bisque topped with minced lobster; vinaigrette-tossed salad and shrimp-stuffed ravioli with lobster was the second and third course. He'd put the entire meal together within thirty-five minutes.

The homemade ravioli literally melted on her tongue, and there was just enough heat in the shrimp to offset the creamy pasta covering. "May I invite myself up for lunch every day?"

"The door is always open. Come up whenever you want."

"You may come to regret those words, Asa Monroe."

Asa smiled at Deborah over the rim of his wineglass. "I doubt that, Debs."

Asa didn't know why but opening night seemed so very long ago, when it'd only been a little more than three weeks. He felt as if he'd known Deborah even longer. She'd hired him to work no more than twenty hours a week, yet he spent more time in the bookstore than he did in his apartment.

In the mornings Deborah came in at nine to dust,

vacuum, and straighten books before opening at nine-thirty. He usually came down around ten, filled the urn with hot water, and then went to the Muffin Corner to pick up an assortment of sweet breads. Throughout the day he checked the bathroom, making certain it was well-stocked and clean. Whenever there was a shipment of books he entered the quantity and ISBNs into the computer for accurate recordkeeping.

Most nights Deborah left at six in order to share dinner with her children, and this was when he missed her most.

He managed to fill up his days talking to customers, playing the piano and fielding phone calls, but at night when the lights were out and the store was silent, he was unable to hold back the sadness. Sometimes it crept up on him, as if on the silent paws of a stalking cat, catching him unaware, where he wanted to cry. Other times, after he'd locked the rear door and watched Deborah get into her car and drive away, he wanted to scream at the top of his lungs. He wanted to release the grief that reminded him that when he climbed the staircase and lay in bed he would be all alone.

It wasn't that he needed a woman for sex as much as he needed her for companionship, and of all the women he'd seen and met since becoming a widower it was Deborah Robinson he wanted. Asa knew their time together wouldn't be long, but that no longer mattered. He would take whatever morsels of affection she was willing to offer.

He'd ignored Deborah's warning about Hannah Forsyth, but when the woman's gossiping became a reality Asa knew he had reacted badly. He knew it wasn't his reputation that concerned him, but Deborah's, and Asa didn't want to think of how her children might react hearing that their mother was sleeping with a man so soon after losing their father. He knew it had been wrong to call her endearments in front of the nosy old woman, or to purchase condoms to fan the rumors, but he hadn't been able to help himself. And the truth was that even though he told himself over and over that he didn't want to make love to Deborah, as soon as the thought entered his head he knew it was a lie. There were times when he did withdraw from her, shut down, but only because he wanted Deborah with him 24/7. He resented her having to go home to her children, but then became racked with guilt for harboring selfish thoughts. He picked up his wineglass, staring at Deborah over the rim.

Leaning back in her chair, Deborah studied the man sitting across from her. Although they spent most of their days together he still was an enigma. She touched the edge of her napkin to her mouth. Asa *was* her friend but a part of her wanted him to become more.

Tenting his fingers, Asa stared at them. "It seems you have something on your mind. Why don't you tell me what it is?"

With an exasperated breath, Deborah told Asa about her mother's promise to her daughter about the dog. Once the words left her lips she felt silly for being bothered by such a small thing. But Asa didn't judge her and instead offered soothing words to help calm her sudden agitation.

"Sorry to hit you with my problems."

"It's not as if you divulged top secret information. You were upset and you needed to vent. I just happened to be here. There's nothing wrong with that."

"I shouldn't have dumped on you."

Pushing back his chair, Asa stood and came around the table, pulling her gently to her feet. "Stop it, Deborah. Stop beating up on yourself. You had a small disagreement with your mother. It probably wasn't the first time, and it certainly won't be the last."

Curving her arms under his shoulders, Deborah rested her head on his chest. "My mother hardly ever disagrees with me."

"Was that the first time?"

"No."

"So, what's the problem? The next time you talk to her you'll kiss and make up."

Deborah tightened her hold on Asa as if he were her lifeline. "Did I make a mistake?" she mumbled against his chest.

"What are you talking about?"

"Maybe I shouldn't have reopened the bookstore."

"Why? Where is this coming from?"

"My children need me. Especially my daughter."

"You shouldn't blame yourself for wanting to continue your business," he said tenderly. "Or is this about Miss Hannah Forsyth?" He led her over to the window, twirling her around as he swayed in time to the music. They glided toward the bed, Asa pulling her down to lie beside him. "Your children are not babies, Deborah. They are young adults, and don't need you to watch them 24/7. They go to school, have their friends and extracurricular activities. If you were home they would resent you monitoring their every move. The bookstore also provides you with an income so you can take care of them."

Deborah wanted to tell Asa that she really didn't need to work to support her children but she didn't. The monies she'd received from Louis's insurance policies and the money from the sale of the house in Charleston had given her financial stability. There was no mortgage on the house in the Cove, and she'd repaid the home equity loan she'd taken out to update the property. Even when she and Louis had needed to watch every penny Deborah never accepted money outright from her parents. They'd accepted the down payment as a wedding gift, and whenever her mother or father sent a monetary gift for her birthday or Christmas she would always use the money to pay off the mortgage. They had paid off a thirty-year mortgage in fifteen years. But the real issue now was Hannah's words, making Deborah second-guess her parenting skills.

"The bookstore keeps me sane," she admitted.

Placing an arm over her waist, Asa pulled her closer. "What would you do if you didn't have the store?"

A dreamy expression crossed her face. "I'd probably teach."

"Did you like teaching?" he asked.

"Yes. Especially on the college level. Nowadays I don't think I could cut it teaching high school students. There's too much crap going on with them."

"Define 'crap.'"

"Bullying, gangs, drugs, etcetera."

Asa smiled. "That was going on when I was in high school, and definitely when you were, too. It appears to be more prevalent because we're living in an electronic age when everything happens in nanoseconds."

"Were you ever bullied, Asa?"

"No. Only because nobody messed with my brother Jesse. He is four years older than me, and he put the word out that if anyone stepped to me then they had to deal with him." Asa smiled, remembering. "If you looked at him sideways he'd just walk over and knock the hell outta you. He could pull A's without opening a textbook. He breezed through college and medical school, graduating at the top of his class." The smile faded. "Then he met a woman who turned him onto drugs. He started writing prescriptions to support their habit, and when he was afraid of getting caught he started stealing drugs from the hospital. The hospital administration couldn't prove he was stealing, but they always had someone watching him.

"When crack became popular he was in hog heaven. It was cheap and readily available, so he literally lost his mind. He would disappear for weeks, and when he'd finally surface he looked more dead than alive. Jesse would go cold turkey, clean up for a while, and then when he met another woman he'd relapse. Whenever he was low on money he'd go to the casino to gamble. Even in his drug haze he still had the ability to count cards. He'd win enough money to pick up a prostitute and score his drugs. Then it would start all over again, until he was banned from several casinos.

"He put my mother in an early grave and I saw my father age before my eyes the first time Jesse came home after spending several weeks in a crack house. My mother would wash him as if he were a baby and nurse him back to health, but whenever one of his women came around he would disappear. When Mom died after suffering a massive coronary, we held the body as long as we could while we waited for Jesse to show up. But he didn't reappear until two days after we'd buried her. When Dad told him what had happened he turned and walked out without saying a word. The last time I saw him he'd come to me asking me for money so he could leave Delaware. I don't know who or what was after him but I gave him all the cash I had in the house. I didn't ask who the people were because I didn't want to know. If it wasn't drug dealers, then it had to be loan sharks."

"Do you ever think about him?"

A wry smile parted Asa's lips. "Yes. I wonder where he is. What he's been doing and whether he's clean."

"I'll say a prayer for him."

Tightening his hold on Deborah's waist, Asa buried his face in her hair. "I'm sure he would appreciate it wherever he is."

"I'd like to invite you to my home for Sunday dinner."

She glanced up at him at the same time he lowered his head and brushed his mouth over hers. "Are you certain you want me to come?"

"Of course. You've met Whitney and Crystal, so it's not as if they don't know who you are."

"What time is dinner?"

"We usually sit down to eat around four, but you can get there about three-thirty."

"Do you want me to bring anything?" he asked.

"Yes. Yourself."

"Now you know I can't show up empty-handed."

Smiling and shaking her head, Deborah said, "Why is it so important to show up with something?"

Asa lifted his shoulder. "I don't know. I guess it's a black thing."

"It is a black thing," she confirmed. "I remember when a woman who my dad had grown up with invited us to Christmas dinner. We arrived empty-handed and even before we darkened the door the word had spread that Herman Williams had forgotten his home-training. He, his highfalutin' clean skin wife, and child came, ate and drank and left with only a thank you. Two days later she had to eat her words when a twenty-five pound Smithfield ham was delivered to her house with a thank-you note from my mother. It was apparent she had forgotten that highfalutin' folks don't tote food because it just might spill and ruin their fancy clothes. Back in the day they had their help bring over the hospitality offering."

"What the heck is clean skin?"

"It refers to a light complexion. Most folks around here believed my mother was mixed race because she has a short button nose and very curly hair."

"But, you said she is white."

"You know skin color means nothing; there are a lot of fair-skinned black folk. Around here people tend to look at the hair, features, and skin undertones. If it's yellow then you're suspect. But here on Cavanaugh there has been a lot of race mixing. So because of my mother's features, every-one assumed one of her parents must have been black."

"Gullah talk and superstitions. It's as if the Lowcountry isn't a part of the United States," Asa said.

Deborah laughed softly. "There's a lot of history here most folks don't know about. Over on Angels Landing there are people who practice putting spells on and off folks. All that talk about working roots and ghosts would scare the bejedus outta me when I was younger."

"What the heck is bejedus?"

"Jedus is 'Jesus' in Gullah talk."

"Say something else and let me try and translate it."

Deborah searched her head for something she was cer-tain would stump Asa. "E onrabble e mout."

Unconsciously his brow furrowed. "I understand mouth. Onrabble sounds like rattling on. You talk too much."

"Yeah, you're good. What's bonkey?" He gave her a blank expression. "That's behind," she explained. "We'll try another easy one: 'Waffuh do?'"

"What you do?"

"Close. It's what *to* do. If you listen closely you'll understand most of the words only because they've become a part of the black dialect and lexicon. Gullah is a blend of African and European languages. I'm certain you've heard people drop the ending to 'with' and it becomes wid. 'Tater' is potato. Now we even have tater tots. 'Jook'um' is to poke or stick. 'Sat-day' is Saturday. 'Ting' is thing. 'Nuff' is enough and the phrase I like is: 'E yent crack e teet.' That means he didn't open his mouth to speak. Some of the words are of African origin, from various tribes in West Africa, and the lilting accent makes it sound Caribbean."

"The culture sounds intriguing."

"It is. It's rich, colorful, and fraught with a lot of superstition."

Asa reached over and brushed a wayward curl off Deborah's cheek. "Are you superstitious?"

A mysterious smile softened her mouth. "The only thing I'm going to admit to is that I respect the superstitions, because I've seen many of them come to fruition. Are they unexplainable? Yes. But I still respect them."

"Give me an example."

"If an older person decides to '*put de mout on you*' then you'd better watch out, because depending upon who he or she is your life isn't worth spit."

Throwing back his head, Asa laughed. "That's crazy."

Deborah's eyes narrowed as she glared at him. "So were the folks who had the *mout* on them."

Without warning, he sobered. "Are you telling me they went crazy?"

She nodded. "My grandmother left me her journals and the other night I read how a woman she knew was messing around with another's husband. The wife dressed her husband, and after he slept with the loose heifer her stomach *swole up* so big folks thought she was going to have triplets."

"Was she pregnant?" Asa asked.

Deborah landed a soft punch to his shoulder. "You're missing the point, Asa. No, she wasn't pregnant. But you thought she was when you could see things moving around her belly under her clothes. Grandmomma wrote: *de doctuh couldn't do nothin' to help de po chile.* Even though my grandmother was college-educated she would sometimes lapse into speaking and writing Gullah."

"What happened to the loose heifer?"

"Grandmomma wrote she got skinnier and skinnier while her belly continued to grow. When she finally passed away the doctors opened her up and found a tumor the size of a watermelon, weighing about thirty pounds. Word went around that the growth looked like a hairy baby pig."

Asa rubbed the back of his neck, clearly agitated. "As a medical student I have witnessed medical procedures where tumors were removed from human bodies that were so hideous that some students bolted from the room or lost the contents of their stomachs. It only took one incident for me to learn not to eat before observing an autopsy or a surgical procedure. This definitely sounds like one of those cases." Asa shook his head as if trying to clear the images from his mind. "What happened to the cheating husband?"

"Grandmomma said his penis shriveled up like a newborn's and that put an end to his tomcattin'."

"Ouch!"

"My grandmother's journals are fascinating. After I finish reading them I'm going to give them to Whitney to read, because one day he may want to write a book about her."

"I read his article about the bookstore opening in the *Chronicle*. It was intelligent and impartial, considering he was writing about his mother."

"He plans to major in Communications."

"What college is he going to?"

"Howard has accepted him, and so has Bennett in Columbia. He doesn't have much more time before he makes his decision."

"Why is he waffling?"

"He'd decided on Howard before Louis died. Now, he feels as if he has to be close to home."

"Close to home or close to his mama?"

"Probably both. I've told him that I don't have a problem with him going to an out-of-state school, but it's apparent I haven't been too convincing."

"Columbia isn't Charleston," Asa reminded Deborah.

"I know. But it's only two hours away by car."

"Where do you want him to go?"

"I'm leaning toward Howard, because there are more employment opportunities in D.C. Wherever he decides to go, I'll support him one hundred percent."

"Where are you going?" Asa asked when she pulled out of his embrace and slipped off the bed.

"I need to clean up the kitchen." Deborah walked over to the table and picked up the soup bowls, cursing under her breath when a spoon slipped, falling against the sweater before it landed on the floor.

"Yuck! Now I'll smell like fish." Luckily the spoon missed her slacks.

Asa walked over and picked up the spoon. "Why don't you bring a change of clothes with you and leave it here since you've been spending so much time in the store?

That way you won't have to go home to shower and change."

"That's a good idea," she said, frowning at the damp spot under her right breast.

"Take it off. I'll give you a shirt."

"Let me see the shirt."

"Don't worry, Debs; it will come at least to your knees." Asa walked to the wardrobe. He returned with a laundered long-sleeved shirt on a hanger. "Will this do?"

Smiling, Deborah nodded. "It will."

Taking the shirt, she went into the bathroom to change; she added a dollop of liquid soap on the spot, rubbed it gently before rinsing it with cold water, then hung the sweater over the shower rod. Slipping out of her pants, she folded them neatly over her arm. Asa was in the kitchen clearing away the remains of their lunch while she hung her blouse and slacks on a hanger and then on a rod in the wardrobe next to rows of slacks, shirts, two suits, and a navy blazer. His outerwear also included a trench coat, barn jacket, and a leather bomber. Shoes, ranging from sandals to two pairs of wingtips, lined a shoe rack. Slipping her feet into her ballet-type flats, she rejoined him in the kitchen.

Asa angled his head and stared at the woman wearing his shirt. Never would he have imagined having her there with him. With her tussled hair she looked as if she'd just been made love to and he instantly hardened at the thought. His gaze traveled downward to her bare legs, realizing it was the first time he'd seen them. They were long and smooth with curvy calves and slender ankles. His mouth watered.

"You look sexy," he croaked, when really he'd wanted to say how much he needed her in his bed, and not just for a few minutes. He wanted her to spend the night.

Chapter Sixteen

The Parlor was brightly lit. Rows of folding chairs took up more than half the space. The men had come as promised and had moved tables, chairs, and rugs toward the back of the store, leaving space for people to maneuver to the restroom and the rear exit. Deborah's treasured piano was pushed close to the plate glass window. Despite the inclement weather there was the usual number of attendees.

Mabel walked in with her husband and headed straight for Deborah. "Have you heard?" she whispered softly.

Deborah leaned closer. "Heard what?"

"Some strange dudes with fat pockets were asking around about abandoned properties here on the Cove."

"I thought I overheard someone mention developers the other day, but I try not to get into the business of my customers because I don't want them in mine."

"Well, Debs, I can't help but hear when they sit in my

shop for hours drinking coffee and beatin' their gums. Even Lester, who hates these meetings, decided to come. He owns some land north of your place that he inherited from his uncle. Someone called him the other day and asked if he was willing to sell it and Lester said *'hell no'* and hung up before the man could leave his name and number. To say he cussed a blue streak is putting it mildly."

"I suppose this is going to be a very interesting meeting."

"Sho 'nuff," Mabel drawled.

Deborah sat down in the back row while Asa elected to stand, leaning against the door leading to his apartment. Spencer White walked in wearing a sweatshirt, jeans, and boots, his expression solemn. The members of the town council were similarly dressed for the rainy weather. Jeff arrived a moment later, removing his cap and taking his seat on the end of the row of seats facing the assembled.

Spencer cleared his voice. "As soon as Eddie arrives we'll start the meeting."

The words were barely off his tongue when the newspaper editor walked in, struggling to close the outer door until Jeff got up to assist him. Before it had just been rain; now it was wind and rain. Eddie, sitting in the front row, removed a handheld tape recorder from his jacket pocket and turned it on.

"I'm ready, Mayor White."

Spencer cleared his voice again. "I'd like to thank everyone for turning out with the weather such as it is. If what I have to tell you wasn't so important for the Cove's future I would have canceled tonight's meeting."

"Quit jawin' and spit it out, son. You're not in the courtroom," said an elderly woman. "I'm certain these good folks want to get back home jest I like do."

A rush of color suffused Spencer's face. "Okay, Grandma," he said, apologizing to his great-grandmother. "I've been approached by several men who represent a developer who want to buy up vacant homes and land to put in a casino, a golf resort with a number of hotels, and a conference center." There came murmurs and whispers until Spencer raised his hand for silence. "They not only approached me, but also the mayors of Angels Landing and Haven Creek."

"What did they say?" Lester asked. "Because I hope those bastards didn't ask you what they asked me."

"I spoke with Allen over in Haven Creek and they want no part of it. He claims it will inflate property values, forcing his people to move."

Luvina Jackson raised her hand. "What about the folks in Angels Landing?"

"The mayor said he took a survey and the vote is split fifty-fifty."

Rachel Dukes stood up. "If they decide to let them fat cats in, it will be a disaster. Everyone knows most of the land in Angels Landing is cursed." Nods and murmurs followed her pronouncement. It was a known fact that Rachel had been born with a caul over her face, which meant she had the gift of sight. Whatever Rachel predicted usually came to fruition. "Let them build and it will become nothing more than a fancy cemetery."

"I don't want them to build anywhere on Cavanaugh Island!" shouted Hannah Forsyth. "It shouldn't matter if the land is cursed or blessed. I've seen what developers have done to Hilton Head, Jekyll Island, and parts of St. Simons. They carve out sections where they put up fancy homes with gates. Then they have folks with guns patrolling the land we'd worked and claimed as our own for generations."

Spencer waited for Rachel to sit, then said, "We've heard the downside of permitting developers to build here. What if we limit their building? Give them an area of, say, eight hundred acres and let them deal with that?"

Elias Fletcher stood up. His formerly long red hair was now snow-white and hung midway down his back. He wore every year of the thirty he'd spent as a fisherman on his leathery face. Blue eyes flashing, he shook his fist at Spencer. "What's in it for you, Mayor Spencer? Did those sons of bitches offer to grease your palm if you convinced us to go along with their crooked scheme?"

"Watch your mouth, Elias," Spencer warned.

"No, Mayor, you watch yours. I've spent all of my life here in Sanctuary Cove and I have seen people come and go because they felt there was something better for them away from here. You were one of those who cut and run for a while when you were chasing that actress's skirt. So don't start with me, Sonny, because I'll give you more than you can take. We on the Cove have survived when so many other Lowcountry politicians have sold out their folks. Just make certain you don't become one of those, *Mayor White*." He'd spat out the title as applause followed his outburst.

Alice Parker stood up, waiting to be acknowledged and heard. Spencer, obviously shaken and embarrassed, pointed to her. "Yes, Mrs. Parker."

"It's Alice. I'm not one of those people Mr. Fletcher spoke about, but my husband is. His roots on this island go back more than three hundred years, and though he lived in other places, when it was time to start a family he had to come back. He wanted our children to benefit from the values this town believes in, and grow up in a place with a strong sense of history. If we sell to developers, then it's the same as selling our birthright. In a couple of generations you won't be able to find anyone with roots that go back years on Cavanaugh Island, because everyone will be a newcomer or outsider. If Cavanaugh Island has survived without golf courses, overpriced hotels, and companies that pollute our waters so fishermen will be forced out of business, then I say to hell with the developers. Sheriff Hamilton, you need to give them a personal police escort off the island with a warning if they come back they'll be shot on sight." The entire assembly rose as one, applauding, shouting, and whistling their approval.

Spencer waited until everyone was seated again. He smiled at Alice. "Are you certain you're not campaigning for something?"

She returned his smile, her complexion flushed. "Yes, Mayor White. I intend to run against you when you're up for re-election."

"Well damn," Mabel whispered under her breath. "The sister ain't no joke."

"I like her," Deborah whispered back. "We've never had a female mayor. It's time we get one."

"You ain't lyin'."

Spencer, who seemed to have recovered his composure, forced a too-sweet smile. "I'm going to poll the council, something we usually do behind closed doors, to get their take on what we've discussed tonight." One by one he called names. No one was in favor of permitting the developers to purchase land in Sanctuary Cove. "It's unanimous. I'll have my secretary send a letter to the gentlemen to let them know that we're unable to entertain their proposal at this time."

Grady, Hannah's husband, raised his hand. The pharmacist also doubled as the Cove's postmaster. "What is it you don't understand, Mayor White? The people have spoken. They don't want outsiders coming in and chopping up their land and offering others outrageous sums to sell out their legacy. Not now and not ever. So, when you word that letter make certain you don't say *at this time*. It's *never ever*!"

Hannah patted his back. "That's *my* man!"

Eddie spoke up for the first time. "Would you mind, Mayor White, if I print a copy of your letter in the *Chronicle*?"

Spencer, knowing he'd been overruled, nodded. "I'll make certain you get a signed copy. There's not much else to report except that repairs have begun on the library and the town hall. However, I'd like Sheriff Hamilton to bring us up to date on what he's uncovered about some suspicious activity in and around the business district."

All eyes were focused on the ex-Marine. A few sighs from women were heard when Jeffrey leaned forward. "Our surveillance cameras picked up two individuals lurking behind several stores after closing time. Business folk—make certain you check to see that all of your back doors are locked before you leave. And, because many of the parking lots are not lit, I suggest you install lights over the rear doors. Not only would it deter someone from breaking in, but their images would be more identifiable when we go through camera footage. I'm not certain what they're looking for, but let's not make it too easy for them."

"Are they kids, Sheriff?" asked the pharmacist.

"It's hard to tell, Grady. I'll let you know if I happen to catch them. I've begun nighttime foot patrols, so tell your kids not to hang around behind the stores once the business district closes down for the night."

Deborah noted the thickness in Jeff's neck for the first time. He was massive. Unless someone was heavily armed, she felt sorry for anyone willing to go up against him. Jeff was handsome, although not nearly as handsome as Asa.

But Deborah didn't want to think about her growing attraction to the man living above her store. She related to him in a way she never had with Louis. Their relationship was smooth and easy.

The loud hum of voices and movement of furniture snapped Deborah out of her thoughts. The meeting had ended, and one by one everyone filed out except the men assigned the task of putting all of the furniture back. Working in tandem, they repositioned the piano, buffet server, desk, writing table, and seating arrangement, leaving Asa and Deborah to rearrange the plants and beanbag chairs.

Asa, having closed and locked the door behind them, turned to Deborah. "That was quite a heated meeting."

"That's because it's about the island's survival," Deborah said.

"How can the island survive if it's stuck in time? Bringing in a hotel or a casino would inject new life in the island's economy."

"New life and all the social ills we don't need," she argued softly. "Developers have been good and bad for the Lowcountry Sea Islands, but in my opinion the negative outweighs the positives. It's like letting Wal-Mart, Sam's Club, Target, or Home Depot set up shop on Cavanaugh. Every independent and mom-and-pop shop in the three towns would go out of business. The only exceptions would probably be Jack's Fish House, the movie theater, and the Cove Inn. Everyone else, including myself, would have to close down. The big companies claim they can lower unemployment rates, but at what cost, Asa?"

"What I found surprising is that no one wanted to entertain limiting how much land the developers could purchase and what they build."

"This isn't the first time developers have expressed an interest in Cavanaugh. Every few years they come back, hoping they'll get the residents to change their minds. What frightens everyone is the pollution that comes with growth. In the 1950s a growing industry along the nearby Savannah River polluted many of the marshes and creeks around Daufuskie. Health officials cited and closed up most of the valuable oyster beds. The fishermen lost their livelihood and moved away. One by one the stores closed and then there were none."

"Personally, I don't think they should have written off the entire proposal."

Deborah exhaled an audible breath. "You can't understand where we're coming from because you don't live here."

"Why should not living here make a difference when you're talking about progress?"

"Are you saying we're backward?"

"No, Debs. I'm just saying things could be better."

"For whom?" she argued. "It can't be for me and my children."

"That's because you have options," Asa retorted. "Your grandmother was educated; so was your father and so are you. Your children will be the fourth generation to attend college. How many others in the Cove can claim that distinction?"

"I don't know, Asa. However, that's not as important as making certain our predictable way of life doesn't change so much that we can't recognize it. Jason Parker moved back because he wanted to give his children a better quality of life than they would have in Charleston. Everyone looks out for one another. You saw how supportive they were at my grand opening."

Her eyelids fluttered wildly and then her expression softened. "When I wake up in the morning, I stand on the front porch and take a deep breath. Then I close my eyes and try to identify the different smells: the ocean, palmetto leaves, and sweet-grass. Even the earth smells are different. When I go to bed I'm not jolted awake by the sounds of police and fire sirens, or kids drag-racing down the street. I go to bed listening to crickets and wake up to them. I don't have to concern myself with traffic lights or stop signs. I love my little house, and there are times when I can almost imagine my grandmother calling me to come in and wash up before we sit down to dinner." She saw the strange look on Asa's face. "You probably think I'm a little crazy, but I don't want anything to change. At least not in my lifetime."

He shook his head. "No, Deborah. I don't think you're crazy. You're just passionate about what you believe in, and there's nothing wrong with that."

"It's been a long day and I'm a little tired." Going on tiptoe, Deborah kissed his cheek. "Good night and thanks for everything."

Asa rubbed her back. "I'll walk you out."

She retrieved her handbag from the desk drawer as Asa grabbed a large umbrella. "Don't forget to lock the door."

"Aye, aye, captain!"

Deborah rolled her eyes at him. Outside, he leaned over and opened the driver's side door for her. She got in and started the engine at the same time Asa closed the door. He stood back, arms crossed over his chest, while she put the car in reverse and maneuvered out of the lot with her wiper blades turned to the highest speed, then he bolted back inside out of the heavy rain.

Deborah pulled into her driveway, got out of her car, and sprinted to the porch and out of the rain. Crystal, singing at the top of her lungs, greeted Deborah when she opened the door. Unlike her mother, who was tone deaf, Crystal had a strong singing voice. She was sprawled on the living room sofa watching *Glee*.

Leaning down, Deborah kissed her cheek. "Hi, baby."

Crystal picked up the remote, muting the television. "Hey, Mom."

"Why are you watching TV down here?"

Crystal sat up straight. "I was waiting to talk to you."

Deborah sat down and stretched out her legs, crossing her feet at the ankles. She rested her head on the back of the sofa and closed her eyes. "What do you want to talk about?"

"Can you meet me after school on Monday so we can go shopping? I know what kind of dress I want."

"Of course. Where is it?"

Crystal chewed her lip. "It's in a boutique on King Street called Finicky Filly. And I also found my shoes. They're Kate Spade." She scrunched up her nose. "They cost three hundred dollars."

Deborah's expression did not change. "Are they also at Finicky Filly?"

"No, Mom. I saw them at the Copper Penny."

"What else do you need?"

"I'm going to have to get my hair and nails done."

"What else, Crystal?"

The teenager rolled her eyes upward, then squinted. "I don't know."

"You're going to need a jacket or shrug in case it gets chilly. And probably a little purse with a strap you can wear across your body. A woman never goes out without a purse. It shouldn't be too big but large enough for your keys, lip-gloss, cash, and other personal items."

"This is my first dance and I want to really look good."

Deborah dropped an arm around Crystal's shoulders, pulling her close. "I'll make certain you'll look beautiful. You should think about letting your hair grow out. Not that it doesn't look nice, but I can tell you from experience that guys like girls with hair they can touch."

"Mom!"

"Don't Mom me. It's true. You'll find out once you're allowed to get a boyfriend. When I met your dad I had hair down my back, and whenever I set it or blew it out he couldn't stop touching it."

"How many boyfriends did you have before you married Daddy?"

Deborah hesitated, then decided to be truthful with her daughter. "Your father was my first serious boyfriend."

"Had you gone out with other boys before him?"

"Yes. They were more like group dates, when six or eight of us would get together and either go to the movies or the mall. It was different when I spent summers here. There was only one movie theater and no mall."

"Where did you go? What did you do?"

"Me and my friends hung out at the beach. Most times we'd go swimming. By the time I was in my teens my parents would let me go to the beach on Friday nights. Every teenager in the Cove would show up with food and pop. We'd light a fire and have a clambake, then sing and dance to a boom box. Somebody's mother or father would come by and check to see if we had any alcohol, and then leave."

"Did you?"

"No. We knew if they caught us it was all she wrote. It wasn't so much about drinking, getting high, or having sex as it was about not having our parents clocking us."

"How late were you allowed to stay out?"

"We had a midnight curfew. That was long enough because we'd start gathering around seven, and with the heat and salt water we were plenty tired by midnight. I fell asleep many a night on the sand, and when I got back I still had to shampoo my hair and wash sand from every crevice on my body."

"Mom?"

"What is it, sweetheart?"

"Do you think you will ever date or marry again?"

"Would you want me to start dating?" Deborah asked, answering Crystal's question with a question.

Crystal lifted her shoulders. "I don't know. Daddy's gone and once I leave for college you'll be alone."

Deborah kissed her daughter's forehead, smiling and thinking about Asa. "I don't want you to worry about me. I'll be okay."

"Which friends did you like best? The ones in Charleston or here?"

"It's not about which ones I liked best, but who they were. The folks on the Cove are more laid-back. It's not about what you're wearing, what make and model car you drive, or the size of the diamonds in your ears. Don't get me wrong, Crystal. There are people who live on Cavanaugh that have a lot of money, but they don't flaunt or talk about it. And there are people who don't have enough, but you won't see them living in homeless shelters or waiting on line at a food pantry, because their neighbors take care of them. You're going to grow more veggies than we can eat or store, right?"

"What do I do with the extra?"

"Call Reverend Crawford and let him know. He'll arrange for you to bring them to the church, where they will be distributed to needy families. Even though Samara Lambert is a teacher, she is having a hard time making ends meet without her husband's salary. She is someone who would benefit from a food donation."

"Tell me about your prom."

Deborah thought about Eddie Wilkes. He'd asked her and she'd said yes. "I had a date for the prom. Why so many questions, baby girl?"

"A lot of girls in my grade have boyfriends, but I told them I couldn't have one because number one I'm too young, and secondly it would interfere with my schoolwork."

Deborah kissed her hair. "When did my daughter get so smart?"

"I was always smart." There was a hint of smugness in her voice.

"I'm not saying you're not smart, Crystal. What I mean is that you're able to stand up for yourself and not give in to peer pressure."

Crystal sucked her teeth. "I don't have a choice. You said I can't have a boyfriend and I can't even sneak around with Whitney shadowing me like I'm about to do something."

"Your brother is just trying to protect you."

"That was okay when the other kids were talking about Daddy. But there's no need for him to watch me now."

"I would've given anything to have had a brother. Even one who would've read my diary or snapped the heads off my dolls."

Crystal laughed. "Whitney never did those things."

"Well then, I guess he's a pretty good brother."

Crystal rolled her eyes, but smiled as she did. "Thanks, Mom."

"For what?"

"For agreeing to take me shopping."

"I told you I'd take you."

Crystal lowered her head and her eyes. "I thought you were still mad about Grandma and the puppy."

"You're giving it too much energy. I said what I wanted and needed to say to my mother, and as far as I'm concerned it's over." Deborah rose to her feet and picked up her handbag. "Don't stay up too late. And don't forget to turn off the lights before you go upstairs."

"I won't." Crystal unmuted the sound, folded her arms under her head, and went back to watching her favorite show.

After settling into her room, Deborah opened the drawer to the bedside table and took out her journal. It had been almost a week since she'd written anything in it. Uncapping her gel pen, she wrote the date:

February 6th—Asa prepared dinner for me. We danced together again—and I find myself growing closer and closer to him. It is as if I need to connect to someone other than Whitney, Crystal, and the customers that come into the bookstore. The more time we spend together the more I like him. He is a wonderful friend and I know I'm going to miss him when he leaves to return to Delaware.

If she were truly honest then she would admit that Asa was becoming more than a friend. A knowing glance, a gentle caress, and a chaste kiss. These were hardly things shared by friends—especially between a man and a woman. When, she mused, had she become a coward?

Recapping the pen, she returned it and the journal to the drawer. She couldn't write anymore. Not tonight.

Chapter Seventeen

Don't forget to come straight home after practice."

"I know, Mom."

Deborah stared at Whitney's impassive expression, her hand resting on the door handle. "Is something wrong, Whitney?"

"No, Mom. I was just thinking about something." He exhaled audibly. "I'm going to have to leave now if I'm going to get to practice on time."

"I'll see you later," Deborah said as she pushed open the car door and got out. She stood on the macadam staring at the Corolla's taillights as Whitney drove off. They'd gone to early service without Crystal. Her daughter had overslept and Deborah had kept her promise not to become the girl's alarm clock.

She'd reminded Whitney not to hang out with his teammates following basketball practice because she wanted him home when Asa arrived for dinner. Having her children there made it look less like a date than an invitation—which it was.

Deborah mounted the porch steps, pausing before unlocking and opening the door. It was only after she'd announced to her son and daughter that she'd invited Asa to eat with them that she'd noticed a change in Whitney's demeanor. He'd looked at her, then mumbled "that's nice." Crystal had lifted her shoulders, but didn't say anything.

Then Deborah began to question herself. Had she acted impulsively when she'd asked Asa to come to her house? Or was the invitation one she would've extended to anyone of whom she'd become fond? It wasn't as if they hadn't had company for Sunday dinner before.

When Louis was alive they'd had Barbara and Terrell Nash and their children, Mabel and Lester Kelly, and of course her parents, Herman and Pearl Williams, as house guests and for holiday celebrations. She wasn't going to let her children's reaction to her inviting her friend spoil her excitement.

Tossing her keys into the small sweet-grass basket on the table in the entryway, she made her way to the half-bath off the kitchen to wash her hands. It was nine-thirty and Crystal still wasn't up. How, she thought, was her daughter going to get up and make it to class on time once she was in college? Or worse—to work when she got a job? Deborah knew she couldn't continue to agonize over Crystal's inability to wake up on time, because they'd talked about it over and over until she was at a loss for words.

She left the bathroom and flicked on the coffeemaker. There had been a time when Deborah would brew a four-cup carafe and drink four cups of coffee a day. That changed when Louis gave her a single-cup brewing system for Mother's Day, and she'd gone from four cups to one, or sometimes two, cups a day. She had always switched from caffeinated to decaf because she'd had a problem falling asleep.

Deborah had finished her coffee and a slice of cracked wheat toast topped with strawberry preserves when Crystal walked barefoot into the kitchen in a pair of pajama pants and a tank top. Her hair stood out like tiny spikes on her head.

"Good morning, Mom. Why didn't you wake me so I could go to church?"

"You know I stopped waking you up months ago. If you'd wanted to go, then you should have set your clock."

Crystal sat on a high stool at the cooking island. "I did. But I guess I didn't hear it."

"You didn't hear it, or you hit the snooze button?"

"I remember hitting snooze, but then I guess I went back to sleep." She ignored her mother's pointed stare. "I have cheerleading practice today."

Deborah did not respond. In the past Louis would've driven her to practice. He would pick up the slack, or pitch in whenever Deborah was unable to make a meeting or arrive home in time to start dinner. But Louis wasn't here.

Deborah rinsed her coffee mug, placing it in the dishwasher before opening the refrigerator to take out the fresh turkey she'd marinated the night before.

"Are you taking me to practice?"

Deborah set the large glass-covered dish with the turkey on the countertop. "No, Crystal, I am not taking you to practice."

Crystal pushed out her lip, slid off the stool, and

stomped out of the kitchen. "It's not fair! I'm going to get kicked off the squad."

Deborah wanted to tell her that life wasn't fair. It had taken her husband and the father of her children from her in the prime of his life. And if Crystal was going to get booted off the cheerleading squad, she had no one to blame but herself.

"You can't live your life expecting people to wake you up, Chrissie. If you got up when you were supposed to, then you could've caught a ride with Whitney. Why don't you move your clock to a place where you can't reach over and hit the snooze button? Put it on your dresser, then you'll be forced to get out of bed to turn it off."

"It's still not fair."

Mentally dismissing Crystal and her antics, Deborah busied herself setting the dining room table with a hand-made crocheted tablecloth, china, silver, and crystal. A bouquet of flowers in a Waterford vase doubled as the centerpiece.

She'd ordered the fresh turkey from the supermarket. The produce section was stocked with a cornucopia of locally grown vegetables, and she'd selected fresh mustard and turnip greens and enough sweet potatoes for two pies.

Deborah had planned her menu to include roast turkey with herb/sausage stuffing, white long-grain Carolina rice, giblet gravy, greens with smoked turkey, and cornbread. She would cook enough so there would be leftovers. She'd just placed the turkey on the rack in a roasting pan when the telephone rang. Wiping her hands on a towel, she picked up the cordless receiver.

"Hello."

"Hi, Deborah. Babs."

"Hey! How are you?"

"Good, girl. I'm calling to ask you whether Whitney and Crystal can spend the night at my place after the school dance. You know Janelle's birthday is the fourteenth, and instead of a party I told her she could have a sleepover. I know Whitney's not going to want to be around a bunch of giggling girls, so he'll probably hang out with Nate."

"Crystal didn't tell me about the sleepover."

"I just thought of it this morning. I'd planned to have something at a restaurant at the end of the month, but then remembered Crystal and Whitney were going to Florida for the break."

"I don't have a problem with them staying over," Deborah said.

"Good," Barbara said. "Nate will tell Whitney and he'll give Crystal an invitation. I know I should have my head examined for entertaining a houseful of teenagers, but I'd rather have them here where I can keep an eye on them rather than drop them off at a restaurant. Janelle wants a D.J., but I told her I don't want the neighbors calling the police if it gets too loud."

"How many kids do you plan to invite?"

"No more than a dozen. That's why I'm handing out invitations. If anyone shows up without one, then they're not coming in. And you know how these kids do when they hear about a party. It becomes a mob scene and when you try putting them out or not letting any more in, they get stupid and come back with guns. I swear before goodness that I will not have a bunch of thugs crash my child's party."

"Have Terrell act as bouncer. I'm certain he could toss a few of them like he used to throw a football when he was a college quarterback."

"Please, Deborah. All the kids know my husband is all bark and no bite."

"I'm willing to bet he won't just bark when it comes to his daughter."

Barbara's high-pitched laugh came through the earpiece. "Anyone messing with Janelle will turn my teddy bear of a husband into a beast. And that's one side of him I witnessed once and don't want to see again. I just want you to know that your kids will be safe while they're here."

It wouldn't be the first time Crystal and Whitney would stay with their former neighbors, but it would be the first time they would attend a house party there while Deborah remained so far away on the Cove. She knew Barbara was apprehensive about hosting the party because there had been a rash of shootings when uninvited partygoers were denied access, but Deborah trusted Terrell and Barbara and was certain they would take the necessary steps to avoid a similar situation.

"I know they will."

Anchoring the receiver between her chin and shoulder, Deborah continued to talk while she put up a pot of boiling water for the sweet potatoes, then went into the pantry for a canister of flour to make pie crusts. She brought Barbara up-to-date about the bookstore. Deborah didn't mention Asa because she wasn't certain when Crystal would walk into the kitchen.

"I've been working double shifts," Barbara said. "We had eleven nurses retire at the end of last year and so far administration has only hired two to replace them. I am working harder than a pack mule going down the Grand Canyon. I keep telling Terrell that I'm going to quit and find a position as a school nurse. At least I'll have holidays and summers off."

"That was why I loved teaching, Babs."

"I know you have the bookstore, but would you ever consider teaching again?"

"That's something I thought about after Louis died and I closed the store," Deborah admitted. "I knew I was going to move to Sanctuary Cove, so I went online to look into vacancies for the schools on the island."

"Did you find any?"

"There is one opening for a language arts teacher in Haven Creek, for the upcoming school year. While I was thinking about whether to fill out the online application I found the vacant store, and you know the rest."

"It's nice that you have options, Debs. You have three elementary/junior high schools on the island from which to choose if you decide to go back to teaching. You'll probably have no more than an eight-to-one student-teacher ratio and field trips will be picking up seashells along the beach."

"Stop it, Babs. You know I'm a visual person. All you have to do is mention the beach and I'm there."

"Have you been to the beach since moving back?"

"Not yet. But soon."

"I envy you, Deborah. Every time I go to Cavanaugh Island I get mad as hell when I come back. Please, don't get me wrong. Charleston is beautiful, but the older I get the more I want a slower pace. I've been telling Terrell that as soon as the kids are up and out of the house we are moving. I wouldn't mind buying a little place in Sanctuary Cove and commuting."

"I know there are a few houses on the market. Some are fixer uppers and one or two are close to move-in condition. Remember Congressman Jason Parker?"

"The Ken doll?"

Deborah laughed. "He's the one."

"What about him?"

"He moved to the Cove."

"No!"

"Yes. I saw his wife and kids in church last Sunday."

"But they live in a mansion on South Battery."

"They don't live there anymore," Deborah stated. "They bought a dilapidated house that had belonged to an eighteenth-century shipping merchant and renovated it. I've heard talk that it is one of the grandest homes on the Cove. It's apparent they wanted a slower, simpler way of life for themselves and their children. I happen to know of a foreclosed abandoned property that's going for around thirty thousand. It's small, but it would be the perfect vacation home. There's even enough land where you can build out and up. And with developers sniffing around like hounds after a rabbit, it's not going to stay on the market long."

She gave Barbara an overview of the last town council meeting. "I don't want to believe they're the type to cut and run. They'll probably resort to underhanded tactics, like having their people buy up vacant lots and homes and hold on to them while waiting for sentiment to change in their favor."

"I'm definitely going to talk to Terrell about looking into buying property on Cavanaugh. Maybe before the year is out we'll be neighbors again," Barbara told her, then said, "What's up with you and Asa?"

"He's coming for dinner," she whispered into the mouthpiece.

"Are you home alone?"

"No."

"Then you have to call me once he leaves and fill me in."

"I will," Deborah said in a normal tone.

By the time Deborah ended the call, she'd rolled out two pie crusts and boiled the potatoes. Crystal, having showered and combed her hair, returned to the kitchen to prepare breakfast for herself. She seemed to have recovered from missing practice when she talked excitedly about attending her first high school dance. Deborah told her about Janelle's birthday party and sleepover.

Mother and daughter worked together cutting, chopping, and sautéing as the kitchen was filled with delicious smells that tantalized their olfactory nerves. The basted turkey had taken on a light golden color, and the aromas from the roasting bird permeated the space.

Deborah finished preparing her dinner at one-forty, then retreated to her en suite bath to shower and change her clothes. Whitney, who had returned at two claiming he was starved, knew he wouldn't sit down to eat until their customary four o'clock. He showered quickly, also changing his clothes. When the doorbell rang at three-thirty, he went to answer it.

Asa smiled at the tall, lanky young man. "Good afternoon, Whitney."

Whitney opened the door wider. "Good afternoon, Mr. Monroe. Please come in."

Asa handed the boy a shopping bag. "This is a little something for dessert."

Whitney peered into the bag. "What is it?" he whispered conspiratorially.

"Mississippi pecan pie. I hope no one is allergic to nuts."

Whitney's eyes danced with excitement. "No one in this house. Come in," he urged when Asa held back. Going to the staircase, he called out, "Mom! Mr. Monroe is here."

Deborah skipped down the staircase and slowed when she saw Asa staring up at her. A slight smile parted her lips as she took in the sight of him. He wore a pair of black, sharply creased slacks, slip-ons, a white silk shirt opened at the throat, and a pale-gray lightweight jacket.

She stepped off the stair, extending her hand. "Thank you for coming."

Asa inclined his head. "Thank you for inviting me. Something smells good."

Crystal, who had come from the kitchen, stopped when she saw Asa standing in the entryway. She tilted her head to the side as if trying to remember where she knew him from, then her gaze shifted between Asa and her mother. She closed the distance between them, holding out her hand.

"Hello again, Mr. Monroe," she said, finally recognizing him from the bookstore.

Asa smiled at Deborah's daughter and shook the proffered hand. "Hello to you, too, Crystal."

Crystal released his hand. "Come and I'll show you where you can wash your hands. My mom has a cow every time we come to the table without washing our hands. Well, you do, Mom," she added when Deborah gave her a *no you didn't say that* look.

Whitney handed his mother the shopping bag. "Mr. Monroe bought a pecan pie."

"I told him not to bring anything."

"No biggie, Mom. I'll eat it," Whitney volunteered.

"You do that, you'll be bouncing off the walls from a

sugar rush." Looping her arm over her son's, they walked toward the kitchen. "Put the pie on the countertop with the others." When Asa emerged from the half-bath, she took his hand and led him to the dining room where Crystal had taken her seat. Deborah had removed the leaf in the dining room table and took away two of the six chairs for a more intimate seating. "You can sit here," she said, directing Asa to sit at one end of the walnut pedestal table.

Crystal stilled, glaring at Asa. Deborah noticed the change in her daughter's demeanor, wondering what had caused her to bristle.

"Asa, would you mind saying grace?" Deborah asked.

With wide eyes filling with tears, Crystal glared at her mother. The tears overflowed as she bit her lip to stifle the sobs. It wasn't until a sob echoed in the room that Deborah turned to look at her daughter.

A frown of concern lined her forehead. "What's the matter?"

"How could you, Mama?"

Whitney, who had entered the dining room, stared at his sister. "What's going on?"

Crystal pointed to Deborah. "Ask the *traitor.*"

Deborah wanted to disappear on the spot. "Traitor? Crystal, honey, why would you say something like that?" she said, clasping her daughter's hands. "I'm not a traitor. I'm your mother," she responded softly. "What's wrong?"

Crystal's chin trembled as the tears continued to flow. "How...how can you have him sit in Daddy's chair when..." Her words trailed off in another round of heart-wrenching sobs.

Pushing back the chair, Asa stood up. "I'm sorry, but I think I need to leave."

Resting her hands on her hips, Deborah's eyes went from Asa to Crystal and back again. "No, Asa. You don't have to leave."

He held up his hands. "But..."

"Please, sit down, Asa. You too, Whitney," she said in a voice that made her children stare at her as if they'd never seen her before. Although spoken softly, it held a hard edge.

Deborah sat opposite Asa, her eyes moving slowly around the table before coming to rest on Crystal. "If you have a problem, then speak on it. After that I intend to have a civil Sunday dinner without your disrespect."

Picking up the damask napkin at her place setting, Crystal dabbed her eyes. "I...I just remember Daddy sit... sitting there and I don't think it's fair that someone else should sit there when..."

"When what?" Deborah asked.

"I understand where Crystal is coming from," Asa said when the girl didn't answer her mother's query. "She feels betrayed because she believes I'm taking her father's place." He lowered his gaze, staring down at the tablecloth. He was so still he could have been carved from stone. A shuddering sigh escaped him. "I know how she feels to lose someone, because I lost my wife...and son...last year." He registered a gasp, and knew it had come from Deborah. "I waited a long time to become a father, but I would only have Isaac for six years."

Resting his elbows on the table, Whitney asked, "What happened to them?"

Pushing back his chair, Asa stood up and walked out of the dining room, then stopped. He didn't move for several minutes, then returned and sat down again. "My wife had taken our son with her when she went Christmas shopping.

She was on her way back home when it started sleeting. The road had become very icy and when she came around a sharp turn she lost control of her car, crashing through the guardrail and slamming into a tree. The car exploded into a fireball and they were unable to get out. The medical examiner used their dental records to confirm their identities.

"I'd stopped eating and sleeping, and there were times when I thought about taking my own life because I had nothing to live for. It would've been so easy to die by injecting myself with a double dose of morphine."

"You're a doctor?" Crystal whispered.

Asa nodded. "Yes, I am a doctor, and my brother was a doctor, as were my father and his father. I'd planned for my son to become the fourth generation Dr. Monroe, but it was not to be."

"Why are you working in a bookstore instead of practicing medicine?" Whitney asked.

"I sold my home and my practice, because there was nothing for me in Delaware. It's been more than a year and I still hurt. I don't know whether I will ever stop hurting when I see a little boy my son's age."

"We miss our dad, too," Whitney confessed. "We were lucky because our father was cool. Maybe it was because he taught at a high school, but he understood where kids were coming from. In fact, he was voted the most popular teacher for three consecutive years. Kids went to him instead of their guidance counselors when they had a problem."

Deborah did not want to believe her children had opened up to Asa—a near stranger. And now she knew that whenever she'd glimpsed sadness in him it hadn't

come from his estrangement with his brother, but because
he'd lost his wife and child. Now she understood what he'd
meant when he said that although she'd lost her spouse
she had her children. He, on the other hand, had lost his
spouse *and* child.

"I came here today because your mother invited me.
And I have no intention of replacing your father. I'll be leaving Sanctuary Cove in a couple of months."

Crystal sniffled. "I'm sorry, Mr. Monroe. I didn't…"

"It's okay, Crystal," Asa said softly. "There's no need to
apologize."

Whitney met his mother's eyes. "I also apologize. Not
for my sister but for having similar thoughts. We weren't
raised to be disrespectful, and I know we're going to hear
it once you leave. Although this is my mom's house I'd like
you to come back and give us a second chance to show you
that we do have home training."

Asa smiled. "If your mother invites me back, then I will
definitely come, if only to enjoy a home-cooked meal."

A new and unexpected warmth eddied through Deborah
when she met Asa's gaze. Her son's offer to invite him back
was as shocking as Asa's revelation that he was a widower.
She'd assumed a soured relationship, even divorce. They'd
worked closely together, talked about any and everything,
yet he had given no indication that he'd recently lost his
wife and child. In fact, he had revealed only that he was
a doctor, had worked in a hospital, had been married, and
didn't have any children. She'd asked, and even though he
hadn't been forthcoming, he had been truthful.

Now she said, "We'll talk about that later. Let's say
grace, then eat before everything gets cold."

Asa bowed his head, as Deborah blessed the table. He

picked up the platter of sliced turkey, holding it for Crystal while she speared several slices. He took some for himself, then handed the platter off to Whitney who held it for his mother, then served himself. The ritual continued until plates were filled, the food eaten then washed down with goblets of homemade brewed sweet tea and lemonade.

Asa took second helpings of everything, stating numerous times that Deborah had missed her calling and that she should have gone into the culinary arts. "Who taught you to cook?" he asked her.

Deborah set down her tea. "My grandmother."

"Mom said our grandmother couldn't cook until she took cooking courses," Crystal blurted out. Crystal swallowed a forkful of stuffing. "I would never have somebody cook for me."

"What if you had a career that took you away from home for days at a time? Or if you had to host a dinner party for twelve? Would you do your own cooking?"

She lifted her shoulders. "Probably."

"I doubt it," he said. "After standing on your feet for hours cutting, slicing, dicing, and checking meat for doneness, do you think you'd have enough energy to entertain your guests?"

"I don't think so," Whitney chimed in.

"Whitney's right," Asa concurred. "You wouldn't. That's why people have their parties catered. Perhaps you could be the one to cater the events, leaving the hosting to someone else. Have you ever considered going to culinary school?"

Crystal nodded with excitement.

"Where did you go to school, Mr. Monroe?" Whitney asked.

"Howard. Undergraduate and medical school."

"I've been accepted at Howard," Whitney said proudly.

"It's an excellent school, Whitney."

"That's what my mom says."

"Your mom is right."

Deborah felt a rush of emotion she couldn't explain. Whitney and Crystal were so comfortable with Asa and had told him things they never would have divulged to a stranger. She wanted Whitney to go to Howard and hoped that his conversation with Asa convinced him the school was the best college for his career choice.

Dinner became a leisurely affair, the quartet sitting at the table long after they'd eaten their fill. The discussion segued from college to the recent Super Bowl and high school sports. Whitney admitted to joining the basketball team because he needed another extracurricular activity.

When Deborah stood up to clear the table, Asa also stood. "Whitney and I will clean up."

Whitney popped up like a jack-in-the-box. "Of course."

Crystal placed a hand over her mouth to hide her grin. "That's a first," she whispered when they disappeared into the kitchen.

Deborah met her daughter's eyes. "You can help me serve dessert as soon as the men are finished."

Crystal leaned to her left. "I like him, Mom."

"Who?"

"Mr. Monroe. He's real nice."

"That he is," Deborah said in agreement. Crystal thought he was nice, the women who came into the bookstore thought he was nice, and she knew he was nice. Her feelings for him were growing stronger with each passing day. What she didn't want was to rely on him for her emotional well-being because she would have him for a very short amount of time.

Deborah didn't want to think of his pending departure as she invited everyone back into the kitchen for dessert. She brewed coffee for Asa and herself and filled glasses with ice-cold milk for Whitney and Crystal. Slices of pecan pie and sweet potato pie were topped with scoops of vanilla ice cream from De Fountain and dollops of fresh whipped cream.

Asa patted his flat belly. "I don't know how you guys stay so thin, but if I ate like this every Sunday I'd blow up like a blimp."

Crystal drained her glass. "I burn a lot of calories cheer-leading, and Whitney is on the basketball team. And Mom won't let us eat fast food more than once a week."

Asa gave Deborah a surreptitious wink. "That's because fast foods are loaded with calories."

Crystal nodded. "That's what Mom says."

"What position do you play?" Asa asked Whitney.

"Small forward."

"How many points do you average per game?"

"Fifteen."

Asa lifted his eyebrows. "Not bad."

"I stink, Mr. Monroe. There are guys on the team who hit twenty to thirty points every game."

Asa nodded, his expression serene. "Call me Asa. Those are the guys who, if they make it to Howard, will do so on an athletic scholarship. And who will have to be tutored in order to keep their scholarship. And if they're lucky enough to make it to the NBA, will mess up off the court during their first season and all the practicing and tutoring will be for naught. I went to high school with a couple of guys who did make it to the NBA, and wound up with six kids and four baby mamas between them before they were twenty-five. One couldn't stay away from the white powder and weed, and the other refused to go into alcohol rehab because he was in denial about his drinking problem." Asa shook his head. "It was tragic, Whitney. They had so much natural talent, but it was wasted because their actions had dire consequences."

Crystal stared at her brother. "I'm glad I'm not a boy."

"Don't start crowing, baby girl," Deborah crooned. "Girls are not exempt from drugs, alcohol, and stair-step babies from a bunch of different baby daddies."

"Like Doreena," the teenagers said in unison.

"Let's not repeat gossip," Deborah chastised.

Crystal rolled her head. "It's not gossip, Mom. Everyone in Charleston knows that she had babies from two brothers and their cousin. Kids call her Chuck Town Ho."

"Crystal!"

"It's true, Mom."

Leaning back, Asa crossed one leg over the opposite knee. "Don't mind me. I've heard worse."

Deborah held her forehead. What was she going to do with her daughter other than love her? And Asa appeared to enjoy her kids' antics. Reaching across the table, she removed plates, forks, and glasses, stacking them in the dishwasher. She turned it on.

"Asa, do you want me to pack up some leftovers for you?"

"But of course. I'll take a little of everything."

Whitney and Crystal stood up, Asa rising with them. They thanked him for coming for dinner. Whitney, after extracting a promise from Asa that he would come back again, dropped an arm over his sister's shoulder and led her out of the kitchen.

"Mom, we're going to Angels Landing to hang out at Simeon's house for a while," Whitney called out.

"Don't come home too late."

"We won't," they chorused.

"You have great kids," Asa said when he and Deborah were alone.

"Even with my daughter going off on you?"

Asa walked over, stood behind Deborah and rested his hands on her shoulders. "It was understandable."

Deborah looked up at him over her shoulder. "Why didn't you tell me you'd lost your wife and son?"

"You didn't ask." Lowering his head, he pressed a kiss to the column of her scented neck. "How can I thank you for the best day I've had in more than a year?"

"Just say thank you."

He chuckled. "That's not enough."

Deborah turned until they were facing each other. "What else is there?"

Asa angled his head, his mouth covering hers in an explosive joining that weakened her knees, forcing her to hold on to him to keep her balance. Her fingers caught the front of his shirt, tightening as her lips parted.

Anchoring her arms under his shoulders, she went on tiptoe to get even closer. Her breathing quickened, her breasts grew heavy, and the area between her thighs was moist and throbbing, reminding her how long it had been since she'd had sex.

Deborah wanted Asa. She wanted to be in his bed and with him inside her. But somewhere between sanity and insanity, she surfaced from the sensual fog clouding her brain and regained her common sense.

"No, Asa." The protest came out weak.

"Come home with me, baby. I need to hold you, taste you. I have protection."

She shook her head. "I can't."

"I'll bring you back before your children return."

Breathing through parted lips, Deborah felt slightly lightheaded. "It's not about them."

Asa pressed his mouth to the side of her neck again as if he wanted to sink his teeth into her skin. There were other places on her body on which he could feast that would remain hidden to everyone except her. The thought made her blush.

"What is it about, then?" he asked, rousing Deborah from her thoughts.

"Asa, when we make love I want to savor the moment. I want to give you my undivided attention without having to rush."

He smiled. "When?"

"Tomorrow. I'll come before noon and stay until it's time for me to pick up Crystal from school. I'd promised to take her shopping for the school's Valentine's Day dance."

Asa's hand caressed her back in a circular motion as he stared at her mouth. Her thoroughly kissed lips felt fuller. He nodded his approval, then watched as she packed plastic containers with food, then stacked them neatly in a shopping bag.

He took the bag, his eyes seemingly searching her face. She'd pulled her hair back in a chignon; giving him an unobstructed view, highlighting her sprinkling of freckles and high cheekbones.

"I'll walk you out," Deborah said with a mysterious smile. They left the brick-walled kitchen and walked down the narrow hall that led past the dining room and into the living room. She stood on the porch, watching as Asa got into the Range Rover and slowly backed out of her driveway. Lifting her hand, she waved to him. She wasn't disappointed when he put his hand out the window and returned her wave. She stood there a long time, staring at the space where his truck had been, then turned and went back into the house.

"I'm falling in love with him," she whispered. She was falling in love with a man she'd known a month—with whom she shared a similar fate. Both had loved and lost, but with Asa the loss was more complete.

Deborah, although knowing he was going to leave Sanctuary Cove, had agreed to sleep with him. She was a thirty-eight-year-old widow with two teenaged children and she was about to embark on a short-lived affair with a transient widower. Neither of them were kids, so there wouldn't be any promises of a commitment or declarations of love. They would enjoy their time together and when it ended they would be left with memories of the time they shared.

Chapter Eighteen

Deborah got out of the car, carrying her handbag and another larger bag filled with several changes of clothes and toiletries. She'd managed to finish cleaning her house by the time Whitney and Crystal left for school. Dusting, vacuuming, and changing beds had kept her busy so she wouldn't have to think about what would happen once she arrived at the bookstore. She was filled with nervous energy as she stopped to deposit her weekly receipts, before driving the short distance to the lot behind the store.

The back door opened and Asa smiled down at her. "Hey, beautiful."

Deborah returned his smile and, rising on tiptoe, brushed her mouth over his. "Hey yourself."

He took the bags, then closed and locked the door behind her. Wrapping an arm around her waist, Asa pulled Deborah close. "Let me escort you up to the penthouse."

Deborah giggled like a schoolgirl. "How are the views?"

"They're all right."

"Just all right, Asa?"

His hand moved from her waist to her backside. "This view is a lot better," he crooned in her ear.

Her free hand went to his tight butt in a pair of relaxed jeans. "And this one isn't too bad either."

"You haven't even seen it."

Deborah laughed again. "My hands have special powers."

"Ah-h! So, my girl is a superhero."

"Super heroine, thank you very much."

Asa set the bag on the floor, then bending at the knees scooped Deborah up in his arms and carried her up the staircase and over to the bed. He placed her gently on the mattress, his body following hers down. Supporting his weight on his elbows, he covered her like a warm blanket. "Are you okay?"

"I'm wonderful. You know, you're good for me."

"Why is that, baby?"

"Because you make me laugh. I've laughed more with you in the past couple of weeks than I have in months. And you make me feel like a woman. It's been a very long time since I've felt that way."

No more words followed; only the sound of measured breathing could be heard in the room. The lowered blinds only allowed for slivers of light to slip through the slats covering the windows.

Deborah turned on her side to face Asa. "I can't promise—"

"Don't," he interrupted, placing a finger on her lips. "Please don't say what I think you're about to say. I don't want any promises."

"What do you want, Asa?"

"I don't want yesterday or tomorrow. I want right now. I'm sorry but that is all I can offer you."

"Why are you always apologizing?" she asked him.

Asa sat up and straddled her. "I find myself doing that a lot with you."

Deborah closed her eyes when she felt his hands brush her breasts, and then slowly unbutton her blouse. She heard his intake of breath when he stared at her breasts in her sheer bra, the color of *café con leche*. It seemed like an eternity before he removed each article of her clothing, until she lay completely naked.

She watched him undress, removing his shirt, jeans, and briefs and throwing them in a pile with hers at the foot of the bed. Asa's clothes had concealed a lean, hard body that belied his age. A light dusting of hair covered his broad chest, and her gaze travelled downward to his flat belly, on to the inverted triangle where his semi-erect penis hung heavily between his thighs. The side of the mattress dipped as he slid in beside her, his hand going under the pillow to retrieve a condom. He quickly opened the packet and slipped on the latex sheath.

Asa gave her breasts his undivided attention, suckling one breast, then the other. Waves of pleasure raced through her body, and her hips bucked upward to meet him. Deborah's fingers dug into his biceps, trembling uncontrollably as a rush of moisture flowed down her inner thighs onto the sheets. He reached down, stroking her clitoris as he continued feasting on her nipples.

Deborah was losing control and didn't want to come without him inside her.

"Please," she pleaded shamelessly, her body on fire.

Heat, followed by chills, then more heat singed her sensitive flesh. Asa kissed her mouth, the hollow in her throat, his lips charting a course down her body. He kissed her breasts, her belly, the inside of her thighs, retracing his path as he explored every inch of her. She didn't want him to stop. He'd discovered erogenous zones on her body she hadn't known existed. Her heart pumped so hard she was certain it could be seen through her chest.

Holding his hard length in one hand, Asa parted her legs with his knees and positioned his erection at the entrance to her sex. He pressed into her body, watching as his hardened flesh finally slipped inside her. She was so tight but managed to take all of him. They'd become a perfect fit.

Deborah gloried in the hard body atop hers, his swollen member sliding in and out of her wetness. A shiver of delight washed over her, a moan slipping past her lips as she felt ready to climax. Finally letting go, her first orgasm took over, holding Deborah captive for mere seconds before another earth-shattering release rocked through her core, taking her straight to heaven.

"You are incredibly beautiful," Asa whispered in Deborah's ear as her body calmed from release. What he wanted to tell her was that he loved her passion, her strength and loyalty to those she loved. Actually, he was beginning to love everything about her and had come to depend on her emotionally. He went to bed thinking of her. Woke looking for her. The moment she walked into the bookstore his day brightened, and when she left he found himself waiting for her to return. He felt like a mouse on a tread wheel, going around and around and not being able to stop.

Again, he grew hard for her, the blood rushing so quickly to his penis that for a moment he felt lightheaded. Asa took a deep breath, held it, and then let it out slowly. He wanted to savor this moment before taking her again. All of his senses were heightened: the soft sounds of Deborah's moans, his own groans, the silken feel of her body against his, and the smell of her perfume mingling with the tantalizing aroma from their lovemaking. It had become an aphrodisiac.

Reaching for Deborah's hand, he cradled it gently, his thumb making tiny circles on her inner wrist. Making love with Deborah was more than he'd hoped for, and he did what he hadn't done in some time. He prayed. He prayed he would be able to leave when the time came for him to join Doctors Without Borders.

"Are you all right, darling?"

Deborah sighed softly, then suddenly tensed beside him. "Yes."

"I didn't hurt you, did I?" he asked, now concerned by the change in her mood.

"No," she said after a long silence.

Asa knew something was bothering Deborah. He wondered if she was conflicted because they'd slept together. Had she felt as if she'd dishonored her husband's memory?

"I want you to tell me about him, Deborah."

She glanced up at him, tears in her eyes.

"How did he die?"

Deborah knew eventually she would have to tell Asa about Louis. Taking a deep breath, she willed herself to begin. "Louis taught high school math," she said in a soft voice. "He'd go in early to work with students that needed extra help. Louis was aware of the school policy that required the door to remain open whenever he had a student in his office, so I don't know why he'd chosen to ignore the rule when a female student came to his office early one morning. I suppose it was because she was crying and told him she didn't want anyone to overhear what she wanted to tell him.

"She was a sixteen-year-old junior who'd found herself pregnant after she got involved with a much older man she'd met on the Internet. Louis asked if she'd told her parents and she claimed she couldn't because they were ultra-religious. When she told her boyfriend about her dilemma he'd suggested she have the baby and sell it to a childless couple willing to pay thousands of dollars for a newborn. The poor girl didn't know what to do, because to her abortion was not an option.

"Louis told me she started to cry. He put his arms around her in an attempt to comfort her, and that was when the principal walked in on them. Louis was suspended without pay pending a school board hearing, and the news spread that Louis Robinson had been caught in a compromising position with a female student."

"Didn't the girl set the record straight?"

"No. If she'd told why she was in her math teacher's office, then she would have had to recount their conversation. It was the first time in eighteen years that I saw my husband depressed. He stopped eating and would sit in the dark regardless of the time of day. I kept begging him to tell the principal why Melissa was in his office, but he refused. Meanwhile, my own kids were catching hell from other students who were as cruel as their parents, who were divided into pro- and anti–Louis Robinson factions.

People whom I'd believed were my friends turned on me. Even the woman who worked for me in the bookstore quit. Then one day he told me he was tired of hiding and left the house."

"Did you know where he was going?"

She nodded, then said, "Yes. Louis loved the beach. He would spend hours sitting on the sand staring at the water.

"The weather was cool that day, the water choppy, and there were marine warnings about riptides and dangerous undertows. A group of high school students who'd cut classes were fooling around in the water. Several of them swam out too far and were caught in an undertow. Witnesses said Louis didn't hesitate when he jumped in in an attempt to save the drowning boys. He pulled two back to the beach and went back into the water for the third one. But he was larger and much stronger than Louis. He panicked, pulling them both under. By the time the police got to the scene Louis and the kid had disappeared. Divers managed to recover the boy's body but Louis was listed as missing and presumed dead."

Asa buried his face in Deborah's moist curls that smelled like fresh coconut. "Did they ever find his body?"

"Yes. Days later his body washed up on the beach a mile from the accident. Once the news got out that Louis had sacrificed his life in order to save three boys everything changed. The ones who were ready to lynch him became remorseful. And those who'd believed Louis would never harm a child pointed fingers at the hypocrites. I had a private ceremony with my family and closest friends, followed by a cremation. I sprinkled his ashes in the very waters that had taken his life.

"Overwhelmed with grief, Melissa told her parents

about her pregnancy. They pressured her to tell the principal why she'd come to Mr. Robinson's office that morning. Eventually the board voted unanimously to reinstate Louis's salary and that made me eligible for his pension and life insurance. The people who were quick to condemn Louis made a complete one-eighty and they sent flowers and condolence cards, and my neighbor became a buffer, answering my phone and the door. But once my parents returned to Florida I realized I could no longer live in Charleston. I sat down with Crystal and Whitney, asking whether they would be opposed to living here. They were ecstatic. Though living here put distance between them and the kids who *had* been their friends, they were okay with it because they would continue to attend the same school."

"What happened to Melissa?"

"Her parents sent her to California to live with an older married sister. Before she left she called to tell me she'd planned to have the baby, and then give it up for adoption. I don't blame Melissa as much as I do the principal. She was a frightened girl, but Francis is a mean-spirited SOB who was jealous of Louis's relationship with the students. He didn't have to suspend Louis. He could've pulled him out of the classroom and put him on administrative desk duty, but he just had to get him out of *his school*."

"I can understand your animosity, Deborah, but you can't blame anyone for your husband's death. It was an accident. A very tragic accident where he'd made the ultimate sacrifice to give up his life to save someone else's. I know it hurts, and the pain is like a deep hole you believe will never be filled, but you will heal."

"Have you healed, Asa?"

"Not completely."

"I suppose it's going to take time—for both of us. However, living here has changed me," Deborah admitted, "and I don't think that would've happened if I'd stayed in Charleston. I've let go of the anger and resentment that gnawed at me like a malignancy, because if I hadn't I'm certain it would have eventually destroyed me. I don't live for myself. I live for my children. I'm all they have, and the way Louis gave up his life to save that boy I would do the same for Crystal and Whitney."

Deborah sat in her car in the visitor's parking waiting for Crystal to come out of school. Each time she moved she was reminded of what she had shared with Asa earlier that morning. They'd made love twice. Once in bed and again when they'd shared a shower. This second coupling had been more uninhibited, when she went to her knees and took him in her mouth and suckled him until he bellowed for her to stop. Then it was his turn, when he carried her out of the bathroom and to the bed, and his teeth and tongue worked their magic as they climaxed simultaneously. It wasn't until she was slipping on her panties that she felt the slight ache from muscles she hadn't used in a while.

During the ferry ride she'd stood at the railing thinking about what had happened between her and Asa, realizing she was confused. Asa made her feel very feminine and desirable, but sleeping with him reminded her of what she'd shared with Louis.

A tapping on the window caught her attention and she smiled at Crystal. Pushing a button, she unlocked the car. Leaning over, Deborah offered her cheek for a kiss and was happy when Crystal kissed her.

"How was your day?"

Crystal tossed her tote onto the rear seat. "Good. How was your day?"

Deborah smiled. "It was very good." She started up the car and drove slowly out of the parking lot. Students were pouring out of the building and strolling across the street to student parking. "Did you tell Whitney that you were going with me?"

"He knows. He's staying late to work on the paper."

"What do you do when he stays late?"

"I either hang out in the library and do my homework, or I go to the newspaper office and take a nap on one of the sofas."

"What color is the dress you want?"

"Red."

Deborah gave Crystal a quick glance before returning her attention to the traffic in front of her. "Do you also want red shoes?"

"Nope. I want them in black; that way I can wear them with other outfits," she said decisively. "Whitney told me Nate gave him two invitations for Janelle's party."

"You're going to be doing a lot of partying that night. First the dance and then the sleepover."

Crystal snapped her fingers. "That's how we Robbies roll."

"Robbies?"

"That's what the girls call Whitney. 'Robbie' is short for Robinson."

"Interesting," Deborah drawled. She tapped her horn to get the attention of a driver drifting into her lane. "I really don't miss this."

"When are you going to let me drive?"

"When you get your license."

"I plan to take the road test this summer."

"As soon as you take the test and get your license, then you can drive me around."

Crystal gave her mother a puzzled look. "You don't like driving?"

"Not really. I drive because I have to, not because I want to."

"If that's the case, then I'll be your driver."

Deborah wanted to tell Crystal that when she did get her license the last thing she'd want to do was chauffeur her mother around, but decided not to. She turned and drove down King Street. "Where do you want to go first?"

"Finicky Filly."

Within minutes of entering the elegant boutique Crystal found the dress she wanted. It was red with spaghetti straps, a fitted bodice, and a skirt with four tiers of ruffles that ended at the knee. It was a perfect fit. Finding shoes proved a bit more challenging. The pair that Crystal wanted was in stock but they didn't have her size. After trying on half a dozen pairs, she finally selected a black silk pump with a three-inch heel that flattered her long, slender legs.

When Deborah suggested they eat out, Crystal said she wanted to go home because she had a history test the next day. During the return trip to the island Deborah did something she'd never done before: she took the causeway. She thought she'd imagined it, but the hair stood up on the back of her neck when she passed the marker for Angels Landing. People had talked about the town being haunted and now she believed it. She wasn't able to relax until they were back in the Cove.

Once there, Deborah prepared a quick dinner for herself

and Crystal, using leftovers from Sunday's dinner. After cleaning up the kitchen, she retreated to her bedroom and closed the door. Walking into the bathroom Deborah stripped off her clothes and stared at her naked body in the full-length mirror on the back of the door. Evidence of the time she'd spent with Asa showed on her breasts and thighs. There was no way she would have been able to explain to her children how she'd gotten the red splotches if he'd bitten her neck.

She smiled at her reflection. It had been years since she'd gotten a hickey. "Shame on you, Dr. Monroe." Her smile faded when she said his title aloud. She couldn't believe he'd spent so many years studying to become a doctor, only to give it up when his wife and son died. At forty-six he was too young to retire, and she wondered what he intended to do once he left the Cove.

Deborah washed her face and brushed her teeth before pulling a nightgown over her head. She got into bed and reached for her journal. What she was feeling, what she had done earlier was still so intense that she had to write it down on paper.

February 12th—Asa and I made love for the first, second, *and* third time. It was as if I'd been dying of thirst and he was an oasis. I just couldn't get enough of him.

Making love with him was very different from what I had ever experienced, because Asa is totally uninhibited. I love it and I'm in love with him.

It was Thursday, The Parlor's late night, and as announced, the night of the raffle drawing. This was the first Thursday

Deborah had worked since the bookstore opened. Usually on Thursdays Asa worked until eight, assuming responsibility for closing up. The bookstore was crowded and the excitement palpable; three gaily wrapped sweet-grass baskets were on display for those who'd dropped their tickets into the fishbowl.

Deborah signaled for silence. "I'd like to thank everyone who came out tonight for our first Valentine's Day raffle drawing. There will be other drawings for Easter, Mother's, and Father's Days."

"How about Grandparents' Day?" someone called out.

"That, too," she said, smiling. "How could I forget that day?" She picked up the fishbowl and stirred up the red tickets. "The first drawing will be for the basket with fruit, cheese, and sparkling cider. All of the baskets were made by our own Rachel Dukes-Walker." A smattering of applause followed this announcement. "Asa, will you please pick the first ticket?"

A murmur of approval rippled through the assembly when he came over and put his hand into the bowl and took out a ticket. He read the name and a scream went up as a young woman ran over to retrieve her basket. At the last possible moment, she put her arms around Asa's neck and kissed his cheek.

"Why she got to be so shameless?" whispered an elderly woman standing next to Deborah, who wanted to agree with her.

"The next basket is also a sweet-grass basket from A Tisket A Basket. This one contains bottles of red and white wine, cheese, crackers, Baci, and nuts." Asa pulled a ticket, but the person wasn't present. He pulled two more before they finally got a winner.

"The third and certainly not the least basket contains a bottle of Möet champagne, Godiva chocolate, and an assortment of gourmet cookies. And before we pull a ticket for this basket I'd like to tell the winners there is a bookstore gift certificate in each of the baskets." She nodded to Asa. He pulled the last ticket.

"The grand prize winner is Mabel Kelly."

Mabel ran over to claim her prize. "That's what I'm talking about!" she shouted. "Oh, damn! It's heavy." Everyone laughed.

"I'll carry it for you," Asa volunteered.

Mabel fluttered her lashes at him. "Thank you so much."

Deborah placed the bowl on the table. "I'd like to thank everyone for participating and for coming out tonight. And don't forget to be nice to your valentine."

She waited until the store had emptied, then lowered and closed the blinds, locked the front door, and went through the ritual of turning off lights and lamps, leaving one on at the back of the store. Punching in the PIN for the cash register, she counted the cash, leaving enough in the drawer to make change for the early morning customers.

The Parlor was thriving. The response to the book club discussions had generated a waiting list to join, and the same women attended afternoon teas. Asa alternated playing the piano with pre-recorded music, and customers seemed to sense whenever he was in the store because they came in droves.

She and Asa spent siestas upstairs in his apartment where they shared lunch *and* the bed, and when Deborah reopened at two she couldn't stop blushing or smiling. Making love in the afternoon had become a thrilling experience.

The back door opened and Asa entered. "It's beginning to rain."

Deborah closed the distance between them. "I'd better get home before it comes down too hard."

Cradling her face, Asa brushed his mouth over hers. "Can't you stay a little longer?"

She deepened the kiss, and then forced herself to pull away. "I would love to, but I have to make certain Crystal packs everything she needs for her sleepover."

Resting his hand on her hip, he pulled her closer. "When are we going to have a sleepover?"

"Tomorrow night. The kids are staying over in Charleston. I'll call you after they leave and you can come and get me. If my car is parked out back all night I think it would raise a lot of suspicion as to why I'm hanging out here after closing." Ironically the gossip Hannah had spread about her sleeping with Asa had died, when in reality they were *now* actually sleeping together.

"Tell them you're celebrating Valentine's Day with your man."

Deborah's eyebrows shot up. "Are you really my man, Asa? I didn't think so," she said when he didn't answer. "We're two ships passing in the night. And when it's over I'm certain I won't have any regrets and neither should you. Good night."

Asa stood there, amazed and very shaken that Deborah could be that disconnected when it came to their relationship. Yes, they were friends, but they had become much more. They were now lovers and every time he made love to her he found it more and more difficult not to blurt out what lay in his heart. He didn't want to leave her or

Sanctuary Cove, but knew his leaving was inevitable. The last time he'd checked his e-mail the reply was that he would receive a determination as to his status within three weeks. He'd looked at the calendar and had begun counting the days. Between now and March fourth he would know his fate.

Asa was suddenly attacked by a gamut of emotions. He was in love with Deborah, wanted to marry her, but he also wanted to fulfill his dream of working for DWB. Long ago, he'd talked to his son, telling Isaac that once he became a doctor and took over his father's practice Asa would become a humanitarian physician, offering free medical care to those in need and in war zones. But now, instead of joining Doctors Without Borders at sixty-five, it would become a reality at forty-six.

Chapter Nineteen

This isn't the way to the bookstore, Asa."

"I know."

"You're driving toward the causeway. Where are we going?"

"Out."

"Out where?"

"I'm taking you to a place where we can have a proper Valentine's Day celebration."

She glanced down at her peach-colored twinset and chocolate-brown slacks. "I'm not dressed."

Asa gave her a quick glance. "You look okay."

"I don't want to look just okay, Asa. You could've told me beforehand and I would have at least put on some makeup."

"You look beautiful without it."

"If you don't tell me where we're going I'll—"

"You'll what?" He smiled. "You're not going to do anything but sit back and enjoy the ride *and* the night."

Pouting, she folded her arms under her breasts. "This will be the first and the very last time I'll agree to a sleepover with you," she said, trying to hide her excitement.

They rode in silence and Asa wanted to tell Deborah she was probably right; that was why he wanted this night for lovers to be a special one for them. He touched a button on the wheel and music flowed around them. Traffic was heavier than usual heading toward Charleston. Following the GPS, once they were on the mainland, he turned down a street and maneuvered into the drive leading to a small boutique hotel. "Don't move," he told Deborah as he parked, then got out and retrieved their bags from behind the front seats. Setting them on the ground, he opened the passenger-side door and extended his hand to help her out.

As Deborah looked around, Asa could see the realization in her eyes. "No, you didn't," she said softly.

He smiled and winked at her. "Yes, I did. See, I planned something special for us, and you caught a major attitude."

"I wouldn't have had an attitude if you'd told me where we were going."

"If I did, then it wouldn't have been a surprise."

A bellman came out to greet them. "Dr. and Mrs. Monroe?"

"Yes," Asa replied.

"Welcome, sir. I'll take these to your room while you check in."

Reaching into the pocket of his slacks, he handed the man a bill. "Thank you."

The bellman nodded. "Thank you, sir."

Asa rested his hand at the small of Deborah's back. "Come, darling. Let's check in, and then we can relax."

"When you made the reservation did you put me down as Mrs. Monroe?"

"No. He probably assumed you're my wife."

They walked into the converted mansion. Chandeliers, marble flooring, stately antiques, and reproductions of oil paintings of bewigged men graced the ornate lobby. She stood beside Asa as he gave the clerk a credit card and his driver's license.

The woman, with a peaches-and-cream complexion and friendly light-brown eyes, gave him a smile. "Your suite is ready. Go down the hall on your right. Suite 147 is at the end of the hall." She gave him two cardkeys. "Enjoy your stay."

Deborah looped her arm over Asa's as they walked down the carpeted hallway. "You are chock-full of surprises."

"I aim to please," he drawled.

"I'm pleased."

"Good."

Asa patted the hand on his arm. He slipped the key in the slot, waiting for the green signal, then pushed it open. Dozens of candles flickered in the semi-dark suite. When he'd called to make the reservation he had requested the special Valentine's package with candles, flowers, chocolate, and dinner with wine and champagne. He'd ordered wine because he remembered Deborah had little or no tolerance for bubbly.

He closed the door and caught her hand. "Let's see what the bedroom looks like." There were more candles in the bedroom, and there was enough illumination to see the California-king four-poster bed. Rose petals littered the sheets and pile of pillows.

They walked through the bedroom and into the bath. More candles lined a garden tub and the ledge of twin marble sinks. Porcelain dishes were filled with chocolate and flower petals. She returned to the bedroom to find their bags on luggage racks, and thick bathrobes spread over the foot of the bed.

"I love it, Asa. Thank you."

He walked over to her, took her face in his hands and nibbled her lip. "I'm the one who should be thanking you. Come over here. I ordered a little something to eat before we begin our sleepover."

They sat at the table in the dining area, eating steak frites, an Asian slaw, and a fruit salad with fresh pineapple, pears, strawberries, and shredded coconut. Asa drank two glasses of rosé to her one, and she didn't protest when he carried her into the bathroom and undressed her and then himself while the tub filled with water. She settled into the warm water, resting her head on a bath pillow. Asa stepped in and sat behind her and started up the Jacuzzi.

"Are you falling asleep on me?" he whispered in her ear.

"No. I'm just relaxing my eyes. Do you know what?" she asked, after a pregnant pause.

"What, baby?"

"I'll always remember this Valentine's Day."

Asa kissed her hair. "And I'll always remember you."

Deborah took a deep breath, trying to will away the negative thoughts that threatened the magic. She didn't know why she felt like crying. Maybe it was because something told her this would be their last time together even though Asa planned to stay until spring. But if he was going to leave, then she told herself she preferred now rather than later, before she found herself in too deep.

Did she know what she wanted from Asa aside from their lovemaking? Did she want him to be a part of her future? Or could she hope to become a part of his?

"What's frightened you, Debs? Your heart is beating so fast."

Deborah stared at the hand cradling her left breast. How had she forgotten he was a doctor and no doubt tuned into subtle changes in her body? "I was thinking about making love with you," she lied smoothly.

"That makes two of us. There are very few times when I'm *not* thinking about making love to you. If you were a drug, then you would be an opiate. Every time I hear the word 'siesta' it will remind me of making love with you."

"I'm that addictive?"

"Crazy addictive."

"That sounds serious, Dr. Monroe."

"You just don't know how serious I am."

Deborah reclined against Asa's chest while bubbles eddied over her body; moisture beaded her face and curled her hair. Her apprehension was slowly replaced by an inner peace that swept away her fear, uneasiness, and confusion. She was resigned to let Asa go.

"Are you ready to go to bed?"

She exhaled a lingering sigh. "I think so."

Asa stood up and stepped out of the tub. Reaching for a towel from a stack on a chair, he dried his body. He helped her from the tub, blotting the moisture from her body.

Deborah lay on her side, waiting for Asa to join her in bed. The suite was exquisite, the food and wine delicious, and her date generous, attentive, and sexy. *He* was the addictive drug—she never got enough of him. Whenever they made love during siesta, it was never enough for her, because she wanted seconds and thirds. Despite his asking her to delay going home after closing, she never did; she and Asa were consenting adults but she didn't want to flaunt her affair, risking that her children might become fodder for gossip.

A soft gasp escaped her when his hand slipped between her thighs. Deborah managed to turn until she was facing him. Her hand closed on his flaccid flesh, stroking gently until he grew hard and heavy against her palm. They had time to explore, arouse, and offer each other ultimate pleasure. Her fingers moved over the hard planes of his body like a sculptor admiring her design.

She snuggled against him, their limbs entwined. Her hand reached lower. Her fingers tightened until he gasped before she eased her grip. She repeated the touch over and over until Deborah found herself on her back with Asa inside her. The ferocity of his penetration sent her libido into overdrive. Grunts, groans, moans, arching, and thrusting punctuated the coupling—not lovemaking this time, but mating. They strained to get closer and together they found a tempo where their bodies were in perfect harmony. Waves of ecstasy held them captive until the dam broke, and they surrendered to a passion that left them shuddering from release.

It wasn't long after his heart rate slowed and erection had gone down that Asa realized the enormity of what had happened. He hadn't used a condom. Even when he'd been a randy teenage boy he'd never not used protection when sleeping with a woman. The only exception had been his wife. "Forgive me," he whispered hoarsely. "Please forgive me," he repeated over and over, his voice breaking.

Deborah cradled Asa's head to her chest. "Don't, Asa. I'm safe."

His head came up. "Are you sure?"

"Ninety percent sure."

Asa's eyes searched Deborah's. They were calm. "It won't happen again."

He pulled away from Deborah and lay on his back. Asa knew he had to tell her about what he'd planned for the next year. She had to know he wasn't some nomad wandering about the country, stopping only when he was too mentally and physically exhausted to go further.

"Deborah." Reaching over, he pulled her close to his body. "I need to tell you something."

"You're leaving."

"How did you know?"

"I feel it. Here in my heart," she whispered. "When?"

"As soon as I'm notified that I've been accepted by Doctors Without Borders."

Asa felt Deborah's heart skip a beat. "Doctors Without Borders?"

"Yes. I'd always planned to work as a humanitarian doctor when I retired, but after Claire and Isaac died I filled out an application. I'll know within three weeks whether I'll be going."

Deborah wanted to cry. But she didn't.

She wanted to scream and throw things. But she wouldn't.

"How...long have you been planning this, Asa?"

"I just told you..."

"No. How long did you plan to sleep with me before

you leave town?" Jerking away from Asa, she sat up. "Why didn't you tell me your hopes before we started sleeping together?"

Asa pushed into a sitting position. "I never deceived you. You knew I wasn't going to stay."

She extended her hand, caressing his face gently. "You know, you're right, Asa," she said with a sad smile. "This is my mistake. It's just . . . when you announced at the town council meeting you were a snowbird I thought you would probably stay for the winter. And then when you came into the bookstore for a job, I was more than aware you were transient and temporary, but I guess I thought I meant enough for you to stay."

"You're wrong. It wasn't like that."

"I know, Asa, because it isn't like that." She turned to gaze into his eyes as she caressed his cheek. "You are a very special man, Asa Monroe. What kind of monster would I be to deny you the chance to help people who need you?"

"Deborah, I—"

"But I can't pretend this doesn't change things." A gentle kiss on the lips silenced him. "Good night, Asa."

Asa drove back to Sanctuary Cove and dropped Deborah at her house, then headed for the bookstore. Everything had changed when he decided to tell her about DWB last night. He knew she had a reason to be angry. She was right. He should've told her about his dream of practicing abroad even before he'd blurted out that he was a widower.

He hadn't told Deborah about Claire and Isaac; he'd told her children. He'd wanted to tell her that he loved her, but he thought she probably wouldn't believe that. What

Asa hadn't wanted to acknowledge was his fear of losing her if he told her about DWB. He knew she was comfortable with his disclosure that he was a snowbird, because that left open the possibility that he would return the following winter. But once he was assigned to work in Africa he doubted whether he would ever return to Sanctuary Cove—or even the States, for that matter.

The thought pained Asa. He realized how much he was going to miss Deborah *and* her children. He wanted to get to know them better—form a relationship with them, especially after Crystal's heartfelt outburst at Sunday's dinner. She'd resented him for taking her father's position at the table, but he had been able to ease her fears. That made him feel good and had also helped him to deal with his own grief.

However, he hadn't been completely honest. When he'd returned to his apartment he realized that he did want to occupy that place at Deborah's table and in their lives, not just on Sundays but every day. Asa wanted to fill the void that Louis had left.

Asa had reminded Deborah over and over that despite losing her husband she still had her children, and now him, while all he had were memories. Painfully, he knew what he had to do. He had to make a clean break and leave Sanctuary Cove. The bookstore was doing well and it could practically run itself. And one thing he knew about Deborah Robinson: she was a survivor. She'd survived a scandal to protect her children. And she would survive what she viewed as his duplicity.

Deborah entered through the rear door of The Parlor, expecting to see Asa, and she wasn't disappointed to find him standing there waiting for her. "You're leaving today." The query was a statement.

"Tomorrow."

"You're welcome to stay until you hear from DWB."

Asa angled his head. "That would complicate everything. It doesn't matter what you think or believe, because this, what we have, isn't about sex. It was never about sex."

"What was it about, Asa?"

"You. Me. Friendship and feelings that go so deep they are impossible to explain. That's what it *is* all about. I'll write you. Every day. And that's a promise."

Placing a hand over her mouth, Deborah willed the tears filling her eyes not to fall. Not now, or she would blurt out how much she loved him. She sniffled. "I'll accept your promise, but never an apology."

He winked at her. "That's a promise. Now, close the door and give me a hug."

Deborah pushed the door closed and stepped into Asa's outstretched arms. She inhaled his familiar scent, committing it to memory. "Thanks for everything, friend."

Asa dropped a kiss on her curls. "You're welcome, friend."

Chapter Twenty

⌒

It was April and spring had come to the Lowcountry, bringing a foreshadowing of the intense summer heat that would make it impossible to remain outdoors for long periods of time.

Asa kept his promise to write every day. The postcards had stamps from Myrtle Beach, Brunswick, Savannah, Jacksonville, and Miami. Then they stopped for three weeks before they started up again, this time from South Africa.

She read the latest one:

Hi Debs,

Arrived in South Africa yesterday.

It's beautiful and hot. For the first time in my life I own a firearm. It's not to protect me from criminals, but from the wildlife.

I love my work and the people—especially the children. When I get a chance to go shopping I'll send you something for the bookstore.

Give Whitney and Crystal my best.

Love, Asa

"Mrs. Robinson, you're next."

Deborah put the postcard in her handbag and stood up. She'd made an appointment to see her doctor because she hadn't been feeling well. She woke up tired and went to bed tired. Maybe she needed vitamins or iron pills.

Forty-five minutes later she knew why she'd been so tired. She was pregnant! Deborah had told Asa she was ninety percent certain she wouldn't get pregnant, but she was wrong. The only reason she'd been so adamant was because she thought she knew her body. For years she and Louis had used the rhythm method and she'd never gotten pregnant, but apparently it hadn't worked with Asa. After all her preaching to Crystal about teenage pregnancy, safe sex, and marriage, she was going to be an unwed mother.

She drove back to Sanctuary Cove instead of taking the ferry, which would have made her nauseous. Deborah didn't want to believe that as a thirty-eight-year-old widowed mother of two teens she was going to start all over again with an infant. When her doctor mentioned she had options, her comeback was that her only option was to give birth to a healthy baby.

Deborah climbed the stairs to the porch and opened the door. She wanted to get into bed and sleep. When her children came in from school she would tell them that come Thanksgiving they could look forward to a new baby brother or sister.

• • •

Deborah sat on the living room sofa. Whitney was on one side of her, Crystal on the other. "I need to tell you guys something that will change your lives," she said quietly as she took their hands.

"Mama, you're scaring me." Crystal's eyes searched hers.

She squeezed Crystal's hand. "I don't mean to frighten you, honey, but you have to know."

"Know what, Mom?" Whitney asked.

"I'm pregnant." There, she'd said it. The two words Deborah were certain would rock her children's world.

"You can't be," Whitney retorted.

"But you're too old," Crystal cried.

"I am and I'm not too old," Deborah argued softly.

Crystal eased her hand out her mother's loose grip. "It's not Dad's."

"No!" Whitney shouted. "It's not Dad's. If it was she wouldn't have waited this long to tell us."

"Then, whose is it, Mom?"

Deborah sat up straight. "Asa Monroe's."

"Shit!"

"Whitney!"

"Where's your baby daddy?" he sneered.

"You're forgetting who you are talking to." She closed her eyes and squeezed the bridge of her nose, trying to relax. "I understand how you two must feel right now, but please adjust your attitude and watch your language."

Whitney didn't say anything further and neither did Crystal, although she rolled her eyes.

"I wanted to be honest with you both because this baby will be, is, your brother or sister, and I really need your support on this. You're my family and I love you." She smiled. "Besides, I won't ask you to babysit too often."

Whitney managed to look contrite. "I didn't mean for it to come out like that, Mom, but it's April and in four months I'll be leaving for D.C. You're going to need someone to look after you."

Deborah patted his cheek. "I want you to stop worrying about me, Whit, and take care of yourself. You're going to live away from home for the first time, and trust me when I say it's not easy adjusting to living with strangers."

Placing a hand over her mother's flat belly, Crystal leaned into her. "Don't worry, Mama. You still have me. I'll help with the cooking and housework."

Wrapping an arm around Crystal's shoulders, Deborah kissed her daughter's hair. She'd taken her advice and was letting it grow out. "I'm going to pay someone to clean the house and the bookstore. We can take turns cooking." She kissed her again. "Okay, baby girl?"

"If you have a girl, then she'll be baby girl."

"No, Chrissie. You will *always* be my baby girl."

"Does Mr. Monroe know about the baby, Mom?" Whitney asked.

"No."

Deborah caught the look Crystal gave her brother as their eyes met. "Are you going to tell him, Mama?"

"No."

Crystal opened her mouth to ask why not when Whitney shook his head, warning her to let it go. "How are you feeling?" she asked instead.

"I tire easily. That's why I take naps," Deborah admitted, smothering a yawn with her hand. "You guys are on your own tonight, because Mama is going upstairs to lie down."

Waiting until their mother was seemingly out of ear-shot, Crystal pulled her legs up under her body and leaned closer to Whitney. "Why won't she tell him that he's going to be a dad?"

"I don't know, Chrissie. Maybe they had a fight before he left."

"Fight or no fight, Mr. Monroe should know about the baby. And it's up to us to find him."

Whitney scratched his chin. "We have his name, he's a doctor, and his car had a Delaware plate. I'll go online and see what I can come up with." He lowered his hand. "If he was Mom's employee, then she had to have some paper-work on him. Maybe you can go to the bookstore and see if you can find anything."

"The store is closed today," Crystal whispered. "Maybe if I get the key you can drop me off and we can check out her desk."

"I have a set of keys to the shop." Whitney rose, pulling Crystal up with him. "Let's go."

"Wait, Whitney. I'm going to leave a note for Mom to let her know we're going downtown. She doesn't have to know exactly where downtown."

"Okay, Sherlock. I'll be outside in the car."

Chapter Twenty-One

⌒

Lilongwe, Malawi

Dr. Asa Monroe's step was slow and heavy as his booted feet echoed on the rickety staircase leading to his quarters. He didn't think he would ever get used to triple-digit heat, the odor of sickness, and the smell of death.

He'd spent the past two weeks working at a remote village delivering babies, inoculating adults and children, and treating patients with diseases that had been eradicated in the States more than fifty years ago. And he still didn't have enough anti-venom to treat the snake-bite victims.

He unlocked the door and the exiting buildup of heat from within caused him to step back as if someone had opened the door to a blast oven. Setting his medical bag and rucksack on the floor, he flipped the switch for the ceiling fans. When he'd moved in there had been only one fan in the one-bedroom apartment, and that was in the bedroom. The next day he'd gone out and bought fans for the living/dining area and the kitchen.

Asa paid a woman to come and clean the apartment twice a week, although he was rarely there. It was simply his home base, where he picked up his mail and where he'd unwind while waiting for his next assignment. Sitting on a stool, he unlaced his boots, leaving them on the rush mat. Thick cotton socks followed. Within minutes he'd stripped off all his clothes and walked into the bathroom to shower away nearly three weeks of dirt, dust, and grime.

He brushed his teeth, and then opened the door to the stall, turned on the water, and stood under the spray of tepid water that was akin to rain soaking the dry, parched earth after a prolonged drought.

It wasn't until he'd returned to the apartment that Asa realized how bone-tired he was. Sleeping thirty-six consecutive hours still wasn't going to be enough. He felt every one of his forty-six years of living. Sleeping in a tent, with his hand grasping a high-powered automatic pistol in the event a wild animal would find its way inside, had disrupted his sleep pattern.

It was ironic how quickly he'd come to think of the apartment as home when home had once been a stately Colonial in a Dover suburb, or the space above the bookstore where he'd made love to Deborah. He'd continued to write her—every day—but had yet to receive a response. Asa had decided to give her until the end of the year and if she didn't write back then he would let her go—in his head and in his heart.

Asa never would've imagined having to grieve twice in just a year because he'd fallen in love for only the second time in his life.

Once the water ran clear, he picked up a bar of soap and began lathering his body from head to toe. Although he'd been given a battery of inoculations he still feared succumbing to a parasitic infection.

He rinsed off, then repeated the ritual until he felt clean. A loud buzzing sound caught his attention, and Asa glanced up to find a large bug against the window screen. The bathroom had been a breeding ground for insects and reptiles before he'd requested the owner of the building replace all the damaged screens. Turning off the water, he stepped out of the stall, slipping his feet into a pair of rubber shower shoes. He smiled. The cleaning woman had remembered to leave the shoes where he'd instructed.

It was still so hot that he didn't need a towel to blot the water from his body. Walking into the bedroom, he sat on the side of the bed and picked up the letters that had been left there. Fanning the envelopes he looked for one with a Sanctuary Cove return address. His heart sank. Deborah still hadn't written. Falling back on the clean sheets, he supported his head on folded arms and fell asleep.

Suddenly, Asa jolted awake, totally disoriented. He didn't know whether it was night or day, or how long he'd slept. Swinging his legs over the side of the bed, he turned on the lamp, opened the drawer in the bedside table and took out his Netbook. He was thirsty and hungry but he needed to go online and connect with a world beyond the one into which he'd been assigned.

One of the reasons he'd accepted an apartment in this building was because it was wired for the Internet, and he had excellent cell phone reception. The tiny computer booted up and he was online in no time. There were ten new e-mails. A slight frown furrowed his forehead when he saw one with an e-mail address he didn't recognize, with the subject line: Urgent.

He opened it, his gaze scanning it quickly. Asa read it once, twice, and then a third time.

Dr. Monroe,

    Please call my mother because there is something she needs to tell you.

Respectfully,
Whitney L. Robinson

He glanced at the date of the e-mail. It was almost three weeks old. Rubbing his hands over his bearded face, Asa did something he hadn't done in more than six months: he prayed.

Slipping off the bed, he opened a drawer to the dresser and took out a pair of boxers and pulled them on. Retrieving his rucksack, he took out his cell phone and turned it on. It was of no use to him in the bush, but he'd tried to keep it charged.

The time on his computer indicated it was eight o'clock at night. That meant it was one o'clock in the afternoon in South Carolina. Asa scrolled through the phone's directory and dialed the number to the bookstore. If Deborah was in the store, then she would be alone because it was siesta. It rang three times before there was a connection.

"The Parlor Bookstore. This is Deborah. How may I help you?"

"Debs? Asa."

"Asa! How are you?"

"I'm good, but you already know that from my post-cards. You did get my postcards, right?"

"I did, Asa. Every one."

"Is...there something you need to tell me, Debs?"

"Yes, there is something I need to tell you," she replied quietly.

"Debs...hello?..."

"Are you sitting, Asa?"

"Should I?"

"Yes."

He moved over to a rattan chair with a distinctive kente cloth pattern and sat down. "I'm sitting."

"I'm pregnant. With your baby."

His eyes narrowed. "I thought you said you—"

"I know, Asa. Clearly I was wrong."

He was glad Deborah couldn't see him because his hands *and* knees were shaking. "Were you going to have my child and not tell me?"

"Yes."

"Why?"

"Why, Asa? Because I didn't want to use this baby to get you to come back to me."

Counting slowly to ten, he tried to compose himself. "I'm sorry."

"Don't you dare apologize. Just don't do it."

"What do you want, Deborah?"

He heard her breathing through the earpiece. "I want to carry to term and give birth to a healthy baby."

Asa smiled for the first time since hearing her voice. "I want that, too. What about your baby's father?"

"What...what about you?"

"Will you allow me to be in your life?"

"I won't keep you from the child, if that's what you're worried about."

"My God, Debs. How can you say that? This isn't only about the baby, Debs. It's about us. I love you. I love you with or without a baby, and if we're going to be together, then it has to be for each other."

"You love me and I love you, but we can't be together, Asa. You're so far away. You're on the other side of the world."

"I can apply for a hardship waiver. I'll probably have to wait for a replacement before I'm able to return to the States, but...I want to marry you, Deborah. I want to try to be a father to Whitney and Crystal and to that precious gift inside you."

"Can I give you my answer when you get back?"

"Of course, but..."

"We have so much to talk about...nothing to do with the baby...trust, and commitment, and..."

Asa clutched his chest. "You're not going to make this easy for me, are you?"

"I'm not trying to give you a hard time, Asa. I've decided to take a chance on love, and I don't want to go through what I did with Louis."

"And what's that?"

"He left me with his children."

"Okay." The single word was whispered.

"Can you answer one question for me?" Deborah asked.

"Sure. Anything."

"Why did you call me?"

"One of the kids e-mailed me."

"Please don't tell me it was Whitney?"

Asa laughed when he heard her incredulous tone. "Yes, Whitney."

"I told him about—"

"Leave the boy alone, Deborah. He's only trying to protect you. He won't have to do that much longer because once I get back that will be my responsibility."

"When do you think you're coming home?"

"I don't know, but I hope it's soon."

"Asa?"

"Yes, baby?"

"I love you."

Asa pulled his lip between his teeth, biting until it throbbed like a pulse. "I love you more." When he finally ended the call he knew he had been given a second chance.

A second chance at love.

A second chance to be a husband.

And a second chance at becoming a father.

Chapter Twenty-Two

Three months later

Deborah tried to adjust the neckline of her dress in an attempt not to reveal too much cleavage. "I'm spilling out of this," she said when she saw Asa's reflection in the full-length mirror. She turned to face her fiancé. "Look at my breasts."

Asa angled his head. "They're like lush fruit."

She gave his shoulder a playful slap before staring at the man who, within the hour, would become her husband. He looked incredibly handsome in a tuxedo, white shirt, and Winsor-knotted pearl-gray silk tie. The African sun had darkened his skin to a rich sable-brown.

When she'd seen him come through the terminal at the airport Deborah had hardly recognized the man she'd fallen in love with. He was bearded and noticeably thinner.

Instead of dropping him off at the bookstore, she'd brought him home where he'd showered and then closed the door to her bedroom and slept for twelve straight hours. It had taken almost a month for his appetite to return, and he'd regained six of the twenty pounds he'd lost.

Once he'd applied for a hardship waiver, it had taken nearly three months for DWB to get a doctor to replace him. But now he'd returned to Sanctuary Cove to live and set up a practice. It would be the first of its kind in the Cove, as residents had relied on midwives to deliver their children and on facilities in Charleston for all other medical emergencies.

A contractor had begun work to renovate the vacant storefront only doors from The Parlor where he would hang out his shingle for his family practice.

"The dress is scandalous, Asa. I'm going to faint if Reverend Crawford stares at my breasts instead of my face."

He chuckled then, easing her fears. They would marry at the Abundant Life Church, then host a reception under more than a dozen tents along the beach for everyone in the Cove. When Deborah had decided to come home she never would have imagined she'd love again while continuing the cycle of perpetuating the precious Gullah culture.

Cradling her to his chest, Asa kissed her forehead. Her hair, brushed off her face, was pinned into a chignon. Miniature roses and baby's breath had taken the place of a veil. The off-white, empire-waist dress with its seeded-pearl bodice artfully concealed her swollen belly.

She was in the last month of her second trimester and had only gained fifteen of the twenty pounds recommended by her obstetrician. Although high-risk, her pregnancy to date had been complication-free.

"Every man in Sanctuary Cove will be looking at you this afternoon," Asa crooned. "You are just that beautiful. And the best part is, you'll be coming home with me." He rested a hand on her belly, feeling the baby's movements. A sonogram had revealed that he and Deborah were going to have a boy.

There came a knock on the door and Asa and Deborah found Herman and Pearl Williams outside the bedroom. Pearl's eyes filled with tears when she saw her daughter and soon-to-be son-in-law. "Oh, darling, you look beautiful." Pearl was stunning in a pale gray chiffon gown that flattered her tall, slender body. Her curly hair was more gray than red, and there were tiny lines around her eyes that had come from squinting in the brilliant Florida sunshine.

Deborah hugged her mother. "Oh, Mom, I am *so* happy!"

"Darling, you deserve it."

"I feel truly blessed, Mom," Deborah said as both of them brushed happy tears from their eyes.

Pearl placed a hand on Asa's arm, leaning in to press her cheek to his. "I know you'll take care of my precious babies," Deborah heard her mother whisper in his ear.

"That is something you'll never have to worry about, Pearl. I will take care of and cherish my family."

Whitney and Crystal walked into the room, stopping short when they saw their mother in her wedding dress. Whitney had flown in from Washington, D.C., for the weekend to stand in as best man at his mother's wedding.

"You look great, Mom. Wow!" Whitney complimented.

"You look kinda hot for a pregnant lady," Crystal quipped.

Herman Williams shook his head and smiled at his grandchildren. His features were Gullah and his speech still had a lingering trace of an accent that Gullahs recognized as their own. "Let's go, Crystal. The limo and the driver are waiting downstairs to take us to the church."

As Crystal headed for the staircase, Herman reached for his daughter's hand and gave it a squeeze before the two embraced.

"I'm so happy for you, sweetheart. You look gorgeous."

"Thanks, Dad," she said, gleaming.

"I'm looking forward to giving you away in marriage. I didn't have the privilege the first time, but I knew the moment I was introduced to Asa Monroe that you'd chosen a man who would not only take care of you, but my grandchildren, too."

"Oh, Dad," Deborah beamed.

They hugged again before Asa put an arm around her waist and led her out of the bedroom and down the staircase.

Soon, Deborah stood in the vestibule of the church with her father and Whitney, waiting for the familiar sound of the "Wedding March." Even as a little girl she'd fantasized about having a string quartet at her wedding and now it was finally happening. Whitney had shocked her when he'd announced he was doing double duty as Asa's best man, while sharing the honor of giving her away with his grandfather. She'd given her bouquet of miniature white roses and a delicate gardenia to Crystal when she realized she wouldn't have a free hand.

Whitney peered through the oval window in the door leading directly into the church. "There's standing room only, Mom."

Before she could reply, the opening of the "Wedding March" filled the church.

"I'm ready."

Those were the last two words she said before the ushers opened the door and Herman and Whitney led her down the white carpet to where Asa stood at the altar, smiling.

Her fingers tightened on her father's and son's arms as she saw familiar faces of the Cove residents in the pews. Her mother was dabbing her eyes, Barbara was grinning like a Cheshire cat, and Mabel gave her a thumbs-up.

Reverend Malcolm Crawford pulled back his shoulders under a flowing black robe. "Who gives this woman in marriage?" he asked, his sonorous voice carrying easily in the large church.

"We do," Herman and Whitney said in unison.

They took Deborah's hands, placing them in Asa's when he reached out for her. Whitney took his position on Asa's right, while Herman turned and sat down next to his wife.

Deborah smiled at Crystal, who looked ravishing in a rose-pink empire silk chiffon gown, before she turned her adoring gaze on the man who unknowingly had changed her and her life the instant their eyes had met in the Muffin Corner.

She felt as if she were a spectator instead of a participant in her wedding as she listened to Reverend Crawford talk about the significance of marriage as he recounted the story of the wedding at Cana. Her gaze never wavered when she and Asa repeated their vows. Whitney had given Asa the diamond eternity band to slip on her finger, and Crystal repeated the motion when Deborah slipped the wide gold band on Asa's hand.

"By the power vested in me by the state of South Carolina, I now pronounce you husband and wife. Asa, you may kiss your bride."

Deborah didn't have time to catch her breath before she found herself in her husband's arms, his mouth covering hers in a passionate kiss that nearly sucked the breath from her lungs as the baby kicked vigorously in her womb.

Placing a hand over her belly, Deborah pressed closer to Asa. "I love you so much," she whispered.

Asa kissed her hair. "I love you, too, Mrs. Monroe."

Her chest swelled with love *and* happiness. She'd wept, mourned, and laughed. Now it was time to dance, and never stop dancing, with the man with whom she would share her love and her life.

Reverend Crawford raised his hands in a prayerful gesture. "My brothers and sisters, I'd like to present Dr. and Mrs. Asa Monroe."

There came a loud applause as Deborah hugged and kissed Crystal, then Whitney. Her eyes filled with happy tears when Asa hugged Whitney and patted his back. The two had grown close since Whitney had enrolled in Howard.

She and Asa proceeded down the aisle and out of the church, where they were showered with rice, bird seed, and flower petals. They stood long enough to pose for photographs before the wedding party went over to the fountain in the town square for official wedding photos.

Water flowed from the marble fountain as Asa wound one arm around his wife's expanding waist, the other around Crystal's lithe body. The realization that he was now a husband, a father to a teenaged son and daughter, and looking forward to becoming a father again when Deborah gave birth to their baby boy, was almost overwhelming.

He was going to open a family practice only doors from

The Parlor, and when he closed up and went home for dinner it would be to share it with his family. "Is that your stomach growling?" he whispered in Deborah's ear.

Smiling, she nodded. "Mama's hungry and so is baby."

Asa raised his hand, signaling the photographer. "Let's finish up here, so we can go down to the beach. My wife needs to eat."

After a half dozen more frames, Herman, Pearl, Crystal, Whitney, Deborah, and Asa headed for the beach. There all of Sanctuary Cove, as well as the mayors and town council members from Haven Creek and Angels Landing, had gathered under tents to celebrate the traditional Cavanaugh Island wedding reception.

Once they'd arrived, Asa asked a member of the waitstaff to prepare a plate for Deborah, then sat beside her and fed her portions of broiled fish and steamed vegetables. "Please, no more," she pleaded quietly a little while later. "I can't eat another bite."

Leaning closer, he kissed her ear then gazed at her gorgeous face, unable to take his eyes off her as she rocked slowly to the music. A deejay had set up his equipment in a tent and was spinning tunes that had people singing, dancing, and swaying to the infectious music.

Reaching under the tablecloth, Deborah squeezed his hand. "I'm going to make mad, crazy love to you tonight."

Throwing back his head, Asa laughed loudly. "You won't get an argument from me, Sunshine. In fact, I'm looking forward to it."

Angels Landing

Angels Landing is *dedicated to my Gullah ancestors for their pride, strength, and determination to survive.*

Intracoas...

MARSH

Black Bay

ANGELS LA...

CAUSEWAY
TO
CHARLESTON

Morgan's House

Patton Family Compound

HAVEN CREEK

MARSH

Happy Hour

Shipley Patton
• Groveyard

Ar...

HAVEN CREEK

ATLANTIC OCEAN

CAVANAUGH ISLAND

Who is left among you that saw this house in its former glory? And how do you see it now? Does it not seem like nothing in your eyes?

—Haggai 2:3

Chapter One

Good morning, ma'am. May I help you?"

Kara returned the receptionist's friendly smile with a bright one of her own. She'd recently celebrated her thirty-third birthday, and it was the first time she'd ever been called "ma'am"; but then she had to remind herself that she wasn't in New York but in the South. Here it was customary to greet people with "yes, ma'am" and "sir," rather than "missy" or "yo, my man."

"I'm Kara Newell, and I have a ten o'clock appointment with Mr. Sullivan," she said, introducing herself.

The receptionist's smile was still in place when she replied, "Please have a seat, Miss Newell. Mr. Sullivan will be with you shortly."

Kara sat down in a plush armchair in the law firm's waiting area. The walls were covered with a wheatlike fabric and artwork depicting fox hunting scenes. She'd planned to take a break from her social worker position at a New York City agency by visiting her family in Little Rock, Arkansas. She never anticipated having to travel to Charleston, South Carolina, instead.

The certified letter from Sullivan, Webster, Matthews and Sullivan requesting her attendance at the reading of a will had come as a complete shock. When she'd spoken to Mr. David Sullivan Jr. to inform him that she didn't know a Taylor Patton, the attorney reassured her that his client had been more than familiar with her.

Kara had called her parents to let them know she wouldn't be coming to Little Rock as scheduled because she had to take care of some business. She didn't tell her mother what that business was because it was still a mystery to her as to why she'd been summoned to the reading of a stranger's will. It was only when the attorney mentioned it had something to do with a relative she wasn't familiar with that she'd decided to make the trip.

She unbuttoned the jacket to her wool pantsuit. Although the temperatures had been below freezing when she'd boarded the flight in New York City, it was at least fifty degrees warmer in Charleston. One of the things she'd missed most about living in the South was the mild winters. By the time the jet touched down, Kara barely had time to hail a taxi, check into her downtown Charleston hotel room, shower, and grab a quick bite to eat before it was time to leave. She sat up straight when a tall, slender black man approached her.

"Miss Newell?"

Pushing off the chair, Kara smiled. "Yes."

"Good morning, Miss Newell. David Sullivan," he said in introduction, extending his hand.

His hand was soft, his grip firm, which took her by surprise. As she took in the sight of him, she realized he didn't quite fit the description she'd had. The one time she'd spoken to Mr. Sullivan, there was something in his tone that made her think he was much older than he looked. Now she realized they were about the same age. Conservatively dressed in a navy-blue pin-striped suit, white shirt, blue-and-white dotted tie, and black wing tips, he released her hand.

"It's nice meeting you, Mr. Sullivan."

David inclined his head. "Same here, Miss Newell. It's nice having a face to go along with the voice." Taking her elbow, he led her out of the waiting room and down a carpeted hallway to a set of double ornately carved oak doors at the end of the hallway. "I'd like to caution you before we go in. I don't want you to reply or react to anything directed toward you. Taylor Patton was my client, and that means indirectly you are also my client."

A shiver of uneasiness swept over Kara like a blast of frigid air. What, she mused, was she about to walk into? For the first time since she'd read the letter, she chided herself for not revealing its contents to her mother.

"What do you mean?" Kara asked.

"I can't explain it now, Miss Newell. But I want you to trust me enough to know that I'm going to make certain to protect your interests."

When the doors opened, Kara suddenly felt as if she were about to go on trial. The room was filled with people sitting around a massive rosewood conference table. She heard a slight gasp from the man sitting nearest the door, but he recovered quickly when she stared at him. The hazel eyes glaring at her—so much like her own—were cold, angry. The resemblance between her and the man was remarkable. So much so that they could have been brother and sister. But Kara didn't have a brother—at least not one she was aware of. She was an only child.

David directed her to a chair at the opposite end of the room, seating her on his left while he took his place at the head of the table. He still hadn't revealed to Kara why he'd wanted her to attend the reading of the will of Taylor Patton, but his cautioning was enough to let her know she was involved in something that was about to change her life. The fact that she resembled several of those in the conference room led Kara to believe there was a possibility she just might be related to the deceased.

Resting her hands in her lap, Kara listened as David informed everyone that a stenographer would record the proceedings, asking those present to introduce themselves for the record. Kara glanced at the stenographer sitting in a corner, fingers poised on the keys of the stenotype machine resting on a tripod.

David touched her hand, nodding. "Kara Elise Newell," she said, beginning the introductions. One by one the eleven others gave their names.

The men were Pattons, while the women were hyphenated Pattons, with one exception. Kara glanced at Analeigh Patton's hands. Unlike the others, her fingers were bare. A hint of a smile inched up the corners of Analeigh's mouth, and a slow smile found its way to Kara's eyes.

Everyone's attention was directed toward David when he cleared his voice, slipped on a pair of black horn-rimmed glasses, and opened the folder in front of him. " 'I, Taylor Scott Patton of Palmetto Lane, Cavanaugh Island, South Carolina, do hereby make, publish, and declare this to be my Last Will and Testament, hereby expressly revoking all wills and codicils, heretofore made by me.' "

Kara felt her mind wandering when David mentioned that as the executor he would judicially pay the deceased's enforceable debts and administrative expenses of Taylor's estate as soon as possible. Taylor hadn't married; therefore, there was no spouse to whom he would have bequeathed his belongings. All of the Pattons leaned forward as if the motion had been choreographed in advance when David paused briefly. Then he continued to read.

" 'I do give and bequeath to my daughter, Kara Elise Newell, all my personal effects and all my tangible personal property, including automobiles owned by me and held for my personal use at the time of my death, cash on hand in bank accounts in my own name, securities, or other intangibles.' "

Kara went completely still, unable to utter a sound as pandemonium followed. The room was full of screams, tears, shouts of fraud, and threats to her person. Another two minutes passed before David was able to restore a modicum of civility. "Ladies, gentlemen, please restrain yourselves. Remember, this proceeding is being recorded, so please refrain from threatening my client. By the way, there is more."

The man who'd glared at Kara stood up. "What's left? My uncle has given this *impostor* everything."

"Please sit down, Harlan. I can assure you that Miss Newell is not an impostor," David said.

Kara wanted to agree with the Pattons. Austin Newell, not Taylor Patton, was her father. She closed her eyes, her heart pounding a runaway rhythm, as David outlined the conditions of what she'd inherited: She must restore Angels

Landing to its original condition; make Angels Landing her legal residence for the next five years; and allow the groundskeeper and his wife, who would receive a lump sum of fifty thousand dollars, to continue to live out their natural lives in one of the two guesthouses. In addition, she could not sell any parcel of land to a nonfamily member without unanimous approval of all Cavanaugh Island Pattons, and the house and its contents could only be deeded to a Patton.

She opened her eyes and let out an inaudible sigh when David enumerated names and monies set aside in trust for three grandnephews and two grandnieces for their college education. This pronouncement satisfied some, but not all. There were yet more threats and promises to contest the will.

Forty-five minutes after she'd entered the conference room, Kara found herself alone with Taylor Patton's attorney. Holding her head in her hands, she tried to grasp what had just happened. She hadn't risen with the others because she wasn't certain whether her legs would've supported her body. David had warned her not to say anything, and she hadn't, but only because she couldn't. Reaching for the glass of water that had been placed before each chair, she took a sip.

David removed his glasses and laced his fingers together. "So, Miss Newell, you are now the owner of a house listed on the National Register of Historic Places and two thousand acres of prime land on Cavanaugh Island."

Kara's eyelids fluttered as if she'd just surfaced from a trance. "I'm sorry to inform you, but Taylor Patton is not my father."

David's eyes narrowed. "Did your mother ever mention Taylor Patton's name?"

She shook her head. "No. The only father I know is Austin Newell."

"Well, I can assure you that you *are* Taylor's biological daughter. In fact, you are his only child."

Kara closed her eyes. When she opened them, they were filled with fear and confusion. "How is that possible?" The query was a whisper.

"That is something you'll have to discuss with your mother."

She would talk to her mother, but not over the phone. What she and Jeannette Newell needed to discuss had to be done face-to-face. Combing her fingers through her hair, Kara held it off her forehead. "Please tell me this is a dream."

David sat on the edge of the table, staring at Kara's bowed head, a look of compassion across his features. "Even if I did, it still wouldn't change anything." Reaching into the breast pocket of his suit jacket, he took out a small kraft envelope, spilling its contents on the table in front of her. "These are keys to the house in Angels Landing, Taylor's car, and his safe-deposit box in a bank in Sanctuary Cove."

Kara released her hair, the chin-length, chemically straightened strands falling into place. "Where's Sanctuary Cove?"

"It's on Cavanaugh Island, southeast of Angels Landing. You only have ten days to transfer the accounts from Taylor's to your name. By the way, do you have a rental?"

"No. I took a taxi from the airport to the hotel."

"Good."

"Good?" Kara repeated.

David smiled. "Yes. It means I don't have to get someone

to drop it off for you. I'm going to have our driver take you back to the hotel so you can pick up your luggage, and then he'll take you to Angels Landing."

"I'm sorry, but I'm planning to leave for Little Rock tomorrow."

"Can you hold off leaving for a few days?"

"David. May I call you David?" He nodded. "When you wrote and asked me to come here, I never could've imagined that the man I've believed was my father all these years is not my father. Not to mention that I now have a bunch of cousins who can't wait to put out a hit on me so they can inherit my unforeseen assets, assets I don't need or want."

"Are you saying you're going to walk away from your birthright?"

"A birthright I knew nothing about."

David leaned in closer. "A birthright you need to protect, Kara. If you walk away from this, then you'll be playing right into the hands of the developers who've preyed on the folks who've lived on the Sea Island and who'll turn their inhabitants' birthright into a playground for millionaires."

Kara felt as if her emotions were under attack. "But... but the will states I can only sell the land to a Patton."

"Pattons who want to sell more than half of Angels Landing."

"Why would they want to do that?" A pregnant silence filled the room as she and David stared at each other.

"Greed, Kara. If they can get you to go along with their way of thinking and you sell your two thousand acres, the monies they'll receive for the sale will be divided among them evenly."

An expression of confusion crossed her face. "How many acres do they hold collectively?"

"Probably about four hundred," David said.

"Hypothetically, if I decide to hand over my shares and we sell twenty-four hundred acres at let's say a thousand dollars per acre. Are you telling me two-point-four million will be divided among twelve of us?"

He didn't respond. Instead, she did the calculations in her head. Instead of $2 million she would get $200,000. "The split seems a little inequitable, especially if I hold the majority shares."

David's dark eyebrows lifted a fraction. "They see you as an outsider, someone who will take the money and run. Please don't prove them right."

"What do you expect me to do?"

"I'd like you to give yourself a week to think about it. Stay at the house, tour the island. If you decide you prefer the Big Apple to the Lowcountry, then you walk away and..."

"I walk away and what?" Kara asked when David didn't finish his statement.

"The surviving heirs will contest the will, it will go into probate, and after the state of South Carolina gets its share, the family will get what's left."

She gave the dapper attorney a long, penetrating stare. He was asking for a week while her supposed biological father had asked her for five years. Right now Kara had three weeks of vacation time: one she could spend in Angels Landing and the other two in Arkansas before returning to New York. She hadn't told her parents when to expect her, so Kara decided to change her travel plans yet again.

"Okay. I'll try it for a week."

David blew out an audible breath. "Thank you." He stood, walked over to the wall phone, and pushed the speaker feature. "Please tell Linc I need him to drive a client to her hotel. He's to wait for her to check out, and then I want him to take her to Taylor Patton's house." He ended the call and came over to cup Kara's elbow when she stood up. "I'm going to call my cousin, Jeffrey Hamilton, who's the island's sheriff and have him stop in to check on you. I'll be in court for the next two days, but as soon as there is a recess, I'll come out to see you. Meanwhile, Jeff or one of his deputies will help you if you need anything."

Kara nodded her head in agreement, trying to keep her emotions in check. Taylor Patton was her biological father?

Jeffrey Hamilton leaned back in his chair, booted feet propped up on the corner of the scarred desk. He'd submitted his department's budget to the mayor and town council at the January meeting, yet it was mid-March and he was still awaiting delivery of new office furniture. Ever since he'd been appointed sheriff of Cavanaugh Island, Jeff had attempted to refurbish his office and expand the force from three deputies to four. Sadly, things seemed to be taking a lot longer than he'd first thought.

The cell phone on his desk rang. Glancing at the display, Jeff answered it on the second ring. "What's up, David?"

"Is there anyone in your jail that needs legal counsel?"

He laughed softly. "Sorry, Cuz, but I haven't locked up anyone in more than three weeks. Are you calling to let me know that you're ready to pop the question to that gorgeous oral surgeon you've been seeing?"

"We're not even close to that. I'd like you to go out to

Angels Landing and check on the new owner. Her name is Kara Newell."

"Is there anything I should know about her?" Jeff asked.

"I may as well tell you now because gossip about her is going to spread across the island faster than a cat can lick its whiskers. She's Taylor Patton's daughter."

"I was under the impression that Taylor didn't have any children."

"Most of us thought the same thing."

Jeff shifted, and his chair groaned like someone in pain. "How are the others taking the news?"

"Let's just say they're not too happy that she exists. That's why I'm calling you."

"Don't worry, David. I'll keep an eye on her." He knew his cousin couldn't divulge how he'd come by the proof because he was still bound by attorney-client privilege, even in death.

"Thanks, Jeff. By the way, how is Aunt Corrine?"

"Grandmomma's good. Have you made plans for Easter?"

"Yep. Petra and I are going down to St. Thomas for a few days. You're welcome to join us."

Jeff stared at his spit-shined boots. After spending twenty years in the Marine Corps, he still enjoyed the age-old tradition of shining his shoes and boots. "I'd love to, but I gave my deputies time off to spend with their families."

"Speaking of families, Jeff, when are you going to settle down and have a couple of kids?"

He sat up and lowered his feet. "After you get married and have one."

David's chuckle came through the earpiece. "You've

got a few years on me, Cuz, so you're first. I have to hang up because I have a meeting with a new client. Call me if Kara is having trouble with her new family."

"No problem," Jeff promised.

He ended the call, then slipped the cell phone into the case attached to his gun belt. He was walking out of his office when his clerk, Winnie Powell, entered the police station through the back door.

Winnie smiled, her bright blue eyes sparkling like blue topaz. She fluffed up her short, curly hair. "It looks like rain."

He returned her smile. "We could use a little of that." The winter had been unusually dry. "I'm going over to Angels Landing."

Winnie nodded as Jeff headed out of the station. Once in the parking lot that served the town hall, courthouse, and police station, the humidity wrapped around him like a wet blanket. He got into the Jeep and started the engine. The vehicle had been emblazoned with a sheriff logo on the passenger-side doors and refitted with a partition separating the front seats from the rear ones. Within minutes of driving, the rain had begun as Winnie predicted, the sound of the wipers breaking the silence.

Slowing to ten miles an hour, Jeff drove through downtown Sanctuary Cove, passing Jack's Fish House, the town square with its fountain and marble statue of patriot militia General Francis Marion atop a stallion, and the Cove Inn, the town's boardinghouse. Once he'd taken over as sheriff, he'd convinced the town council to lower the town's speed limit to fifteen miles an hour because there were no traffic lights in the Cove and to discourage teenagers from drag racing. Amazingly, there hadn't been posted speed limits for years.

Maneuvering onto an unpaved road, he shifted into

four-wheel drive. A marker pointing the way to Angels Landing came into view, and Jeff turned onto Palmetto Lane and headed to the house that had given this section of Cavanaugh Island its name. The few times he'd come to Angels Landing, Jeff felt as if he'd stepped back in time. The antebellum mansion at the end of a live oak allée was breathtaking with its columned, wraparound porch. The rose-colored limestone Greek Revival home, with its pale pink marble columns and black-shuttered tall windows, had been one of the finest homes on the island.

Jeff parked next to the vintage Mercedes-Benz sedan that had belonged to Taylor Patton. Reaching for his cap on the passenger seat, he pulled it on. The rain was now a steady drizzle as he sprinted to the front door, which opened as he wiped his boots on the thick rush mat.

"Why, if it isn't Corrine Hamilton's grandbaby boy. What brings you out this way?"

Jeff took off his cap and curbed the urge to roll his eyes upward. The petite woman and her groundskeeper husband had worked for the Pattons for longer than he could remember. He also wanted to remind Mrs. Todd that at forty he had left boyhood behind many years before.

"Good afternoon, Miss Iris. I'm here to see Ms. Kara Newell. Is she in?"

Mrs. Todd's dark eyes narrowed suspiciously behind her rimless glasses. "Did she do something, son?"

Jeff tightened his grip on his cap. It was apparent that the housekeeper had transferred her loyalty from Taylor to his daughter within weeks of his death. Those who lived on Cavanaugh Island joked that it was easier to gain access to the Oval Office than to cross the threshold to this historic house.

"No, she didn't, Miss Iris. David Sullivan asked me to look in on her."

Mrs. Todd opened the door wider. "Why didn't you say that in the first place?" She smiled. "Follow me. She's in the garden room."

Jeff shook his head in amazement as he followed the elderly woman, who was dressed in a crisp gray uniform that matched the coronet of braids atop her head. It had been years since he'd stepped foot into the house, but like the exterior, nothing had changed. It had the same vases, lamps, tables, and chairs. Mrs. Todd directed him down a narrow carpeted hallway to a doorway on the south side of the property.

He stopped at the entrance to a room filled with potted plants, trees, and flowers. The sound of soft music flowed from somewhere in the indoor oasis. His gaze shifted to the housekeeper when she approached the woman reclining in a cushioned chaise and spoke quietly to her.

Jeff felt his heart stop when Kara Newell swung her long, slender, bare legs over the chaise and stood up to face him.

She was absolutely stunning. Anyone familiar with the Pattons would recognize the startling resemblance between Kara and her paternal grandmother Theodora— or Teddy as she had been affectionately called by her husband. His gaze went from her tousled hair, pulled up in a short ponytail, to the tawny face with large hazel eyes, cute button nose, and lushly curved full lips, then lower to a white tank top and olive-green shorts. Each time she took a breath, the swell of her breasts were visible above the top's neckline. Scolding himself, he focused his attention on her face rather than staring at her chest. She was slim but had curves in all the right places.

He inclined his head. "Ms. Newell."

Kara smiled and offered her hand. "Please call me Kara."

Taking three long strides, Jeff grasped her hand, holding it gently within his much larger one. "Jeff Hamilton."

"David told me you would stop by. Would you like to sit down?"

"Thank you." He waited until Kara sat on a pull-up chair at a small round table covered with a floral tablecloth before sitting on the matching one.

A pair of eyes with glints of gold and green met his. "May I offer you something to eat or drink?" Kara asked Jeff.

"No, thank you." He crossed one jean-covered knee over the other. "Have you settled in?"

Kara assumed a similar pose, staring at the polish on her bare toes. "There's not going to be much settling in. I'll only be here a week."

Leaning forward, Jeff lowered his leg, planting both feet on the worn rug. "Are you telling me that you don't plan to live here?"

"No, I'm not telling you that."

"Then what is it you're *not* saying?"

"Why do I get the impression that you're interrogating me, Sheriff Hamilton?"

Jeff's impassive expression did not change with her accusation. "If I were interrogating you, Kara, you wouldn't have to ask. All I want is a yes or no as to whether you plan to live on Cavanaugh Island."

"I can't give you a yes or no, Sheriff Hamilton."

"It's Jeff."

"Okay, Jeff. As I said, I can't answer that question right

now. I promised David I would spend a week on the island before making a decision. Only two hours ago I was told the man I believed to be my father isn't." She looked away from him, trying to hold back the tears forming in her eyes. "When I walked into that conference room earlier this morning and saw people staring at me who look like me... to say it was a shock is putting it mildly. Then I was told that I've inherited a house, two thousand acres of land that my so-called relatives want me to sell to a group of greedy developers, and I must live here for five years. If I do so, it means I have to resign from my job, give up my Manhattan apartment, which has an incredible view of the East River, and lose contact with a group of friends I've become extremely close to."

"Yes, I can understand how difficult that may be. Not only will you have to uproot your entire life, but you'll also have to deal with the family issue." Jeff lifted his broad shoulders under a long-sleeved chambray shirt. "The upside is you can always get another job and make new friends. And instead of views of the river, you'll have views of the ocean."

Kara folded her arms across her chest. "You make it sound so easy."

A hint of a smile tilted the corners of Jeff's mouth. "Because it is. I gave up a military career to come back here to take care of my grandmother."

"That's different."

"You think so, Kara?"

"Of course it is. There is no discussion when it comes to family. You do what you have to do," Kara said.

"Like you have to accept your birthright and honor your father's last wishes."

"What's with this birthright thing?" she asked.

Jeff stood up. "I'll tell you sometime soon. Right now, I have to get back."

Kara also rose to her feet. "When will I see you again?"

"Tomorrow. I'm off, and if you don't have anything planned, I'll come by and take you to Jack's for lunch and give you a crash course in Lowcountry culture."

"I'd like you to answer one question for me, Jeff."

"What's that?"

"Do you have something against the Pattons?"

"Nothing personal. I just don't like it when people threaten others."

Her eyes grew wider. "Did David tell you what happened?"

"He didn't have to. You can say I read between the lines. As sheriff of Cavanaugh, I have zero tolerance for those who break the law. And to me threats are a serious offense. I'll pick you up at twelve."

Jeff didn't give Kara a chance to accept or reject his offer when he turned on his heels and walked out of the room. He'd been back for almost a year, and it was the first time that a woman had captured his attention for more than a few minutes.

There was something about Kara, other than her natural beauty, that had him enthralled. He didn't know whether it was her big-city attitude, but whatever it was, he intended to discover it before the week ended and Kara was out of his life for good.

Chapter Two

Kara sat motionless, her gaze fixed on a potted palm. It had been more than two hours since David had informed her that Austin Newell was not her biological father; instead, her father was a dead man who knew about her when she hadn't known he existed. The news had stunned her, the hostility exhibited by the Pattons frightened her, and Sheriff Hamilton coming to see her made their threats even more terrifying.

Any normal person would've been overjoyed to inherit a house listed on the National Register of Historic Places and two thousand acres of land and four automobiles—three of which were classics—cash on hand, securities, and other tangibles in Taylor Patton's name. And if the house, its contents, the cars, and the land was an indication, then there was no doubt she'd become a very wealthy woman.

Kara knew she had to call her mother because only

Jeannette Newell could give her the answers she needed as to her true paternity. What she didn't want to think about was her mother's duplicity. How could she hide the true identity of the man who'd fathered her for more than three decades, while Austin, the only father she'd ever known, had become a coconspirator?

She also knew she couldn't avoid the inevitable but decided to wait—wait until her mother was at home before calling her. Normally Kara would've called Jeannette at the senior residence where she headed the nursing unit, but she couldn't find the nerve to talk to her mother just yet. She also wanted to tell her mother that her travel plans had changed and not to expect her the following day.

David has asked if she would stay on the island for a week, and she'd said she would. A week was more than enough time to uncover what David and Jeff Hamilton had warned her about giving up: her birthright.

Kara bit her lower lip. Whenever she heard the word *birthright*, she thought of her Sunday school lesson about twin brothers Esau and Jacob. Firstborn Esau cared little for his birthright, so he sold it under oath to Jacob for bread and lentil soup because he was hungry. She also recalled that Jacob had not only taken Esau's birthright, but also his dying father's blessing.

Was that what she was going to do? Walk away and give her birthright to relatives who in turn would sell it to developers? Or would they sell her two thousand acres and keep the money—a sale that would drastically affect the lives of the residents of Angels Landing and Cavanaugh Island forever?

She could take the proceeds and buy a co-op or condo in an upscale Manhattan neighborhood, maybe a house in the suburbs where she could park her own car in her driveway instead of hailing taxis or renting cars to take her whenever she wanted to go. She could also plant a rose garden and even get a little dog that would have a backyard to run in.

Kara could do a lot with her newfound wealth, but in reality it really wasn't her money, even though Taylor had believed she was entitled to all his worldly possessions. She didn't want to think that he had included her in his will out of a perverted sense of guilt. Had Jeannette come to him with the news that she was carrying his child, and he'd turned his back on her?

The questions assaulted Kara like barbs, and she was unable to parry them. Combing her fingers through her hair, Kara dug her nails into her scalp, welcoming the pain. She knew she had to pull herself together or lose it completely.

"Miss Kara?"

Her hands came down, and she turned to find Mrs. Todd standing only a few feet away. Kara hadn't heard her come into the room. She stood up. "Please call me Kara, Mrs. Todd."

The older woman inclined her head. "Miss...I mean, Kara. I made lunch. Would you like to have it in the breakfast room or on the back porch?"

Kara smiled. "In the breakfast room."

She hadn't believed how quickly her life had changed. She now had someone to cook and clean up after her—something that made her uncomfortable. Iris Todd had introduced herself and then informed Kara that Angels Landing had been her only home for the past fifty-five years; she'd worked for Taylor Patton's mother, Theodora, then stayed on after her death to assume total responsibility of running the household for Mr. Taylor.

She followed the tiny, doll-like woman with a sable-brown complexion and snow-white hair. "Mrs. Todd, I'd like you to tell me about my ... Taylor Patton." Kara had caught herself before calling him "father."

Mrs. Todd shook her head. "Cain't do that. Not up to me to talk his business. God bless the dead."

"I'm not asking you to divulge his secrets."

Mrs. Todd stopped midstep, turned, and faced Kara. "There are no secrets because around here, there is no such thing as a secret. This town is so small, everybody knows everyone's business."

"What did he do?"

A network of faint lines fanned out around the housekeeper's eyes when she smiled. "David didn't tell you?"

A look of confusion crossed Kara's face. "Tell me what?"

"Mr. Taylor was an investment banker. He handled rich folks' money jest like it was his own. Made tons of money for them even though they didn't need no more."

Kara sucked in her breath, held it, and then let it out slowly. If Taylor Patton had made his rich clients even richer, then there was no doubt he had done the same for himself. "Is there a safe in this house?"

"No. Why you asking?"

"I thought perhaps Mr. Patton kept his important papers there."

Mrs. Todd squinted behind her glasses. "Why do you keep calling him Mr. Patton instead of your daddy?"

"Because I'm not certain if he *is* my daddy."

"Oh, he your father all right. You look jest like Miss Theodora. Or Teddy as the fancy folks around here used to call her. Yes, Kara. You the spitting image of your grandmomma."

So that's why the Pattons had looked at her as if she were an apparition, Kara recalled. It was obvious they'd known something she hadn't when she'd walked into the law firm's conference room, even before the reading of the will. They knew just by looking at her that she was a Patton. So why had they tried to deny her?

Kara still couldn't bring herself to think of Taylor Patton as her father and certainly not as *daddy*.

Mrs. Todd angled her head, appearing deep in thought. "I don't know if Mr. Taylor had a safe. He took his papers to the bank in Sanctuary Cove."

Again she was reminded of the envelope David had given her with keys to the house, cars, and safe-deposit box. The first thing on her agenda the following day was to go to the bank and go through the contents of the box.

Mrs. Todd took a step, resting a hand on Kara's arm. "Don't you worry yourself none, honey. Everything will work out in its own time. All you need is a little faith."

That's what I'm hoping for, Kara thought. She wanted to tell Mrs. Todd she needed an abundance of faith. She also wanted everything to work out so she could visit with her family in Little Rock; return to New York; and pick up her life as if she'd never heard of David Sullivan, Taylor Patton, or the Angels Landing Pattons.

"How did he die?" Kara asked.

"Mr. Taylor had problems with his heart. He went to bed one night and never woke up. My husband tried reviving him, but when the doctor from the Cove came and covered him with a sheet, we knew it was too late. It's a shame because he was only fifty-six."

Taylor Patton was fifty-six, the same age as her mother. Kara followed Mrs. Todd down a narrow hallway, into the kitchen, and to an alcove that overlooked the rear of the house. Upon close inspection she saw the shabbiness of the worn carpets and fading wallpaper. The antebellum mansion was antiquated; whoever did the interior decorating must have been arrested in a past time period. Yet despite all that needed to be done, Kara knew it could be elegant and beautiful again if restored to its original condition. Unfortunately, she knew she wouldn't have the time needed to make the repairs. She'd promised David and Jeff she would stay on Cavanaugh Island a week, and she would. But there was no way she could supervise restoring the property in that short amount of time.

After a lunch of lobster bisque, shrimp salad, and sweet tea, Kara returned to the bedroom Mrs. Todd had chosen for her. She picked up her cell phone that she'd left on a side table. She'd missed one call. Tapping the voice mail icon, she listened to her roommate's message, then tapped the key for Dawn Ramsey's number.

"Hey, Miss Dee," Kara said in her usual greeting. Walking over to an armchair, she sat down.

"Hey yourself, Miss Kay. I'd called to find out if you'd made it home safely."

Kara exhaled an audible sigh. "Yes, I did. But..."

"But what, Kara?" Dawn asked when she didn't finish the sentence.

"I'm not in Arkansas."

"If you're not in Little Rock, then where the hell are you?"

"I'm in Angels Landing. It's on Cavanaugh Island."

There was silence on the other end of the line. "I know I didn't do well in geography, but could you please tell me where Cavanaugh Island is? Is that even in the United States?"

"Yes. It's a Sea Island off the coast of Charleston, South Carolina."

"South Carolina! Why are you in South Carolina? Have you been holding out on me, girl? Do you have a man there you don't want me to know about?"

If the situation into which she'd found herself wasn't so serious, Kara would've laughed. But it wasn't funny. Far from it. "No, I don't have a man here. You, better than anyone, should know that I don't want to deal with any man after that last loser. Too bad I didn't have the good sense to walk away before it even started."

Dawn sucked her teeth. "You dated him for all of four months, and that was more than two years ago, Kara."

Kara stared at the threadbare rug and the fading drapes of the floor-to-ceiling windows. "I wish it'd been four seconds and two hundred years ago."

The sound of Dawn sucking her teeth again came through the earpiece. "You weren't alive two hundred years ago."

Shaking her head, Kara held her forehead. There were times when she didn't know if Dawn actually worked at being obtuse or if she was that gullible. When she'd mentioned this to her roommate, the dance teacher claimed men liked her best whenever she pretended to be an airhead. There had to be an awful lot of men who liked Dawn because Kara had lost count of the number of them who'd crossed the threshold of their East Harlem apartment.

There were times when she'd come home to a living room filled with people. She'd go directly into her bedroom, close and lock the door, and wait for the revelry to end. It did end, but not until the early-morning hours when she had to get up and go to work, while Dawn slept well into the afternoon when it was time for her to get up and go into the dance studio where she taught ballet, jazz, and tap.

"I'm here because I need to work out a few things that have to do with someone's estate."

"What are you talking about, Kara?"

She told Dawn everything, beginning with the letter from David up to and including her meeting with the sheriff. What she left out was her relationship to Taylor Patton. She wasn't ready to approach that can of worms when she could barely wrap her own head around things. "Right now, I've committed to staying here a week to sort out a few details."

"Have you lost your mind?" Dawn asked. "You just found some long-lost relatives are ready to take you out, and you talk about hanging around and giving them the opportunity for a drive-by?"

The laughter began, shaking Kara until she found it almost impossible to talk. She could always count on Dawn to make her laugh. And lately there hadn't been that much for her to laugh about. Her position as a social worker for at-risk children had her close to being burned out, and the steady stream of people coming and going at the apartment she shared with Dawn had also begun to take its toll, leaving her sleep deprived. If she could afford to move, she would have, but with exorbitant and prohibitive Manhattan rents, Kara felt trapped.

She loved Dawn like a sister, but her roommate allowing unemployed actors and dancers to occasionally crash at their apartment went beyond being a good friend. And as much as she tried to explain to Dawn that they were *her* friends, not their friends, nothing changed until Dawn asked a few of them to leave and not return because several valuables had disappeared from the apartment.

"It's not that easy to execute a drive-by down here. First of all it's an island, and there are only two ways on and off it, the ferry and the causeway, so how would they get away? And then there's the sheriff. He's definitely no-nonsense."

"Is he a good old boy?"

Kara scrunched up her nose when she recalled Jeff Hamilton. If she hadn't been so agitated, she knew she would've noticed that he probably wasn't much older than she was and that he was tall and well-spoken. He'd denied interrogating her when that was exactly what he'd done. Also like his cousin David, he had tried to convince her to remain in Angels Landing and claim her birthright.

"Not quite," Kara responded.

"What does the house look like?"

"It's a twenty-room antebellum mansion. It's rather run-down but not falling apart."

"Damn, Kara," Dawn drawled. "We could party for days in a place that big."

"That's where you're wrong. I'm not going to be here long enough to throw anything."

"Good for you. You come on back home where you belong. It's taken me awhile to turn you into a Big Apple diva, so I can't imagine you turning into a Scarlett O'Hara Southern belle, rocking on the front porch with a tall glass of sweet tea, while servants fan your moist face."

"Stop it, Dawn!" Kara said, laughing.

"Is there someone who takes care of the house?"

"Yes."

"Then you have a servant."

"She's a housekeeper."

"We won't argue about terminology, but on a more serious note, I'm worried about you, Kara. You can't dismiss the threats because you don't know how far these folks will go to get what they feel is legally theirs."

"It's not legally theirs," Kara argued softly.

There came a beat; then Dawn asked, "Are you certain?"

"Very certain."

"What aren't you telling me?"

"It's something I can't talk about right now."

"Hold up, Kara. You know you can tell me anything. We're more than friends, we're sisters. Let me be there for you...help you with this."

"No lie, Dawn, because if I didn't think of you as my sister, I would've moved out a long time ago." Kara chuckled uneasily.

"I know you're not talking about my friends hanging out at *our* place."

"They don't hang out, Dawn. They move in."

There came another pregnant pause from Dawn. "Why didn't you tell me you felt like this?"

Kara rolled her eyes upward even though Dawn couldn't see her. "I've told you I didn't mind them staying over for a night or two, but they'd come and never leave." Having lived with Dawn for so long, Kara knew how hard it was for an actor, singer, or dancer to wait for his or her big break. Kara was the social worker, but Dawn had become their Mother Teresa.

"I can understand. Honestly...I used to think you were jealous of them, particularly my guy friends."

This time Kara was at a loss for words. "Jealous, Dawn? No way! I don't have a boyfriend because I'm too stressed out from dealing with women who let their husbands or boyfriends abuse their children, then lie because they don't want to lose the man. I put myself at risk every time I report a case of abuse or neglect. And I never know when the parents are going to turn on me.

"Then there are the times when I'm on call. Do you think any man is going to understand me getting up in the middle of the night to remove a child from his or her home? And every time I have to go to the hospital to see a battered child with tubes attached to their little bruised body, I lose a little bit of myself." Tears filled Kara's eyes, and she clasped a hand over her mouth to stifle the sobs. "I have to go. I'll call you in a few days."

"Kara?"

"Bye, Dawn."

She broke the connection. Wiping the tears with the back of her hand, Kara attempted to bring herself under control. She knew feeling emotionally exhausted had something to do with her current situation. Although she'd been a social worker for ten years, she was still shocked and amazed by the amount of adults abusing helpless and vulnerable children and prayed she would never get so jaded that she'd accept it as commonplace rather than the exception.

She lost track of time as she sat in the chair, staring into nothingness. Kara had always prided herself on being strong, yet this was one of those times when she didn't know what to do.

Her situation wasn't unique. There were thousands who'd uncovered they were adopted or that one parent wasn't their biological parent. The use of DNA had become quite popular to determine paternity. Maury Povich's "You *are* or you're *not* the father!" had become the show's catchphrase. Despite her startling resemblance to the Pattons,

Kara knew some of them would demand she submit to a DNA test to validate Taylor's claim that she was his child and sole heir.

Pushing off the chair, Kara plugged the cell into the charger. She stood in the middle of the bedroom, her eyes shifting from one object to another. The room reminded her of those she'd seen in museums, and she was uncertain whether the massive mahogany four-poster bed was an antique or a reproduction. The posts were elaborately carved with pineapples, leaves, and vines. The design was repeated on the legs of the highboy, writing table, the drawers on the bedside tables, and on the front of an armoire. Age and countless footsteps had worn away the color and woven threads of area rugs, and the design on the wallpaper had faded.

Mrs. Todd had offered her a choice of the six bedrooms, and she'd chosen this one because the casement windows opened out onto a veranda that overlooked the rear of the property while offering panoramic views of the water. What had kept the mansion from appearing decrepit was its cleanliness. There wasn't a speck of dust anywhere.

Kara didn't know why, but suddenly she felt as if she were smothering and had to get out of the house if only for a few minutes. She exchanged her tank top and shorts for a blouse and black cropped pants. Slipping her feet into a pair of sandals, she picked up her cross-body bag and walked out of the bedroom, nearly colliding with Mrs. Todd; she'd just come out of a room carrying a plastic bucket with cleaning supplies.

"Now that it's stopped raining, I'm going out for a while."

"Are you going to walk or drive?"

Kara paused. "I think I'll drive. Where do you suggest I go?"

Mrs. Todd switched the handle of the pail from one hand to the other. "I think you should start with Haven Creek."

"Where's Haven Creek?"

"It's west of here. It's the first town off the causeway." The older woman squinted. "You do know east and west don't you?"

Kara smiled, nodding. "Yes, I do." She'd noticed Mrs. Todd squinting and wondered if she needed to have her eyes examined, then reminded herself Mrs. Todd wasn't her client and she wasn't in Angels Landing to evaluate her.

Mrs. Todd nodded. "Will you be back in time for dinner?"

She glanced at her watch. It was after 3:20. "Yes. I'm only going to be gone for about an hour."

"Until you learn the island you shouldn't be out after dark."

"Now you're scaring me, Mrs. Todd."

"I don't mean to scare you, but some of the roads don't have lights. Don't drive too fast or you'll get a ticket. The second time you're caught speeding the sheriff will impound your car for thirty days."

"Isn't that a little harsh?" Kara asked. "What if you need your car to go to work?"

"That's the law. The sheriff doesn't make exceptions."

"I'm not going to be out too late. And I'm definitely not going to speed."

The older woman nodded before Kara headed out of the door.

Minutes later, Kara drove slowly, staring out the window of the car that made her feel as if she were riding on air. The sedan was at least twenty-five years old, and kept in mint condition. There wasn't a hint of rust on the black, shiny exterior and the saddle-tan leather interior was as supple as soft butter.

As she lowered the driver's side window, the scent of salt water wafted into the car. Decelerating to ten miles an hour, Kara became a tourist and sightseer. One- and two-story homes, palmetto and Spanish moss–draped trees dotted the landscape. She spied a marker indicating the number of miles to Haven Creek.

A cyclist coming in the opposite direction waved to her as he passed, and she returned the wave. How different, she mused, Cavanaugh Island was from Manhattan where cyclists and bike messengers whizzed in and out of traffic while coming dangerously close to the many taxis playing chicken with pedestrians. Here the street and road names were flora: Magnolia, Palmetto, Honeysuckle, Oak, Gardenia, Peach, Carnation, and Cherry. In Manhattan there were street numbers running east and west and avenues running north and south.

The most profound difference was the absence of noise—no sirens or honking horns. The apartment she shared with Dawn was on the eighteenth floor, and once she closed the door all street noises ceased to exist. Kara had spent hours sitting on the balcony outside her bedroom, reading or taking in the sight of pleasure boats and barges gliding along the East River. Winter was her favorite time of the year with the falling snow making it almost impossible for her to see the lights on the many bridges connecting Manhattan with the other boroughs.

And if she hadn't had to come home and step over people in sleeping bags in the living and dining rooms, her home life would have been close to perfect. She also resented not being able to watch television in the living room because of strangers sprawled over the sofa and chairs drinking beer and eating chips. Kara loved Dawn but hated that her dogged need to take care of a bunch of freeloaders allowed her to constantly be used as a doormat.

She'd also found it hard to accept twenty- and thirty-something educated people traveling around with all of their worldly goods in a bedroll or backpack. Perhaps if she hadn't had such a stressful job, then she probably would've been more tolerant. The deliberation whether or not to leave or remove a child from his or her home was never an easy decision for Kara. Even after she'd made the decision, there were doubts. Those were the occasions when she wanted to come home to peace and familiarity.

Kara knew she could find the peace she craved at Angels Landing. She would be the only one living in a six-bedroom, eight-bathroom house with a small and grand ballroom, two kitchens, a formal dining room, a solarium, and front and back porches. Mrs. Todd told her Taylor had lived alone, rarely had visitors, and conducted business using the telephone or Internet. She could understand his need for solidarity.

A wry smile twisted her mouth. She couldn't believe Taylor had known so much about her, yet she knew very little about him. However, in the week that she remained on the island, she would find out as much as she could about the man who supposedly had fathered her.

The landscape changed again, becoming more wooded with trees lining both sides of the two-lane road. The houses in this section of Angels Landing were smaller replicas of the house she'd inherited.

"Pattons." The name had slipped unbidden from her lips. They couldn't live in the big house, so they'd built their own Angels Landing mini-mansions.

Kara slowed and turned off the road at the marker

pointing the way to Haven Creek's business district. Waning afternoon shadows slanted over a street that could've been in any small town in America. There was a sign prohibiting vehicles on the street, and she maneuvered into an area set aside for parking. She walked the short distance from the parking lot to Oak Street. Cobblestone streets, bricked sidewalks in a herringbone design, and black-and-white striped awnings shading storefronts gave the main thoroughfare a picture postcard appearance.

Peering through a window, Kara stared at a group of women sitting in a circle quilting. She'd always wanted to learn how to hand quilt. The shelves in the next shop were filled with sweet-grass baskets.

Moving along the street, Kara soon realized the area was an artists' colony. Haven Creek was a Lowcountry Taos with businesses offering photographs and paintings depicting the scenes of the Sea Islands; another shop displayed an ironworker's creations reminiscent of the late Philip Simmons's, the most celebrated of Charleston ironworkers; she passed a jewelry store featuring gold and silver pieces, another of a furniture maker, and an architectural firm. She stopped abruptly when she came face-to-face with Jeff.

He touched the worn brim of his Atlanta Braves baseball cap. "Good afternoon, Kara. I thought I wouldn't see you again until tomorrow."

Kara felt her breath catch in her throat when she met the dark, deep-set eyes of the man who'd promised to protect her. Why, she thought, hadn't she noticed the perfection of his masculine face? He wasn't just a good old boy, but tall, dark, and very handsome.

She inclined her head. "Good afternoon. I thought I'd get out and do a little sightseeing."

"I told you I'd take you around."

Kara focused on his face rather than the automatic handgun holstered at his waist. "I suppose I felt a little restless. I'm not used to sitting around doing nothing."

Jeff nodded to a shopkeeper and stepped to his left to allow him to pass. "What is it you do, Kara?" he asked.

Her gaze moved to the badge and name tag pinned on the chambray shirt over his heart. "I'm a social worker for a child protective agency."

Crossing his arms over his chest, Jeff whistled softly. "That can't be easy, especially in a big city."

"It isn't."

"Overworked and underpaid?"

"How did you know?"

Jeff smiled, drawing her eyes to the slight cleft in his strong chin. "I've met a few social workers in my travels, and they all complained about carrying too many clients on their caseloads and are paid a pittance for performing miracles."

Kara laughed for the second time that afternoon. "I've never heard it put quite that way."

"It's not much different for law enforcement when the bad guys outnumber the good guys."

She sobered quickly. "Are you saying there's a lot of crime on Cavanaugh Island?"

"Quite the contrary. There's little or no crime, especially with an islandwide policy of zero tolerance. You break the law, you pay the price."

"Like speeding?" Kara asked.

"Especially speeding because there're no stop signs or traffic lights on the island."

"I noticed there are no posted speed limits."

Jeff's right eyebrow lifted a fraction. "Do you see that as a problem?"

"It smacks of entrapment, Jeff."

He leaned closer. "How's that?"

"Just say I'm stopped for going thirty miles an hour, and you tell me the speed limit is twenty when nowhere on the island is it posted that the limit is twenty. You hit me up for a hundred dollar—"

"Two hundred," he said, interrupting her.

Kara's jaw dropped. "Two hundred dollars? That's excessive."

"So is speeding," Jeff countered. "We don't have drag racing or hit-and-runs."

"What about DWI and DUI?"

"Those fall under Charleston PD's jurisdiction." The small walkie-talkie clipped to his shirt collar crackled. "Please excuse me," he said, then took a backward step, his gaze meeting and fusing with Kara's before he turned his back.

Kara stared at the width of Jeff's broad shoulders, his trim waist and hips. He'd admitted to having been military, and his ramrod posture validated his claim. She didn't know whether he was married or involved with someone, but there was something about Jeffrey Hamilton that reminded her of what she'd been missing: male companionship.

She'd told Dawn that she was too busy, tired, or stressed out to deal with a man, when in reality she hadn't met one who could hold her interest. She'd accused her roommate of being Mother Teresa, wanting to house and feed the homeless, when she could've become a spokesperson for Save the Children. Her supervisor had cautioned that she was too involved with some of her clients, but Kara's mantra was "No child will fall between the cracks on my watch."

Glancing at the time on her cell phone, Kara knew if she didn't cross the street to see the other shops, it would be dark before she returned to Angels Landing. She'd just stepped off the sidewalk when a large hand around her upper arm stopped her.

"Where are you going?"

She glanced over her shoulder to find Jeff's gaze riveted on her face. "I'm going to check out the shops across the street. I plan to head back to Angels Landing before it gets dark."

His fingers tightened, then fell away. "You probably won't have much time to look around. You can follow me back to Angels Landing, and I'll bring you back tomorrow and introduce you around."

Kara wanted to tell Jeff she didn't want to meet anyone; she wanted answers about Taylor Patton. And if anyone knew everything about anyone on the island, then it would be the sheriff.

For a long moment, she returned his stare. There was something in his entrancement that ignited a tingling in the pit of her stomach. "Okay."

Reaching for her hand, Jeff led her to the parking lot, waiting until she was seated and belted in. "I'll head out first."

Kara wagged her finger at him. "No speeding."

He flashed a white-toothed smile. "Just try and keep up."

Her eyes grew wider when she registered his veiled challenge. "Please close my door."

He bowed from the waist. "Yes, ma'am."

Starting up her car, Kara waited for the Jeep to maneuver

out of the parking lot, she following close behind. When he'd said for her to try and keep up, she knew he would exceed the unofficial island speed limit. The Mercedes's speedometer hovered close to forty miles an hour as she stared at the taillights on the vehicle in front of hers.

Palmetto Lane came up so quickly Kara hit the brakes to keep from passing it. Jeff tapped his horn, she tapping hers in response. He sped off while she drove on the sandy road under a canopy of live oaks, draped with Spanish moss. Angels Landing came into view at the end of the allée, her breath catching in her throat. Waning sunlight reflected off the columns in shimmering shades of rose-gold.

In that instant Kara wondered how different her life would have been if she'd grown up in this house. Would she have viewed things differently if Taylor Patton had raised her instead of Austin Newell?

She parked the car, got out, and walked around to the door that led directly into the kitchen. She made it to her bedroom without encountering Mrs. Todd or her husband Willie. Picking up her cell phone, Kara stood at the window as she tapped speed dial. Her mother's sultry drawl came through the earpiece.

"Hi, baby. What time should your daddy pick you up at the airport tomorrow?"

Kara closed her eyes for several seconds. "I'm not coming in tomorrow."

"What's going on, Kara?"

She knew she had to choose her words carefully. "Mama, I need you to answer one question for me." Kara had decided not to wait for a face-to-face encounter with her mother to ask her about Taylor because she knew it would nag at her for the week.

A beat passed. "What is it?"

"Why didn't you tell me Taylor Patton was my father?"

Jeannette gasped. "Who told you?"

"Mama, please. Was he my father?"

"I can't talk now."

"When can you talk?" Kara asked.

"Not over the phone, Kara."

Kara knew by her mother's evasiveness that she'd validated David's claim that she *was* Taylor's daughter. "Is Daddy there with you?"

"Yes."

It was obvious her mother didn't want to talk about Taylor in front of Austin. "I'm not coming to Little Rock." She told Jeannette that she'd committed to staying on Cavanaugh Island for at least a week. "Can you get off and come here?"

"Right now I'm short staffed. Two nurses called in today with the flu. They're going to be out at least a week."

"Can you come here next week?"

"I'll try, baby."

Kara pulled her lower lip between her teeth. "You don't have to explain anything until you get here. But I need to know now. Yes or no?"

The seconds made a full revolution before her mother said, "Yes."

Walking on shaky legs, Kara sat on the padded bench at the foot of the bed. "Thank you, Mama."

"It's not what you think, Kara."

"I'm not judging you, Mama. I just needed to know the truth."

"I love you, baby."

"And I love you, too. Let me know when you're coming, and I'll meet you at the airport."

"You take care of yourself."

"You, too, Mama."

Kara ended the call filled with a powerful relief that she knew the truth. She would now be able to face whatever challenges came her way with new objectivity. And knowing she was Taylor's daughter gave her the ammunition she needed to handle her newfound relatives' threats and intimidation.

Chapter Three

Jeff had always been a light sleeper, so when he heard the distinctive ringtone he woke, reaching for the cell phone on the bedside table. Glancing at the clock, he moaned softly. It was 3:48 in the morning. Turning on the lamp, he punched a button.

"Hamilton."

"I'm sorry to bother you, Jeff, but I have a situation down here at the station."

Groaning under his breath, he ran a hand over his face. "Is it a situation or an emergency, Kenny?" Jeff had hired Kenneth Collins to replace a part-time deputy who'd remarried his wife, then relocated to Orlando to be close to their grandchildren.

"It's a situation that will soon be an emergency. Patty Calhoun called because her ex showed up drunk and threatening to kick down the door if she didn't let him in. I arrested him because of the restraining order."

"Where is he?"

"I locked him up."

"Did you call Charleston PD and tell them to pick him up?"

"Yes."

"Then what's the situation?" Jeff asked.

"Patty's here pitching a fit because she doesn't want her man to get locked up. And Jimmy's threatening to kill himself if I don't let him out."

Throwing an arm over his face, Jeff cursed softly. "She should've thought of that before she took out a restraining order. Make certain there isn't anything in the cell he can use to hurt himself."

"What about Patty?"

"Tell her to go home or you're going to lock her up, too. Is that her screaming?" Jeff asked when he heard a screeching sound.

"Yeah."

Lowering his arm, he sat up. "Put her on the phone, Kenny....Patty, this is Sheriff Hamilton." Normally he would've introduced himself as Jeff, but right now he and Patricia McFarland weren't former classmates. She was a resident of Sanctuary Cove and he sheriff of the island.

"Yesss," came her tearful reply.

"Where are your kids?"

"They...they're at home."

"Are they home alone?"

"Yes...but—"

"But nothing, Patty!" Jeff practically shouted. "You left

your kids home alone to follow a man who beats you on a regular basis. Either you get home and take care of your kids or when the Charleston police come for Jimmy I'll have them pick up your kids, too. Both you and Jimmy will have to stand before a judge. You for abandoning your children and he for ignoring the order to stay away from you. It's your choice. Let me know now what you plan to do."

There came a pause. "I'm going home."

"Don't play games with me, Patty."

"I'm going home, Jeff. I swear."

Jeff hated playing the bad guy, especially with someone he'd grown up with. Life hadn't been kind to Patty. She'd grown up with an abusive alcoholic father and had found herself in the same situation when she married a man like her father.

"I'm going to give you five minutes to get home; then I'm going to call your house. If one of your kids answers the phone, then I'm coming to arrest you, but not before I call child protective services to have them remove the children from your home."

"Please don't, Jeff. I'm going home now."

"Put Kenny back on the phone."

He heard muffled voices before his deputy returned. "She just left, Jeff."

"Give her ten minutes to get home, then call the house," he ordered. "Call me right away if she doesn't pick up."

"What are you going to do if she doesn't pick up?"

"I'll call CPS and have them put her children in foster care. Between Patty and Jimmy, those poor kids are going to be messed up."

"I hear you, boss," Kenny intoned.

"How's Jimmy?"

"He's quieted down, but I know he's going to start up again when they come to get him."

"It won't matter because he'll no longer be our responsibility."

"You're right, Jeff. I'm sorry to disturb you, but you have a better relationship with the people on the island than I do."

Sliding back to the mound of pillows supporting his shoulders, Jeff smiled. "That's because I grew up here and you didn't." His smile faded as quickly as it appeared. He was scheduled to be off for the next two days, hoping his deputies would be able to handle whatever came up until his return. "Good night, Kenny. Or should I say good morning?"

"Good morning, Jeff. I'll try not to call you again."

"You do that."

He ended the call, turned off the lamp, and readjusted the pillows. Threatening to remove Patty's children from their home reminded him of Kara. As a social worker she'd been entrusted to protect children from situations that threatened their safety.

Jeff had consciously tried not to think about Kara, but the image of her face and body lingered around the fringes of his mind when he least expected it. When his cousin had called to ask him to check on Taylor Patton's daughter, to say he was shocked was putting it mildly because he along with others who'd spent their lives on Cavanaugh Island believed Taylor didn't have any children.

Although Jeff had spent twenty years in the corps, returning home whenever he had leave, he knew if Taylor had fathered a child, he definitely would've heard about it only because there were very few secrets on Cavanaugh Island. And he knew not to ask David how he'd learned that Taylor had a daughter because his cousin would've claimed attorney-client privilege.

Resting his head on folded arms, he closed his eyes and attempted to go back to sleep, but it proved elusive. Reaching for the television remote, he turned on the flat screen and began channel surfing, passing numerous infomercials until he found a sports channel. The Super Bowl was over, baseball's spring training had begun, and the NBA and NHL seasons were in full swing. Jeff would be the first to admit he was a rabid sports fan, becoming an armchair spectator only because South Carolina did not have a professional sports team. He always took his dinner hour at Jack's Fish House just to watch the televised games on the many flat screens installed at the island's popular restaurant.

He muted the sound, turned on the closed caption feature, staring at the images until he felt his eyes closing. When he woke hours later, the television was watching him, and Jeff felt more tired than he had when he'd gone to bed and turned off the TV.

Bright sunshine filtered through the blinds at the windows, threading its way over the hardwood floor. Sitting up and swinging his legs over the side of the bed, he walked on bare feet out of the bedroom and across the hall to the bathroom. The first thing he'd done once he returned to Sanctuary Cove was to have an architect draw up plans to expand the house by adding a first-floor bedroom, bath en suite, and sunroom for his grandmother after her cardiologist cautioned her about climbing stairs. Corrine had pouted whenever he carried her up and down the staircase until the renovations were completed; then her attitude changed once he suggested they go into Charleston to shop for furnishings to decorate her new living quarters.

It had become role reversal when he looked after his seventy-nine-year-old maternal grandmother much like she'd cared for him after his mother died in childbirth. Corrine had become mother, father, and grandmother, and after his grandfather passed away, she'd also stepped into that role. She'd been forthcoming when it came time for her to tell him about sex. She was emphatic about his using protection whenever he slept with a woman and cautioned him about using women just to relieve his own sexual urges. What had surprised Jeff was he was more embarrassed about the discussion than his grandmother. Always taller than the boys his age, he hung out with older boys, most of whom were sexually active and proud of their exploits and conquests. However, his respect for the woman who'd raised him outweighed that of his peers, and he was discriminating and very discreet whenever he'd become involved with any woman.

Jeff did what he'd always done on his days off: yard work. He mowed the lawn, raked leaves, and bagged everything for the weekly trash pickup. His grandmother had voiced her concern whenever he opted to stay home with her instead of going out with a woman, fearing he would go through life alone. At forty he wasn't as concerned about marriage or fathering children as he was about taking care of the woman who'd sacrificed so much for him.

He'd been back a year, and his love life was nonexistent. There were single women on the island, but none had interested him. He'd found them shallow, immature, and gauche, unlike the women with whom he'd been involved when he was stationed in the States or abroad. Jeff had had two serious relationships—one that had prompted him to propose marriage—yet at forty he was still a bachelor. There was a time when he'd looked forward to marriage and becoming a father, but lately he'd reconciled to the possibility of that not happening in his immediate future. This didn't mean he wasn't looking for a woman with whom he could have a comfortable ongoing relationship. He just wasn't sure if he'd found her yet.

Twenty minutes later, dressed in sweats, Jeff walked into the kitchen and kissed his grandmother's cheek. "Don't you know how to sleep late?"

Corrine patted his stubble. "It's your day off. Don't *you* know how to sleep late?"

He smiled tenderly at the tall, thin woman with smooth skin the color of café au lait, tugging gently at the silver curls hugging her scalp. There were a few lines around her eyes whenever she smiled. "Remember, I have to clean up the yard."

"The yard can wait until next week, Jeffrey."

"No it can't, Gram. Then I would have twice as much to do." He only called her Gram whenever they were together and usually referred to her as Grandmomma when speaking of her to others.

Corrine filled a mug with freshly brewed coffee from the blue enameled pot on the stove, handing it to him. "What else do you have to do on your days off? You get up the same time as when you'd go to the station, you work in the yard, and then you come back inside and watch every game imaginable on that darn idiotic box."

Jeff cut his eyes at her. "Would you prefer I go to a bar, pick up women, guzzle beer, and chomp on peanuts all day?"

"No. I'd like you to find a nice young woman to marry and give me a few great-grandchildren before I die."

"Please, Gram, don't start on that again."

Corrine pushed her hands into the pockets of the bibbed apron covering a floral shirtwaist dress. "You gave up something you loved for me, son."

"And you gave up your life for me, Grandmomma!" Jeff shouted. "I'm sorry about raising my voice," he apologized when her jaw dropped. "You had the chance to marry again after Grandpapa died, but you didn't because you didn't want to put a man ahead of me." He held up a hand when she opened her mouth. "I overheard you when you were talking to Miss Dean about Mr. Hawkins wanting to marry you, and you said I came first in your life."

"You were eavesdropping on grown folks' business?" Corrine asked accusingly.

Opening the door to the stainless steel refrigerator-freezer, Jeff removed a container of cream, poured a dollop into his mug, then replaced it and closed the door. His grandmother had also balked when he updated the kitchen with top-of-the-line appliances, complaining that she liked her old stove. He'd also bought a single-cup coffeemaker that she refused to use, declaring her enamel pot made better coffee. How, he mused, would she know that when she hadn't drunk coffee for more than a year?

"No. I was bringing something to your classroom when I heard you talking with Miss Dean. That's all I heard before I waited at the end of the hall for her to leave."

"You couldn't have been more than six."

"I was seven, Gram."

Corrine removed her hands from her apron, clasping them in front of her. "And you waited all this time to tell me this, Jeffrey?"

Jeff took a sip of the warm brew, staring at his grandmother over the rim of the mug. Corrine Jefferson

Hamilton's life was measured in numbers. She'd graduated high school at fifteen, married her high school sweetheart at eighteen, graduated college at nineteen, gave birth to her only child at twenty, became a grandmother at thirty-eight, and was widowed at forty. A former teacher and elementary school principal, she was the only one on Cavanaugh Island who called him Jeffrey. To everyone else he was Jeff, Sheriff Hamilton, or Corrine Hamilton's grandbaby boy.

"I didn't say anything because at that time I'd felt as if I was in the way and also a burden on you."

"What do you mean by 'in the way'?"

"There was talk, Gram. Folks used to say it was a shame that you'd raised a child and then you had to turn around and raise your grandchild when you had the chance to remarry after Grandpapa died. Some said I was standing in the way of your happiness, while others—most of them—praised you for your selflessness. It wasn't until I was older when I realized that if you'd wanted to remarry, then you would have."

Corrine walked to the table in the corner of the eat-in kitchen and sat down. She traced the design of the hand-stitched embroidery with her fingertips. "I did what I had to do, Jeffrey. Your mother died giving birth to you, and there was no way I was going to let you go to some foster home or let some strangers adopt you. Not when I still had breath in my body. I didn't marry Mr. Hawkins because I found out later that he was as mean as a junkyard dog whenever he drank. Your gramps never raised his hand or his voice to me, and I wasn't about to involve you in a situation where that may happen. Even if I would've put up with it, I know you never would once you got older."

Jeff sat opposite Corrine. Placing his hand over hers, he gave her fingers a gentle squeeze. "No one will ever hurt you, Gram. Not while I have breath in *my* body."

Eyelids fluttering, Corrine blinked back tears. "Drink your coffee, and take care of the lawn. I'll have breakfast ready for you when you're finished."

Leaning over, he kissed her cheek. "I'm going to pass on breakfast this morning because I'm meeting somebody for lunch."

"Who is she? It is a she, isn't it?"

He smiled. "Of course, it's a she."

"Who, Jeffrey? Do I know her?"

"No, you don't know her, but there's no doubt you'll hear about her before the sun goes down."

Reversing their hands, it was Corrine's turn to squeeze her grandson's fingers. "I guess I can wait for the rumor mill to start working overtime."

Kara had just come out of the bathroom when she heard soft knocking on the bedroom door. "Good morning, Mr. Todd."

The groundskeeper stood in the hallway outside her bedroom. He was the complete opposite of his wife in looks and personality. Tall, light-skinned with a face covered with freckles, and his once reddish hair now liberally sprinkled with gray, he spent most of his day landscaping the many acres that made up Angels Landing, sitting on the riding mower and pruning trees.

Mr. Todd crushed a battered straw hat between his large hands. "The sheriff is here to see you, Miss Kara."

She nodded. "Thank you. Please call me Kara," she

reminded him. The man was old enough to be her grandfather, yet he'd insisted on calling her Miss Kara.

Mr. Todd's solemn expression didn't change. "As I said, the sheriff is downstairs."

"Thank you, Mr. Todd."

A hint of a smile tilted the corners of his full lips. "And you can call me Willie."

Kara plucked the navy-blue pashmina shawl off the back of the armchair, looping it around her neck, then picked up her handbag. "I can't do that, *Mr. Willie.*" If Mr. Todd had spent his life in the South, then he knew children were taught to address older people by miss or mister, regardless of first or surnames.

He stepped aside. "You should leave now. The sheriff isn't a very patient man."

Kara glanced at the clock on the fireplace mantel. It was 11:45, fifteen minutes earlier than when Jeff had promised to pick her up. "Please let him know I'm coming down." She waited until Mr. Todd left, then followed him, he taking the back staircase and she taking the one that led to the front of the house.

Her pace slowed as she stepped off the last stair. Jeff stood in the middle of the living room, staring at the paintings of former owners of the house that had given the town its name. He looked a little sinister dressed in black: slacks, sweater, and jacket. Facets of light from the massive chandelier shimmered on his smooth jaw and dark brown skin. There was something about Jeff that was so masculine, virile that she found swallowing and breathing difficult.

"Good morning." Jeff turned at the sound of her voice. He stared at her as if she were an apparition. "Is there something wrong?" Kara asked.

• • •

Jeff blinked, his gaze moving slowly from her face to her feet. Kara appeared quite the chic, urban sophisticate. "No, Kara. Everything is fine." He closed the distance between them while extending his hands. Kara placed her hands on his outstretched palms, he leaning down to kiss her cheek. "You look beautiful."

Kara glanced down at the navy-blue wool gabardine pantsuit and matching patent leather pumps with a sturdy four-inch heel. "Thank you." Her head popped up. "I hope I'm not too overdressed for lunch at Jack's."

Tucking her hand in the crook of his arm, Jeff gave her a reassuring smile. "No. If anything, you'll bring a little class to the joint."

She pulled back, but he tightened his grip on her much smaller hand. "I'll go up and change into something less businesslike."

"Please don't. Our lunch will be a combination of business and pleasure."

Jeff didn't want to tell Kara she was like a breath of fresh air. The ponytail was missing, and in its place was a sleek hairdo, parted off center to frame her face, the blunt-cut ends falling inches above her shoulders. A light cover of makeup accentuated her best features: her eyes and lips. His gaze lingered on the curve of her mouth outlined in a soft orange-brown shade.

"Pleasure?"

"The food at Jack's is pleasure personified. You don't believe me, do you?" he asked when she gave him a skeptical look. "I know you have good restaurants in New York, but they can't compare to Jack's."

"We'll see."

"Okay, Big Apple skeptic, let's go find out." Jeff led Kara out of the house and to his parked car. He released her hand, seating her in the low-slung, silver two seater.

"Nice, sexy little car," she crooned.

He hadn't thought of the Miata as sexy but practical for his lifestyle. In essence, it was a bachelor's car. His grandmother had accused him of being selfish when he'd first purchased the two seater, but after he'd taken her into Charleston for a test-drive, she changed her mind. The only thing Corrine complained about was that it was too low to the ground and she much preferred her four-door Camry. Jeff wasn't certain how much longer she would continue to drive, leaving that decision up to her doctors. What he wanted was for his grandmother to remain independent for as long as possible.

"Thank you," Jeff said to Kara as he slid in behind the wheel.

"It smells new."

The engine of the Mazda MX-5 Miata roared to life when he pushed the Start Engine button. "It is. I picked it up from the dealer a couple of months ago. My last car was eighteen years old, and I used to work on it whenever I came home on leave, but then after a while, I was unable to replace the parts, so I sold it for scrap."

"Did you give it a proper farewell?"

Throwing back his head, Jeff laughed, the rich sound bouncing off the roof inside the small vehicle. "To be honest, I couldn't look when the tow truck driver hooked it up and drove away."

There was a comfortable silence as he continued in an easterly direction toward the Cove, Jeff more than aware of the woman sitting less than a foot away. Everything about her screamed big-city sophisticate: coiffed hair, pantsuit, shoes, and the pearl studs in her ears. He'd told a little lie when he said she wasn't overdressed because it'd been awhile since he'd gone out with a woman like Kara. It wasn't that the women on the island didn't dress up, but those who were stay-at-home mothers or shopkeepers tended to be more casual.

"How large is Cavanaugh Island?" Kara asked, breaking into his musings.

"The entire island is about eight square miles."

"If it's that small, then why is it divided into towns?"

Jeff met her eyes for a second. Sunlight coming through the windshield had turned them into large pools of green and gold. "There were rumors that Thomas Cavanaugh, whom many suspected was a pirate, used the island as his home base. He and his band of men would lay in wait in the marshes and fire on merchant ships moored off the coast. Although British authorities could never prove he was responsible for the dastardly acts, they forced him to give up his claim to the island when he was impressed into their navy. Others came seeking their fortune in what had been the American colonies, and they were awarded land grants for their service to the king."

"Why is the house called Angels Landing when the town is also called Angels Landing?"

Jeff shifted into a lower gear as he approached the newly built road connecting Angels Landing with Sanctuary Cove. "Now that's a long story."

"Remember, Jeff, I'm not leaving tomorrow."

He laughed again. "It definitely won't take a week to tell, but I want to warn you that it has everything to do with your people."

She went completely still. "When you say my people, are you talking about the Pattons?"

"Yes."

"Is it something I don't need to know?"

A beat passed. "There's an old Gullah saying that 'you can't know where you're going if you don't know where you've come from.' "

"Are you saying I'm Gullah?"

"If you're Taylor Patton's daughter, then yes, you *are* Gullah."

Kara closed her eyes. "I still don't want to believe the man I thought to be my father for all these years isn't."

"That happens to a lot of us."

She opened her eyes. "Us?"

"I never knew my father," Jeff stated in a strained tone. "I wouldn't know him if I met him on the street. But it's different with you because you don't have to share DNA with a man for him to assume the role as dad."

"The man I call Daddy is awesome."

"That's all that counts, Kara."

He maneuvered into the parking lot at Jack's Fish House, pulling into the last space. The lot was filled with pickup trucks belonging to the fishermen who came to the restaurant for the luncheon specials. There were also out-of-state license plates belonging to snowbirds that came down to spend the winter on the island.

"Is the lot always this crowded?" Kara asked.

Jeff realized Kara had asked a lot of questions because she was trying to sort things out for herself. Some he could answer, and others she would have to uncover on her own. He'd grown up not knowing his mother or father, yet he'd never felt disconnected. He didn't remember his grandfather, but the stories Corrine told him about her beloved husband and photographs she'd saved of him made Malachi Hamilton come alive in Jeff's imagination.

"Most of the time. By twelve thirty nearly all of the fishermen on the island come for lunch, then around five or six it's the dinner crowd."

Kara gave Jeff a tender smile. "Well, Gullah man, you promised me a wonderful lunch, so let's go."

Jeff opened his door, planting one spit-shined, booted foot on the ground, then turned and smiled at Kara over his shoulder. "It appears as if I'm not the only Gullah here."

She ran an imaginary line down the middle of her body. "Only half."

His smile grew wider. "One drop of Gullah blood makes you Gullah."

Waiting until he came around to assist her, Kara tilted her chin. Jeff's eyes sparkled in amusement. "Do you speak Gullah?"

He shook his head. "But I do understand it."

"I was hoping you'd give me a crash course. Sometimes Mrs. Todd will lapse into dialect, and it takes a while before I realize what she's saying."

"My grandmother could teach you, but a week isn't long enough for you to pick up even the simplest phrases."

Kara wrapped her arms around her body to ward off a gust of cold wind coming off the ocean. "I'm staying more than a week."

Jeff stared wordlessly as if he couldn't believe what she'd said. He replayed her statement over and over in his head. "You're staying longer than a week?" She nodded. At that instant he didn't know whether to shout like a crazy man or kiss Kara. Twenty-four hours ago he hadn't known she existed. But now it was different. David had told him she wasn't married, yet that still didn't mean she wasn't committed to someone back in New York.

He didn't know what it was that drew him to Kara other than she was different than any of the women on the island. She was a transplanted Southern girl who wasn't reticent when she'd accused him of interrogating her, yet underneath the feigned tough-girl exterior, she was a vulnerable woman whose very existence had proven to be a lie.

Their eyes met, and he smiled. "I'll introduce you to my grandmother. She was a teacher for forty-five years, and I know she'd like nothing else better than having you as her student."

Kara's expression changed. It stilled, becoming serious. "I can't impose on her like that."

Wrapping an arm around her waist, Jeff led her out of the parking lot toward the restaurant. "I wouldn't have mentioned it if I thought it was an imposition. If it will make you feel more comfortable, you can ask her yourself."

Opening the door, he held it for Kara, watching her reaction as she walked inside the restaurant where the cuisine had become legendary throughout the Lowcountry. Tantalizing and mouthwatering aromas filled the air as the waitstaff pushed their way into and out of the kitchen's swinging door, trays laden with dishes piled high with lunch orders.

Kara's eyes were as large as silver dollars. "Oh my..." Her words trailed off when a waitress placed platters of fried chicken, catfish, biscuits, red rice and sausage, collards and chitlins on the table of six diners who'd tucked napkins under their chins.

"Did I not tell you?" Jeff whispered in her ear when she leaned back against his chest.

"If that's lunch, then what are they going to eat for dinner?" she asked softly under her breath.

"I don't know."

The waitress beckoned to them. "Jeff, there's a table for two near the side door. If you don't want to sit there, then you can wait for an empty one."

Jeff lowered his head, pressing his mouth to Kara's ear. "Do you want to wait?"

"No!"

Her reply was so emphatic that he was hard-pressed not to laugh. Resting a hand at the small of her back, Jeff directed her to the table. As if on cue, the entire restaurant fell silent, all eyes directed at them. He knew most of the locals were either curious or shocked to see him bringing a woman into Jack's. In fact, they hadn't seen him with a woman since he'd returned to the Cove to live. Whenever he ate at the restaurant, it was usually alone, with his deputies, or his grandmother.

"Damn, Jeff! She's hotter than a bushel of peppers!" boomed a male voice.

Jeff never broke stride. "Watch your mouth, Bossier. And you will respect the lady, or I'll lock you up for disturbing the peace!"

A few guffaws and titters followed his warning. Those who didn't laugh knew he never issued idle threats. Jeff seated Kara, then came around the scarred oak table hewn from massive tree trunks. "What's the matter?" he asked when she looked at him, a strange expression on her face.

"Does this usually happen whenever you bring a woman here?"

Leaning back in his chair, he gave her a long, penetrating

stare. "No, it's happening because I don't bring women here. The exception is my grandmother."

"What about your wife?"

His eyebrows flickered slightly. "I don't have a wife."

It was Kara's turned to lift her eyebrows. "What about a girlfriend?"

"I don't have a girlfriend."

She angled her head. "I know this is a little personal, but do you like women?"

Jeff smiled, flashing his teeth. "I happen to love women."

"But you don't date local women," Kara said perceptively. Her question was a statement.

He nodded. "Not from the Cove, Landing, or the Creek."

"What's wrong with them, Jeff?"

"Nothing."

"Nothing?" Kara repeated. "There has to be a reason why they don't appeal to you."

Propping an elbow on the table, he rested his chin on his fist. "Do you want me to set up a session where you can analyze me?" He knew he'd embarrassed Kara when a rush of color darkened her face. "I'm sorry," he apologized quickly. "That was uncalled for. Will you forgive me?"

Kara stared at something over his shoulder. Her eyes were now a deep green. "I'll think about it."

Reaching across the table, Jeff grasped her hand, tightening his grip on her fingers when she tried pulling away. "I'm really sorry, Kara, for not answering your question." He thought for a moment. "I don't know why, but I've never been attracted to the girls on the island."

Her gaze swung back to meet his. "Is it because you resent being Gullah?"

"No! Why would you think that?" he asked, letting go of her hand.

"I don't know, Jeff. It just seems odd that you don't find any woman on an eight-square-mile island attractive."

Jeff lowered his arm. "That's where you're wrong. I find you attractive."

Kara blushed again. "I don't count."

"And why not?"

"Because I don't live on Cavanaugh Island."

A pregnant silence ensued as they stared at each other. "What if you do decide to stay?" Jeff asked, "would you be opposed to going out with me?"

There, he'd said it. Depending on Kara's answer he would know whether she was or wasn't involved with someone either in New York or Little Rock. And he hoped it was the latter.

A hint of a smile softened Kara's mouth. "I'm having lunch with you, aren't I?"

Crossing his arms over his chest, he nodded slowly. "Yes, you are. But it's not really a date."

"Then what is it, Jeff?"

"It's keeping a promise to my cousin that I would look after you. And that includes showing you around and making sure that certain people like that jerk who disrespected you won't do it again."

"So I'm safe as long as I'm with you?"

Lines fanned out around his eyes when he smiled. "As safe as you'd be if you were locked in a bank's vault."

"You just reminded me of something."

"What's that?"

"I have to go to the bank. I have power of attorney to open Taylor's safe-deposit box."

"Do you have the key?"

"Yes. David gave me an envelope yesterday with the key and some other papers that I never took out of my bag."

"After lunch I'll take you to the bank."

Kara let out an audible sigh. "How can I thank you?"

"Go to the movies with me," he said quickly. "I'm off duty tomorrow."

"Is there a movie theater here on the island?"

"There's one on the Cove, but most of the films are at least two to three months behind the ones they show in Charleston. There's also a small theater in the Creek. They only feature foreign films and black-and-white movies from the thirties and forties. The Creek is our artist community. Most of the people who live there are artisans and farmers. All of the chickens sold on the island come from the Creek. There's still a dairy farm and a couple of hog farms. Every Wednesday the farmers set up an outdoor market where you can buy fruits, veggies, and home-baked goods.

"Angels Landing is different because it is solely residential. The Cove offers both. It has a bank, post office, pharmacy, bakery, boardinghouse, supermarket, liquor store, ice cream parlor, and bookstore. It also has a unisex salon. Last year the island got its first resident doctor in more than a decade. Dr. Monroe has an office off Main Street and Moss Alley, and he makes house calls."

"So folks really don't have to leave the island if they don't want to."

Jeff shook his head. "No, they don't. Every town has a school with grades one through eight. Once they graduate they go into Charleston for high school."

"Do the kids from Charleston ever come to the island?"

"Many of them do once they form friendships with the kids who live here. It's like culture shock for many of them because life here is very laid-back. Everyone knows one another, and there is zero tolerance for crime. Old folks say kids can cut the fool on the mainland, but we don't tolerate that here."

"What about churches?"

"Each town has its own church."

A waitress with neatly braided hair covered with a hairnet came over to their table. Her dark skin glistened with good health as she nodded to Jeff, then Kara. "Would you like to see a menu?"

"Yes," Jeff said, answering for himself and Kara.

Within seconds, menus were placed on the table along with a pitcher of sweet tea, two tall glasses, and a plate of biscuits. "We are a little backed up in the kitchen, so it may take awhile before you get your food. But I could start you off with a bowl of gumbo."

"Would you like to try the gumbo?" Jeff asked Kara.

"Yes, please."

Chapter Four

Kara was tempted to undo the button on her slacks. She couldn't remember the last time she'd eaten so much. The gumbo could've been a meal because it wasn't just celery, okra, tomato, onion, corn, and peppers; the chef had added pieces of smoked meat, spicy sausage, crabmeat, oysters, and shrimp.

When she couldn't decide what to order she'd insisted that Jeff order for her, and much to her delight he'd selected red rice and sausage, shrimp, crab and salmon cakes, and mustard greens with cornmeal dumplings.

Kara placed her napkin beside her plate. "I can't eat like this every day."

"You hardly ate anything. Are you sure you don't want dessert?"

She groaned. "Quite sure. Lunch for me is usually a tuna salad or a half a bagel left over from breakfast."

Jeff dabbed the corners of his mouth with the napkin. "I hope you're not one of those women who monitors everything they put into their mouths because they don't want to gain two pounds."

"No way. It's just that I don't have time to eat. Between seeing clients and field visits I'm lucky if I eat two meals a day."

"Do you ever take a vacation and just chill out?"

"That's what I'm doing now," Kara explained. "I've accrued so much vacation leave that if I hadn't taken at least three weeks I would've lost it."

"Oh, so you can stay three weeks."

Kara bit back a smile when she saw the look of expectation on Jeff's handsome face. There was something about the man sitting across from her that was intriguing. He still had the drawl verifying that he'd grown up in the American South; however, there was a worldliness about him that probably had come from his time in the military.

"I can stay a maximum of three weeks, then it's back to New York and the grind." She saw Jeff angle his head and stare at her as if he were committing her face to memory. "What's the matter?"

"Why do you work at something you refer to as a grind, Kara?"

"I only say that because it's the same routine day in and day out. I'm certain it was the same with you when you were in the military."

"Not when you're in a war zone."

A slight gasp escaped Kara. "You were in Iraq?" Jeff's expression changed, the warmth in his eyes was replaced by something she could only interpret as pain.

"Afghanistan. Two tours."

She slumped back in her chair. "I'm sorry if what I said sounded so glib."

"It's all right. You didn't know."

"Were you in the army?"

"Hell no."

"Ouch!" Kara held up her hand, palm facing Jeff. "You must have been a jarhead."

"You've got it," Jeff admitted proudly.

"Once a marine, always a marine?" she teased.

"You better believe it." He shrugged out of his jacket, pushed up the sleeve to his sweater, and showed her the insignia and motto of the corps on his left forearm.

She stared at the tattoo of an eagle, globe, anchor, and *Semper fidelis* on his muscular arm. "How long have you had your tattoo?"

"Almost twenty years. I got it after successfully completing OCS and the NROTC program."

Kara tucked a thick lock of hair behind her right ear. "So, you were an officer."

"I'd attained the rank of captain in the military police before I put in my discharge papers."

Shock after shock slapped at Kara with this disclosure. "My dad was also in the corps as military police. He retired last year after thirty years as a sergeant major."

"Hot damn! My man!"

She brought her hand up to stifle a giggle. "It can't be all that, Jeff."

"Baby, you just don't know what it means to be a marine."

"I do know," Kara countered. "My mother lived on base with Dad for the first eight years of my life. She didn't like it, and I didn't like moving from base to base and leaving my friends. We moved back to Little Rock, and I lived there until I left to go to college."

She felt as if she'd known Jeff for years when she told him about moving to New York to attend college, earning an undergraduate degree and MSW, and sharing an apartment with a professional dancer.

"Do you like New York?" he asked.

"There was a period of adjustment, but I've grown used to the noise, grittiness, and the pulsing excitement that's so contagious. The first time I went to Times Square during the summer I couldn't believe I had to jostle for space on the sidewalk at three in the morning."

"Well, it is touted as the city that never sleeps," Jeff reminded her.

"And it doesn't. What made you decide on a military career?" Kara asked, deftly steering the focus of conversation from her to Jeff.

"A recruiter approached me within days of my enrolling in college, and his pitch sounded so good I signed up."

"Do you miss it, Jeff?" Her voice was soft, almost a whisper.

He pulled down his sleeve and stared at the initials carved into the table. "Yes and no. I miss the brotherhood, seeing the drills, the dress parades, and the silent drill platoon. I still get together with some of the officers whenever they come to Charleston."

"Your mother must be very proud of you." Without warning Jeff sobered, and instinctually she knew she'd mentioned something that should've been left unsaid. She also recalled he'd talked about his grandmother, but not his mother. "I'll understand if you don't want to talk about her."

"There's not much to talk about. My mother died giving birth to me."

Kara's eyelids fluttered as she attempted to bring her emotions under control. She'd been trained as a therapist to remain detached, not get emotionally involved with her clients, but Jeff wasn't a client. He was the man whom she'd found herself drawn to; a man who made her feel things and react to him when she didn't want to.

He'd openly admitted he was attracted to her, while she didn't and couldn't tell him she felt the same. There was no way she would permit herself to get involved with Jeff when she knew she would be leaving Cavanaugh Island in three weeks or maybe even less. It had taken only one devastating relationship for Kara to learn never to let her heart rule her head. If she had planned to relocate to Angels Landing, she would seriously consider dating Jeff. He was intelligent, a wonderful conversationalist, and very easy on the eyes.

"I'm sorry, Jeff." She exhaled a breath. "Why is it we keeping apologizing to each other?" He angled his head in a gesture she found endearing and had come to look for.

"I don't know, Kara. Actually there isn't anything to apologize for. I—" Whatever he was going to say was preempted when the waitress approached their table.

"Is there anything else I can get you, Sheriff Hamilton?"

"Just the check, Bessie."

Reaching into the pocket of her apron, Bessie placed the check facedown on the table. She stared openly at Kara. "You have to be a Patton because you look just like those folks in the Landing. Which one are—"

"Thank you, Bessie, and keep the change," Jeff said, handing her several twenties and cutting her off. He pushed to his feet, came around the table, and pulled back Kara's chair. "Please let Otis and Miss Vina know that everything was delicious."

"That wasn't very nice," Kara chastised once they were out in the parking lot.

"It wasn't very nice that she tried to get in your business like that," he countered.

"I am a Patton, Jeff, and that means I don't have any business—at least not on Cavanugh Island. Right now, I feel as if my life is a puzzle with several missing pieces. Meanwhile, I have to wait until my mother gets here before she can give me the piece about her relationship with Taylor. Then there's the financial component and the mandate to restore Angels Landing. It's not only a lot to take in, but a great deal to handle in just a couple of weeks. The only constant is that I'm still Kara Newell and Austin Newell is and will always be my father."

Jeff glanced at his watch. "Speaking of finances, I'd better get you over to the bank before it closes."

Three minutes later, Jeff sat in his car in the business district parking lot behind the bank waiting for Kara. He'd revealed things about himself that he never would have said to another woman during their first encounter. He'd thought of it as an encounter and not a date. David had asked him to keep an eye on her, yet keeping an eye on Kara did not translate into asking her to go to the movies with him. She hadn't said yes or no to his offer, so as an optimist he'd hoped she would go with him.

Jeff reclined the seat, crossed his arms over his chest, and closed his eyes. He didn't know what prompted him to tell Kara about his mother, because whenever anyone asked about Juanita Hamilton his reply was she was dead. His mother had died in childbirth, but the details of the events leading up to her death were imprinted on his brain like a permanent tattoo.

Whenever kids asked about his father, he'd either refuse to talk about him or say he'd died a hero. It was easier to lie and tell them his father had died in Vietnam than say he didn't know who his father was.

The drawback to growing up on Cavanaugh Island was no one had to ask who your folks were because everyone knew everyone. Although he rarely interacted with the Pattons, Jeff knew them all. Even when he'd been away for years and returned on leave, his grandmother would catch him up on what had been going on not only in the Cove, but also in Haven Creek and Angels Landing. She'd given him an update on who'd died, gotten married, divorced, moved back and the names and sex of newborns, some who'd been delivered by a midwife and some who were born in hospitals on the mainland.

It wasn't until the year he'd celebrated his tenth birthday that his grandmother felt he was ready to deal with the circumstances behind his birth. Juanita left the island to go to college and had found herself involved with an older student. Corrine had believed she was living on campus when in reality Juanita had moved in with her boyfriend. Juanita hadn't realized she was pregnant until she went into labor late one night. It was only when she'd begun hemorrhaging that her baby's father drove her to the hospital; he'd panicked, leaving her in the hospital's parking lot and drove away. Her body was found the following morning, barely conscious. Juanita was lucid enough to give the ER doctor her contact information and how she'd gotten to the hospital. What she did not reveal was who'd left her there. She delivered a three-pound baby boy but did not survive the ordeal because she'd lost too much blood.

When Corrine and Malachi came to claim her body, they were unable to bring home their grandson until he was able to breathe on his own. Jeff was four months old when his grandparents finally brought him to the Cove. When asked, Corrine told everyone the baby was their grandchild and their daughter had died giving birth to him.

There was gossip that if Corrine hadn't kept her daughter on such a tight leash, Juanita wouldn't have gone buck wild when it came time to leave home for college because Corrine had established a reputation as a strict teacher and an even stricter no-nonsense principal.

Jeff never got to see that side of his grandmother; he'd never had her as a teacher and had only known her as a soft-spoken and somewhat overindulgent grandparent. He didn't know whether her spoiling him was because she'd wanted to make up for him not knowing either of his parents, but that aside he realized he'd had a wonderful childhood. He knew how much his grandmother valued education and Jeff studied longer and harder than necessary, eventually becoming an overachiever.

Once he'd become sexually active there was never a time when he hadn't assumed the responsibility of using protection. Even when a woman claimed she was using an oral contraceptive, he still wore a condom.

A light tapping on the window garnered his attention, and Jeff sat up. Kara had returned. He got out of the car. The wind had picked up, blowing her hair around her face. The temperature had dropped twenty degrees from the day before, topping out at forty instead of the average sixty. He tucked several strands behind her ear. "Did you finish what you had to do?"

Kara shook her head, her windblown hair moving with the motion. "No. I left a message with the manager's secretary that I'd like to see him tomorrow morning. I decided on a morning meeting because I didn't know when you wanted to go to the movies."

Jeff was hard-pressed not to pump his fist. Kara had given him her answer. She would go out with him. However, he had to be careful, very, very careful not to become too emotionally involved only because she was going to leave, just like the other women in his life. He'd lost his mother, past girlfriends, fiancée, and it was inevitable he would eventually lose his grandmother.

"Would you like to take in a matinee, then eat afterward, or see a later show?"

"I'll leave that up to you," Kara said.

"Are you all right?" he asked when he saw her chewing her lip.

Kara flashed a quick, too bright smile, then looked away. "Of course."

Cradling her face in his hands, Jeff forced her to look at him. "What's the matter, Kara?" He lowered his head, their mouths inches apart. "Whatever it is, I want you to remember that I'm here to help you."

Kara anchored her arms under Jeff's shoulders, feeding on his warmth and the strength in his muscular upper body. How could a man she'd known twenty-four hours make her feel so safe, protected? There were men she'd dated for months, a few for years, and she'd continued to see them because it was better than sitting home alone. They took up the empty hours when she wanted and needed to get out of the apartment. However, none of them made her feel quite like she did with Jeff. He'd parried the outburst from the man in the restaurant with a warning about disrespecting her, while she'd lost count of the number of ribald comments and lecherous gazes directed at her whenever she walked down a street or entered a traditional male bastion with another man who'd kept walking as if he were deaf *and* mute.

Going on tiptoe, she pressed her mouth to his ear. "Taylor has been hiding cash in a deposit box," she whispered. "Lots of money."

Jeff froze. "How much are you talking about?"

"I don't know. I stopped counting at fifty thousand."

He buried his face in her hair. "Call David and ask him what you should do."

Kara patted his back when she wanted to kiss him. "Thanks for reminding me. I'll call him later."

Turning his head, Jeff kissed her hair. "I want you to forget about what you found inside the bank and come with me. I'm going to give you an up close and personal guided tour of the island." He glanced down at her feet. "Are you comfortable walking in those shoes?"

"I'm good."

She'd been truthful. Given their height, the shoes were very comfortable. She could wear them all day, walk up and down stairs, and then go out dancing in them. However, she couldn't remember the last time she'd danced. Dancing around the apartment whenever one of her favorite songs came on the radio didn't count. Dawn had accused her of not knowing how to have fun. What the dancer failed to understand was that she would've been more animated if their living arrangements hadn't impacted her very essence.

Kara wanted to be able to walk around in a state of half-dress, hang out in the kitchen on weekends and cook enough food to last her and Dawn for several meals, because her friend and roommate's cooking skills were wholly deficient.

Suddenly she realized spending time on Cavanaugh Island was a respite from the fast pace and noise of her adopted city; the revolving door of people coming and going in the apartment; and not having to deal with clients, updating case records, and listening to her supervisor's critical assessment of the work she did every two weeks. Jeff took her hand, holding it protectively. She hadn't realized how tall and powerfully built he was until they stood side by side. She giggled like a little girl when he bowed gracefully.

"We'll begin the tour with the bank. They are now open on Saturdays in keeping with the banks on the mainland. Next we have the pharmacy, which also houses the post office."

"Does each town have a post office?" Kara asked, shading her eyes with her free hand when she peered through the plate glass window.

"No. It's always been here on the Cove. Before the state built the causeway, mail was delivered by ferry, and the ferry only docks at this end of the island."

She strolled with Jeff, stopping when he entered each store and introduced her to the owners. There was no mistaking their shock when Jeff introduced her as Newell and not Patton.

They'd just walked out of Rose Dukes-Walker's sweetgrass basket shop, A Tisket A Basket, when Jeff waved to a slender blonde woman pushing a stroller with a flaxen-haired little boy. "That's Alice Parker. Her husband is US Representative Jason Parker. His folks were originally from Haven Creek, and they moved from Charleston to the Cove last year. It turned out to be a good thing for the Cove and Landing because it was Jason who made certain we got enough money from the Department of Transportation to build the road between the two towns."

"Where to next?" she asked.

"We won't stop at De Fountain because it's impossible to go there and not buy something. All of the ice cream, sorbet, and gelato are made on the premises. During the summer months there is always a line out the door. Folks come from Charleston just to buy ice cream."

Kara gave him a sidelong glance. "It's *that* good?"

He nodded, smiling. "It's that good."

"The next time I come to the Cove I'll be certain to pick some up."

They strolled past a wine and liquor store, a florist, and a supermarket with a deli and gourmet food sections. "This is Dr. Monroe's office, and his wife's bookstore is on the corner."

Tugging on Jeff's hand, her eyes dancing in excitement, Kara said, "I need to go to the bookstore."

He gave a smile parents usually reserved for their children. "Slow down, baby. If someone sees you running, they'll think I'm chasing you."

"People don't run on Cavanaugh Island?"

"Only on the beach."

"Let go of my hand, Jeff."

"Jeff Hamilton, when did you start dating a Patton?"

Kara heard Jeff when he mumbled an expletive. He

smiled, but the gesture did not reach his eyes. "Good afternoon, Miss Hannah."

Bright green eyes darted between Jeff and Kara. The frames on the oversized glasses perched on the end of her nose matched the vermilion color on her mouth, while clashing with a head of teased champagne-pink hair.

"Good afternoon, Jeff. Aren't you going to introduce me to your *girlfriend*?"

Kara opened her mouth to tell the garish-looking woman that Jeff wasn't her boyfriend, but the slight pressure on her hand when he tightened his grip on her fingers stopped her.

"Kara, this is Mrs. Hannah Forsyth. She's the Cove's librarian and the island's historian. Miss Hannah, Kara Newell."

Hannah blinked, reminding Kara of a heavily lidded owl. "You're not Kara Patton?"

"No, ma'am."

"You have to be related to them because you look just like Theodora Patton when she was your age."

"We're sorry to rush off, Miss Hannah, but we have to get to the bookstore."

The librarian patted her cotton candy wisps. "I just came from there to welcome Deborah back from her maternity leave. Deborah opening the bookstore, and she marrying Dr. Monroe is just wonderful for the Cove."

"I agree," Jeff said at the same time he moved past the librarian. "Have a good evening, Miss Hannah."

"You, too," she said to his departing back.

"What was that all about?" Kara asked when they were out of earshot.

"I should've introduced her as the island gossip instead of the historian. She's a walking tabloid."

Kara couldn't fathom how Jeff knew everyone on the island whereas she didn't know all of the people who lived in the six apartments on her floor of the twenty-two-story high-rise. She'd recognized a few whenever they rode the elevator together but didn't know their names. Most New Yorkers were too busy and self-absorbed with making it in a city that offered something for everyone. They didn't have time to dawdle because they were always going or coming from somewhere.

She didn't know why, but Kara hadn't expected to find a bookstore on the island. So many bookstore chains in large cities had gone out of business or were closing with the advent of the super bookstores that offered coffee shops and reading rooms.

Jeff opened the door to the Parlor Bookstore, and the inviting warmth of a parlor enveloped Kara. The concert piano, comfortable leather grouping, area rugs, Tiffany-style floor lamps and hanging fixtures, low tables, flat screen, and wall-to-wall, floor-to-ceiling shelves packed tightly with books beckoned her to come and stay awhile. It was the perfect place to relax and read.

A tall, slender woman with a profusion of curly hair framing her bare face greeted Jeff with a hug and kiss. She appeared casually chic in a pair of fitted jeans, ballet-type flats, and man-tailored white shirt. He lifted her effortlessly off her feet with one arm.

"Welcome back. How's the family, Debs?"

She rested a hand on Jeff's cheek. "Everyone's well. Georgia told me you stopped by every day when you're out on foot patrol to check on the store."

He nodded. "How's the baby?"

Deborah smiled. "He's getting so big."

Curving an arm around Deborah's waist, he led her to where Kara stood watching the interaction. "Kara, this is Deborah Robinson-Monroe, owner of the Parlor. Debs, Kara Newell."

Kara and Deborah shared a handshake and smile. "It's nice meeting you, Mrs. Monroe."

Deborah waved a hand. "It's Deborah. You're welcome to look around, and as a first-time customer you'll be entitled to a fifteen percent discount—that is, if you decide to buy something."

There was something about Deborah that Kara liked immediately. She had an infectious smile that lit up her entire face. "Thank you."

"There's tea and sweet breads on the table," Deborah offered.

"Oh, no thank you. Jeff and I just came from Jack's."

"Was it your first time there?"

"Yes. And it definitely won't be my last. Do you have any books on gardening?" Kara asked Deborah.

"Yes. They're at the end of this row on the right."

Kara found the section and was surprised to find quite a few books on the subject. Although she hadn't planned on living in Angels Landing, she'd thought about putting in a rose garden.

After a quarter of an hour she decided on a coffee-table book on designing gardens. Deborah processed her credit card, taking off 15 percent and placing the book in a recyclable bag with the bookstore's logo.

"I hope you'll come again."

Kara and Jeff exchanged a glance. "I'm certain I will."

Deborah hugged Jeff again. "I want you and your grandmother to come by the house during Easter week.

Whitney will be home from college, and it will be the first
time we'll all be together since Christmas."

"I'll make certain to bring her by."

"I like Deborah," Kara told Jeff once they left the bookstore to return to where he'd parked his car.

He took the shopping bag from her. "Debs and I go way
back. Her grandmother was the first black teacher to integrate the Cove's white school."

"Don't you think it's strange that she's the only one who
didn't mention my resemblance to the Pattons?"

"Maybe that has something to do with Debs not growing up on the island. She doesn't have the same sensibilities as the rest of us."

"Where did she grow up?"

"Charleston. She used to spend her summers here with
her grandparents."

Kara smiled. "I bet spending summers here was better
than going to a sleepaway camp."

"It was wonderful for kids. After we did our chores we
used to hang out on the beach. Once we were teenagers we
were allowed to hang out on the beach at night. We'd light
a fire and roast marshmallows and make s'mores. The trick
was eating them without ingesting sand. The only thing
we couldn't do was swim at night. Years before a couple of
kids had gone swimming at night and one drowned. It was
weeks before his body washed up off Saint Helena Sound."

"The island is like living in a huge gated community."

Jeff angled his head. "I never thought of it in that way.
But you're right. Everyone looks out for one another. The
kids who live here are careful not to do anything they're not
supposed to do because they never know who's watching
them. It's not like kids on the mainland when parents take

the keys to the car because of an infraction. Here they're truly on lockdown. Once the news gets out that Jamal or Keisha are grounded, it spreads through the island like a lighted fuse. Some of them call me and ask that I stop by the house to check and see if their kids are there."

"That's invasive, Jeff."

"No, it's not. It's about concerned parents, Kara. How many stories have you heard about kids sneaking out and getting into trouble, or they were at the wrong place at the wrong time?"

"Unfortunately too many," she confirmed. "There's no fast-food restaurant or Starbucks on the island, so where do the kids hang out?" Kara asked Jeff.

"There's always the beach, and the Cove and Creek have town squares. Many of them gather there on weekends and in the summer. Most of them entertain their friends in their backyards. A few who have cars drive to Charleston, and those who don't take the ferry. However, the ferry doesn't run all night, so that acts like an unofficial curfew."

"What happens if they miss the ferry?"

"Then they'll have to come out of their pocket for a taxi. The mayor of the towns negotiated with the taxi companies on the mainland to charge a flat fee; otherwise it would be prohibitive to pay what's on the meter."

"Why isn't Cavanaugh Island listed as one of the best places in the country to live and raise children?"

"We want that to be our little secret. That's one of the reasons why we don't want developers buying land here. They'll put up condos, golf courses, and country clubs, and the folks who live here will become second-class citizens in their own towns. Taxes will probably triple and quadruple, and when someone on a fixed income whose family has owned a plot of land for more than a hundred and fifty years can't pay the taxes, they'll lose everything."

Kara thought about her dilemma. Developers wanted Angels Landing and the two thousand acres it sat on. If she did sell it, then it would only impact two people: Willie and Iris Todd. Taylor Patton's will stated that the grounds-keeper and his wife would continue to live out their natural lives in one of the two guesthouses. That might prove problematic if the developer who purchased the land sought to displace them. She couldn't do that to the friendly couple.

"You can't do what?" Jeff asked.

Giving him a confused look, Kara then realized she'd spoken her thoughts aloud. "I can't sell Angels Landing."

His eyebrows lifted. "You were thinking of selling it?"

"Not consciously. But what am I going to do with a house with twenty rooms?"

"The same as Taylor did once his mother passed away. Live in it. Angels Landing is on the National Register of Historic Places; its contents and the land are worth millions and much too important to give away to a bunch of greedy developers."

Kara slipped into the car when Jeff held the door for her. She'd complained to him about living alone in a house with double-digit rooms yet complained to Dawn about the number of people crowding their two-bedroom apartment, aware that she couldn't have it both ways. Either she return to New York and accept Dawn's need to take care of the less fortunate or accept her birthright and restore the house as stated in Taylor Patton's will. Settling back against the leather seat, she stared out the side window. She had time in which to make a decision to stay or leave.

Jeff drove slowly enough for her to see the town hall,

the courthouse, and the library. She noticed signs pointing to the school, ferry, and the Cove Inn, the town's boardinghouse.

"Where are we going?" she asked when he turned off Main Street and onto a road that didn't lead to Angels Landing.

"I want you to meet my grandmother."

"I'm not ready to meet your grandmother."

Jeff gave her a quick glance. "When will you be ready?"

"I don't know."

"Are you always this indecisive?"

"No. And I'm not indecisive."

"You're not ready to meet my grandmother, you don't know whether you'll sell Angels Landing, and you haven't decided whether you're going to stay or leave. In my book, that adds up to indecisiveness."

Kara pushed out her lower lip as she'd done as a child when she was angry or bothered. "You're reading the wrong book."

"I don't think so, Kara. If you want to know about Taylor, then you have to ask Corrine Hamilton, because Gram and Theodora Haynes Patton were once what kids refer to nowadays as BFFs."

Chapter Five

Corrine Hamilton stared at the young woman standing next to her grandson, feeling as if she'd stepped back in time, a time when she and Theodora Haynes were as close as sisters.

An uncertain smile flitted across her features. "Please come and rest yourself."

Jeff placed a hand at the small of Kara's back. "Gram, this is Kara Newell. Kara, my grandmother, Corrine Hamilton."

Kara inclined her head. "It's a pleasure to meet you, Miss Corrine. Jeff speaks very highly of you."

Corrine waved a hand. "That's because Jeffrey is quite biased when it comes to me, and I must admit I'm a bit partisan with him, too." She nodded to the object of her admiration. "Jeffrey, please take Kara into the sunroom. I'll be in directly."

What she didn't tell him was that she had to spend a few moments alone just to compose herself. Jeff had introduced the young woman as Kara Newell when he should've said Kara Patton. She looked enough like her childhood friend to have been her clone.

Walking into the kitchen, Corrine sat down because she didn't think her shaking knees would support her body. She was still sitting when Jeff entered the kitchen. "I'm coming as soon as I get some sweet tea from the refrigerator."

Jeff hunkered down in front of her. "Are you all right, Gram?"

She nodded. "I'm fine, Jeffrey. It's just seeing that girl gave me quite a shock because it's like seeing Teddy come back to life."

Jeff held her hands. "Don't worry about the tea, Gram. I'll bring it in for you."

Corrine stared into a pair of eyes so much like her own. "She's Taylor's daughter." The statement was also a query.

"Yes," he confirmed. "She just found out yesterday when David read the will."

"That poor child must have been shocked."

"She's that and more." Jeff told her about the Pattons' reaction when they were told that Kara had inherited everything. "David asked me to keep an eye on her."

Placing a hand over her mouth, Corrine tried to process what she'd just heard. "You know they want to sell that land," she said after lowering her hand.

"They've been quite vocal about that. And it's not about improvement or growth progress, but greed."

"How does Kara feel about this?"

"She's mentioned that she doesn't want to sell, but…"

"But what, Jeffrey?"

He didn't meet Corrine's eyes. "The will states she has to make Angels Landing her legal residence for five years and restore it or the house and the land will revert to her money-grubbing relatives who don't give a damn about anything or anyone but themselves. And you know they'll sell the land quicker than a cat can flick its tail."

Corrine closed her eyes and shook her head. "I've seen what happened to folks on the other islands in the Lowcountry when developers buy their land, but I thought it would never happen here." She opened her eyes, the dark orbs flashing fire. "Kara can't sell it, and she can't leave."

"I've tried to be subtle when I kind of said that. But subtlety has never been my strong suit," Jeff admitted.

"You're about as subtle as a runaway locomotive."

Leaning forward, Jeff kissed her cheek. "Thanks, Gram."

The seconds ticked by as grandmother and grandson stared at each other, Corrine seeing something in his eyes that she hadn't seen in a while. "I know David asked you to look after her, but what is it about this girl that makes you take a more than passing interest in her?"

There came another pause. "I like her, Gram."

"Like her how?"

He smiled. "Enough to ask her to go to the movies with me tomorrow."

Corrine leaned back in the chair, her gaze narrowing. "You asked her out after knowing her for one day?" There was no mistaking the slight trace of wonder in her voice.

"I had to, Gram, because she was only going to be here a week." Corrine's jaw dropped. "But that's before she told me she would extend her stay to three weeks." He paused. "It's not what you think."

"Now, how do you know what I'm thinking?" Corrine asked.

"Because you have the same look on your face that you

had when I told you I'd proposed to Pamela. It's nothing like that," Jeff added.

Corrine gave him a skeptical look, deciding to drop the subject. "Let me get up and entertain that girl before she thinks we've forgotten our manners." Extending her hands, Corrine allowed Jeff to ease her up off the chair, thinking of how their roles had changed.

From the time she and Malachi had brought their grandson back to Cavanaugh Island, there had never been a time when she'd made a decision without taking into consideration how it would affect Jeff. Most of the time she was left to raise the boy on her own whenever her merchant seaman husband went to sea for months at a time. He'd return with souvenirs from the countries he'd visited, while always bringing her exquisite bolts of fabric from which she fashioned the latest styles she saw in magazines or pattern books.

Her Malachi had died much too young, leaving her to raise Jeffrey on her own. Her period of mourning was brief because she had to focus all of her energies on a toddler that relied solely on her for his very existence. Although she'd had several opportunities to see men and/or remarry, Corrine knew that wasn't going to be possible as long as she had to take care of her grandchild. Her mantra was that she would never put a man before him.

She entered the sunroom to find Kara studying the framed artwork of renowned Southern painter Jonathan Green mounted on a wall of the room that had become her sanctuary. Kara must have sensed she wasn't alone because she turned slowly, eyebrows lifted questionably.

"Yes," Corrine confirmed with a smile, "they are originals. *Majestic Sheets, Richard's Piano,* and *Red Lips* are three of his newer paintings."

Kara turned back to the artwork. "They don't look like oil or watercolor."

"They're acrylic on paper. That's why I could afford to purchase all three." She approached Kara, pointing to a larger painting. "He painted *Grays Hill Blankets* in oh eight, and it was the only oil on canvas I was willing to pay five figures for."

Kara's eyes shimmered with excitement. "You have a very valuable art collection."

Corrine smiled. "It would be a lot more valuable if I bought the one I really want, but I can't see myself putting out a hundred fifty thousand for *Young Bride*. How did you come to know about Jonathan Green's work?"

"There are a lot of street vendors in New York, and one in particular carries reproductions of his artwork."

"Please sit down, Kara." She gestured to a love seat covered with a sunny-yellow fabric with bright green leaves. Waiting until her guest sat, Corrine took her seat in a matching armchair opposite her and rested her feet on a like-patterned footstool. Her sharp gaze took in everything about the young woman who unknowingly had enthralled her grandson, even if he wasn't willing to admit it. She'd noticed the proprietary way Jeffrey had placed his hand at the small of her back and the softening of his gaze whenever he looked at Kara. He was in denial with a capital *D* and unaware that she knew him as well as she knew her own mind.

Corrine knew Jeffrey had been less than lucky in the romance department and that he'd sworn off forming lasting relationships with women, but that was when he was in the military. What he still hadn't accepted was that the life of a civilian was vastly different from that of a career soldier. Her fervent prayer was he'd realize that before she passed on.

Crossing her feet at the ankles, she met Kara's steady gaze. "Does it bother you when folks say you look exactly like Taylor's mother?"

"Do I?" Kara asked softly.

Corrine was preempted from answering when Jeff entered the room with a pitcher of tea. He placed it on a glass-covered table. "Aren't you going to join us?" she asked him when she saw he'd brought only two iced tea glasses.

"Not right now. I just got a call from Dr. Monroe that some kid came into his office with a superficial gunshot wound. The boy claims his older brother was cleaning his handgun and hadn't realized there was still a bullet in the chamber. Apparently he pulled the trigger and the gun went off, the bullet grazing the fleshy part of his upper arm."

"But you're off duty, Jeffrey."

Leaning down, Jeff kissed her hair. "I'm never off duty. I'll be back as soon as I check out their story and file a report." He gave Kara a long, penetrating stare, then turned on his heel and walked out.

Kara pushed off the love seat. "Do you mind if I pour the tea?"

Corrine smiled. "Not at all. Thank you," she said when Kara handed her a glass. Waiting until Kara had filled her glass, she took a sip, then set it on a coaster. "Is it sweet enough for you, Kara?"

"It's perfect."

"Good. Now, back to your question about you looking like Theodora Patton. The answer is yes. Teddy was one of my best friends even though kids from the Cove didn't mix too freely with those from the Landing or the Creek."

"Why was that?"

Corrine ran a hand over her short, silver curls. "I don't

know. It'd been that way for years and continues to this day."

"How did you meet her?"

"At that time all of the black children on the island took the ferry to a segregated mainland school. We socialized in school, but once the ferry dropped us off, we went our separate ways. However, it was different for Teddy and me. I'd beg my mother to let me have playdates with her, and it continued until they finally integrated the schools on the island. She made new friends, and I bonded with the kids here."

"Did you continue to keep in touch?" Kara asked.

Corrine toyed with the tiny gold hoop in her left ear. "Yes. We'd call each other, and once we left for college, we'd write. Teddy shocked everyone when she announced her engagement to Cornelius Patton because no one knew they were seeing each other. The Haynes were working-class folks who brainwashed Teddy into believing that she had to marry up, and landing a Patton was like having the cake with the icing and the cherry. They had a big, lavish wedding at the mansion, and I knew then we'd moved in different directions because I wasn't invited to the wedding."

Kara gasped. "That's horrible."

"I'd thought so, too. I later learned her mother said she didn't want me in the wedding party because I'd lowered my standards to take up with a man without a college education. She was a fine one to talk because she hadn't finished high school. My late husband worked for the post office before he signed up as a cook on a merchant ship. It was hard at first because he was out to sea nine months out of the year, but whenever he came home, it was Christmas and New Year's all rolled into one. My parents took care of our daughter while I taught, and when she was old enough to go to school, I took her with me.

"Every time Teddy had a baby she threw a lavish party with everyone bearing gifts as if the new baby was royalty. She had two sons and three daughters before she had Taylor. He was a beautiful baby with a wonderful disposition. Everyone doted on him: his parents, grandparents, and his sisters. Once he became a teenager and showed an interest in girls, Teddy sabotaged every relationship he had."

Unconsciously Kara's brow furrowed. "But why, Miss Corrine?"

"There were rumors that she wanted him for herself."

"Oh no," Kara drawled at the same time she scrunched up her nose.

"As I said, there were rumors. By this time Cornelius was a deputy solicitor general, and when the Supreme Court was in session, he divided his time between South Carolina and Washington, DC. The girls went off to college and married and had a bunch of babies. When it came time for Taylor to go to college, Teddy wouldn't allow him to attend an out-of-state school."

"But he had to go to an out-of-state college if he'd met my mother."

Corrine paused to take a sip of tea. "She relented when Cornelius resigned his position and came back to South Carolina and opened a practice in Charleston. That's when Taylor left to enroll in Morehouse."

Kara bent her head and studied her clasped hands. "My mother went to Spelman." Her head came up slowly as she awkwardly cleared her throat. "I suppose that's where they met." Spelman and Morehouse were brother and sister colleges. Her eyes filled with tears, and she blinked them back.

"Are you all right, baby?"

"I'm fine, Miss Corrine."

"I can stop now if you want."

"No, please don't. I need...want to hear as much about...Taylor before I talk to my mother."

Kara's expectant stare bore into Corrine. The poor child didn't know who she was because someone had lied to her about her paternity. She didn't blame the girl's mother as much as she did Taylor Patton. He knew he was her father, yet he'd withheld that information, revealing it only in death. As far as Corrine was concerned, it was the coward's way of settling an old score.

"Taylor came home changed."

"Changed how, Miss Corinne?"

"It was like he'd grown up overnight. He'd left South Carolina a boy and had returned a man. Many said it was because he'd gotten out from under Teddy's thumb. After he graduated he went to work in a bank in Columbia. His daddy died, and Teddy was like a lost soul. Then his oldest sister was diagnosed with an inoperable brain tumor, and she died. Teddy became an emotional cripple and rarely was seen outside the house. She neglected her award-winning garden, most of the flowers going to seed, and she had the plaque designating Angels Landing a National Register of Historic Places removed because she claimed it reminded her too much of Cornelius. Last year it made National Historic Landmark status.

"There was talk that Teddy had come down with insomnia. Lights burned at the house twenty-four hours a day, seven days a week. Iris was concerned because she'd stopped eating. Taylor held onto his mother for as long as he could, but toward the end she had to be confined to a nursing home."

"How long did she live there?"

"She didn't last a month. The family had a private funeral with just a graveside service. I don't know if you've had a chance to tour the property, but there is a cemetery... No, I take that back. There are two cemeteries at Angels Landing. One white and one black. That practice ended with Cornelius when he was buried in the white section. I always thought it so asinine that people have separate cemeteries based on race and religion when dirt is dirt, and the Lord said he would be the one doing the separating."

Kara smiled for the first time since Corrine began her discourse on the Pattons. "I agree. Was Angels Landing a working plantation?"

Corrine nodded. "It was the largest plantation producing Sea Island cotton, rice, and indigo. The east end of your property is a swamp with poisonous snakes and gators, and heaven knows what else is lurking below the surface of the water. There are also egrets, herons, and someone took a picture of an eagle's nest in a cypress tree. Cabins were built near the swamp as a deterrent for slaves attempting to run away."

"Where would they go, Miss Corrine? After all, they were on an island surrounded by water. And if they did make it to the mainland, where would they hide?"

"Not everyone in the South was pro-slavery. There was a wealthy cotton merchant, James Whitcomb, who hid runaways, then took them North with him, passing them off as his slaves. He'd managed to get away with the ruse for a year until a patroller recognized him, called the authorities, and he was sentenced to hang. The governor commuted his sentence to twenty years because James was a distant cousin. He was sent to Old Jail, the same prison where Denmark Vesey spent his last days in the tower before being hanged. It remains a mystery to this day, but James had managed to escape and stow away in a ship transporting cotton to the mills in the North. After that, increased restrictions were placed on slaves and free blacks in Charleston as a result of the Vesey insurrection, and at that time the law required that all black seamen be housed in the Old Jail while they were in port."

Leaning forward, Kara caught and held Corrine's eyes. "Were any of those escaped slaves from Angels Landing?"

"A few. But they weren't your ancestors."

"Are you saying that Taylor's ancestors were so wedded to their servitude they made no attempt to escape?"

"Why would you run away when you were already free?" Corrine had answered Kara's question with a question of her own. "Please excuse me," she said when the phone rang. She picked up the receiver, listening to the velvety soft, deep voice. "Okay. No problem." She hung up, watching Kara staring at her. She did look like Theodora, but upon closer inspection she was softer, prettier. Her face was rounder, cheekbones higher, and her mouth was lush. It was her eyes with glints of greenish-gray and gold that reminded her so much of Theodora.

"That was Jeffrey. He's tied up at the station house and won't be able to drive you back to Angels Landing. I'll take you back."

"Are you certain I won't put you out, because I could always call Mrs. Todd and ask her to pick me up?"

Corrine lowered her feet and stood up. "Of course you're not putting me out. Since I retired I have to find things to do to keep myself busy. Last year I had a health scare when I found myself in the hospital with a blocked artery. It weakened my heart, so I have to be careful not to get exhausted."

Kara rose to her feet. "I'm going to be here for at least three weeks, and if there is anything you want me to help you with, just let me know."

"Thanks for asking, baby, but I'm okay here. Jeffrey hired someone to come in twice a week to clean, so there's not much for me to do except cook. Speaking of cooking, I'd like to invite you over for Sunday dinner."

"I'd love to come, but I'm not certain when my mother is coming to town."

"Bring her with you. I'm certain she'll be tired from traveling and would enjoy sitting down to a home-cooked meal."

"Thank you, Miss Corrine. That's very kind of you."

"It has nothing to do with kindness and everything to do with Lowcountry hospitality."

It wasn't until she was back at Angels Landing that Kara thought about what Jeffrey's grandmother had said about Lowcountry hospitality. Her newfound relatives hadn't shown her the warmth and welcome but blatant hostility. They viewed her as an interloper, taking what they'd considered theirs because they were legitimate Pattons.

Sitting on a rocker on the front porch, she stared out at the verdant landscape that resembled green velvet. Countless trees, draped in Spanish moss, stood like sentinels along the path leading up to the historic house. Closing her eyes, she imagined horse-drawn carriages filled with men and women in their silks and finery coming up the unpaved path to Angels Landing for a ball.

Instead of horses it was now cars that brought people to the house. She opened her eyes. Mrs. Todd told her that not much had changed over the years with the exception of indoor plumbing and electricity and updated appliances, while the antebellum mansion upon close inspection still looked run-down. The smaller kitchen hadn't changed. There was still the massive black wood-burning stove with an oven large enough to roast a small pig.

Something Corrine said about the property receiving landmark status the year before made her think of Taylor's mandate that she had to restore the house to its original condition while making Angels Landing her residence for the next five years. She wasn't certain how long it would take to complete the restoration; however, she knew the cash in the safe-deposit box was more than enough to pay an engineer to ascertain the house's structural stability and to refinish floors and replace wallpaper, drapes, and rugs. And she had to make sure that Mr. and Mrs. Todd received a lump sum of fifty thousand dollars for their dedication and loyalty.

Opening the door, she switched on the light, staring at the space where Taylor had probably spent hours working for his clients. It was quintessentially masculine from the massive carved antique mahogany desk and cordovan leather sofa and chairs. She stared at the faded rug with a narrow strip lighter than the rest, leading her to believe this was where Taylor had paced up and down its length.

Built-in bookshelves were packed tightly with books, some with worn leather bindings. Kara walked over to an armoire and attempted to open it, but the doors didn't budge. Then she realized it was locked. She thought of the envelope David had given her with keys. There had to be one that unlocked the armoire.

She retrieved the envelope, spilling the keys out on the

top of the desk. There was one skeleton-type key, and when she inserted it into the lock and turned it, Kara wondered what she would find behind its locked doors.

She couldn't control the runaway beating of her heart when opening a drawer to find bank statements with staggering balances. There were statements from five different mainland banks and the one in Sanctuary Cove. She opened another drawer, finding copies of Taylor's tax returns for the past ten years. He'd reported income from his corporation, interest and dividends from bank accounts and bonds. There were copies of checks on the taxes owing attached to the forms.

Sinking down to the floor, Kara clapped a hand over her mouth. She felt faint and had begun to hyperventilate. How could she go from a middle-income, overworked social worker who was lucky if she could save fifty dollars a month to someone with enough money to buy an apartment in Trump Tower?

It was all too much for her take in so quickly. She lay back on the rug, staring up at the ceiling. Even if she didn't work another day in her life, she would have enough money to last her for the rest of her days.

"She must restore Angels Landing to its original condition." David's words echoed in her head as if he were in the room with her. He wasn't talking about the house but the entire plantation: the house, gardens, and outbuildings.

The doorbell chimed throughout the house, and Kara scrambled to her feet. Mrs. Todd worked from eight to six, then retreated to her two-bedroom guesthouse to spend the evening with her husband.

Kara made her way down the hallway to the staircase, curbing a childish urge to slide down the banister.

The marble floor in the living room and entryway felt cool under her bare feet. Going on tiptoe, she peered through the security eye, seeing the distorted image of a familiar face. She unlocked the door and opened it. Standing on the porch wearing a black T-shirt and jeans was Jeff, and seeing him caused her mouth to suddenly go dry. She had only caught a glimpse of his upper body when he'd taken off his jacket to show her his tattoo, but the cotton fabric stretched over broad shoulders, massive pectorals, and bulging biceps left little to the imagination.

"Hi." The single word was torn from the back of her throat.

"May I come in?"

"Of course." She stepped aside and he walked in, and that's when she saw what he held in his hand. "You brought my book."

Jeff felt as if he'd been punched in the stomach. He knew Kara was sexy, but seeing her in a skimpy tank top and shorts made him feel things he didn't want to feel at that time, as he thought of what he'd wanted to do with her. And because of his height advantage he could see her breasts.

He handed her the book. "I thought you'd want to read it."

"Thank you." A blush darkened her cheeks. "I'm forgetting my manners. Would you like something to eat or drink?"

Jeff had just stopped by to drop off the book but quickly changed his mind. "I'll take coffee if it's not too much trouble for you."

"Of course not." Kara gave him a sensual smile. "I usually have a cup before I go to bed because drinking something hot helps me fall asleep."

He wanted to tell her there were other things guaranteed

to help her sleep but quickly banished his traitorous musings. Perhaps his grandmother was right. He'd been without a woman much too long.

He loved how she looked from the front but didn't mind the view as she walked away. He followed her, his gaze fixed on the shape of her behind in the shorts that revealed more than they covered. If he didn't get it together, Jeff knew he was going to embarrass himself. At forty he still had a healthy libido, but he'd learned to control his urges with strenuous physical workouts. There were mornings when he would get up and run the length of the island or do a hundred push-ups. The "once a marine, always a marine" motto carried over to daily physical training and conditioning. At six four he'd managed to keep his weight at 225, and if he went five pounds above what he considered his peak weight, he substituted more fruit, vegetables, and protein for the carbs.

He'd accused Kara of having a possible eating disorder but seeing so much of her body proved him wrong. She was slender but definitely not skinny. Women he'd found himself attracted to usually were more full figured, yet that hadn't stopped him from pursuing Kara. He was definitely interested in her and had to admit that bringing her the book was just an excuse to see her again.

"My grandmother said she loved talking with you this afternoon."

Kara stared at him over her shoulder. "All I did was ask questions. She did most of the talking. Please sit down." She gestured to a chair in the dining nook. "I'm glad I did get a chance to talk to her because she helped me to make up my mind about something."

Jeff watched as Kara washed her hands and went

through the motions of measuring coffee into an automatic coffeemaker. "What was that?"

"I'm going to stay."

He went still. "What do you mean stay?"

"I'm going to stay and restore the property."

"How long will that take?"

She filled the carafe with water from the sink and poured it into the well. "I don't know. I have to call an architect and have them come out and inspect the house and outbuildings. I'll also have to hire a landscape architect to see if the gardens can be revived."

"That's not going to take three weeks, Kara."

Resting a hip against the countertop, she folded her arms under her breasts. "Very funny, Jeff."

He smiled, coming to his feet and closing the distance between them. Wrapping his arms around her waist, he lifted her off her feet until their faces were level. Not giving her a chance to react, he brushed his mouth over hers in a light kiss. "I'd like to offer you a very special welcome to Cavanaugh Island."

Curving her arms around his thick neck, Kara pressed her cheek to his. "Do you welcome everyone like this?"

"Hell no! Just the pretty women."

Jeff didn't want to believe Kara felt as good as she looked and smelled. He buried his face against the column of her neck, not wanting to let go. But he knew he had to because he was becoming more aroused with each passing second.

Kara kissed his cheek. "Thank you for the very special welcome."

Slowly, deliberately, he let her down until her feet touched the floor. He cleared his throat. "You made this decision without talking with your mother?"

Her catlike eyes smiled at him. "Yes. The pieces of the puzzle are coming together."

"I'm happy for you, Kara."

"Thank you."

His expression stilled, becoming somber. "You know this news isn't going to sit too well with your cousins."

Kara sobered. "Even if I give them what they want, they still won't be satisfied. When it comes to greed, you have to ask yourself, when is enough, enough? And the answer is it's never enough."

Cradling her face in his large hands, Jeff kissed the end of her nose when it was her mouth he wanted to kiss and smiled when he heard the soft intake of breath. It was as if he couldn't stop touching her. "I'm still going to stop by whenever I go on patrol. I'll tell my deputies to do the same."

"Don't you think you're overreacting?" she asked.

"No, I'm not. After all greed is one of the seven deadly sins."

Kara patted his shoulder. "I promise I'll be careful. Would you mind if we postpone going to the movies tomorrow?"

"No," he said when he wanted to say the opposite. "Now that you're staying we can go anytime."

"Thank you for being so understanding."

"What I understand is that you're going to be a very busy woman. I'm not going anywhere, and neither are you."

Easing out of his embrace, Kara stared at the middle of his chest. "I think the coffee is ready."

"Aren't you going to join me?" Jeff asked when he noticed she'd only taken down one cup.

"I'll have mine later. I'm not ready to go to bed now." She set the cup on the table, then opened the refrigerator to get a small container of cream. "There's sugar on the table if you want it."

"No thanks. I usually drink my coffee without sugar."

Standing behind him, Kara rested a hand in the middle of his back. He went completely still when he felt the warmth of her palm through his T-shirt. Jeff knew they were playing a dangerous game touching each other, but he didn't want it to stop.

"What's the matter, Sheriff Hamilton? You're sweet enough?"

Reaching around his body, he pulled her to stand between his outspread legs. "Oh, sweet thing. Don't you know you're my everything?" he sang.

"Uh-ah, Chaka Khan wannabe."

"Don't knock her, baby. The girl can still blow."

"I know that," Kara admitted. "Drink your coffee before it gets cold. I'm sorry I don't have any doughnuts in the house. Maybe next time."

Jeff gave her a layered look. "Now you're trying to stereotype me. Not all cops drink coffee and eat doughnuts."

"The ones in New York do."

"Again, that's a stereotype. What if I said all social workers are bleeding heart liberals?"

"It wouldn't bother me none because I am."

Jeff gave her a long look. "Good for you."

Her eyebrows lifted a fraction. "You approve?"

"I approve." He took her hand. "Come sit with me." Jeff took longer than he normally would to drink the coffee, taking furtive sips to prolong the time spent with Kara. "Thanks for the coffee," he said after he'd drained the cup.

She stood up, took the cup, and placed it in the sink. "I'll walk you out. I don't know if your grandmother told you, but she invited me to Sunday dinner."

This disclosure shocked Jeff. When he'd returned, his grandmother hadn't mentioned this to him. "Are you coming?"

"I told her I would if my mother doesn't come in before then."

"Bring her with you."

"That's what Miss Corrine said."

Jeff stopped at the door. "The deputy will probably come by tomorrow, but I'll definitely see you Sunday afternoon."

Going on tiptoe, Kara kissed his cheek. "Thank you for showing me around."

"Remember, we still have to see Haven Creek."

She nodded as he opened the door, then closed it behind him. Standing on the porch, Jeff waited until he heard the locks click into place. Walking to his car, he didn't know what to make of Kara. His past experience with women had always been tenuous because of his dedication to the military. Many of them had become Miss Right Now. Pamela Singleton had been the exception. He'd found himself in love with her and proposed marriage; however, she'd ended the engagement once she realized she hadn't wanted to become an officer's wife.

Jeff knew it would be different with Kara. He was now a civilian, and she'd made a commitment to live on the island. He'd thought of her as a distraction—a very welcome distraction that he couldn't help wanting to be around.

Other than reuniting with his grandmother, Jeff was glad he'd come home.

Chapter Six

Kara woke more tired than she had been when she'd crawled into bed after two in the morning. She spent hours going through Taylor's financial records. She also found a slip of paper in an envelope marked "computer password." His password was the month and day of her birth: Kara1219. Once she logged on, Kara lost track of time as she researched design companies specializing in historic restoration. She'd found two based in Charleston. There was also the architectural firm in Haven Creek she planned to contact.

Her eyes were blurry by the time she'd searched out historic places and landmarks in South Carolina and other Southern states. If she was going to restore Angels Landing, then she wanted to know what it entailed. Kara's fatigue disappeared when she happened upon the website for Middleton Place on Ashley River Road in between

North Charleston and Summerville. Her excitement escalated once she realized there were tours of the house and
the landscaped gardens. Transfixed by the colorful photographs of the well-preserved, mid-eighteenth-century
house, ideas were swirling around in her head as she
printed out the pages. Corrine had mentioned Theodora's
garden, and Kara believed it was a coincidence that she'd
purchased a book devoted to designing gardens.

Jeff and Corrine had answered her questions, yet she
still had more. The issue of her paternity would come
from her mother, but would anyone tell her why Theodora
had elected to leave the house to her bachelor son rather
than her children who'd married and had children of their
own? Wouldn't it have been better to hear the footsteps and
laughter of her grandchildren in the twenty-room mansion
than near or complete silence by a single soul?

Rising slightly on an elbow, she peered at the clock on
the bedside table. It was after eight, time to get up and start
the day.

Fortified with a breakfast of grits, eggs and strips of
melt-in-your-mouth Smithfield ham, and a cup of coffee, Kara set off for Haven Creek. She'd left a voice mail
message for David, and he'd returned her call. When she
explained what she'd found in the safe-deposit box, David
revealed he was aware that Taylor had stored cash in the
box the same way people either put money under their
mattresses or in shoe boxes. He'd reminded her she had
power of attorney and that she should close out Taylor's
accounts and reopen them in her name within ten days from
the reading of the will.

Her decision to contact the local architectural firm was
predicated on their familiarity with the island. There was

no doubt their archives would have plans and photographs of the 160-year-old house and outbuildings. Decelerating to less than ten miles an hour, Kara maneuvered into the parking lot behind the two-story building. Her appointment was for eleven and she was ten minutes early.

Walking around to the front, she opened the door and stepped into a reception area. Rattan chairs and love seats covered with plush colorful seat and back cushions, a raffia rug, and ceiling fans made her feel as if she'd stepped into a Caribbean bungalow. She gave the receptionist her name, then sat down to wait for Morgan Dane.

Kara's head popped up when a woman approached her. Tall, slender, and dressed entirely in black—turtleneck, stretch pants, and high-heeled booties—she'd pulled her braided hair into a ponytail. The large turquoise pendant suspended from a thick silver chain matched the studs in her ears. With her flawless sable-brown skin, delicate features, and thin body, she could've been a model.

"Miss Newell?"

Kara stood up. "Yes."

"I'm Morgan Dane." Her dark eyes sparkled when she smiled. "I know you were probably expecting a man, but my mama decided to name me after my granddaddy."

"Kara."

Morgan offered her hand, smiling. "Please call me Morgan. Come with me. We'll talk in the conference room because workmen are painting my office."

They sat at a small round table in a conference room with walls covered with black-and-white photographs of historic buildings and homes. Kara recognized Middleton Place and Drayton Hall.

"Are you familiar with Angels Landing?"

"The house or the plantation?" Morgan asked.

"The entire property. I've just inherited the house and—"

"So you're the one who has the Pattons going ballistic," Morgan interrupted.

Momentarily speechless, Kara thought the woman was mocking her until she saw her smirk. "You've heard?"

"Who hasn't?" Morgan's expression and tone changed when she said, "When the receptionist gave me your name, I had no idea who you were. This is not gossip, but you should know that a few of the Pattons have been less than complimentary where it concerns you. Harlan in particular."

Kara's jaw tightened. "What I'm about to propose is going to make them even more upset. I plan to restore the property, and I'd like an appraisal from your firm. I also want to be candid and let you know I intend to check out two other architectural firms before I make a final decision."

Morgan laced her fingers together in her lap. "I appreciate your candor. However, I doubt whether the other firms would be as familiar with the property as I am since I live here. Would they know that the east end of Angels Landing is a cypress swamp? That there is evidence of several winnowing barns? And that seven of the original cabins in the slave village are still intact?

"I'm certain they could," Morgan said, answering her own questions, "but it would take them a lot longer to gather all the information than I would because I've lived on Cavanaugh all my life. I left to attend the Savannah College of Art and Design, and instead of accepting a position with a very prestigious firm in California, I decided to return home because I wanted to preserve the Gullah culture, and that can only be done if Gullahs take care of what has been passed down for generations."

"You sound very passionate about what you do," Kara said, smiling.

"I'm as serious as a heart attack. I'm more than aware of developers sniffing around the Landing like bloodhounds chasing an escaped prisoner, and I don't like it. If one person sells out, then that translates into everyone selling out. All they have to do is wave some paper around, and it's all she wrote. If you sell off ten acres and the developers put up a hotel or an inn—they prefer the term *inn* because it sounds warmer and fuzzier than hotel—what do you think is going to happen to the Cove Inn?"

"It'll probably lose business."

"No, Kara. It won't lose business. It will go *out* of business. Once you build an inn, you'll have to feed your guests. A restaurant will be in direct competition with Jack's Fish House. And of course they'll have to have a souvenir shop. That would put folks here on Haven Creek in direct competition with what they're selling in their shops."

Kara stared at Morgan, complete surprise freezing her features. She'd sought out the architectural design firm to get an idea of what it would cost to restore her property, not to get a history lesson or listen to a rant defaming developers. First it was David, then Jeff, and now Morgan.

Slowly, as if pulled by a taut wire, Kara leaned forward. "I did not come here to talk about selling the property, Morgan. I'm here because I need an estimate of how much it would cost and how long it will take for your firm to restore Angels Landing Plantation to its original state circa 1854. I understand your opposition to developers coming in and literally changing the landscape and their impact on the lives of the people who live here because I'm now one of those people. I may be a couple of things, but I've never been accused of being a sellout." Morgan lowered her eyes in a gesture Kara could only interpret as embarrassment.

"I'm sorry if I offended—"

"I'm not offended," Kara said, interrupting her. "It's just that I didn't expect to be reminded about giving away my birthright yet again."

"I'm not the first person to tell you?"

Kara laughed, the sound seemingly shattering the tension. "No. I've heard it from David Sullivan and Sheriff Hamilton. There are probably a few others who feel the same way but haven't said anything to me. At least not yet."

Twin dimples kissed Morgan's cheeks when she smiled. "Folks here usually don't bite their tongues when they have something to say."

"Like you?"

Morgan nodded. "Yes, like me."

Kara stared at the photograph of Middleton Place. "When it comes to historical restoration I know we're on the same page." Her gaze swung back to the woman sitting across the table from her. "This is only my third day on the island, and I have yet to tour what you call the Angels Landing Plantation; so other than the guesthouses, I haven't seen any of the outbuildings."

"Do you want me to go with you to see them?"

Taken aback by the question, Kara hesitated. "When would you like to see it?"

"What about now? That is if you don't have anything planned for this afternoon."

Kara glanced down at her pencil skirt. When she'd gotten dressed earlier that morning, she hadn't planned on traipsing over several thousand acres in a fitted skirt, cashmere twinset, and pumps. She smiled. It was about time she looked over what Taylor had bequeathed to her and what her cousins so passionately coveted.

"No, I can't right now. What other time would you be able to meet?"

Morgan checked her watch. "Let's make it one."

Pushing back her chair, Kara stood up and extended her hand. "Great, then I'll see you at one."

Kara returned to Angels Landing, Mrs. Todd opening the door before she could turn the knob. The house remained unlocked during the day. It was only at night that Kara felt uncomfortable leaving the doors unlocked, especially since she lived there alone.

"Good afternoon, Mrs. Todd."

"Good afternoon. I was just leaving to bring my Willie his lunch." She held up a cloth-covered wicker basket. "Once that man gets on his riding mower he doesn't want to get off."

Men and their toys, Kara thought. "I know. It's like getting a brand-new car. I've known men to sleep in theirs. Someone is coming here at one, and we're going to tour the property to ascertain what needs to be done to make this place beautiful again."

Mrs. Todd nodded slowly. "Mr. Taylor knew what he was doing when he left everything to you. If some of his nieces or nephews got this property, the scavengers would've been here minutes after the will was read to start taking this place apart."

"Don't worry, Mrs. Todd. That's not going to happen. Not now or years from now. I'll make certain of that."

"You may look like your grandmomma, but you got your daddy's heart. Out of all of Miss Teddy's children, Taylor

was the best. Enough jawin'. Let me get this to Willie 'fore
it gets cold. I left your lunch in the warming drawer."

Bending slightly, Kara kissed her cheek. "Thank you."
Knowing she'd shocked the housekeeper with the display
of affection, Kara walked into the house, leaving Mrs.
Todd staring at her back.

With a light step, she raced up the staircase to her bedroom to change. Fortunately she had packed a pair of rain
boots. Kara entered her bedroom, stopping abruptly when
she saw the bouquet of pale pink roses on the table in the
sitting area. Attached to the vase was a balloon stamped
with "Welcome Home."

Walking over to the table, she picked up the card. A
smile curved her mouth when she read the bold script:
"Thank you for staying. Hugs, Jeff."

"You're welcome," she whispered to the empty room,
reminding herself to call Jeff and thank him for the
thoughtful gesture.

If he was glad she'd decided to live on the island, she
was equally excited she'd made the decision to stay. This is
not to say it had been an easy decision because she would
have to resign her job and give up a way of life she'd grown
accustomed to for fifteen years. She'd come to New York
to attend college and stayed. Except for her noticeably
Southern drawl, she'd become a New Yorker in every sense
of the word.

Kara had learned to walk quickly in order to navigate the sidewalks teeming with pedestrians, and she
also learned to push her way into a crowded subway car
so she wouldn't have to wait for another that would be
just as crowded. She'd adopted the practice of not making eye contact with anyone on the street; not speaking

to strangers; not responding to ribald catcalls from men; and not picking up her drink at a bar, a club, or party once she'd averted her gaze. And she didn't give out her address, home or cell numbers arbitrarily.

The men she'd dated were usually friends of friends. Several had progressed beyond the platonic stage, and a few ended before they'd begun. Kara could not get used to men expecting her to take off her panties on the first date. Firstly she hadn't known them well enough to take their relationship to the next level, and secondly she didn't know whether they were some crazed deviant who would rape or, even worse, kill her.

Kara knew she had to call Dawn and let her know that she'd decided to relocate. She retrieved her cell and punched in Dawn's number, activating the speaker feature as she undressed. "Hey, Miss Dee."

"Hey you," Dawn drawled.

"Did I wake you up?"

"No. I was just taking a power nap before I go into the studio. Kara?"

"What is it, Dawn?"

"You're right about the apartment becoming an SRO. Jackie stopped by yesterday with a couple of guys, and they stayed up all night drinking beer while playing poker. I didn't get more than an hour of sleep. And you know I have to be alert when working with my students. Their parents pay big bucks for me to teach the little cherubs to dance."

Kara slipped into a pair of jeans, buttoning the waistband. They fit a bit more snugly than they had when she'd worn them before, and she knew it had come from eating three meals a day. She made a mental note to begin walking along the beach for exercise.

"I'm not going to say I told you so."

"Tell me, girl, so I can experience a reality check."

"I told you so, Dawn Ramsey."

"Thanks. Now I can get rid of the guilt."

"Since you're newly guilt-free, what are you going to do about it?"

"I'm going to take a break from friends. Maybe your pep talk and not having you around for a few days brought me to my senses."

"You're not going to have me around for more than a few days, Dawn."

"What aren't you saying? And please don't tell me something I'm not equipped to deal with right now."

Kara knew putting off the inevitable wouldn't make it any easier for Dawn or herself. "I'm staying." The two words made her heart sink like a stone in her chest.

"You can't, Kara."

"I have to, Dawn."

Kara told her why she'd decided to relocate to Angels Landing. "I can't walk away, not when I have a chance to possibly build a relationship with a family I never knew I had."

There came a pregnant pause until Dawn said, "I understand where you're coming from because you told me you don't have a large family, but that still doesn't make me feel any better."

"I'm not going to leave you hanging, Dee. I'm going to send you a check for my share of the rent until the lease expires."

"You've got it like that?"

Kara smiled. "Yes, Dee. I've got it like that."

"Well, damn! Did you hit the mother lode?"

"Just about," she admitted. "I want you to take off and come visit me."

Dawn's distinctive Eddie Murphy laugh came through the earpiece. "I thought you'd never ask."

"Come on, sister. You know you can come hang out with me anytime. The only thing I'm going to ask is that you not bring your funky bunch with you."

Dawn laughed again. "Have you forgotten that I'm trying to rid myself of the funky bunch?"

"That should be easy, Dawn. We live in a building with a doorman, and when he calls to ask if he should let Freeloader Freddie in, just say no. Or you could call management and tell them that you're not accepting visitors. That way you can save face whenever you run into them. Better yet. Blame it on management, and tell them that your neighbors are complaining about the number of people who are hanging out at the apartment, and if it continues, then you're going to lose your lease."

"You're a genius, Kara."

"No, I'm not. I'm just a little more practical than you are. Look, Dee, I have to go. But I promise to call you in a couple of days with an update of my life in the Lowcountry."

Kara didn't know why, but she felt like crying. She'd heard the pain and indecision in her former roommate's voice when Dawn said she understood why Kara had decided to live in South Carolina but still wasn't too happy about it.

What she hadn't told Dawn was that she was frightened, more frightened than she'd ever been in her life. New York City had become her second home. Of course, she'd experienced some anxiety moving from Little Rock to New York, but that was normal for college students when they attended out-of-state schools. They were little birds ready, yet hesitant to leave the nest. First there was the college tours, then the monumental decision of what college they would attend.

Her parents didn't want her to move so far away. After all, she was their only child, and both tried to hold onto her for as long as possible. She'd reassured them New York wasn't that far away, and in the end they relented. Kara suspected they were more concerned with her living in a big city than the actual distance, and for the first six months she called them weekly to let them know how she was doing.

After a while the calls decreased to every other week, then finally to once or twice a month. She had made new friends and had her first serious boyfriend, who'd eventually become her lover. They parted amicably during her junior year, and Kara concentrated on pulling up her grades because she'd planned to enroll in graduate school.

She dated sporadically throughout grad school and had a serious liaison with another social work intern. She wanted a commitment while he wanted an open relationship wherein they would date other people. Doubt and cynicism dogged Kara whenever she was introduced to a man, and after a while she could care less whether she dated or not.

Kara knew the decision to relocate to Angels Landing would've been a lot more difficult if she had someone with whom she was in love. She'd always told her mother she wanted what Jeannette had: a loving, loyal, and protective husband.

Opening a drawer in the triple dresser, she took out a lightweight wool sweater. Daytime temperatures were in the low forties, almost twenty degrees lower than the average high for the region. She pulled on her patterned houndstooth rain boots and pushed her cell into the back pocket of her jeans. Running a large-toothed comb through her hair, she swept it up in a ponytail and secured it with an elastic band. The doorbell chimed as she reached for a baseball cap and a pair of sunglasses.

Quickening her pace, she jogged down the hallway to the stairs. Kara was halfway across the expansive living room when the bell rang again. She opened the door, expecting to see Morgan, but the woman standing on the porch elicited a shiver of uneasiness.

"Hello, Analeigh."

The petite woman with sandy-brown twists and dark eyes smiled. Her white midi blouse, navy-blue pleated skirt, and penny loafers were better suited for a schoolgirl. "I'm surprised you remember my name."

"I remembered because you were the only one who didn't give me a screwface." Kara estimated she and Analeigh were about the same age.

"May I come in?"

Kara opened the door wider. "I'd love to sit and chat with you, but I'm expecting someone any moment. Is there another time when you can come back?"

"Tomorrow. Same time."

"Do you want to give me an idea of what you'd like to talk about?" Kara asked.

"I'll wait until tomorrow."

"I'd rather know now if you don't mind."

Exhaling a breath, Analeigh twisted her mouth. "I thought we could be friends."

"Friends?" Kara questioned. "I thought we were cousins."

"We are, but I'd like for us to get to know each other."

Something told Kara not to trust Analeigh, but on the other hand she'd never been one to reject an offer of friendship. "Okay. Please come back tomorrow, and we'll have lunch."

Analeigh pressed her palms together. "Should I bring something?"

"Yes."

"What would you like me to bring?"

"Yourself."

Analeigh's face fell like someone pulling down a window shade. "Me?" The single word sounded like a squeak.

Kara would've laughed if her cousin's eyes hadn't filled with tears. She hugged her instead. "Yes, you. You're the guest of honor." She gasped when Analeigh put her arms around her neck, squeezing her tightly. "Please, Analeigh. You're choking me."

"Thank you, Kara. I told the others you were nice, but they wouldn't listen to me."

Reaching up, she pried Analeigh's arms from around her neck. "Thank you for speaking up for me."

"Are you nice, Kara?"

Kara saw movement out of the corner of her eye. A Jeep came to a stop in front of the house. The passenger-side door bore the logo of the sheriff's department. "Excuse me, Analeigh." She walked out onto the porch, watching as the stocky-built man climbed the steps. The buttons on his red flannel shirt strained across his broad chest. A round face, ruddy cheeks, and beer belly made him the perfect candidate to play Santa.

He touched the brim of his baseball cap. "Afternoon, Miss Newell. I'm Deputy Sheriff Collins. I'm just stopping to check on folks in the Landing."

"I'm well, thank you."

Analeigh stepped from behind Kara, flashing a lop-sided smile. "Hi, Mr. Deputy. How you doing today?"

Deputy Collins stared at her as if she were an apparition. "What are you doing here, Analeigh?"

Wrapping her arms around her body, Analeigh angled her head and closed her eyes. "I came to see my cousin. Did you know she is my cousin?"

He glanced around. "No. How did you get here?"

Analeigh moved closer to Kenny. "I walked."

"You walked all the way from your house?"

She took another step. "Yes, sir."

Kara blinked as if coming out of a trance. She realized Analeigh's childlike behavior wasn't an act. "Deputy Collins, can you please drop Analeigh off at home?"

He touched his hat again. "Of course. I'll let Jeff know you're good here."

A nervous smile found its way across Kara's features. She wanted to tell Deputy Collins that she wasn't so good. An obviously mentally or emotionally disturbed woman had come to her home with the intent to befriend her. The uneasiness when she'd opened the door to find Analeigh standing there wasn't imagined, but real.

"Thank you, Deputy. If you speak to Jeff, please tell him to call me on the house phone."

"No problem, Miss Newell."

Crossing her arms under her breasts, Kara watched as the deputy escorted Analeigh to his truck, helped her inside, and drove away. She was still on the porch when Morgan drove up in a white late-model Cadillac Escalade. "I just have to get my sunglasses," Kara told Morgan when she got out of the vehicle.

"I'd like to do a once-over of the interior of the house first." Morgan held up a digital camera. "A picture is worth a thousand words once you look at the before and after photos."

"Do you want me to go with you?"

"No. I won't take long."

Kara nodded. "I'll wait on the porch." She folded her body down to the white wicker rocker with baby-blue cushions, recalling what Dawn said about her turning into a Southern belle while sitting on a porch drinking sweet tea. Even though she'd spent the last fifteen years of her life in New York, she was still a Southern girl at heart.

She rocked slowly, marveling at how the dictates of a dead man were determining her future. Kara knew she didn't have to follow the mandates set down in Taylor's will, yet strangely, she felt compelled to honor his wishes.

If she had known Taylor was her biological father, would he have been willing to share her with Austin or would he have legally exercised his right to share custody with Jeannette? Or would her mother have agreed to let her spend her summers on Cavanaugh Island? The maybes nagged at Kara until Morgan returned, camera in hand.

Kara rose to her feet. "What do you think?"

"The house and the furnishings are magnificent. Of course, the wallpaper has to be replaced. You'll also have to replace the drapes, and the rugs will need to be cleaned. The rugs are Aubusson, and that alone makes them price-less. I suggest once they're restored you use them as tap-estry wall hangings. Some of the floors are warped, so they'll have to be replaced. An engineer will examine the foundation to make certain it's sound and can hold up to some of the brick and plasterwork. An electrician should rewire the entire house, and I recommend heating registers installed in the floors to make them less conspicuous."

"Where would you find the people to do the restoration?" Kara asked Morgan.

"Most of them would come from Haven Creek. There are at least four master carpenters, and a few that are experts in brick and plasterwork. There is also a father and son team that put in parquet floors with herringbone or inlaid designs that will take your breath away. The advantage to using local artisans is that they're always available and take a lot of pride in their work because they have to maintain their reputations. The fabric for the chairs can be ordered from a firm on the mainland that specializes in patterns that are almost an exact match to what you have."

Kara put on her sunglasses. "We can talk while we walk." She knew there was a lot of land to cover, and she wanted to see as much as she could before nightfall. She waited until Morgan drove her SUV around to the rear of the house, then they took off walking.

Afternoon shadows had fallen, and the air was much cooler when they finally returned to the main house. Morgan gave her an overview of life in the Sea Islands when rice-producing plantations provided much of Europe with "Carolina Gold." It was African American slave labor that had perfected irrigation techniques using tidal water and man-made dikes.

She saw the ruins of what Morgan had referred to as winnowing barns where rice grains were processed for shipment. The architectural historian compared Angels Landing to Mansfield Plantation as only two American plantations to be saved from development and reclaimed by a direct descendant of the original owner.

Kara didn't want to believe she was a direct descendant of the men in the paintings. Uncovering who her ancestors were and how Cornelius Patton had come into possession of Angels Landing was another missing piece of the puzzle. *You can't know where you are going if you don't know where you've come from.* The Gullah saying wasn't far from the truth as it referred to her.

Morgan had pointed out that the original owners had built the main house on a hill to provide them with views of the ocean and river. There were more buildings: a schoolhouse, a chapel, and a dilapidated shed filled with blacksmith tools. There were two cemeteries, one for the white family and the other for blacks. The area in the undeveloped northeast section was made up of a densely forested woodland and swamp.

Kara felt like crying when she saw the cabins that had made up the slave village. The one-room shacks were structurally unsafe to enter, but when she'd peered through the windows she saw items that had been essential to those who'd lived there: broken pottery, spoons, a chair, table, and frames for several beds. Morgan took pictures of everything: trees, several ponds, outbuildings, and what had once been gardens.

"I don't know if you realize what you have here," Morgan said to Kara.

"Yes, I do. Angels Landing is like a pretty girl covered in dirt and grime. And I know it's going to take time to clean her up where everyone sees her beauty."

"You're very lucky Angels Landing is here instead of on the mainland because it probably wouldn't have escaped the Civil War when Union soldiers either occupied or burned plantations when they came through Charleston. I took photos of the books in your father's office, and many of the titles go back more than one hundred years. They alone are worth a small fortune. I'm certain private collectors would act like rabid fans at a music concert if they saw them."

Kara stared at the avenue of live oak trees leading up to the main house. "How long do you think it would take to restore everything?"

Morgan supported her back against one of the massive pale pink marble columns. "Probably two, maybe even three years."

She closed her eyes. "That long?"

"That's not very long, Kara. As a student at SCAD, I'd worked on projects that were ongoing for more than six years. My recommendation would be to start with the house and the gardens. The outbuildings would be the last because I would have to search for authentic artifacts to re-create life as it was more than 150 years ago."

Kara opened her eyes, staring at Morgan. As they walked she'd also regaled Kara with how she'd become an historical architect. Morgan had admitted her first choice when enrolling in Howard University's College of Engineering, Architecture and Computer Sciences was engineering but quickly changed her concentration when she took an architecture course. She graduated as an architect, then returned to South Carolina to enroll in the Savannah College of Art and Design to pursue a degree in historic preservation.

"Who would supervise the project, Morgan?"

Morgan stared off into the distance. "Most likely it would be one of the partners."

"You do all the legwork, and they get to supervise? No pun intended," she added when Morgan looked at her. "Right now my legs are screaming for mercy. I can't remember when I'd walked so much."

Morgan nodded. "It's like running a half marathon. And to answer your question as to supervision. I'm only an assistant. One of the partners or senior architects will probably oversee the project."

"How long have you been with the firm?"

"Two years."

"If you don't mind my asking, how old are you?"

"Thirty-two."

"How many years will it take before you're more than an assistant?"

Morgan lifted a shoulder. "I don't know. Probably at least another ten years, give or take a few."

Kara took a deep breath, held it, then exhaled slowly. She'd known she was going to use Morgan's firm within an hour of their surveying the property. However, she'd hoped to work directly with her, not the owners of the architectural and design firm.

"How would you like your own firm?"

Morgan stood up straight. "What are you talking about?"

"I just came into more money than I know what to do with. Taylor . . . my father's will states I have to restore this property, and that's what I intend to do. Right now, I don't have the patience to go through what I've just gone through with you. I'll hire you if you set up your own firm."

"But I don't have my own firm," Morgan whispered.

"Open an office here on Cavanaugh Island, and I'll be your first client."

Morgan's eyelids fluttered wildly. "I don't have that kind of money. And besides, I'd never open an office in

Haven Creek. I'd be in direct competition with Ellison and Murphy."

"What about Sanctuary Cove? I noticed there were a few vacant stores in their business district. I'll loan you the money you'll need to be operational."

"Why are you doing this, Kara?"

"Why wouldn't I, Morgan?" She'd answered her question with one of her own. "We're both young, single black women who have to fight to make our way in this world. I'm an overworked and underpaid social worker with a male supervisor who refuses to give me a favorable evaluation even though I go above and beyond what is called for in my job description. I've lost track of the number of times I was tempted to resign and set up a private practice. That is virtually impossible in Manhattan because I'd have to rent an office or a desk with another group of social workers and/or psychologists.

"I barely make enough money to pay rent on the apartment I share with a friend, buy food and a monthly Metro-Card for the bus and subway. Then there are movie tickets that are nearly twenty dollars, and please don't buy popcorn or a soda. If I go to a club and give the bartender a twenty for a drink, I'm lucky if I get back two dollars, which becomes his tip. It's not easy for us, Morgan, and if you don't want to accept my offer, then I'll respect your decision."

"Damn, Kara. You really know how to pile on the guilt."

"That's what my roommate says."

Morgan smiled. "What do *we* have to do to make this a reality?"

"Are you familiar with the law firm of Sullivan, Webster, Matthews and Sullivan?"

"No."

"David Sullivan Jr. was Taylor Patton's attorney and is also my attorney. I'll ask him to draw up an agreement stating that I'm an investor and silent partner in your firm."

"Aren't you afraid I'd run out with your money?" Morgan asked.

Kara chuckled. "Where are you going, Morgan? Didn't you tell me you live here? And I have to assume your family still lives here."

Morgan nodded. "They do."

"Would you embarrass your family when word got out that you're a thief? I don't think so," she added when Morgan gave her a wide-eyed stare. "I'm giving up a lifestyle I've come to like and a career I love despite all my bitchin' and moanin' to fulfill a dead man's wish. Together we can make it happen, or the new owners of Angels Landing may not look like you or me. And I don't have to tell you that developers couldn't care less about preserving the Gullah culture once they put in their golf courses, condos, and country clubs."

"I won't say anything to my supervisor until I'm ready to leave."

"Good for you."

"I'll take time off and check out the vacant stores in the Cove. Once the news gets out that I'm renting space in the Cove, the proverbial shit will hit the fan."

"What's the worst they can do, Morgan? Fire you?"

Morgan laughed until tears ran down her face. "By that time it'll be too late." She sobered. "I'll need office furniture and equipment."

"What about employees?"

"All I need is a receptionist who will handle the phone

and paperwork. I have a good working relationship with the artisans in the Creek, so that eliminates looking for them. You know, Kara, I think this is going to work."

"Of course it is. I don't want to be rude, but I'm going inside to soak in the tub for a while. My calves are singing the hallelujah chorus right about now. You have my numbers, and I have the one to your cell. I'll call you tomorrow after I speak to David."

Morgan threw her arms around Kara's neck. "Thank you, girlfriend."

"You're welcome, girlfriend."

Kara opened the door and walked into the house that held memories and secrets of those who'd lived before her. Hiring Morgan to restore the house was another piece of the puzzle that would soon be in place.

Chapter Seven

Jeff couldn't wait to return home. He'd played phone tag with Kara even before he'd left the island to attend a crime prevention conference. With the proliferation of illegal firearms and an increase in drug-related crimes, the governor and law enforcement officials had convened with a joint task force that included police departments from as many as two hundred small towns.

By the time Kenny called to say that Kara wanted him to call her at home, it was after eleven and much too late to call. Then Spencer White woke him at dawn, apologizing because his secretary had misplaced a letter from the governor requesting his presence at the conference and he had to leave for Columbia posthaste. Jeff was tempted to refuse the mayor's directive because he suspected Spencer was so busy campaigning for his upcoming reelection that he had misplaced the letter and decided to blame the secretary.

He'd asked his closest neighbor to look in on his grand-mother during his absence, although he doubted she would do anything to exert herself. The cardiologist had inserted a shunt into her heart to divert the flow of blood from one chamber to another because he'd wanted to avoid a bypass procedure.

Jeff knew Corrine didn't like curtailing her normal activities yet resigned herself to following the doctor's directives. Corrine had been very active up until the attack, and she still talked about not being able to bowl. For years she'd belonged to a bowling league that met every Sunday night at the Charleston bowling alley. She'd also been an avid swimmer and like most children on the island had learned to swim by jumping off the pier.

He wasn't certain why Kara wanted him to call her, but when he'd checked in with his deputies, they reported back that Mrs. Todd said Kara was spending a lot of time in Charleston. Sending her flowers and the balloon had been a knee-jerk reaction when he'd passed the florist. Jeff hadn't wanted to believe it had taken less than a week for Kara to change her mind and move to the island. She'd revealed that she was required to stay for five years, but five years was a great deal longer than one or even three weeks.

Jeff felt his mind drifting when thunderous applause shook him from his reverie. He still hadn't figured out what it was about Kara that he'd found so attractive. He knew it wasn't her looks because he'd dated beautiful women before and a few that were so overtly sexy they turned heads wherever they went. Unfortunately their looks weren't enough to get him to commit to something other than a physical relationship. The only one who'd gotten him to commit was a North Carolina schoolteacher he'd met when he was assigned to Marine Corps Base Camp Lejeune.

Pamela wasn't as pretty as she was charismatic. Her infectious smile, the timbre of her sultry voice, and the dedication she'd shown her students were what had won him over. He'd waited thirty-six years to find someone like Pamela, and when he'd proposed marriage, she accepted without hesitation. Then when he was transferred from Camp Lejeune to Camp Pendleton, Jeff realized their relationship was on shaky ground. Pamela had been appointed to assistant principal, and she'd postponed their wedding date because she had to think about whether she'd wanted to become a military wife. A month later she returned his ring, declaring she'd made a mistake accepting it when she knew he would never give up his military career to live a normal, more stable life.

A scraping of chairs and more than three hundred men and women representing police forces all over the state filed out of the auditorium. Gathering the many handouts they were given, Jeff shoved them into his plastic folder stamped with the conference title and made his way out to the parking lot. He'd left Cavanaugh Island Wednesday morning, and it was now Friday afternoon. The drive between Columbia and Charleston would take approximately two hours, barring traffic delays. He was anxious to see his grandmother...and Kara.

One hour and forty-five minutes later, Jeff smiled when he saw his grandmother sitting on the porch knitting. She hated sitting around doing nothing, so she'd picked up her needlework. If he had to recall one thing from his childhood, it was a basket filled with squares of fabric for quilting or colorful skeins of yarn Corrine used for her knitting, crocheting, or embroidery projects. She even knitted or crocheted when watching television.

He parked his car under the carport beside her Camry and came around to the front porch. Leaning over, he kissed her forehead. "How's my favorite girl?"

Corrine gazed up at him with loving eyes. "Your grandmother is just fine. You should be asking that question to that cute little girl you brought here earlier in the week."

"She's just a friend, Gram."

"She needs to be more than a friend, Jeffrey. I may not leave this house every day, but I do manage to hear the gossip."

Flopping down on a chair beside her, Jeff stretched out long legs. "What gossip now, Gram?"

"She's staying. And someone saw that pretty little architect from the Creek over at the house. That can only mean that Kara plans to fix it up. And there has been other talk…"

Jeff shook his head. He was away from the Cove for three days, and the gossipmongers were busy. "Spit it out, Gram."

"You had flowers delivered to Angels Landing."

Taking off his hat, Jeff placed it on his knee. "Since when is buying flowers for someone a crime?"

"It's not a crime, Jeffrey. It just sends a message that you're interested in the young lady."

"Do you want me to say that I'm not interested in Kara?"

"Oh no! I think it's wonderful that you are. It's just that I want you to be prepared in case you start keeping company with her."

"Prepared for what, Gram?"

"For all the talk about you and Kara."

Running his hand over his face, Jeff closed his eyes. "Grandmomma, I couldn't care less about what folks say. Spending two years in Afghanistan taught me to take one second at a time. When I saw men who'd become my brothers in every sense of the word get blown up right in front of my eyes, I promised myself that nothing or no one could get to me. The exception is you." He pushed to his feet. "I'm going inside to shower and catch a few winks before I go over to the station house."

"Don't you want something to eat?" Corrine asked.

"No thank you. I'll grab something from Jack's before they close if I get hungry." Leaning down, he kissed her again. "It's good to be home."

Kara sat at the table in the kitchen drinking coffee and flipping through the pages of the book she'd bought from the Parlor Bookstore. Not only did she want to revive Theodora's garden, but she also wanted to plant a vegetable and herb garden.

Even though Mrs. Todd prepared most of the meals, she wanted to begin cooking for herself, even if it was only the evening meal. She'd thought she would be bored, but she'd been anything but. It had taken three trips to Charleston to complete her banking. The accounts in Taylor Patton's name were closed and reopened in her name. She'd met with an investment banker at each branch who'd recommended which accounts she should utilize to maximize the greatest yield. What she'd refused to do was put her money into accounts that weren't insured by the FDIC.

Morgan had called to say she found a small shop two doors from the Muffin Corner on Moss Alley. It was perfect because it was off Main Street. The owner of the property had waived the security fee and the first month's rent because he'd been trying to rent the space for more than a year and a half. Morgan said she would take the space, then made him swear an oath that he would not reveal who the new tenant was until it came time for her grand opening.

Kara had David draw up the papers making her a silent partner in M. Dane Architecture and Interior Design. He'd met with Morgan and convinced her to set up a corporation for which he would file the necessary paperwork.

Morgan had given her a projected budget of what she would need to start up the business, and Kara had checks drawn on her Charleston accounts to minimize someone inadvertently leaking the news that Kara had given Morgan a check for six figures. What they didn't know was the amount on the check was minuscule compared to the price of restoring the property and would be deducted from the final cost.

She studied a page featuring a pond in a meadow surrounded by ornamental grasses and irises. When walking the property, Kara had discovered several ponds and an underground stream. She jumped when she heard the doorbell chime and glanced at the clock on the microwave. It was 10:50.

Lowering her feet she'd rested on another chair, she went to answer the door. It hadn't taken her long to get used to locking the door right after Mrs. Todd left for the evening.

Peering through the security eye, she saw Jeff standing on the porch. When he hadn't returned her call, she thought either he forgot or had intended to call her. He'd done what David had asked him to do and was keeping an eye on her. His deputies continued to stop by every day to ask about her as they did with most residents and business-people on the island. It was something Jeff had instituted to stay connected. Morgan said the former sheriff was distant, reinforcing the stereotype that people shouldn't trust law enforcement.

She opened the door to find him grinning at her like a Cheshire cat. He was wearing his badge and gun, so she assumed he was on duty. "Good evening, Sheriff Hamilton."

He nodded and angled his head. "Good evening, Miss Newell. I heard you were asking for me."

Kara shivered slightly. Not from the cool night air but from the way Jeff was staring at her. Pulling back her shoulders, she managed a tight smile. "Yes. I wanted to thank you for the balloon and the flowers." She noticed he was staring at a spot below her neck, and when she glanced down, she saw her distended nipples were clearly visible under the cotton fabric of her pajama top.

Jeff's gaze inched up to her face. "May I come in?" Taking a step back, Kara opened the door, and he stepped into the entryway. "I would've come sooner, but I was away at a conference."

Kara closed the door but didn't turn around. "You don't have to explain yourself to me, Jeff."

He took a step, pressing his chest to her back. "What if I feel the need to explain myself?"

"Why?"

Her heart was pounding in her chest like a trip-hammer. Jeff dwarfed her as she stood there in her bare feet. His heat, the scent of his cologne, and the solid wall of his chest against her back reminded her of what she'd missed and had been missing for years. She wanted to trust him but couldn't because of the men in her life: Taylor and the other men in her past. Even Austin had deceived her when he'd elected not to tell her he wasn't her biological father. And yet despite her angst, her body betrayed her at the exact time his arm went around her waist.

"Because I missed you," he whispered in her ear.

"You haven't known me long enough to miss me," she murmured.

"I don't measure my life in days, weeks, or years but in seconds. You look at life differently once you stare death in the face every second of your life. I grew up hearing the old folk talk about tomorrow isn't promised to you. My mantra is today isn't promised, either."

Kara was certain he could feel her trembling. "What is it you want, Jeff?" His deep chuckle caressed her ear.

"You really don't want to know what I want."

She smiled in spite of her pleasurable predicament. "Yes, I do."

"Right now I want to kiss you."

"Is that all?"

He laughed again. "What else were you expecting?"

"Nothing," Kara said much too quickly to sound convincing.

"You're an incredibly beautiful liar." He pressed his mouth to her hair. "I want that too but only when you're ready."

She bit her lip and nodded. "What if I'm never ready?"

"Then we'll have a relationship without the sex. I just want to be with you."

Turning in his loose embrace, Kara met his eyes, looking for a trace of guile. His expression was closed. "You're kidding, aren't you?"

"No, I'm not. Do you believe I'm so self-centered that I think all women want to sleep with me?"

"Most of the men I've known or met expect me to sleep with them."

His eyebrow lifted a fraction. "You've been hanging out with the wrong guys."

"It appears as if I have," she said under her breath. What she couldn't tell Jeff was that if she were given a choice she *would* sleep with him.

She hadn't told anyone (and that included Morgan) that after she restored Angels Landing, she planned to move into the vacant guesthouse and convert the main house into a museum. The revenue she derived from tours would be used for preservation. Once she had lived there for five years, she would decide what she wanted to do with the rest of her life. At thirty-eight she would still be young and wealthy enough to do whatever pleased her.

Jeff cradled her face. His head dipped as if in slow motion, and Kara breathed in his scent seconds before his mouth covered hers in a kiss that stole the breath from her lungs. Going on tiptoe, she anchored her arms under his shoulders, holding onto him as if her life depended on him and only him.

Arousal snaked through her body, scorching her from head to toe. She opened her mouth to his searching tongue, losing herself in the moment and the man. It took herculean strength but Kara managed to tear away before she begged Jeff to take her upstairs and make love to her. A soft groan escaped her parted lips when he fastened his mouth to the column of her neck.

"My grandmother wants to know if you're coming for Sunday dinner."

"Will you be there?"

"I can arrange to be there if you want me to."

"It really doesn't matter," she quipped, offering him a saucy grin.

His eyebrows lifted a fraction. "Oh, really? What do I have to do to make you change your mind?" he teased, pulling her closer and lowering his head to kiss her again.

"Leave before we start something we can't finish."

"Yes, ma'am."

Jeff's arms fell away, and Kara felt his loss even before he walked out of the door. Something about being in his embrace felt so right, so natural, as if they'd done it before in another time and place. "Good night," she said in a hushed whisper.

Amusement shimmered in his eyes. "Oh, that it will be." Turning on his heels, Jeff opened the door. "I'll pick you up on Sunday."

Kara could still see his broad shoulders, cropped hair and remembered the sparkle in his dark eyes long after she'd locked the door. She felt a warm glow of satisfaction when she realized he hadn't forgotten her. In fact, he'd admitted to missing her.

"I missed you, too." She didn't know why it was so hard for her to have admitted that to Jeff.

Kara returned to the kitchen and poured the lukewarm coffee in the sink, rinsed the cup, and put it in the dishwasher. Leaving the light on in the hallway, she walked up the back staircase to her bedroom. When she climbed into bed, she felt a pang of emptiness. She'd slept alone for so long it almost seemed natural for her. Since meeting Jeff, Kara realized she didn't want to sleep alone.

She didn't want to end up like Taylor living in a twenty-room house with no one to tell him that they loved him. He'd grown accustomed to being alone and had died alone.

How sad for a man in the prime of his life and who'd amassed a great deal of wealth to have no one to share it with.

Kara shook her head as she pulled the sheet and blanket up and over her body. No. She would not go out like that. Even if she never married, she would adopt a child or children, anyone who would enjoy their grandfather's legacy.

Kara felt as if she had butterflies in her stomach when she saw her mother's name and number come up on her cell as she prepared to leave the house to walk along the beach.

"Mama?"

"I got someone to cover for me, and I'm on my way to Charleston."

She closed her eyes. It was time to discover another piece of the puzzle. "What time is your plane coming in?"

"I'm driving, Kara."

"Is Daddy with you?"

"No. This is something we need to talk about without him being present."

"Where are you now?" It was about nine hundred miles between Little Rock and Charleston, and Kara hoped her mother hadn't attempted to make the drive without stopping.

"I just crossed into South Carolina. I'm going to stop in Columbia, check into a hotel for a couple of hours, then come on in."

"Mama, you'd better sleep for more than a couple of hours."

"Once I get to Charleston, I'll need directions for Cavanaugh Island."

"Call me and I'll meet you."

"Okay."

"Mama? Please get some sleep."

"Okay, baby."

Kara tapped the button, ending the call. Walking on shaky knees, she managed to make her way over to the bedroom's sitting area. Dropping into a deep armchair, she rested her feet on the footstool. The bottle-green, watered silk fabric was faded and frayed.

She couldn't wait to see her mother—not just to uncover the details of her paternity, but because Jeannette was the stabilizing factor in her life. The last time she'd seen her mother cry was when Austin was being transferred to another base, the third in four years, and Kara had become hysterical because she didn't want to leave her friends. Jeannette had risked her marriage when she told her husband she wasn't going with him, that she was returning to Little Rock to live with her mother and father until he voluntarily resigned or retired from the corps.

Kara knew the ultimatum had shocked Austin, and he'd accused Jeannette of not supporting him, but Jeannette remained resolute when she said her daughter's emotional well-being was first and everything else secondary. It was the first time Kara remembered her mother's reference to her being *her* daughter and not *their* daughter. However at eight years of age she hadn't understood any of the dynamics surrounding her parents' marriage. The only thing that mattered was she was going to go to the same school year after year and she didn't have to leave her new friends.

Kara loved Austin, but even at a young age she knew she didn't like military life when her family moved every few years, and there were times when she rarely got to see him. Would it, she mused, have been that way if Jeff was on active duty and they were in a relationship? She knew whatever they would've had would have failed because she was not willing to embrace that lifestyle.

Sitting and thinking about her past was not helping to ease her nerves about the pending meeting with her mother. And if she didn't get up, she wouldn't, and she wanted to make it to the beach in time to watch the sun rise.

When she got there, Kara discovered she wasn't the only one on the beach. There was an older couple walking slowly while holding hands. She passed two young women jogging at a fast pace who nodded to her but didn't break stride. She walked in the opposite direction, heading for the Cove and where the Black Bay connected with the southwest bank of the Ashley River. Slowing, she watched the magnificent sunrise as the cold, gray, angry surf pounded the beach.

"Awesome, isn't it?"

With wide eyes, she spun around to find Jeff standing several feet away. She forced herself not to stare at his bare chest. Beads of perspiration dotted his forehead and upper body despite the cold wind coming off the water. She could see every one of the abs on his flat belly.

"Yes it is." He was talking about the sun, and she was talking about his body. "Aren't you cold?" She'd elected to wear a cotton turtleneck under her sweats, while Jeff had opted for sweatpants.

He began jogging in place. "You don't feel the cold if you keep moving." He took her hand. "Come jog with me."

"I hadn't planned to jog."

He gave her a sidelong glance. "You don't look as if you're out of condition."

She quickened her pace to keep up with him. Jogging

on sand was much more difficult than on a track. "My mother is coming in today."

"What time is her flight?"

"She's driving. I told her I would meet her in Charleston."

"She's welcome to join us tomorrow."

"I'll tell her." Kara's breathing was becoming more labored. If she'd joined a gym, the extra exertion wouldn't have tested her endurance. "You're either going to have to slow down or let go of my hand. Oh no!" she screamed when he swung her up in his arms and continued running. "Put me down, Jeff," she yelled between clenched teeth.

"Hold on, baby."

She held onto his thick neck to keep her balance. "Are you hard of hearing? I told you to put me down."

"Stop talking and enjoy the ride."

Kara couldn't believe he was carrying her as if she were a child. "You're going to pay for this."

"Ooo-wee! I'm scared." Jeff shook himself for effect.

"I'm not kidding, Jeff."

"Please stop talking, darling."

"I'm not your darling."

"You could be."

"What if I don't want to be?"

"Your mouth says one thing today, while the other night your lips said the opposite."

"Do you have to remind me of that?"

"Why not? I can't forget it."

"Stop it, Jeff. You're embarrassing me."

He slowed, then came to a complete stop. "Are you a virgin?"

Her jaw dropped, heat suffused her face, appalled that he thought her so prudish that she could've been a virgin.

Was it that obvious because it had been a while since she'd been in a man's company? She had been alone for far too long.

"Do you realize how old I am?"

"That's not what I asked you. Have you ever slept with a man?"

"Of course I have. And why would that interest you?"

"There's an innocence about you I find endearing."

"Too innocent for the worldly military man?"

Jeff grinned, his teeth showing whitely against the stubble on his lean jaw. "Never." Bending slightly, he set Kara on her feet. "It's time I start back. Some of us have to work for a living."

She scrunched her nose. "Very funny. Remember, I'm on vacation."

He cradled her face and brushed a light kiss on her mouth. "I'll call you tomorrow."

Kara stood watching as Jeff turned and raced down the beach, sand spewing under bare feet. As she turned to retrace her steps to the parking lot, she noticed two women watching her. By the looks on their faces, they'd seen the entire encounter.

Chapter Eight

Kara and her mother stood at the rail of the ferry, watching the skyline of Charleston growing smaller as the ferryman deftly steered the boat through the narrow inlet until he reached open water.

Jeannette placed a hand over her mouth, smothering a yawn. "I suppose I still didn't get enough sleep."

"That's why you're going straight to bed once we get to Angels Landing." Shifting, Kara leaned back against the rail. "Even with bags under your eyes, you still look beautiful, Mama."

The older woman yawned again. "And you always know what to say to make me feel better."

Kara studied her mother, noticing a few more strands of gray in her thick, stylishly cut, coiffed hair. Kara had inherited her mother's hair and body, but that's where their resemblance ended. Her eyes were hazel, her coloring a golden-brown, while Jeannette always joked that her eyes and skin were an exact match: henna.

"It's the truth. I'm surprised Daddy didn't insist on coming with you. You know he has a jealous streak as wide as the Mississippi."

Jeannette flashed a demure smile. "I told him we were going to have a girls' week. After all, he has his boys' week with his military buddies whenever they go camping and do Lord knows what."

Kara smoothed back the wisps of hair that had escaped her ponytail. It was the last week in March, and spring was definitely in the air. Daytime temperatures now topped out at seventy. "Did his jealousy have anything to do with Taylor?"

An audible breath came from Jeannette. "Come, let's sit down, Kara." They moved over to sit on padded benches, far enough away from the other passengers so they wouldn't be overheard. She smiled when Kara rubbed her back. "Austin and I grew up together. He was my first and only boyfriend until I met Taylor. I'd left home to go to college while Austin enlisted in the Marines. Austin and I hadn't slept together, and he made me promise to wait for him.

"My college roommate was dating a Morehouse brother, and I sort of paired up with his roommate. Taylor and I became real good friends. Outside of class you rarely saw me without him and vice versa. One night when he'd had too much to drink, he told me about his family, his overly protective mother in particular, and how he'd had to fight for his independence. I was close to tears once he admitted that he'd never slept with a woman. He was a handsome, brilliant man who'd been afraid to approach a woman because his mother had turned him into a social cripple.

Then everything changed during our senior year. Instead of going home for spring break, we took off for Virginia Beach, checked into a hotel, and a sorry sight it was with not one but two bumbling virgins. We managed to get it right, and for one glorious week I felt as if I'd died and gone to heaven.

"My period was late, but that didn't raise any warning bells because my cycle was never regular. It wasn't until after I'd graduated and moved back to Little Rock that I realized I was carrying Taylor's baby."

"Did you tell him?"

Her mother nodded. "I'd called his home and left a message for him to return my call, but either he didn't get the message or he'd decided to move on. I wrote him a letter, and that too went unanswered. That's when I knew I had to tell Austin that I was carrying another man's baby. I'd expected him to walk away, but he insisted we marry as quickly as possible. We went to the courthouse, got married, and moved into off-base housing. You were born a week before Christmas, and when Austin held you for the first time and called you his baby girl, I knew I'd been given a second chance. I had a wonderful supportive husband and a beautiful daughter."

"How did Taylor know my birthday?"

A slight frown furrowed Jeannette's smooth forehead. "What are you talking about?"

"His computer password is Kara twelve-nineteen, which just happens to be my birthday."

"I don't know, Kara. After I sent him that letter, I'd mentally exorcised Taylor from my mind."

"It's incredible, but he knew everything about me, Mama. My full name, birthday, my New York City address, and who knows what else. He left me everything: the house, land, antiques, classic cars, cash, bonds, et cetera, et cetera, et cetera. I'm told he never married or had any other children. No one ever saw him with a woman, and he lived and died alone. I'm certain it wasn't too difficult for him to hire an investigator to collect whatever information he needed on me." A beat passed. "You never told him you had given birth to his daughter, yet it wasn't until after he died that I was made aware that Taylor Patton, not Austin Newell, was my biological father. Why didn't you tell me, Mama? Why did I have to find out from a dead man?"

Jeannette took a deep breath, holding it until she was forced to exhale. "Austin and I never talked about it. I was your mama and he was your daddy. It'd become our tainted little secret."

A cynical laugh escaped Kara. "One thing I've learned living here is there are no secrets."

"Living? Don't you mean visiting?"

Kara made circular motions on her mother's back as if to ease the blow of what she was about to tell her. "I'm going to live here, Mama."

"What! You can't, Kara!" Her protest was pregnant with shock and fear.

"I have to," Kara countered. "If Taylor was out for revenge, then he has exacted a heavy price." She revealed the terms of his will.

"How can he ask you to live here for five years?"

"I don't know, but he did. At least the mandate comes at a good time in my life. I'm not married, and I don't have to worry about uprooting a child."

"Are you certain this is what's best for you, Kara? You have a beautiful apartment in one of the greatest cities in the world and a wonderful career. Why would you want to give that up?"

"I own a house here that is listed as a National Register of Historic Places, and the property is a National Historic Landmark District. Don't forget that I'm a CSW, and I can always work as a school-based or hospital social worker in any city. Or I could open a private practice, an option I didn't have in New York because I didn't have the time or money."

Pushing away Kara's arm, Jeannette slid over, putting distance between them. "Don't tell me you're doing this because of money."

"Mama!"

"Don't 'Mama' me, Kara. Is it about money?"

Kara felt as if she'd been stabbed through the heart, left to bleed invisible blood. She did not want to believe that her mother thought she was that greedy, avaricious, and narcissistic. That she'd agreed to carry out a dead man's wishes because he'd made her wealthy. It wasn't just about money; it was about the future of Cavanaugh Island and its inhabitants.

"I can't believe you said that," she whispered. "If I'd wanted to make a lot of money, I never would've become a social worker. Please look at me, Mama," she pleaded. "It's not about me," she continued when Jeannette stared at her.

"What is it about?"

"It's about connecting with relatives I never knew I had. It's also about getting involved in a restoration project that will take years to complete and may even permit me to start up a new business." What she didn't tell her mother was the possibility of a relationship with an attractive man—something she hadn't had in a long time.

"I can't believe it's taken only a week for you to become this impassioned about something you knew nothing about."

"A week ago I had no idea that the man I call Daddy isn't my biological father. But that doesn't change anything because DNA aside, Austin Newell is and will always be my father... even though everyone says I look exactly like Theodora Patton."

"He loves you, baby."

Kara inched over and hugged her mother. "Nothing's changed because I still love him. I don't know why Taylor left me everything when he should've left it to his brother, sisters, nieces, and nephews."

Jeannette's round, sherry-colored eyes grew wider. "He disinherited them?"

"I wouldn't call it disinherit because they're not his heirs."

"That probably didn't make them too happy."

Kara didn't tell her mother about the outburst in the lawyer's office following the reading of the will. "He did set aside monies for some of the younger Pattons' college education, and he has provided for the housekeeper and her husband. The more I think about it, the more I believe my inheritance is attributed to his guilt. Taylor knew about me but was either too much of a coward or too intimidated by his mother to reach out to you."

"I don't know, Kara."

"Would you have married Taylor if he'd asked you?"

"In a heartbeat. I loved Austin, but I was in love with Taylor."

"Are you in love with Daddy now?"

"Yes. Our marriage hasn't been perfect, but we've sacrificed a lot to make it work. I know he felt cheated that I never got pregnant again, and that put a strain on our marriage once he was diagnosed with a low sperm count. My decision not to become a military wife was as difficult for me as it was for Austin. I would've followed him around the world if it'd been just me, but there was someone else to consider, you. It wasn't easy not having my husband with me for your parent-teacher conferences, when your cheerleading team went to Orlando to compete, and your high school graduation."

Kara rested her head on her mother's shoulder like she'd done as a child. "It was never easy for me to make friends, so when we had to move so much, I couldn't deal with it."

"I know." Jeannette gave her daughter a tender glance. "Have you made friends here?"

"Sort of."

"What do you mean 'sort of'?"

"The sheriff is my attorney's cousin, and he's sort of taken me under his wing. I met his grandmother, and we're invited to have dinner with them tomorrow."

"Do they know I'm coming?" Jeannette asked.

"Yes."

"Is the sheriff your only friend?"

"No. I think Morgan and I are going to get along well."

"It appears as if you have guy friends. Don't you think you need at least one girlfriend?"

Kara laughed. "Morgan is a girl."

Jeannette's mouth formed a perfect O. "I see."

The ferry slowed as it neared the dock and landing for Sanctuary Cove. Kara and Jeannette were the last cars off the boat. Kara had paid the ferryman for a bumper sticker for her mother's car. Other than official vehicles no vehicle was allowed on island roads without a permit.

"Follow me," Kara told Jeannette before she slipped in behind the wheel of the Mercedes.

She drove slowly away from the pier and through downtown Sanctuary Cove. It was Saturday morning, and people were out and about shopping. They drove past the town square. The benches were filled with retirees taking advantage of the warmer weather. Kara smiled when she saw Jack's Fish House, remembering her unofficial date with Jeff that seemed so long ago when it'd only been a week. What she couldn't forget were his kisses, kisses that fired her blood while reminding her why she'd been born female: that she was a woman with needs only a man could assuage.

Kara had no preconceived notions about having a relationship with the handsome lawman. He was a forty-year-old confirmed bachelor who lived with his grandmother on an island with a total population of less than 2,300 residents. She'd made home visits to New York City public housing projects with more than 2,300 tenants in the development. And like those on Cavanaugh Island, everybody knew everybody and their business.

She didn't believe she would be able to live on the island and have a normal relationship with a man. Mrs. Todd had revealed Jeff didn't bring the flowers to Angels Landing but had had them delivered. How long, she mused, had it taken for the news to sweep over the island that Jeffrey Hamilton had sent flowers to Kara Newell.

Kara had never been one to flaunt her affairs, and she knew she had to develop a thicker skin *if* she was going to date Jeff. Peering up into her rearview mirror, she saw her mother slowing down. It was apparent she was driving and sightseeing. Jeannette had taken a week's vacation, and that was more than enough time for Kara to show her the island and Charleston's historic district.

Signaling, she took the newly constructed two-lane road to Angels Landing. She maneuvered off the road, signaling again, before driving slowly under a canopy of live oaks draped with Spanish moss. The sight of the pink house at the end of the allée never failed to elicit a feeling of incredulity that the massive trees had survived countless generations that had owned and inhabited the grand house.

She came to a stop, parking in front of a trio of carriage houses that had been converted to two locked garages used to house Taylor's three classic cars. Kara motioned for her mother to pull up alongside her.

"Pop the trunk, and I'll take your bag inside." When she saw the direction of her mother's gaze, she smiled and said, "Close your mouth, Mama." Using the side door, she led her mother into the main kitchen with brick walls and flooring. A massive fireplace took up half of an entire wall.

"Oh my word!" Jeannette gasped. "This reminds me of Williamsburg."

"I read that the house was built sometime around 1832. There was a fire in 1854, and the first floor was completely destroyed. The house remained unoccupied until 1858. After extensive repairs a gambler, who'd won the house on the turn of a card, moved in with his mistress. Then came the Civil War and he joined the Confederate Army and died in the Battle of Rivers Bridge two months before the war ended."

"What happened to the mistress?"

Smiling, Kara shook her head. "I don't know yet. I'm still reading a book about the history of Cavanaugh Island. Come, let me show you to your room. After you're rested I'll give you a tour of the house and introduce you to Mrs.

Todd once she returns from the dentist. She and her husband are off on the weekend."

Jeannette followed Kara down a narrow hallway to a staircase at the rear of the house. "Are you losing weight?"

Kara glanced over her shoulder. "Quite the contrary. I think I've gained now that I'm eating three meals a day. I've also started exercising."

"Where do you exercise?"

"I walk along the beach."

"Don't exercise too much because you look better with a little more weight."

"Spoken like a mother."

"That's because I am a mother, who one day would like to be a grandmother."

"That's definitely not going to happen now. This is your room. You also have a private bathroom."

Kara had chosen the bedroom at the far end of the hall for her mother. Embroidered mosquito netting draped the four-poster bed. Kara had dubbed this the yellow room because of the coverlet, pale pine floors, yellow bed dressing, and green fabric on the settee and chairs embroidered with yellow butterflies.

"How many rooms are in this house?"

"Twenty."

Jeannette closed her eyes. "I can't imagine one person living here alone."

"I guess you get used to it."

She gave her daughter a long, penetrating stare as she placed her luggage on the bench at the foot of the bed. "Is that what you intend to do, Kara? Do you really want to ramble around this...this monstrosity of a house alone like Taylor did?"

Crossing her arms under her breasts, Kara met her mother's glare. "No."

"Didn't you tell me the housekeeper and her husband live in a guesthouse? And if that's true, then you are here alone."

"Can we talk about this later? Right now, I have to draft a letter of resignation because I'd like to put it in the mail on Monday. I'll either be in the kitchen or on the front porch if you need me."

"I'd like to do a little shopping and sightseeing later this afternoon."

"I'll take you to Haven Creek for shopping; then we'll go to Sanctuary Cove for dinner."

Jeannette slipped out of her lightweight wool jacket. "Why don't we eat in Angels Landing?"

"Angels Landing isn't zoned for businesses. It's the only town that's solely residential. Even folks who own large houses with the intent of turning them into boardinghouses can't because the town council won't give them a variance."

Kara had spent most of her spare time researching the history of the island and the house she would now call home. She knew her property was exempt from the town's building codes because of its landmark status; once the restoration was complete, and she made it known she was turning it into a museum, she knew there would be little or no opposition.

"Isn't there some way for them to get around that?"

She smiled. "There is always a way to circumvent the law. All they have to do is apply to the Secretary of the Interior for landmark status."

Resting her hands at her waist, Jeannette's smile matched her daughter's. "What do you plan to do with this place?"

"You can't mention a word of this to anyone, Mama. Not even Daddy."

It took a full minute before Jeannette said, "Okay."

"After the house, the gardens, and the outbuildings are restored, I'm going to turn Angels Landing into a museum. People will be able to purchase tickets for tours. I'll offer discounts to schoolchildren and senior groups. When I spoke to my attorney, he suggested setting up a foundation with a mission to sustain the highest level of preservation. I've been thinking about building an inn not far from the formal gardens to attract corporate groups who wish to hold a conference in a different kind of setting. Then there are always the destination weddings. Why go to the Caribbean when you can marry in the Lowcountry? Again, I would offer discounts on weddings on Fridays and Sundays in May and Friday, Saturday, and Sunday in June."

Staring at her only child, it was as if Jeannette was seeing Kara for the first time. "You are truly *his* child."

"What are you talking about, Mama?"

"Whenever Taylor had to come up with a business plan for any of his business courses, he would always draft two schematics. Then he would submit the least probable of the two while saving the best for himself. His rationale was why give away something he could possibly use for his future."

"I was told he made a lot of money for his clients as an investment banker." A smile played at the corners of Kara's mouth. "And based on his net worth, he also made quite a bit for himself. Aside from the appraised value on this house and the two thousand acres it sits on, Taylor left me close to five million dollars. That's only cash on hand in banks. There are still bonds and other securities that I have to get an accountant to interpret for me."

Jeannette pressed a hand to her throat. "I don't believe it!"

"I must admit, it is a little overwhelming."

"It's mind-boggling, Kara."

"I know you and Daddy refinanced your house, so I'm going to give you an early Christmas gift and pay it off."

"You can't!"

"I can and I will," Kara countered. "You and Daddy struggled to send me to a private college, then paid for grad school out of your pocket because you didn't want me to end up with student loans. I never would've been able to rent an apartment in Manhattan if I'd had loans. Taylor owes you this, and because he's not around to repay you, I will." She held up her hand when Jeannette opened her mouth. "And, Mama, please don't start with me because you're only going to lose this argument."

Jeannette narrowed her eyes. "Are you finished mouthing off to your mother?"

Kara struggled not to laugh. Her mother only pulled rank when she believed she was losing an argument. "Yep. I'll see you later." Turning on her heels, she left the bedroom, closing the door behind her.

Jeannette tugged at Kara's arm. "I want to go inside and look around." They'd stopped in front of a window display of miniature jars of jellies, jams, and relishes.

Kara followed her into the Cannery, the most delicious aromas wafting to her nose. Her mother had slept for more than four hours, and when Jeannette joined her in the kitchen, it was as if they'd never discussed the awkward subject of money and her intent to pay off their mortgage . . . or her biological father.

She liked what could be interpreted as the hustle and

bustle of Sanctuary Cove, but it was the laid-back attitude of the artisans in Haven Creek that really appealed to her. Morgan mentioned hiring many of them for the restoration project, and she wanted to stop by the shops to look at samples of their work.

The tiny bell over the door rang, alerting the shopkeeper that she had a customer. A woman with graying dreadlocks smiled and nodded. "I'll be with you directly. Feel free to sample the spiced apple butter."

Kara walked over to the shelf with mason jars filled with fruit and vegetables: corn, beets, cherries, zucchini, peaches, pears, and an assortment of berries—blackberries, raspberries, and gooseberries. She picked up a small jar of Asian chili/salsa and one of chowchow, placing them in a wire basket. She'd known women in Little Rock who'd canned fruits and vegetables, but she'd never learned the process and neither did her mother.

The bell rang again. Kara turned and froze when her gaze met and fused with one of the women who'd sat in the conference room during the reading of Taylor's will. Her gray eyes and sable-brown skin told Kara she was a Patton. She was casually dressed in a pair of fitted jeans, white silk man-tailored blouse, navy blazer, and black leather slip-ons. The solitaire in her wedding set was much too large for her delicate hand.

Kara was the first to end the stare-down impasse when she smiled. "Hello."

"It's Kara, isn't it?"

"Yes."

"I'm Virginia Patton-Smith. But most folks call me Virgie."

Kara offered her hand and wasn't disappointed when

Virgie took it. "This is my first time coming here. Perhaps you can recommend something."

Virgie picked up a jar of cherries, handing it to Kara. "I use the cherries as a topping for pancakes and ice cream."

She placed the jar in her basket. "What else?"

"You've got to be a Patton because we all have a weakness for chowchow."

"You don't believe I'm a Patton?" The question was out before Kara could censor herself.

"Please, don't get me wrong, Kara. I believe you're one of us because you look exactly like my grandmother. But some of my relatives still believe you're an impostor."

"I can reassure you that I'm not an impostor."

Virgie patted her shoulder. "I wouldn't worry too much if I were you. Give them time, and I'm certain they'll come around. We have a family tradition that we all get together for Sunday dinner. We rotate homes; that way it becomes more equitable. This Sunday it's my turn, and I'd love to invite you, but I don't want you to be blindsided by some of our less than hospitable relatives."

"It's okay. I wouldn't have been able to make it even if *our* relatives were ready to welcome me with open arms. I happen to have a prior engagement."

"Good for you. I'd really like us to get together before you go back to New York."

Hazel eyes met a hoary-gray pair. "I'm not going back. I've decided to make Angels Landing my home." Kara thought Virgie was going to faint when she swayed slightly. She reached out to steady her, but Virgie took a backward step.

"You're kidding, aren't you?"

Kara almost felt sorry for Virgie when she saw her expression of confidence replaced with fear. "Not at all."

"But why?"

"Why? You heard the conditions outlined in my father's will. I've been directed to restore the property and live in the house for five years. And that's—"

"Kara, baby...Oh, I'm sorry I didn't realize you were talking to someone."

She gave her mother a plastic smile. "This isn't just someone, Mama. She's Virginia Patton-Smith, and she happens to be my cousin."

Virgie recovered enough to give Kara's mother a friendly smile. "It's nice meeting you, Ms. Newell."

Jeannette nodded. "Same here."

"I'd invited Kara to share Sunday dinner with the family, but she told me she has a prior engagement. I'd love to stay and chat, but I have to keep to my schedule or I won't get back in time to pick up my daughter from her dance lessons." She wiggled her fingers. "I'll call you, Kara. I hope to see you again, Ms. Newell."

"Why do I get the impression that she didn't mean a word she said," Jeannette whispered in Kara's ear.

"It's called being fake," Kara whispered back. "Let's finish up here so we can stay on schedule."

Jeannette cut her eyes at her daughter. "You know you're bad, don't you?"

"I learned it from my mama," she intoned.

Kara and Jeannette left the Cannery with their purchases in a recyclable shopping bag. Haven Creek's town council had recommended business owners replace plastic bags with recyclable ones to offset polluting the island's environment.

Mother and daughter had become teenagers turned loose in a mall with a no-spending limit. Jeannette couldn't make up her mind which size sweet-grass basket she wanted to buy for her sister while Kara sat on a tall stool patiently waiting.

"Kara, please help me out," Jeannette pleaded.

Sliding off the stool, she walked over to the table. "I like the large tray."

"Do you think it would look nice on a coffee table?"

"Mama, stop wondering where Aunt Denise would put it. It's a beautiful piece."

Jeannette turned it over, staring at the price sticker. "I don't know if I want to spend this much for it."

Kara took the exquisitely woven tray from her mother, walked over to the counter, and gave it to the salesclerk. "I'll take this one, and I'd like you to gift wrap it," she said, handing her a credit card.

"Kara!" Jeannette hissed.

"Mama?"

"What is it?"

"You're giving me a headache."

"That's because you need to eat. The only time you get headaches is when you don't eat. What did you eat today?"

Kara rolled her eyes upward. "Can't you stop being a mother for five minutes?"

Jeannette stood up straight and pulled back her shoulders. "No. Once you become a mother, you'll know exactly what I'm talking about."

"That's not going to happen any time soon." Jeannette moved closer, placing her ear against Kara's chest. "What are you doing?"

"I'm listening to your biological clock. It's getting louder."

"No comment."

Those were the last two words Kara exchanged with Jeannette until they sat at a table for two at Jack's Fish House. They'd had to wait twenty minutes before they were seated because it was Saturday night and the island's date night. She found herself glancing around the crowded restaurant for a glimpse of Jeff. Even if she closed her eyes, she was able to recall every feature of his face, the sound of his mellifluous voice, and his body's clean, masculine scent. What she didn't want to think about was the awesome sight of his magnificent chest or how her body had reacted when he'd kissed her on the beach.

Kara had told her mother Jeff was her friend when she wanted him to be so much more. She didn't think that was possible because on an island as small as Cavanaugh everyone would be in her business, while in New York she didn't know the name of her closest neighbor. The only way she and Jeff could hope for a measure of anonymity would be to go into Charleston.

"I can't believe this menu."

Jeannette's voice had broken into her thoughts. "What about it?"

"It has all of my favorite dishes. I'm beginning to like the Lowcountry."

Kara smiled. She, too, was beginning to like the Lowcountry *and* Sheriff Hamilton.

Chapter Nine

Kara was sitting on the porch with her mother when Jeff drove up the live oak alleé. He'd called the house earlier that morning to let them know he would come by at two.

"He's gorgeous," Jeannette whispered when Jeff got out of the car.

"That he is." Kara sighed, like a vapid heroine in the Regency novels she favored.

"Is he married?"

Kara didn't have time to answer when Jeff placed a booted foot on the first stair. Rising to her feet, she extended her hands. "Hello again," she crooned when he towered over her.

Dipping his head, Jeff kissed her cheek. "How are you?"

"I'm well. How are you?"

His dark eyes shimmered like polished jet. "Wonderful." His gaze shifted to Jeannette. He held out his hand, gently easing Jeannette off the cushioned rocker. "Jeff Hamilton, Mrs. Newell."

"It's Jeannette," she insisted, smiling.

Kara watched the dynamics play out between her mother and the sheriff of Cavanaugh Island. Jeannette stared up at Jeff under lowered lashes. The gesture was unequivocally seductive. Was that how she'd looked at Taylor Patton, where a man who'd never had a physical relationship with a woman had succumbed to her subtle seduction? Or was it Taylor who'd initiated making love after four years of a platonic friendship?

If David hadn't requested her presence at the reading of the will, Kara realized she never would've known the circumstances surrounding her birth. She didn't blame her mother or Austin for keeping her paternity a secret for thirty-three years. After all, Jeannette did reach out to Taylor to inform him that he was going to be a father not once, but twice, and she had no recourse but to get on with her life.

Thankfully Austin hadn't rejected the woman who'd promised to save herself for him, but married her, claiming another man's child as his own. Kara may have shared Taylor's DNA, but she doubted whether he could ever be the father Austin was.

Kara's gaze lingered on Jeff's spit-shined boots, black tailored slacks, and a crisp light blue shirt open at the neck. She smiled when she saw the engraved corps belt buckle. Her smile became a full grin when he offered Jeannette his arm and led her off the porch to his grandmother's Toyota Camry.

"Aren't you coming?" Jeannette called out as Jeff seated her in the passenger seat.

Kara locked the front door and then looped her

cross-body bag over her chest and picked up a decorative shopping bag off the table. Jeff met her as she made her way off the porch. "Your mother is as pampered as she is beautiful," he said in her ear.

She smiled up at him. "Oh, you noticed."

He nodded, patting her free hand tucked into the bend of his arm. "It's no wonder Taylor couldn't resist her."

Kara had no comeback as Jeff escorted her to the sedan, holding the rear door open and waiting for her to get in. Relaxing against the leather seat, she stared at the back of her mother's head. There was no doubt Jeannette was enjoying herself. Kara thought about their meal the previous night. Instead of entrées, they'd ordered appetizers at Jack's, allowing them to sample dishes they liked and some that were unfamiliar.

Jeannette did something Kara rarely saw her do. She ordered a beer with her meal. There had always been beer in the house whenever her father came home on leave. The first few days of his leave he would go into the equivalent of a mancave, sink in his favorite chair, grab a beer, and watch sporting events around the clock. He wouldn't even move to eat, asking his wife to bring his meals to him. By day number three, after he'd gone through twenty-four hours of military withdrawal, he emerged from the cave ready to immerse himself into civilian life.

It took only ten minutes to drive from Angels Landing to Jeff's house, door-to-door. Corrine was standing on the porch when Jeff parked alongside the updated two-story house. During her trips throughout the island, Kara had seen homes ranging from those that were one story, built high off the ground, and some with tin roofs to sprawling two-story colonials along private roads where the owners had named their plots. Jeff's house claimed white vinyl siding, dark green shutters, and a wraparound porch.

Not waiting for Jeff to assist her, Kara exited the car and climbed the porch steps. "Thank you for having us, Miss Corrine," she said, kissing the older woman's smooth, scented cheek.

"I want you to remember that you're always welcome here. And you don't have to wait for Jeffrey to invite you."

"I'll be certain to remember that, Miss Corrine." She handed her the shopping bag. "I hope there's something in here you like."

Corrine peered into the bag, smiling. "Who told you I liked onion and chow relish?"

"I haven't lived in New York that long that I've forgotten Southerners love their relishes."

"You're right. Go on in and rest yourself while I meet your mama. It's going to be at least half an hour before we sit down to eat."

Walking into the parlor, Kara inhaled a plethora of mouthwatering aromas. It smelled like Easter, Thanksgiving, and Christmas all rolled into one. There were a few times when she didn't come home for Thanksgiving and Easter, but she'd never missed spending a Christmas in Little Rock since leaving at eighteen.

She sat on a pale pink love seat with green leaves. There was a green one with pink roses facing her. The parlor was intimate, inviting one to come sit and relax. Live plants in painted bowls sat on side tables, and a trio of flowering begonias sat on a runner lining an oak credenza.

Jeff entered the room and sat down beside her. "Gram just found out that she and your mother are sorority sisters."

"That explains the pink and green," she said, laughing. "Where did your grandmother go to college?"

"B-CU."

"So she's a Bethune-Cookman Wildcat."

Jeff smiled. "So you're familiar with the Wildcats?"

"B-CU was on my college tour list."

"Where did you finally end up?" Jeff asked.

"Columbia."

He whistled. "Miss Ivy League." He draped an arm over her shoulders. "How long is your mama staying?"

"She says a week."

"How does she like the Lowcountry?"

Shifting slightly, Kara turned to look directly at Jeff. "She really likes it."

"Did you tell her you're staying?"

Kara closed her eyes. When she opened them, she saw Jeff staring at her, an impassive expression freezing his features. Whenever he looked at her like that, she felt as if he'd put up a shield to keep her from getting close. Was this the way it had been with the other women in his past? Show an interest and he'd shut down emotionally?

Don't analyze the man, Kara, the silent voice reminded her. It had been that way with all of the men she met. Within minutes of their introduction, she would begin to analyze his body language and everything that came out of his mouth.

"Yes. Even though she's accepted my rationale, she still doesn't like that I'm living alone."

"Do you live alone in New York?"

"No," she said, shaking her head. "I have a roommate."

"I see her point."

"Why are you taking her side?"

Jeff rubbed several strands of her hair between his fingers. "It's not about taking sides, baby. You have to understand where she's coming from. You're her child, and she has a right to be concerned about you."

"I'm a thirty-three-year-old woman, Jeff. I've lived on my own for the past fifteen years, fifteen years in a city of eight million people. If I can survive in New York City, then I believe I can survive anywhere. There are probably more people living in my Manhattan high-rise than in all of Angels Landing."

"And doesn't that make you feel safer in Angels Landing?"

"Yes. I'd never leave my door unlocked in New York."

"We do have crime here, but it's basically with teenagers coming from the mainland."

"What about the kids who live here?"

"They know better. Either they'll get the business from me or from their parents. Within days of installing security cameras in the Cove, the tagging of fishermen's boats stopped. Folks in the Creek and Landing don't want cameras because they feel it's an invasion of their privacy, but I know they'll change their tune once there's a rash of break-ins or vandalism."

Kara leaned into Jeff. "Are you saying I should lock my doors during the day?"

Lowering his head, he buried his face in her hair, seemingly inhaling the scent. "I want you to be careful, Kara. Kenny told me about Analeigh showing up at your house. She doesn't drive, so that meant she walked almost a mile to come to see you. Anyone who comes over on the ferry or causeway could do the same. And I'm certain you'd either open your door or talk to them because you don't know who they are. I make it my business and that of my deputies to do foot patrols. This way they get to familiarize themselves with everyone on the island."

"I'll be careful."

"Say it like you mean it, Kara."

Kara rested her hand alongside his face. "I promise I will be very careful."

Jeff kissed her forehead. "That's better."

"Jeffrey, please turn off the stove and plate the chicken."

Kara and Jeff sprang apart like teenagers who'd been caught doing something they weren't supposed to be doing. She met her mother's questioning gaze. Jeannette winked at the same time, a knowing smile softening her mouth, and Kara returned it with one of her own. There were very few things she could hide from her mother, so she'd learned never to lie to her.

She pushed off the love seat. "Show me where I can wash my hands, and I'll help you," she said, following Jeff as he headed toward the half bath off the kitchen.

"Move over," Kara ordered when they crowded into the small space. "You're hogging the sink."

Shifting, Jeff stood behind her and held his hands under the running water. "I need soap."

Kara felt his breath on the nape of her neck and his hardness pulsing against her hips. "Move back."

He fastened his mouth to the side of her neck. "First it's move over, and now it's move back."

"I can feel you, Jeff."

"Now you know what I feel whenever I'm around you."

Lowering her head, she closed her eyes. "Please don't do this to me."

"Do what?"

"You're getting me aroused."

He laughed softly. "Why should I be the only one aroused?"

"My mother and your grandmother are waiting for us."

"To be continued," Jeff whispered.

Five minutes later they sat at the table, passing serving bowls and chatting casually. "How come you didn't pledge a sorority like your mother?" Corrine asked Kara as she handed her a serving bowl.

Jeff took the bowl from her, holding it while she placed a spoonful of cabbage on her plate. "I didn't have time. I was carrying eighteen credits every semester."

Unfolding her napkin, Jeannette placed it on her lap. "You could pledge as a graduate."

Kara stared across the dining room table at her mother. "I don't have time to pledge, Mama."

"You're going to live here, so what's stopping you from finding a Charleston chapter."

"If you were to pledge, which sorority would you choose?" Jeff asked.

She gave him a sidelong glance. When Corrine set the table, she'd sat her and Jeff together while she and Jeannette sat side by side. "I don't know."

"You don't know?" Jeannette and Corrine chorused.

Kara slowly chewed and then swallowed a forkful of chicken. Corrine had prepared a delicious dinner: stewed chicken with dumplings so light and fluffy they melted on the tongue, steamed cabbage, baked sweet potatoes, and corn bread.

"I don't like the pink-and-green combination."

"It's on and poppin' now," Jeff said under his breath.

Jeannette then Corrine launched into a discourse that

it wasn't about the colors but the organization. Then each went on to talk about all the notable AKAs and their service projects.

Laughing, Kara put up a hand. "Please stop. I feel as if I'm sitting under a hot light being interrogated *and* intimidated into confessing to a crime I didn't commit."

"Easy there, baby," Jeff drawled. "Let's not start with the cop jokes."

Kara pressed her shoulder to Jeff's. "Ooooo. Aren't we touchy," she teased.

"No I'm not."

"Let it go, Jeffrey. She's not intimidated. And I think you've finally met your match."

"To be continued," he said, repeating the promise he'd made to Kara in the bathroom.

The conversation shifted to local politics, Corrine recounting what she'd heard about another developer who'd approached several of the Cove's older residents. "Now they're going after folks who don't have any children or grandchildren to look after their property once they die."

Jeff took a swallow of sweet tea. "I don't know why they continue to sniff around the Cove because they know no one is going to sell to them."

"What about Haven Creek?" Kara asked.

Corrine looked directly at her. "They're sixty-forty against the developers. It's a bit different in Angels Landing."

"The last survey put them at seventy-thirty," Jeff added. "And with the Pattons leading the charge that percentage could go higher."

Kara set down her fork. "Why would they want to sell their land? And if they did, where would they go?"

Corrine dabbed the corners of her mouth with her napkin. "I know you haven't been here long, but how much contact have you had with your relatives?"

"Very little."

"You should try and keep it that way."

"Gram!" Jeff chastised.

Corrine waved her hand. "I'm right and you know it, so don't 'Gram' me. Those folks are not right. Ever since Teddy left everything to Taylor, they've been out for revenge."

A warning voice whispered in Kara's head as she recalled the threats directed at her. "Revenge against who?"

"Whoever is the owner of the house."

Jeff placed a hand over Kara's knee under the table. "Gram, you're frightening her."

"There's no need to sugarcoat it, Jeffrey. She needs to hear the truth."

"Is my daughter in some kind of danger?" Jeannette asked.

"No," Jeff said quickly. "Nothing's going to happen to Kara."

Jeannette massaged the back of her neck. "Can you guarantee that, Jeff? Because right now I don't feel very comfortable with the direction of this conversation."

"Yes. I guarantee it," he said with such conviction that everyone at the table looked at him. "Gram, I think it's time Kara hears the truth about her ancestors."

Corrine pushed back her chair, coming to her feet. "Let's go into the sunroom where it's more comfortable."

Kara stood up when Jeff pulled back her chair. "I'll help clear the table."

Corrine shook her head. "Please leave it. I'll do it later.

After I tell you about your folks, we'll have dessert and coffee."

Jeff rested a hand at the small of Kara's back when they filed out of the dining room and into the expansive enclosed back porch. The space reminded her of the garden room at Angels Landing.

Corrine sat in an easy chair and rested her feet on the ottoman. She waited until everyone was seated, then said, "People have always thought of the Pattons as Lowcountry royalty but the griots tell a much different story. They told stories long before they were written down, passed down from one to another. It began back in 1830-something when Shipley Patton bought land here to start up a rice plantation. He was already growing cotton on the mainland but decided Carolina Gold was much more profitable. He was an architect by profession and drew up plans for what would become the grandest house on the island, calling it Angels Landing. Meanwhile he had the swamps drained so he could plant his rice, Sea Island cotton, and indigo. Shipley was an anomaly in his day because all his skilled laborers were free blacks. It took two years to complete the house and furnish it. He moved his family from what is now Goose Creek, and he and his wife hosted a lavish ball, inviting people from the mainland.

"That summer he lost his wife and two daughters to swamp fever. After that he always took his two remaining sons back to the mainland during the summers. A year later he remarried, and his second wife eventually gave him two sons and four daughters. Even though dueling was outlawed, Shipley challenged another planter to a duel. The man supposedly had spread a rumor that Shipley's youngest son wasn't his and the boy's father was a mulatto slave. Unfortunately Shipley's gun jammed, and he was mortally wounded. It took him two weeks to die."

Kara was barely able to control the gasp that escaped her. "Was he the child of a mulatto?"

"The slaves said yes while his wife denied it. Fortunately for her, Oakes looked more white than black. Mrs. Patton closed up the house and moved her children to Charleston to be closer to her parents. Years later a small-pox epidemic swept through the Lowcountry, and all of the Pattons except Oakes and his half sister were among the many casualties. She joined a convent, and Oakes inherited everything.

"Oakes eventually married a local girl who refused to move to the island because she feared coming down with swamp fever. She hosted glittering parties while he entertained himself at Angels Landing when he made nightly visits to the slave village. He fathered a lot of black children, but when he saw a slave woman from a neighboring plantation, he knew he had to have her. Word was he paid nearly five thousand dollars for her, an unheard-of sum during that time. Once the woman with whom he'd found himself enthralled told him she was pregnant, he moved her into the main house and did something most slaveholders refused to do. He freed her children on their first birthday."

Kara closed her eyes for several seconds. "Why did he free her children when he hadn't freed the others?"

"Wasn't it obvious, Kara? He was in love with her. Their relationship was scandalous because they were living together as husband and wife. Most married men didn't bring their mistresses into their homes."

"How many children did they have?"

"It was either three or four. Everything changed when word got back to his wife, and she'd become the laughingstock of Lowcountry society. And what made it even worse to Rebecca Patton was that he'd refused to sleep with her and give her a child.

"Rebecca waited until her husband had sailed to England to meet with a cotton broker; then she paid several men to bring her to Angels Landing. Waiting until nightfall, she had them douse the house with a flammable liquid and then set it afire. Everyone inside the house died from smoke inhalation. Rebecca believed she'd wiped out her husband's mistress and his bastards, but there was one child who'd escaped the carnage. Jacob was a two-year-old boy who was prone to sleepwalking. That night he'd crawled out of his crib and out of the house. The next morning he was found sleeping under a tree. I'd heard that my great-great-great-grandmother took Jacob in, hiding him in case Rebecca would come back to kill him, too. When Oakes returned to find his home damaged by fire and his mistress and children dead, he abandoned the property and never returned to Angels Landing."

Jeannette held her throat. "What happened to Rebecca?"

A slow smile spread over Corrine's face, a smile so much like Jeff's. "What's the expression about revenge best served cold? Well, Rebecca Patton got hers served hot. Apparently she'd gotten up one night, lit a candle, and went downstairs to sit on the porch because she'd become an insomniac. She probably tripped, and the lighted candle landed on her nightdress, and she went up in flames. By the time house servants heard her screams, she'd been burned over half her body."

"Did she die?" Kara asked.

"The Lord wasn't that merciful. She recovered from the burns, but never left the house because of the scars to her hands, face, and neck. One day she took an overdose of laudanum and never woke up. Oakes started drinking, and he gambled away Angels Landing. Once word reached the island that Becky was dead, Oakes was told that his youngest child had survived the fire. He had someone retrieve the boy, and they went to live in Europe for several years. Jacob had trained to be a doctor at the University of Edinburgh, and once he and his father returned to the States after the Civil War, Jacob was fully fluent in French, Italian, and Spanish.

"Unlike his father, Jacob couldn't pass into the white race, so he lived in Charleston as a free man of color. However, he was treated with polite respect because he was a doctor. After the war, rice production became too expensive, and soon, most plantations on the Sea Islands fell into bankruptcy and were sold off to new owners. Jacob's driving ambition had been to make enough money to buy the house where he'd been born and restore it."

"Did he?" Kara had asked yet another question.

"He couldn't do it directly because antiblack sentiment was rampant throughout the South, and the Klan had begun burning the homes, schools, and churches of former slaves. He finally convinced his father to negotiate the sale for him. Oakes agreed, and once again Angels Landing belonged to a Patton. Jacob relocated his practice to the island, and the folks here had their first colored doctor. He lived in one of the outbuildings while the main house was being renovated. He married a Gullah woman from Edisto Island, and they had eight children, six that lived to adulthood. I remember the old folks talking about how the Pattons, whether dark or light, all had Oakes's gray eyes, and in each succeeding generation they had at least one or two children who'd die young. Some say Rebecca put a curse on her husband's children and his children's children."

Jeff shook his head. "Come on, Gram. That's just superstitious nonsense."

"Is it, Jeffrey?" Corrine asked. "Taylor's sister wasn't thirty when she died from that brain tumor." She turned to Kara. "It's not the men in the family, but the women they marry who turn into villainesses. Cornelius was a gentle soul, but very few people could stand Theodora. Once she became Mrs. Patton you'd think she was the queen of England. She could never keep any help because she systematically bullied them. The only ones who stayed were Willie and Iris Todd.

"She practically destroyed her children when she pitted one against the other. Taylor had become her favorite, and as a result his siblings hated him. He'd tried reaching out to them, but they turned their backs on him. The only time they did come together was when it came time for them to make a decision on whether to put Teddy in a nursing home. That's when it became unanimous because they were glad to be rid of her. Taylor was the only one to visit her, and she rewarded him when she left him everything in her will: house, land, and money.

"His brothers and sisters talked about him as if they didn't share blood, so Taylor withdrew from them completely. He'd put the word out that if any of them stepped foot on his property, he would shoot them on sight for trespassing. I don't believe they were notified of his death until after he was cremated and his ashes were scattered in the ocean. Now you know the story of your people. Their entire lives were shrouded in secrets, lies, illegitimate babies, arson, and murder—all the ingredients for a very interesting novel. I only tell you this because you're not going to know where you're going if you don't know where you've come from."

"Why don't you write the novel, Gram?"

Corrine's mouth tightened into a thin line as she glared at her grandson. "It's not my place to presume to write about someone else's people. It's the past, so let sleeping dogs lie."

Hours later Kara stood on the porch, staring out at the encroaching darkness. It was only now that she was able to react to Corrine's account of her biological father's family.

"Lives . . . shrouded in secrets, lies, illegitimate babies." It was as if Corrine was talking about her. She'd lived more than three decades believing one man was her father when he wasn't. Her mother had lied by omission because she had no intention of telling her Taylor Patton was her biological father if he hadn't written her into his will. And last but certainly not least, illegitimate babies. If Austin hadn't married Jeannette, then Kara would've become one of an endless list of babies out of wedlock. In essence her entire life had been a lie. This is not to say she didn't have a wonderful childhood, but if she couldn't trust her own mother, then who could she trust?

"Kara?"

Her eyelids fluttered. Kara had been so deep in thought that she hadn't heard her mother come up behind her. "Yes, Mama?"

"It's after midnight."

"I know."

"Don't you think it's time you go to bed?"

She shook her head. "I can't sleep."

"Is it because of what Corrine told you this afternoon?"

"Yes," she admitted. "It was and still is a lot to take in."

Jeannette took a step and put her arms around her daughter's waist. "What's bothering you, baby?"

Kara didn't know why, but she felt like crying. "Everything."

"Do you want to talk about it?"

She shook her head. "No, because what you want to talk about is something we should've discussed a long time ago. You say you love me, but it's apparent you didn't love me enough to trust me with your tainted little secret. Did you actually believe I would've loved you or Daddy any less if you'd told me about Taylor? I talk to my clients about trust issues, and right now I'm having a bit of my own."

"Why now, Kara? You didn't seem that upset this morning when I told you about Taylor."

"I guess it's taken a while to sink in."

Jeannette made a sound that came from the back of her throat. "You wouldn't be like this if Corrine hadn't filled your head with all that talk about people who have nothing to do with you."

Kara pushed her mother's arms down, turning around and looking at her. "That's where you're wrong. They have everything to do with me. You may not share blood with the Pattons, but I do. I'm not proud of some of the things they've done, but they are still my family."

"A week ago you didn't know these people existed!" Jeannette shouted, her voice carrying easily in the silent night.

"Don't shift the blame, Mama. I should've known about

them as soon as I was old enough to understand that I had another family. What were you afraid of? That I would judge you for getting pregnant from one man when you were practically engaged to another?"

Jeannette ran her fingers through her hair, pushing feathered bangs off her forehead. "Now that I look back, I realize not telling you was a mistake, but I thought it was best because I didn't want to confuse you. You're angry and you have every right to be, but I did it because I wanted to protect you."

"Protect me from what, Mama? The truth?"

"No, baby. I wanted to protect you from the ugliness that's so insidious to the Pattons. Corrine said a lot of things about Taylor's family I didn't know. But there were other things I did know, and that's why I wanted to protect you from them. They're no better than a pit of vipers turning on themselves. However, you seem so hell-bent on living here among them when it's obvious they would prefer to see you gone."

"I'm not afraid of them. If they expect me to pack my bags and leave, then they don't know who I am. One thing I learned having a marine as a father is that they never ran and never will. I'm going to stay and do what I have to do."

"Do you intend to shoot them if they come on your property like Taylor threatened to do?"

Kara couldn't help but smile. Austin had taught her how to shoot the year she turned thirteen. The recoil from the automatic had nearly knocked her off her feet, but after he'd shown her the two-hand grip, she was proficient enough to hit her target.

"I would if I could find Taylor's gun. If I have any problems with the Pattons, then I'll report it to the sheriff's office."

"What about an emergency, Kara? Do you think the sheriff can get to your place in three minutes or less?"

"If Jeff can't, then one of his deputies can. The deputies live in each town, so response time will be less than three minutes."

"The only thing I'm going to say before I go inside is be careful."

A nervous smile trembled over Kara's mouth. "I will." She moved closer and kissed Jeannette. "Good night, Mama."

Jeannette hugged her as if she feared she would disappear in front of her eyes. "Good night, baby."

Kara waited for her mother to retreat inside the house before she walked over and sat on a rocker. Back and forth, back and forth. She rocked until she felt herself relaxing. Then she rocked some more until her eyelids started to droop. Then something woke her. Sitting up straight, she squinted in the darkness as the shape of a vehicle came closer.

Pushing to her feet, she stood in a corner of the porch to make herself a smaller target. A smile parted her lips when she recognized the Jeep, then the man who stepped out.

"What are you doing here?"

Jeff placed a foot on the first stair. "I'm out on patrol. I didn't expect to see you up this late."

Kara rested a hand on the column, its coolness seeping into her palm. "I'm glad you drove up because I was falling asleep." He mounted two more steps until his head was level with hers.

"Go inside, Kara, and don't forget to lock the door."

She leaned close enough for his moist breath to feather over her mouth. "I'd like to reciprocate and invite you and Miss Corrine to dinner whenever you have a day off."

"Are you catering it?"

Kara pulled back. "No. I'm going to cook."

"You can cook?" he teased.

"You can go home now."

Cradling her face, Jeff brushed a kiss over her parted lips. "Go inside and lock the door."

Easing back she affected a snappy salute. "Yes, captain!"

Jeff's hand cupped her hip, holding her captive. "You're pushing it."

Kara rested her hand over his. "Good night, Jeff."

Tightening his hold, he cupped the back of her head and slanted his mouth over hers, stealing her breath away. It ended as quickly as it'd begun. "Good night, Kara."

With her mouth burning, knees shaking, and her heated blood racing through her body, Kara managed to make her way to the door before she begged Jeff to make love to her. She didn't know what it was about him that elicited a desperate need to lie with him.

She opened, closed, and locked the door like an automaton. Jeff had come at the wrong time to check on her, or she'd picked the wrong time to sit outside. Now she would go to bed aroused, remembering Jeff's confession of his own arousal.

Crossing her legs at the knees, she waited for her traitorous body to return to normal. Kara knew she and Jeff had to stop—stop the sexual teasing before they embarked on something or a situation that could prove disastrous, at least for her. She'd never been able to engage in a physical relationship and remain emotionally detached. She had never learned to love with her head and not her heart.

Maybe, she thought, it was time she learned.

Chapter Ten

Jeff sat opposite Spencer White, the mayor of Sanctuary Cove, acknowledging him with an imperceptible nod. He, not Spencer, would chair the session. When Spencer set up the meeting with the mayors of Angels Landing and Haven Creek, the two men expressed a reluctance to attend because they had always felt like the Cove's stepchildren. Whenever tourists came to Cavanaugh Island, it was the Cove that took in the lion's share of tourist revenue. Lacing his fingers together on the conference table, Jeff curbed the urge to fist his hands and reveal his frustration. "Don't you think your constituents would like to hear what I propose before you preclude to speak for them?" he asked Harlan Patton.

Harlan's hazel eyes narrowed as he leaned forward. "I read Spencer's memo, and I speak for my constituents."

Jeff smiled at the man who was a masculine version of Kara. "No, you don't. You speak for yourself, Harlan."

"It's Mayor Patton to you, Sheriff Hamilton."

Spencer White, an attorney with movie star looks, brought his palm down on the table. "Enough, Harlan! We're here not to attack one another, but to come together for the good of the island. Jeff didn't spend three days in Columbia with more than two hundred other law enforcement officers for you to blow him off."

Haven Creek's mayor, Douglas Rosen, nodded. "Spencer's right. I want to hear more about the governor's small-town crime prevention initiative."

Jeff nodded to the portly man with a thinning pate. Douglas, a direct descendant of Thomas Cavanaugh, the pirate that had given the island its name, was a retired FBI forensic analyst. "Thank you, Doug." He directed his attention to Harlan again. "Perhaps, it's because you're the only mayor on Cavanaugh Island lacking law enforcement experience that you're opposed to installing security cameras in Angels Landing. You've seen the cameras in the Cove's downtown area and know they're not that conspicuous. They would be even less conspicuous in the Landing because it's more densely forested. But just knowing they're there should be enough to deter burglaries."

"Where would you put the cameras?" Harlan asked.

"Along all the roads, both public and private."

"Which means you'll see everyone coming and going."

Jeff leaned back in his chair. "Do you see that as a problem, Harlan?"

"Do you think folks want Big Brother spying on them?"

"Only if they have something to hide," Jeff countered.

"Not only would my deputies spend less time driving around on patrol, but we would also save on fuel."

"I'm in agreement with Jeff," Douglas said. "Fuel costs for our official vehicles this past year were outrageous."

Spencer nodded in agreement. "It's the same in the Cove."

Picking up a pencil, Jeff drew interlocking circles on a pad. "That's because the Creek and the Cove have to cover fire calls for the Landing because they still don't have a fire department. Perhaps, Harlan, it's time the residents of Angels Landing share in the cost of the other two towns responding to fires and medical emergencies."

A rush of color suffused Harlan's face. "Two years ago Spencer and Doug agreed, in a show of good faith, to have their volunteer fire departments cover the Landing because it would be cost-effective rather than erecting a building and having to buy a pumper truck."

Jeff knew it was time to proverbially cut Harlan off at the knees. "That agreement is due to expire before the end of the year, and I suggest you revise your projected budget to include a line for fire prevention, safety, and emergency services."

Harlan's gaze shifted from Jeff to Spencer and Douglas, then back to Jeff. "Are you really going to leave the residents of the Landing without access to a fire department?"

Crossing his arms over his chest, Jeff slowly shook his head. "No, Harlan. I don't have the authority to make that determination. But you can't have it both ways. Last year you saved money by not having to pay the salary and benefits of a full-time sheriff while you managed not to raise property taxes because you don't have a fire department. The security cameras and the command center won't cost us anything. Fortunately, Spencer had the wherewithal to apply for a grant to offset the expense of installing and maintaining it."

Harlan's jaw tightened. "I don't want our people spied on."

The frustration Jeff felt whenever he met with the mayor of Angels Landing escalated. "What the hell do you have to hide, Patton! You keep talking about *'our people'* when I suspect it's you. I shouldn't have to remind you there's crime on Cavanaugh Island. And statistics show there are more domestic situations, vehicle infractions, and 911 calls from Angels Landing than the Cove and Creek combined. My part-time deputies are hardly part-time when they have to work twelve-hour shifts three days a week."

Doug rested a hand on Harlan's shoulder. "Pick your battles, Patton. When your people hear that cameras are a deterrent to crime in the Cove and the Creek and that Spencer and I decided not to renew the fire department agreement, they're going to vote you out of office. And I shouldn't have to remind you that the Landing has the highest property taxes on the island because you don't want a business district."

Harlan shook off the hand. "Is that all you have? Threats and intimidation?"

Jeff blew out a breath. "You can't continue to hide behind the privacy pretext. Excuse me, gentlemen, but I'm still on duty." He rose in one fluid motion, his lethal gaze pinning Kara's cousin to his seat. "I'll see you around, Patton."

"I guess you will whenever you come sniffing around Kara. You think I don't know about your so-called night runs when you supposedly are checking up on her. How is she, Jeff? Is the little schemer a screamer or—" The words were snatched from Harlan's open mouth when Jeff reached across the table and slapped him with an open hand.

In a movement too quick for the eye to follow, Jeff grabbed the front of Harlan's shirt, pulling him half on and half off the table. "If I ever hear something like that come out of that filthy mouth again, I will hit you again. And next time, it won't be a bitch-slap." He released Harlan as if he were throwing away a soiled garment.

"You saw that!" Harlan gasped, pressing his hand to the left side of his face. "I want him arrested for assault."

Spencer stood up, Douglas rising with him. "I didn't see anything. Did you, Doug?"

The forensic analyst shook his head. "Sorry, Harlan, but you must be hallucinating." The three men burst into laughter when Harlan raced out of the office. Doug wiped the tears from his eyes. "Jeff, Spencer, I'd love to stay and talk, but I have to meet my brother who's been bitchin' and moanin' about losing his only female architect because he's too cheap to pay her what she's worth. It would serve him right if she opened her own office next door and gave him some serious competition."

"I'm not going to touch that," Jeff remarked.

Doug inclined his head. "Mayor, sheriff. It's always a pleasure." He shook hands with Spencer and Jeff, then left the room.

Walking over to the door, Spencer closed it, turning to face Jeff. "I know there's always been bad blood between you two. Just don't be surprised if Harlan goes to the Charleston PD to file an assault charge. And if I'm called as a witness, I'll have to tell the truth. I can't afford to risk jeopardizing my license to practice if I'm charged with perjury."

"Don't worry about it, Spencer. I don't think Harlan's going to risk his so-called playboy reputation when he admits I slapped him like he was a girl."

"You're probably right. Harlan's all about image. But does he know something I don't about you and Taylor's daughter?"

Jeff told the mayor about his cousin's phone call following the reading of Taylor's will. "Just say the Pattons were less than hospitable in welcoming their new cousin."

"They've always been a strange lot, Jeff. Collectively they have more money than any family on the island, but what I don't understand is their competing with one another."

"Crabs in a barrel, Spencer. That's the only way to describe them." Picking up his baseball cap, Jeff put it on. "When can I expect to see my new office furniture?"

"I'll have my secretary call the vendor, then get back to you. Now that we have the grant, you and your men will be expected to wear uniforms."

Jeff wanted to remind Spencer that he'd worn a uniform for more than half his life. Getting his deputies to wear one when on duty was another matter. He left the conference room, nodding and smiling at the mayor's administrative assistant. He knew slapping Harlan went against his training, but if he'd hit the potty-mouthed man the way he truly wanted, then Harlan would've wound up with either a broken jaw or, worse, a broken neck.

He and Harlan had never gotten along. As a schoolboy Harlan had put the *b* in bully. Jeff had permitted Harlan to intimidate him because of his grandmother's warning that intelligent people used their brains instead of their fists to settle an argument. It only stopped once they'd entered high school. Jeff had joined the football team, and at six four and weighing close to two hundred pounds, he'd become a human wrecking machine, known for setting a school record by sacking opposing teams' quarterbacks—a record that still stood. Not only was he strong, but he was also very fast.

Instead of taking the tunnel connecting the town hall with the court and the station house, he walked out into the bright sunlight. He needed to get outdoors and clear his head. Reaching for his cell, he hit speed dial. "Winnie, Jeff. I just left Mayor White's office. I'm going down to the Muffin Corner. Do you want me to bring something back for you?...Today, Winnie," he told his clerk when she changed her mind for the third time.

"Can you stop at the supermarket deli and bring me back a tuna salad on a bed of lettuce. Please ask them if it's fresh. If not, then I'll take chicken salad on a bed of lettuce. And make certain they give you crackers and a pickle."

Jeff exhaled an audible sigh. "Aren't you going to give me a third choice, Winnie?"

"You must be feeling good today."

"Why would you say that?"

"Because you're trying to be a comedian. And I must say not a very good one."

He headed in the direction of Main Street. "I'll see you later."

Jeff knew his hitting Harlan had everything to do with Kara and not because he still harbored a grudge against a man who'd made his boyhood a living hell. Although each town had its own elementary-middle school, half the students from the Landing were bused to the Creek and the other half to the Cove when their school burned to the ground from an electrical fire. It'd taken two years for it to be rebuilt. The construction had been delayed for almost a year when the school board had to decide on whether it should be a brick or wooden structure. In the end it was stucco.

It'd been the worst two years of his life, but it taught Jeff something about himself he hadn't known he had: extraordinary self-control. At least he had until Harlan opened his mouth to mention Kara. Harlan hadn't known Jeff to retaliate with a physical attack. He could rationalize and tell himself that it was payback for past bullying, but he would be lying to himself.

It had everything to do with Kara and his growing feelings for her. It'd been so easy for him to use David's warning as an excuse to see her. But how long would he be able to continue in that vein before she saw through the ruse. The more he saw Kara, the more he wanted to be with her. She turned him on, made him want to make love to her, and he couldn't remember when he'd met a woman whose intense appeal triggered a lust he found impossible to ignore. She was easy to talk to, made him laugh because there were times when he took himself and life much too seriously. Kara understood his dedication to his job as island sheriff and the sacrifices he'd made to care for his grandmother.

Jeff was aware that resigning his commission and returning to Sanctuary Cove had changed him. In the past his grandmother had taken care of him, but now it was his turn to take care of her. At that time the military had become his extended family, the men under his command his brothers in arms, and his dedication to his country and corps unwavering.

Then there were his past relationships; they were never smooth or easy. The women complained they would've preferred competing with another woman for love and affection, not his career. He was also aware that his past relationships hadn't worked out because he feared loving and losing.

Resigning his commission and moving back to the

Cove was one of the easiest decisions he'd ever made in his life. It'd become a case of no contest. His grandmother's heart attack had become a reality check that he could lose her like he'd lost his mother, and he intended to hold onto Corrine Hamilton for as long as he could.

A smile tilted the corners of his mouth when he thought of Kara. There was something about her that had slipped under his emotional radar where he felt the need to protect her, too. Harlan's outburst and his distasteful reference as to her moral character spoke volumes, and if the other Pattons felt the same as Harlan, then Kara would fare no better than her father. They'd banded together for a common cause: greed.

"Good afternoon, Jeff."

He waved to the elderly man standing in the doorway to the liquor store. "Good afternoon, Mr. Washington. How's the family?" he asked, slowing his stride.

"Everybody's good. Praise the Lord. I want to tell you that those folks who want to buy us out are back. One of them offered my brother more money than he'd ever made in his life to sell his house."

Jeff stared at the man who'd served with valor during World War II. "What did he tell them?"

"Something I can't repeat in public. But it wasn't nice. Why should he sell his house and land to a stranger when he can save it for his grandchildren? His grandbaby girl just got married, and she and her new husband are trying to buy a house, but the bank wants so much money down. Harry told them they could move in with him."

"Are they going to take him up on his offer?"

"Yup."

Jeff smiled. "Good for them. We need more young

folks living here. Meanwhile, tell your brother stay strong. And you stay well, Mr. Washington."

"You, too."

Jeff hadn't realized how much he'd missed Cavanaugh Island until he'd returned—this time to stay. He still did police work but at a much slower, more laid-back pace. The crime on the island was something he could control, and if it reached the courts, then a stern warning from the judge, a fine, or a couple of nights in jail usually was a deterrent for the defendant not to repeat the offense.

Most cities in the country had surveillance cameras to protect their citizens and to make police work easier. Living on the island had led many of the residents to believe they were immune to a lot of the big-city social ills, but Jeff knew otherwise. Unlike his predecessor he'd begun the practice of foot patrols to reacquaint himself with the townspeople and gain their trust. He'd taken an oath to protect and serve, and he wanted everyone who lived on the island to know that he was there solely for that purpose.

What he or Spencer hadn't revealed to the mayors of Angels Landing and Haven Creek was an increase in the number of residents that were approached with offers for them to sell their land. Installing the security cameras would monitor the comings and goings of those who were not permanent island residents. Everyone was aware that those in Angels Landing wanted to sell out while Haven Creek was split evenly.

Sanctuary Cove had become the only holdout. Several had called to say they believed they were being threatened, while others had felt intimidated. Jeff couldn't stop the developers from coming to the island or even canvassing potential clients, but what he wouldn't tolerate was their scare tactics to force residents to sell their property.

He turned off Main Street and onto Moss Alley, waving to Deborah as she adjusted the bookstore's window blinds. Several doors down from the Parlor he saw workmen inside a vacant storefront. A year ago there had been enough vacant stores in the downtown business district to count on both hands. Now there were less than six. It was apparent the Cove was recovering from the downturn in the economy.

Jeff walked into the Muffin Corner. The smell of brewing coffee and sweet breads was intoxicating. Mabel Kelly came from behind the counter to hug him. He kissed her cheek. "Where have you been hiding yourself? When I asked Lester about you, he said you'd run off with another man."

Pulling back, Mabel gave him her trademark gap-toothed smile. Her braided hair was covered with a black-and-white pin-striped bandana. "I don't think so. There's no way I'd give up my Lester for all the oil in Saudi Arabia and the money in Dubai. I took a couple of weeks off to go up to Atlanta to help my sister with her new baby. She had a C-section and unfortunately had complications. How's life treating you, Jeff?"

"Life is good."

"How's Miss Corrine?"

"She's good."

Mabel stared up at him. "Do you think she would like a little dog?"

Jeff shook his head. "Unfortunately, no. My grandmother is not equipped to run after a dog. Right now, the doctor doesn't want her climbing stairs. What's up with the dog?"

"My sister is a dog breeder and she gave me a little Yorkshire terrier. He's adorable, Jeff, and it's a shame

I have to leave him home all day. I want to give him to someone who has the time to take care of him. He's had all his shots, he's housebroken, and he responds to his name."

"What's his name?"

"Oliver."

Jeff twisted his mouth. "That sounds a little wimpy."

"He's a little dog. Do you know someone who might give him a good home?"

"Don't give him away until I ask around. I'd like a large container of my usual."

"What about something sweet, Jeff?" Mabel asked when she walked over to the commercial espresso coffeemaker.

He peered into the showcase with trays of tarts, cookies, brownies, and mini-doughnuts. "What's the special for the day?"

Mabel added a generous amount of cream to the coffee. "It was apple crumb cake, but it sold out before eleven."

"What do you recommend?"

"The doughnuts are always good." She held up a hand. "It's not because you're a cop, Jeff."

"No harm done, Mabel. Give me a dozen. I'll give them to the staff."

"By the way, I'm sure you heard about the dude going around bugging folks about selling their homes. Every spring and summer the vultures come and roost. When are they going to give it up?"

"I don't know, Mabel. They'll continue to come until everyone on the island is of like mind. If we stand united, then maybe they'll get the message."

He paid for his purchases, then retraced his steps, stopping at the supermarket deli for Winnie's lunch.

When Jeff returned to the station, Winnie Powell

glanced up from working on a crossword puzzle. "A tuna salad on a bed of lettuce with crackers and a pickle for the boss, and doughnuts for the staff," he teased.

Winnie blushed, her cheeks turning pink. "Are you ever going to let me live that down?"

He winked at her. "Never." Before he'd taken over as sheriff, Jeff had overheard Winnie telling someone on the phone that she'd run the police station for more than twenty years, and she would continue to run it no matter who the sheriff was. "I'm going to be in the break room."

Jeff drank his coffee, then lay on the sofa to relax. He hadn't slept well the past two nights; he'd found himself tossing and turning as the sounds and images of war came back vividly, never allowing him to return to sleep. He'd gotten out of bed, went down to the front porch, and sat there until the sun came up. He was still there when his grandmother woke. She'd asked him what time he had to go on duty, and when he told her, she suggested he try and get a few hours of sleep and that she would wake him later. The nightmares didn't come as frequently as they had in the past, but they were still there.

He'd just closed his eyes when he heard Winnie calling his name. "What is it?"

"I just got a call from a Jeannette Newell. She said there's someone out at Angels Landing trying to talk her daughter into selling her house."

Jeff sprang up like a jack-in-the-box, reached for the small two-way radio and gun belt. "Call her back and let her know I'm on my way."

Kara opened the door to find a conservatively dressed young black man standing on the porch. His blue blazer;

buttoned-down light blue shirt; red, white, and blue striped tie; gray flannel slacks; and black slip-ons were prep school chic. The only thing missing was a pair of glasses.

Her gaze lingered on his pleasant features. "Yes?"

"I'm looking for a Ms. Kara Newell."

Nice voice, she thought. "Who's asking?"

"Porter Caldwell."

"I'm afraid I don't know a Porter Caldwell."

His eyebrows shot up. "You're Kara Newell?"

She nodded. "Yes, I am. Why are you looking for me?"

Porter gestured to the half-opened door. "Can we go inside and talk?"

"I'm sorry, but I'm not in the habit of inviting strangers into my home. It comes from living in New York," Kara added quickly. "Would you mind if we sit here on the porch?"

Porter recovered quickly. "Of course not." He moved over and pulled out a chair, waiting for her to sit before sitting across from her. He stared out at the allée of live oak trees. "What a magnificent view."

Kara noticed the direction of his gaze. She didn't think she would ever get used to seeing the century-old trees forming a natural canopy over the road leading up to the house. "It is. Mr. Caldwell, what exactly do you want to talk about?"

Crossing one leg over the opposite knee, Porter stared at the young woman. "Please call me Porter. Mr. Caldwell sounds so formal. I hope you don't mind if I call you Kara."

"Not at all." Kara thought of Porter, as he wanted to be called, as a throwback to men who epitomized the term Southern gentleman. "Before we begin, I'd like to know how you've come to know my name and where I live."

"I'm here on the island looking to purchase property, and someone told me you might be interested in selling."

A slight frown appeared between her eyes. "Who told you that?"

"I don't remember. But you do have a magnificent home. It's obvious it needs some work, and there's no doubt it will be spectacular after the repairs are completed."

Kara leaned forward. "Who do you represent, Mr. Caldwell?"

"Excuse me?"

She smiled, the gesture not reaching her eyes. "I do believe you heard me, Mr. Caldwell. I'm asking who sent you to see me."

He pulled his shoulders back. "No one sent me. I told you I'm looking to purchase property on Cavanaugh Island, and I happen to love old houses."

Kara stared at the rose-pink polish on her toes, paying him no attention, noticing a chip on the big toe of her right foot. She'd missed her regularly scheduled mani-pedi back in New York. She looked up. "Do you have any idea how much this house is worth?"

Porter gave her a direct stare. "I do."

"If I threw out a figure, would you be willing to match it?"

He nodded. "Throw it out."

"Three million. And that doesn't include the furnishings." Kara was surprised that his impassive expression did not change when she'd said the first thing that had come to her mind. "Five million with the furnishings. And that's only a conservative figure because I don't have an updated appraisal."

"That's a little steep for my wallet, but if you exclude the furnishings, then it may be doable."

"Are you saying that you can give me a bank check like yesterday if I decided to sell you my home?"

"That's exactly what I'm saying."

"If you don't mind answering another question, I'd like to know how many people would live in this house if I sold it to you. Because right now I'm the only one living in a twenty-room slightly dilapidated mansion in South Carolina Lowcountry."

"There will be my brother, his fiancée, and myself."

"Are you aware that Angels Landing is listed as privately owned on the National Register of Historic Places and the property on which it sits is a US National Historic Landmark District?"

He whistled through his teeth. "I wasn't aware of those facts."

Kara wanted to tell the young man that she wasn't as gullible as she appeared. If living in New York had taught her anything, it was that hustlers came in all colors, sizes, and manners of dress. "Do you really think I would sell something so valuable for even ten million?"

He wouldn't meet her eyes. "Hypothetically, if you were to sell everything, what would be your asking price?"

"Five hundred million. And that includes the two thousand acres and everything on it."

"A half billion dollars! No property is worth that."

Kara smiled. "That's where you're wrong, Porter. It's worth that and more to developers who plan to turn it into a billionaire's playground. Hypothetically," she drawled, "they could build five thousand-square-foot condos and sell them for five million a pop, and poof, they've recouped most of their money. Then don't forget the golf course fees and country club memberships. That should bring in another cool half billion a year. Mr. Porter Caldwell, just because I speak a little slow that doesn't mean I'm slow up here." She tapped her forehead.

"You're wrong, Kara," Porter said quickly.

She decided to try another approach. "I hope I'm wrong. Leave me your business card, and I'll seriously think about your offer."

Opening his jacket, Porter reached inside his breast pocket, then patted his pants pockets. "I seem to have forgotten my cards. May I set up an appointment to see you again? I promise I'll have my cards."

"Can you go and pick them up now?"

"Today?" he asked.

"Yes, today."

Porter raised his arm and stared at his watch. "That may pose a problem because I have an early dinner meeting." Kara stood up, he rising with her. "Perhaps we can get together again tomorrow?"

"What makes you think I'm going to change my mind?"

He leaned closer. "I was hoping you would change your mind."

"Only if you meet my price."

"What if we meet over dinner? I know a wonderful little intimate restaurant on James Island that serves the most incredible seafood in the Lowcountry."

Kara couldn't wrap her head around the notion that a man she hadn't known fifteen minutes ago had just asked her out to dinner. Did he actually believe he could turn on the charm, and she would be so impressed that she would sign on the dotted line?

"I'm sorry, Porter. That's not possible."

"Why not?"

"Why not?" she repeated. "Isn't it obvious?"

"What is obvious is that I like you, and I'd like to see you again."

Kara didn't know whether to laugh in his face or turn around and walk back into the house and slam the door for dramatic effect. They stared at each other, the seconds becoming a full minute. Then Kara saw movement out of the corner of her eye. Her mother was standing in the doorway watching the exchange, and she wondered how long she'd stood there and how much she'd heard. The sound of an approaching vehicle caught her attention, and Kara turned to find someone speeding up the path to the house.

"What I'd like is for you to leave now."

She walked barefoot down the steps at the same time Jeff stepped out of the Jeep. He extended his arms, and she went into his embrace. "How did you know?"

"Your mama called me. She thought you could use some help."

Kara had her answer. It was apparent her mother had eavesdropped on their conversation. "Please get him to leave," she whispered in Jeff's ear when he dipped his head.

"Did he hurt you?"

"No, but he's annoying."

Jeff kissed her forehead. "Work with me, baby."

With his muscular arm around her waist, Kara climbed the stairs to the porch. "Porter, Sheriff Hamilton. Sweetheart, this is Porter Caldwell. He's interested in buying the house, but I told him he couldn't afford it."

"Isn't that just like a woman," Jeff drawled, shaking his head. "Why do they always presume to make decisions for us? Did she ask you if you could afford it, *son*?"

Porter's face brightened as if he'd just discovered an ally. "No, she didn't."

Jeff squinted at Kara. "Baby, didn't I tell you about that?"

She was hard-pressed not to laugh. "Yes, you did, but I figured he wasn't serious because he doesn't even have a business card."

"I...I forgot my cards, but I offered—" Porter stammered nervously.

"You offered what?" Jeff asked when Porter didn't finish his statement.

"I'd offered to take your girlfriend out to dinner so we could discuss it."

"He wants to take me to James Island for incredible seafood," Kara added innocently when Jeff glared at Porter as if he was ready to attack the man.

It was obvious the developers had sent a boy to do a man's job. Dawn had given her an overview of how neighborhoods, particularly those in New York City, were changed dramatically when they were gentrified. When tenants moved out of rent-controlled or stabilized apartments, landlords allowed them to remain vacant along with a gradual decrease in services. The remaining tenants would eventually move out or the owners would employ more drastic measures by either forcing them out or setting fires. The buildings would remain abandoned, sometimes for years, until a developer would buy up the parcels and rebuild luxury apartments, the selling prices far beyond the means of those who'd lived in the neighborhoods for generations.

Kara had listened to David, Jeff, and Morgan talk about the developers as if they were a small growth, feeding on the residents of the Sea Islands until they became a malignancy, destroying the Gullah culture and their legacy for future generations.

They'd sent a clean-cut, preppy boy wearing a handmade tailored suit and imported footwear, instead of a slick, fast-talking, more experienced man, believing he would be more acceptable and approachable. Well, they were wrong. Even if Kara hadn't decided whether to stay or leave, the impromptu meeting with Porter had justified why she should stay.

Jeff, dropping his gaze, stared out into the distance. "I can't believe you asked my woman to go to James Island with you when it's known that Jack's Fish House is the best seafood restaurant in the Lowcountry. And it just happens to be a few minutes from here." His gaze swung back to Porter who looked as if he was ready to bolt off the porch if Jeff made a sudden motion. "Do you think if you took my woman to James Island, I wouldn't hear about it?" His voice was soft and dangerous.

Porter held up both hands. "Look, man, I wasn't trying to hit on your woman. I just wanted to talk to her about selling the house."

"I'm sorry to tell you," Jeff continued, "but she's not going to sell. Not for you or for me. I've tried to talk her into selling it to come live with me, but she's as stubborn as a mule."

Kara rested her hands at her waist. "I'm not living with you, Jeffrey Hamilton. My mama didn't raise me to shack up with a man, so stop asking me."

Porter lowered his hand. "I'm sorry, but I have to leave now." He nodded to Kara, then Jeff. "It's nice meeting you." Turning on the heels of his imported footwear, he practically ran to his car, jumped in, and started it up in one continuous motion.

Jeff took out his cell phone and punched in several letters and numbers. "No speeding, son!" he called out as the gleaming black BMW swerved before it was able to regain control and drive along the allée of oaks and away from Angels Landing.

Kara began laughing and couldn't stop as tears ran down her face. Jeannette, who'd overhead everything, joined her as they collapsed on the love seat. "Did you see his face, Mama?"

Jeannette held her belly with both hands. "I heard and saw everything. You and Jeff were hilarious."

Sobering, Kara stared at her mother. "How long were you standing there?"

"Long enough to hear his spiel. The boy couldn't sell water in the desert."

Jeff came over and sat on a chair facing the love seat. "I'll find out soon enough exactly who he is and who sent him."

"What are you talking about?" Jeannette asked.

"I got his plate number. Unless that young man has a rich uncle, I doubt whether he'd be able to afford a car with a sticker price starting at six figures."

Kara met his steady gaze. "I told him I'd sell the house for three mil, and he claimed that figure was doable. Either he does have a very rich uncle or he's involved in some criminal activity and just happens to have a few million lying around."

"I'll find out soon enough. I know someone who still has connections at the bureau, and we'll find out who Porter Caldwell is and what he's all about."

Jeannette moved to the edge of the cushion. "Do you think Kara is in any danger?"

Reaching out, Jeff patted her hand. "Of course not. But I'm glad you called me. I'm certain Kara would've gotten rid of him, but if he believes there's something going on between the two of us, he won't approach her again."

Jeannette placed her hand atop Jeff's. "I'm leaving here tomorrow, and I want you to look after my baby."

"Mama!"

"Don't 'Mama' me, Kara. You're my only child, and I don't want anything to happen to you."

"Don't worry, Miss Jeannette. I'll make certain nothing happens to her."

"You promise?"

"I promise." Jeff stood, bringing Jeannette up with him. He smiled, then kissed her cheek. "What time are you leaving tomorrow?"

"Around eight in the morning. Why?"

"I thought I'd treat you to breakfast before you leave."

"I'd like that," Jeannette said quickly.

He kissed her other cheek. "I'll meet you here at six thirty." His eyes met Kara's. "I'd like you to join us."

Smiling, Kara nodded. "Thank you."

Jeff turned to leave, then stopped. "Kara, do you like dogs?"

Her eyes lit up like a child's on Christmas morning. "I love them. Why?" He told her about the Yorkshire puppy. "Oh, please I'd love to have it."

"I'll let Mabel know. I'll call you before I bring him over."

Kara and Jeannette stood together, their arms around each other's waists, watching as Jeff drove away. "This was one time I didn't mind you being the nosy mother," she said softly.

"He's a keeper, Kara."

"What are you talking about, Mama?"

"Jeff. He's a keeper."

"He's a forty-year-old confirmed bachelor," Kara countered.

"That's only because he hasn't met the right woman."

"And you think I'm the right one?"

"I know you are." Jeannette dropped her arm. "I'm going inside to take these rollers out of my hair. Are you coming in?"

"Not yet. I'm going to look around to see where I can put in a rose garden."

"Wait for me to comb my hair, and I'll join you."

"Okay."

Kara had never known her mother to be so clingy. Even when she'd moved to New York, she'd appeared resigned that her little girl had matured enough to make her way in such a big city. She was now thirty-three, living on Cavanaugh Island with a population of 2,300 instead of on Manhattan Island with a million and half, and Jeannette was freaking out.

And if she were to ask her mother about her inconsistent behavior, Jeannette's comeback would be *"wait until you're a mother and you'll understand."*

Well, she was about to become a mother of sorts, and she was looking forward to taking care of what would become her four-legged baby.

Chapter Eleven

Kara didn't realize how much she'd missed her mother until she got up that Sunday morning and waited for Jeannette to join her on the front porch. Both had always been early risers, and not to have her to sit with and watch the sunrise reminded Kara of how sterile her life was. If it hadn't been for her stressful job—a job from which she'd resigned—and Dawn, now her former roommate, her day-to-day existence would've been as exciting as watching paint dry.

Aside from Dawn, she didn't have any close friends. And if Dawn hadn't been her roommate, she wouldn't have had any. She'd lost touch with her childhood buddies, electing not to return to Little Rock for her tenth high school reunion because she hadn't wanted to run into a boy she'd had an intense crush on.

When she'd confided this to whom she'd believed was her BFF at the time, Chantal couldn't wait to tell Chris

Day. The next day Chris approached her in the cafeteria and told her he would consider taking her out, but only if she would do something for him. He then whispered in her ear that he wanted her to go down on him because every girl he went out with did; no girl was going to blame him for getting her pregnant and jeopardize his athletic scholarship. The shock and horror must have been evident when everyone at her lunch table burst into laughter. Unfortunately for Kara, she hadn't been privy to Chris's sexual exploits and spent the last two years of high school as a loner, finding it easier to form relationships with boys than she did girls. It had all come down to trust.

She'd trusted her mother, and even Jeannette had deceived her when she felt she was protecting Kara. In essence, she was protecting her own reputation. Jeannette wasn't the first and she definitely wouldn't be the last woman to have a child and pass it off as another man's. It was ironic that she'd become Jeannette's and Taylor's only child, and now that she knew the circumstances of her birth, Kara wondered if Austin had felt cheated that he hadn't fathered a child with his wife, that *their* daughter was a constant reminder of his wife's affair with another man. Jeannette had called her husband to let him know to expect her arrival in Little Rock late Sunday night and to say that she loved and missed him.

Overhearing that conversation reminded Kara that it'd been a long time since she'd told a man that she loved and had missed him whenever they were separated. She didn't have a husband or lover, and now she didn't have a best girlfriend or even coworkers she could hang out with whenever they got together to celebrate someone's birthday, promotion, wedding, or baby shower.

She'd become Taylor Patton, living alone in a house that had become as sought after as a cure for a communicable disease. The Pattons wanted her to sell the land to them, and in turn they would sell it to developers.

Things weren't going as smoothly as she had hoped, and Kara felt inheriting Angels Landing was more a curse than a blessing. However, she still planned to turn it into a museum.

She knew without a doubt that her decision to stay in Angels Landing had a lot to do with Jeff, but she wasn't ready to openly admit that to anyone. Despite his military experience and extensive travels, he had the small-town sensibilities she found totally charming.

It was now two weeks since she'd last seen Jeff. He'd come by, as promised, early Sunday morning to escort her mother to a Charleston twenty-four-hour diner for breakfast. After she was stuffed with shrimp and grits, a Lowcountry staple, Kara and Jeff waited until the taillights from Jeannette's car disappeared from view as she headed toward the interstate; then they returned to the island on the ferry instead of taking the more direct causeway.

Kara remembered standing at the rail next to Jeff not exchanging a word during the trip. He'd dropped her off at Angels Landing, saying he would see her around, and left with a hug and a kiss. She'd found his behavior puzzling but decided not to make too much of it. He didn't owe her any explanation, and as sheriff of Cavanaugh Island his responsibilities went beyond his becoming her personal bodyguard.

The news of her resignation had generated a firestorm of questions, firstly from her supervisor who wanted to know if he'd been responsible for her abrupt departure.

Kara reassured him he had nothing to do with it and that she'd decided she needed a different lifestyle because she'd been close to burnout. He'd offered to cut her caseload, but Kara refused to relent and wished him the best.

Then came the phone calls from coworkers blowing up her cell. Many wanted to know if she'd found a man in Little Rock and had decided not to come back. A few were gauche enough to ask her if she was pregnant, and that's when she programmed her calls to go directly to voice mail.

She'd called Dawn asking her to box up her personal items and ship them to Angels Landing. She had also invited her to come down during the spring break because Dawn never taught classes at that time. She knew Dawn was still angry with her for leaving when she said she would think about it. What was there to think about when Kara had offered to pay for the flight? Dawn's response dampened her mood for several hours until she left the house and went to the beach. Sitting on the sand and watching the choppy waves and pounding surf wash up on the beach was soothing and hypnotic, and by the time she returned home she'd felt a gentle inner peace.

Kara was on the computer in Taylor's office when Mrs. Todd knocked softly on the door. "Corrine Hamilton's grandbaby boy is here to see you. He's waiting in the kitchen."

She smiled when hearing Jeff announced that way. When, she wondered, would he ever stop being Corrine's grandbaby boy? "Thank you. Tell him I'll be right down."

Kara hadn't realized how fast her heart was beating until she went into her bedroom to exchange a pair of too-short shorts for a pair of capris. At the last possible moment she reached for a brush and put her hair up in a ponytail. She'd put off going into the Cove to have her hair styled. Most times she washed it, let it air-dry, then pulled it into a ponytail. She knew she had to snap out of the rut of not taking care of her appearance, or she would end up like many of the mothers of her former clients who drifted from one day to the next, oblivious of the world going on around them.

It was so easy to become a recluse in the large house that held good and not-so-good memories. She rarely saw Mrs. Todd, who floated in and out of rooms like a specter, leaving only the scent of lemon and gleaming surfaces behind her.

Taking the back staircase, Kara walked into the kitchen, her heart stopping, then starting up again, when she saw Jeff. He was a visual feast in a pair of jeans; a black, waffle-weave, long-sleeved T-shirt; and shiny black leather boots. The badge pinned to his chest and the deadly-looking automatic strapped to his waist told her he was on duty. There was something poignant in seeing a man his size cradling a small puppy to his chest. She began imagining him with an infant.

"Hello, stranger."

Jeff stared numbly at Kara, unable to believe that after two weeks he still could recall everything about her. He'd deliberately stayed away from Angels Landing because of gossip, no doubt spread by Harlan, that he was sleeping with Taylor's impostor daughter. It had been his grandmother who'd warned him about ruining Kara's reputation. He reminded her that it was the twenty-first century and Kara was an independent woman, but his explanation did not sit well with her. Corrine had countered with *"If you don't plan to do right by Kara, then stay away from her."*

He wasn't certain what his grandmother meant, but he had no intention of hurting Kara—directly or indirectly. All he wanted to do was protect and care for her.

And he wasn't about to argue with his grandmother that there wasn't anything going on between him and Kara, but took her advice and had stayed away. Until now. He'd had his deputies stop by to check on her and had got up before the sun came up to run along the beach. It was only when he went to bed that the images of the horrors of war were replaced with her face and the sound of her voice. And when Mabel called for him to pick up the dog, Jeff knew he had to see Kara again.

"It's been a while. I was down one deputy, so I wasn't able to take off," he said truthfully, "but hopefully that's going to change with a new hire."

"Who are you considering?"

He told her about Marine Reserve Sergeant Nelson Lambert who had returned from Iraq and had come to Jeff to apply for the vacant deputy position. As soon as he received approval of Nelson's background check, he would be added to the payroll. Nelson still would have to attend classes at the Charleston police academy during his probationary period.

"With Nelson's hire we'll have deputies living in each of the towns. Kenny will still cover Angels Landing, and Nelson will move from the Cove to Haven Creek. I would love to have a third deputy, but there isn't enough money in the budget."

"Are they part-time or full-time?"

"They're part-time. I'm the only one that's full-time. There was a time when each town had a full-time sheriff, but that wasn't cost-effective. Once I was hired to replace the Cove's sheriff, the mayors decided I would police the entire island, and deputies from the Landing and the Creek would provide part-time oversight in their towns."

"Can they make ends meet on a part-time salary?"

Jeff angled his head. "Always the social worker, aren't you?"

She gave him a wide smile. "I'm not going to apologize."

"And I don't want you to. Kenny is a retired correction officer, and my former deputy was a probation officer. They take on the position to supplement their pensions." He watched Kara approach, her gaze fixed on the terrier. "Don't you want to take him?"

"Will he come to me?" she asked. There was a slight tremor in her voice.

"Hold out your arms." Jeff placed the puppy in her arms, then stepped back. The terrier had whined incessantly when Mabel had placed him in a crate but soon had settled down during the drive. He refused to come out of the crate until Jeff reached in to carry him out, the tiny canine shaking uncontrollably.

Kara smiled when the dog yawned. "What's his name?"

"Oliver."

Her eyebrows lifted. "For Oliver Twist?" '

"I don't know. If it were me I'd call him Killer or Bruiser."

Kara gave him an incredulous stare. "You can't be serious. This little thing probably doesn't weigh more than three pounds."

"Two and a half. I have his papers in the car with his breed and the date of vaccinations. Mabel also gave me a crate, wee-wee pads, food, and a bag of doggy-grooming supplies."

Burying her face in the soft fur, Kara pressed a kiss on the puppy's head. Oliver was gold and gray with round brown eyes and a black dot for a nose. "Why are you shaking, baby? Mama's going to take care good of you."

"I take it you've had dogs before."

Kara nodded. "I've had dogs, cats, birds, fish, rabbits, and guinea pigs."

Jeff crossed his arms over his chest. "It looks as if Oliver is going to have a good home."

"Thank you for thinking of me. This little guy and I are going to have a lot of fun together. I must admit this is the first time I've ever had a dog this small. Most of my other dogs were hounds, and they stayed outdoors. The exception was when temperatures were close to freezing; then my mother would let them in."

"How is your mother?"

"She's good. In fact, she asked about you, and I told her I hadn't seen you in a while."

"Tell her that's going to change."

Kara gave him a blank stare. "What are you talking about?"

"I now have time to fulfill my promise to take you to the movies. And there's still the Sunday dinner you owe me."

"I'm always here, Jeff. You know where to find me."

"You *and* Oliver."

She pressed another kiss to the dog's silky hair. "Me and Oliver. By the way, did you find out anything about Porter Caldwell?"

"We're still checking."

"Will you let me know what you uncover?"

"I will, but only if it doesn't entail police business. And pouting will not get me to change my mind," he added when she pushed out her lips.

"Fine. Be like that, Jeff."

He smiled in spite of the potential seriousness of the situation. "The developers are getting bolder and more aggressive," he said, suddenly sobering. "Millicent Baily, who's a Haven Creek sweet-grass weaving instructor, called me to say someone had come to her, asking whether she was willing to sell her late father's house and farm. When she told him no, he'd asked whether she'd ever seen *The Godfather* when Don Corleone said to make him an offer he can't refuse. She interpreted it as a veiled threat and felt compelled to call and report it."

Kara whistled softly. "That's scary."

Jeff nodded. "My men are on full alert when it comes to strangers hanging around." Having Nelson policing the Creek would make it possible for the recent war combatant to closely monitor what was going on in the smallest and least populated of the three towns.

"How's Miss Corrine?"

Jeff smiled thinking of his grandmother. "She's doing quite well. She just joined a book club discussion group at the bookstore and is talking about coming to the Haven to join a quilting club."

"Good for her. Please let her know I asked about her."

"I will. Let me go and get Mr. O's things." Jeff returned to the Jeep and managed to bring in the crate and a large plastic bag with the supplies. Mabel had vacillated between wanting to keep the terrier and giving him up but in the end decided giving him up was in the canine's best interest. Oliver, bored at being left alone all day, had begun gnawing on furniture and soiling the carpet whenever she came home.

Kara examined the contents of the bag. "Did he have any chew toys?"

Jeff stared down into the eyes that made him feel as if

he were drowning in pools of green and gold. "That's all Mabel gave me."

"It doesn't matter. I'll buy him some."

He took a step toward her, bringing them inches apart. "I have to get back so my clerk can go to lunch. I have your numbers. I'll call you and we'll go out."

"I'd like that," Kara said softly.

Placing an arm around her waist, he dipped his head and kissed her. It had been so long since he'd tasted her mouth that he had almost forgotten how sweet she was. "I promise I won't stay away so long again."

"Don't make promises you can't keep," she whispered against his mouth.

"I never break a promise, baby." Jeff kissed her again, wishing for the first time in his life that he didn't have to go back to work. But he'd never been one to shirk his duties or disobey an order.

Kara patted his chest. "Go before your boss fires you for theft of services."

Jeff laughed loudly, startling Oliver who let out a yelp. "Sorry about that Mr. O. I happen to think I have a rather nice boss."

"Who's that?"

"Me."

"Aren't you appointed by the mayor?" Kara asked.

"No, baby. My position is an elected one. Only the people can vote me in or out. I served several months of my predecessor's term, then ran unopposed a month later. I'm up for reelection in thirty-three months."

"Do you plan on running again?"

"Probably. I'd thought it would be difficult adjusting to small-town life again, but so far it's been good."

A beat passed before Kara asked, "If your grandmother wasn't still living here, would you have come back?"

There came another pause as Jeff replayed Kara's question in his head. "Yes. I've traveled all over the world, and I've never felt the connection with those places that I feel here. This is home, Kara." An expression he could only interpret as indecision filled Kara's eyes. "What's the matter?"

She lowered her gaze. "I keep telling myself this is home when it really doesn't feel like it. Maybe that's because I'm only staying here temporarily."

Pressing his mouth to her forehead, Jeff said, "Don't rush it, Kara. First you were only staying a week, then it became three weeks, and now it's five years. A lot can happen in five years."

"You're right." She turned her head and kissed his cheek. "Go to work before your boss writes you up."

"Do you mind if I stop by when my boss isn't clocking me?" he teased.

"Of course. I'll even cover for you if he comes around looking for you," she said, smiling.

"You're definitely a keeper," he said.

Later that afternoon Kara had another visitor. This time it was Morgan. She put Oliver in his crate and closed the door. She'd finally calmed the puppy enough where he'd stopped shaking. She'd temporarily placed the crate near the back staircase, covered the fleece dog mat with wee-wee paper, and placed bowls of food and water in a corner.

Kara studied the renderings and photographs Morgan had spread out on the dining room table. "It's amazing."

"What's amazing?" Morgan asked.

She pointed to an early photo of one of the guest

bedroom suites. "It looks so shabby when compared to the rendering."

"It's the same room and furniture but with different wallpaper, rugs, windows, and bed dressing. The other accessories in the room will look the way it did a hundred fifty years ago."

Moving along the table, Kara stared at each photo and its accompanying rendering. "What about the fabric on the chairs?"

"I deal with two fabric houses specializing in eighteenth- and nineteenth-century patterns. One is in Charleston on King Street and the other in Atlanta's Buckhead neighborhood."

"Which one do you recommend?"

Morgan smiled, dimples deepening. "The local one of course."

"Do I have to keep the same colors? Because whoever decorated appears to have been obsessed with green."

"I noticed that, too. We can always change the colors. What colors are you thinking about?" Morgan asked, opening a book with fabric samples.

Kara met Morgan's dark eyes. "Every piece of furniture in this house is either light or dark, so I'd like each of the bedrooms to have a different palette."

"How do you like these?" She pointed to swatches of fabric that paired white with blue, rose, black, lavender, and cream. "The light-colored furniture is mid-1700s French. These pieces were probably purchased when the house was first built in 1832. The mahogany pieces came later."

"Are they antiques or reproductions?"

"They're antiques. Why? Are you thinking of auction-ing off a few pieces?"

"No, actually," Kara admitted. "I was thinking of donating a few pieces to a museum. I found several chests filled with china, crystal pieces, and silver. There are duplicates of everything."

"Why don't you give them to an auction house? Of course, they'll take their fee, but you could always use the money for the upkeep of the property. Restoring Angels Landing isn't a onetime endeavor. You're going to have to hire people to maintain the gardens, make repairs and… Why are you looking at me like that, Kara?"

She knew it was time to level with Morgan, inform the historical architect of her future intentions for the property. "If we're going to work together, then we must trust each other."

"You don't want me to restore the property?"

Kara rolled her eyes upward. "Morgan, please don't get melodramatic on me," she remarked when the other woman pressed her palms to her chest as if she was going to faint. "Of course, I want you to restore the property." Morgan twisted a plait around her finger, and Kara saw that her hand was shaking. She knew the architect had taken a huge risk resigning her position to go into business for herself, even if someone had put up the money.

"Remember when you told me why you didn't want developers here?" Morgan nodded. "That they would take business away from island merchants?"

"Yes. Where are you going with this, Kara?"

She told her everything, watching as Morgan's eyes danced with excitement. "I want Angels Landing to become part of the Gullah tours. Those who take the tour would be able to buy sweet-grass baskets from artisans on the island if I decide to open a souvenir shop. In fact, everything in the shop will come from Cavanaugh Island. If it's not made here, then it won't be sold here. Think destination weddings and business meetings. We can have a restaurant on the property that can be a spinoff of Jack's Fish House. And I've heard that Lester Kelly is the island's cake man."

"And he makes the most incredibly beautiful wedding cakes," Morgan added. "You know you've just appealed to my historic gene."

"So you like my idea?"

"Don't play, Kara. You know I love it. What makes it so ingenious is it's like living off the land. You'll use what you have here, not like outsiders that will take from us. That way the plantation will take care of itself."

"I really don't like that word."

"Neither do I," Morgan agreed, "but it is what it was. It's a word that has been around since the fifteenth century, and some of the first plantations were established in Ireland. A lot of tourists come to the island in the summer, but it's the Cove that draws most of the business, then the Creek, and the Landing is last because it's totally residential."

"I went to college with a girl who was from Savannah, and she could trace her family tree back to the Revolution. She told me her house was listed on the Savannah tour of homes and gardens. It could be the same with Angels Landing if some people were willing to open their homes and gardens like they do in Savannah."

Leaning over, Morgan took her iPhone from her bag, touching the Notes icon. "Take a look at this," she said, handing Kara the phone. Kara's smile grew wider as she read the note.

"Yes!" Kara gave Morgan a high five, then did a happy dance while still seated. "I can't believe we've come up with a similar plan."

"What do they say about great minds? Why should the developers reap all the profits? I gave you that little pep talk to get you thinking about the possibilities for Angels Landing. I also didn't want you to think I was trying to coerce you into doing something you weren't comfortable with."

"Were you testing me?" Kara asked.

Pressing against the worn fabric on the back of the dining room chair, Morgan ran her hands over her neatly braided hair. "I wasn't testing you, Kara. This is your property and your project so the final word rests with you. Angels Landing is similar to Middleton Place, Mansfield Plantation, Drayton Hall, or Borough House Plantation in that they have private governing bodies and are registered as a historic place and/or historic landmark. The difference is you're female, African American, and a direct descendant of Shipley Patton. Once the word gets out, Angels Landing will operate like the other historic homes, and I hope it will put a stop to the developers preying on Cavanaugh."

Kara felt as if a weight had been lifted off her shoulders. What she'd planned for the property wasn't an original idea, but after spending hours on the computer researching historic sites throughout the South, she'd felt she could do the same for Angels Landing. She felt a warm glow flow through her. The puzzle was beginning to take shape, and soon she would be able to see the whole picture.

"Let's hope it does. I don't know why, but I feel like celebrating. Is there any place, other than Jack's, where we can go and have a little fun?"

"Hey," Morgan drawled. "I'm down if you are. There's Happy Hour in the Creek. It's the only bar on the island. And it's happy hour from the time it opens around five until it closes. They cater to an under-forty crowd and offer a wonderful buffet."

"Is it a popular place to hang out?"

"It is for the locals. We get a lot of folks from the mainland on Friday and Saturday because of the live music. There is a cover charge, but I always get around that because one of my cousins is a partner in the club."

"Is everyone on the island related?" Kara asked, laughing.

"No. And those who are make it known. We can't have cousins marrying cousins like they do in some states," Morgan joked.

"You know that's wrong. Incest is illegal."

"Tell that to some folks." Morgan checked her watch. "It's a little after five. If we get there before eight, then we should be able to get a table."

"That gives me a couple of hours to wash my hair and flat iron it."

Morgan flipped her braids. "That's why I have low maintenance hair. Wash and go."

"I had my hair braided once, and I had to take them out the next day because they were so tight I sat up all night in ppppaaaaiiiinnnn." Pain had come out in four syllables, causing Morgan to laugh and Kara to laugh with her.

Gathering up the photographs, Morgan left the renderings for Kara. "I'll come back and pick you up between 7:15 and 7:30."

"I'll be ready.

Chapter Twelve

Kara felt as if every eye in the Happy Hour was fixed on her and Morgan when they wove their way through the crowd in the dimly lit club. It could've been a Friday in Manhattan instead of Friday night on Cavanaugh Island. Instead of taxis and car services dropping off passengers in front of clubs sandwiched between buildings in mostly commercial neighborhoods, these clubbers had parked their cars in a lot large enough for one square city block. Young, attractive, and casually chic, they could've come from any major city in the world. Most of the men had shed their ties and suit jackets, their dates preening in designer dresses, power suits, and stilettos.

She wore the ubiquitous New York City black—a sheath dress with an asymmetrical neckline; narrow, black patent leather belt around her waist; and four-inch black patent leather pumps—while Morgan turned heads in black stretch pants, silk blouse, and strappy stilettos. She wouldn't have had anything to wear tonight if she hadn't stopped at a boutique when she'd gone into Charleston to do her banking. She thought of the dress and shoes as an impulse buy that had served her well. And if she was going to socialize with Morgan, then that meant she had to make a few more purchases before Dawn packed up her clothes and shipped them to South Carolina.

A man with a shaved pate leaned in close to Kara, crooning, "Hello, hello, and hel-lo!"

She laughed. "Hello to you, too." Prerecorded music pumped loudly as Kara and Morgan followed the hostess to a small table.

"I called my cousin and told him to save us a table," Morgan shouted over her shoulder as they sat down. She signaled a waiter and ordered a sex on the beach, while Kara ordered an apple martini.

The waiter stared at Kara, a slight smile playing at the corners of his mouth. "I need to see some ID."

She stared at him, tongue-tied. "Excuse me?"

"I need to see some ID," he repeated, his smile now a full grin.

Kara opened her tiny purse unable to believe she was being carded. She handed the man her driver's license. "Nice photo, Kara," he drawled, handing her back the license.

"If you wanted to know my name you could've asked." She smiled at his look of embarrassment.

"I'll be right back with your drinks."

Kara and Morgan waited until he walked away before they burst into laughter. "Do you think I hurt his feelings?"

"I told Damon that asking for a woman's ID is played out, but you can't blame him for trying."

Kara leaned over the table. "I'm certain seeing the New York State license threw him for a loop."

"Don't delude yourself into believing that. People know who you are, Kara. Damon thought asking for your license would flatter you because he wanted you to believe he thought you didn't look old enough to drink."

"It's been a while since I've been carded." What she should've said was that it had been a while since she'd gone out for drinks. Most Friday nights found her at home, in bed, and trying to catch up on lost sleep before Dawn's transients invaded the apartment.

Kara missed her roommate. She missed Dawn coming into her bedroom and flopping down on her bed to talk about what had gone on in her busy life. Kara thought of Dawn, a native New Yorker, as a Big Apple diva. She knew how to talk the talk *and* walk the walk, teaching and helping Kara navigate the frenetic lifestyle of the celebrated city.

"People know who you are."

Now that they knew who she was, what were they going to do with that information? Kara knew the Pattons weren't happy about her being on the island, and she wondered who else felt the same. Had the others thought of her as an outsider, too? Had they also shunned Taylor or had he avoided them as well?

"Should I be concerned, Morgan?"

Morgan stared at the lighted candle on the table. "I don't think so. There's going to be a lot of talk once the repairs begin on Angels Landing. Folks are going to want to drive by and check out what's going on. The supervisor of the work crew will probably put up barriers on the road leading up to the house where only workmen will be permitted to access the property. My former boss—it feels so good to say that—threw a hissy fit when I handed in my resignation, accusing me of being disloyal. Once he finds out that I'm working for you, he'll probably bad-mouth me as if I stole something."

"What's the ditty about sticks and stones?"

"Yeah, I know. Why don't you go and get something to eat before Damon brings the drinks. I'll go after you come back."

Pushing back her chair, Kara stood up and walked over to the buffet table where patrons stood two deep waiting to serve themselves. She liked the vibe in the club. It wasn't as large as some of the ones she'd gone to in Manhattan, but what it lacked in size, it more than made up in atmosphere. A U-shaped bar was the centerpiece, and mirrored walls made everything appear bigger. Tables seating two, four, and six were positioned closely together to maximize capacity. The waitstaff wore white shirts with black ties, armbands, slacks, and shoes. Everyone was patient, polite, and talking softly, but it was the number of people attempting to be heard over the ear-shattering music that increased the noise decibels.

"You can get in front of me."

Kara smiled up at a man with wavy, sandy-brown hair and soulful green eyes. "Thanks, but I'm in no hurry."

"Did you know that you're beautiful?"

She felt heat sting her cheeks. "No."

"Well, you are. Why is it I've never seen you here before?"

Kara knew he was trying to either engage her in conversation or pick her up. She didn't mind talking to him, but she definitely was not going to be receptive if he wanted more than that. "This is my first time."

He extended his hand. "Steve Young."

She shook his moist palm. "Kara Newell."

"Are you here alone?"

Kara groaned inwardly. He wasn't being just friendly; he wanted to pick her up. Any normal woman would've been flattered to have an attractive man come on to her, but she wasn't interested. If he'd been Jeff, then she wouldn't have been so standoffish. She would've been cheesing so much, he would've been able to see her molars.

"No, I'm not."

"My loss."

Picking up a plate and flatware, Kara moved slowly along the table, spearing small portions of salad greens and toppings. There were the customary dipping sauces for wings, sushi, calamari, chicken fingers, and zucchini sticks. She chose an assortment of cold antipasto and mini–crab cakes.

Morgan stood up. "Is that all you're eating?" she asked, looking at Kara's plate.

"It's only the first course."

"Good for you. I know a few women with eating disorders, and I just couldn't be around them because there's only so much lettuce one could eat without passing out."

Kara set her plate on the table. "Not me. I like food too much." She picked up a fork and cut into the crab cake. Her hand halted when she spied David sitting with a woman. She couldn't hear what they were saying, but judging from their expressions, they didn't appear to be a happy couple. Damon returned with their drink order, and Kara paid him, adding a generous tip.

"I paid for the drinks," she told Morgan when she sat down.

"The next round is on me." They touched glasses. "Here's to friendship."

"Friendship and Angels Landing."

The food was delicious, the cocktails perfect, and once the jazz quartet replaced the driving, thumping baseline beat, the music became melodious and soothing. Kara was content to come to the Happy Hour just to listen to the live music. Morgan touched her arm, garnering her attention.

"Your attorney isn't having a good night. It looks as if his girl just walked out on him. And judging from the number of glasses on the table, I think he's had more than enough to drink. I think you'd better do something, Kara."

Shifting slightly, she stared at David. The confident lawyer responsible for monitoring and protecting her legal interests was missing, and in his place was a dejected man. There were several glasses on the table, and he'd motioned the waiter over.

Kara's relationship with David was strictly business, and she didn't want to ingratiate herself into his private life. Opening her purse, she scrolled through the directory and tapped a number.

Jeff had just stepped out of the shower when his cell phone rang. Looping a towel around his waist, he answered the call when Kara's name and number came up on the display. His twelve-hour shift had ended, and he looked forward to relaxing until it was time for him to return for the eight o'clock shift.

"Hey, Kara. What's up?"

"David's here at the Happy Hour. He doesn't look so good, and I think he's had too much to drink—"

"I'll get there as soon as I can," he said, cutting her off.

Jeff could not understand what had sent his cousin over the edge because he rarely drank. Even as teenagers, when they shouldn't have been drinking, David was always the designated driver. He'd taken a lot of ribbing from the rest of the guys in their crowd, but that didn't seem to bother him. Jeff had never known anyone to be more focused than his cousin David. Jeff dressed quickly and bounded down the stairs, stopping to look in on his grandmother.

She was in the sunroom, shades drawn, television tuned in to a cable channel, piecing squares of cotton. "I'm going out, Gram."

Corrine peered at him over a pair of half glasses. "I thought you were staying in tonight because you have to work in the morning."

"I need to meet someone. Don't wait up for me," he teased.

"I stopped that years ago. Be careful, Jeffrey."

Walking over, he kissed her cheek. "I'm always careful, Gram. Love you."

She smiled. "Love you more."

It was a game they'd played when he was a child. He would tell her he loved her, and she would always say she loved him more. They would go back and forth until they lost count of who loved the other more.

He did love his grandmother unconditionally, and Jeff's greatest fear was losing her like all of the other women in his life. Corrine was his only link with a woman who'd given up her life to give birth to him. He'd known kids who didn't know or had never met their fathers, but he had been one of the rare cases where he hadn't met either parent. His grandmother was his only link to his past, and he intended to hold onto her for as long as he could.

David was his grandmother's great-nephew. Corrine's sister had left the island to attend college and never returned. She married a lawyer, and after graduating they put down roots in Charleston where David's father set up a law firm with two of his fraternity brothers. After David graduated law school, he, too, joined the firm, becoming a junior partner. His cousin loved coming to the Cove to spend the summers. When people asked who David was to him, Jeff would say "my little brother" instead of his cousin.

Right now, his little brother was in trouble, and Jeff wondered how or what had shaken the brilliant attorney so much that he was attempting to escape into a bottle of alcohol.

He got into the low-slung sports car and started it, backing out of the driveway faster than he normally would. The no-speeding rule did not apply this night when Jeff pushed the racy car past sixty as he navigated the unlit narrow road. He sped past Angels Landing, slowing only when he reached the town limit for Haven Creek. The downtown business district was dark, quiet. Jeff drove another quarter of a mile before the neon lights of the Happy Hour came into view. Maneuvering into an empty space, he was out of the car as soon as he cut the engine. He opened the door and stepped inside. Track lights appeared like stars against the black ceiling.

"What's up, Jeff?" asked the man at the door with biceps as large as a child's waist.

"Not much, Dwayne," he said, exchanging handshakes before they pounded each other's back.

"Yo, man, you still hard as a rock," Dwayne remarked. "You workin' out?"

Jeff smiled. "I just do push-ups and run along the beach whenever I can."

"Keep doin' what you're doin'. I have to say, I'm surprised to see you here. There hasn't been any trouble."

"I'm here to meet someone."

Jeff had only come to the club whenever there was a problem with a patron or when he stopped by to make certain they weren't serving alcohol to minors. The owners strictly enforced the "we card everyone under twenty-five" rule because they didn't want to risk being fined, have their liquor license suspended, or even worse, close down permanently.

"Go on in."

Waiting until his eyes adjusted to the darkness, Jeff wended his way through tables, around throngs of people waiting at the bar, until he found David standing in a corner with two women. He recognized Morgan Dane immediately, then Kara as she struggled to keep David from falling.

Moving quickly, he took over, holding David under his armpits. The smell of alcohol on his cousin's breath was revolting. "What's going on, Cuz?"

David tried to focus his eyes. "She cheated on me, Jeff."

"Who?"

"Petra. I was going to take her away and propose marriage, but she cheated on me."

Jeff managed to get David to sit without falling off the chair. His gaze swept over Kara in the body-hugging dress. It moved lower to her bare legs in a pair of sexy heels before reversing itself to her face. Seeing her dressed like that made him think that she'd come to the club to meet a man or men, and jealousy rocked him to the core. But he knew in order to feel jealous he had to care about her...a lot.

"Kara, could you please order some black coffee for him."

She gave him a demure smile. "Of course."

His gaze was trained on the gentle sway of her hips as she walked away. He swallowed a groan when the flesh between his thighs stirred to life. Hunkering down in front of his cousin, he placed a hand on the attorney's shoulder. "We're going to sober you up before I take you home."

David's chin touched his chest. "I want to hate her, Jeff, but I can't. I still love her."

Jeff patted his cheek. "Love is overrated, David. What you should've done was let her love you more than you loved her." He felt someone next to him, and when Jeff glanced up, he saw Kara staring at him as if she'd seen a ghost. "What's the matter?"

"Nothing. Someone is bringing the coffee."

Morgan hunkered down next to Jeff. "How will you get him home?"

"I'm going to call someone to follow me in David's car; then I'll drive them back."

"Why don't you let him sleep it off at my house? I have two extra bedrooms," Morgan said quickly when Jeff gave her a questioning look. "After he sobers up he can drive himself to Charleston."

"Are you sure he won't put you out?" Jeff asked Morgan.

She smiled, dimples winking at him. "Come on, Jeff. The worst he can do is throw up, and if he ruins anything in my house, then I'll make him pay for it. Besides, he's probably going to sleep all night."

He thought about her suggestion, deciding it was better than calling someone in the middle of the night to help him take his inebriated cousin home. And it was better David not be left alone. Plus, Jeff could always stop by in the morning to check on him.

"You're right, Mo. As soon as I get some coffee into him, I'll drive him to your place in David's car." He turned to Kara, handing her the key fob to his car. "You'll have to drive my car to Mo's; then I'll take you back to Angels Landing."

Now I know why's he single, Kara thought as she watched Jeff force David to take furtive sips of the scalding-hot brew until he pushed the cup away. Is that how it'd been with Jeff and the women in his life? They loved him while he pretended to love them back?

Why couldn't he see that his cousin was hurting, that he'd truly loved a woman who'd deceived him by sleeping with another man? She blinked as if coming out of a trance. Maybe she'd found herself attracted to the wrong cousin. Despite his disheveled appearance, there was something about David that was refined, urbane while Jeff projected an aura of the bad boy athlete. Kara didn't know why, but she'd always found them far more exciting, yet had been reluctant to take up with one.

Jeff had made it known that he liked her, and he knew it was reciprocated when they'd shared the erotic moment in his grandmother's bathroom. She knew if they'd been alone, there was no doubt she would've asked him to make love to her. It had been a long time since a man had aroused her sexually and even longer since she'd slept with one. Could she, Kara mused, sleep with Jeff and remain emotionally detached? Knowing how he felt about falling in love was certain to make it easier for her.

Her heart turned over in compassion when David patted his shirt pocket, then those in his suit trousers. He extended a trembling hand to Jeff who shook his head. "I need my car keys."

"Not tonight, David. I'm going to drive you to Morgan's house where you're going to sleep it off. I'll stop by in the morning to see you."

David clenched his jaw. "I want to go home."

"I can't let you drive drunk. If you don't hurt yourself, then you'll probably hurt someone else."

David closed his eyes. "I'm not drunk. Now, give me my keys."

Jeff shook his head. "No."

"Give me my keys, Jeff," David insisted between clenched teeth.

Jeff caught his cousin in a savage grip under his shoulders. "Keep mouthing off and I'll charge you with drunk and disorderly conduct. And even in your inebriated state you know that's a minimum one day in lockup. What's it going to be, *counselor*?"

Closing his eyes, he nodded. "Let's go."

"Are you sure you can walk, or should I carry you?"

"Dammit! I...I can walk," he slurred.

Kara and Morgan shared a glance when David exhibited a display of belligerence for the first time. They left the club through a side door, David's uneven gait indicating he was no doubt under the influence.

Kara got into Jeff's car, smiling when she felt the power of the engine after she'd pushed the Start Engine button. It was definitely a pedal to the metal vehicle. The lingering scent of the masculine cologne inside the car was a blatant reminder of the man who made her feel things she'd forgotten, a man whose kisses left her mouth burning and wanting more, a man who made her throw caution to the wind when she'd admitted to him that he'd turned her on. So turned on she'd been ready to beg him to have sex with her instead of making love to her because he'd professed to finding love overrated.

Shifting into gear, she followed Jeff as he drove David's Lexus along pitch-black roads. Occasionally lights from homes in the distance punctuated the night as Kara concentrated on following the taillights of the sedan. No matter how hard she tried, she couldn't forget Jeff's offhanded comment about falling in love. The lyrics to Tina Turner's "What's Love Got to Do with It" came to mind: *It's physical, only logical. You must try to ignore that it means more than that.* Was that how it would be between her and Jeff? Whatever they would share would be purely physical?

Kara waited in the Miata as Morgan parked her SUV, got out, and opened the door to a one-story house with a front porch. She watched Jeff hoist the limp body of his cousin over his shoulder and carry him inside.

The haunting hooting of an owl came through the open window, and Kara pressed a button on the armrest, raising the window. Morgan's house had been built in a clearing surrounded by palmetto trees. Ten minutes seemed like an eternity when Jeff finally stepped out onto the porch with Morgan. He hugged her and then came over to the car.

Kara lowered the window. "Get in. I'll drive back."

He leaned into the window. "Are you sure you know how to get back?"

"Very funny, Jeff. Please get in."

She waited until he folded his long frame into the passenger seat and fastened his seat belt, then executed a perfect U-turn and drove back the way they'd come. "How is David?"

"Sleeping like a baby. I managed to get him out of his shirt and pants, but I didn't want to strip him naked. I wanted him to retain a little of his dignity when he woke up in a strange woman's bed. Thank you for calling me. I'm certain when he's lucid he'll also thank you for protecting his reputation as a straight arrow."

"Morgan's not a stranger to David." The admission had come out before Kara could censor herself.

"How does he know her?"

Kara knew she'd made a faux pas and had to think fast to cover it up. "Morgan went to Charleston with me when I had to take care of some legal business, and I introduced her to David."

"I didn't know you and Morgan were friends. Slow down, baby," Jeff warned. "There's a blind curve coming up, and you won't be able to tell if there's another car coming at you until it's too late."

She downshifted, slowing the car. "I hired Morgan to restore Angels Landing." It would become common knowledge that Morgan was the architect on the restoration project once work began; the fact that they were business partners would remain their secret, known only to her, Morgan, and David.

"So you're the one who lured Morgan away from Lenny Rosen?"

"I didn't lure her away, Jeff. She resigned because she felt stymied, and despite holding degrees in architecture and historical architecture, she probably would never advance beyond an assistant if she'd continued to work for him."

"We'll see."

"What do you mean we'll see?"

"Restoring Angels Landing will become her litmus test."

"Are you saying this because she's a woman?"

"Keep your eyes on the road," Jeff ordered when Kara turned her head to look at him.

"Why aren't there any lights?"

"It's because we don't want lighted roads. Once the sun sets you should either be home or on your way home. And to answer your question about Mo. It has nothing to do with her being a woman. The best commanding officer I ever had was a female lieutenant colonel. She truly was awesome, so please don't presume that I'm sexist."

There was only the sound of their measured breathing and the *slip-slap* of tires on the roadway as Kara turned off on the path leading to Angels Landing. "Will you accept my apology? I didn't mean to imply you were sexist," she said after a lengthy silence.

"I'll think about it."

"Don't you know how to be gracious?"

"I'll think about it," Jeff repeated.

Kara slowed, the car coming to a complete stop, and then shifted into Park. "This stop is Angels Landing. All passengers getting off at Angels Landing please exit the vehicle," she said in a teasing tone. Light from the porch lamps reflected off the pearlescent columns.

"Turn off the car, Kara."

"Why?"

"Because I'm not going to let you go into an empty house alone."

She shut off the engine. Unbuckling her seat belt, she shifted in her seat and stared directly at him. "Have you forgotten that I stay here every night by myself?"

Stretching his left arm over her headrest, Jeff stared at her. "And I worry about you."

"Why?"

His hand touched her hair. "Do I have to wear a sign around my neck that reads, 'Jeffrey Hamilton Likes Kara Newell'?" He leaned closer. "I mean really, really likes her."

Kara stared at the strong masculine mouth. "Show her," she whispered.

Jeff slanted his mouth over Kara's at the same time a sharp sound rent the stillness of the night. He went still, then sprang into action, reaching for the small holstered automatic at his ankle. He pushed open the car door.

"Don't move."

"Jeff!"

He was there, then he wasn't when he disappeared, running around to the back of the house. Kara disobeyed him when she did move. Grabbing her purse off the console, she got out of the car, raced up the porch steps, and unlocked the front door. It was then she heard the sound of breaking glass along with Oliver's frantic barking.

She dropped her bag on the table in the entryway, kicked off her heels, and ran to see about her pet. The terrier was howling and cowering in a corner of the crate. Going to her knees, she unlatched the door and scooped him up.

"It's all right, baby. Mama's here."

"Didn't I tell you not to move!"

Kara spun around to see Jeff standing over her. "Don't you dare talk to me like that!"

He glared at her before his expression changed, softening. "I'm sorry, but you can't disobey an order, Kara."

"This is not the corps, Jeff, and I'm not one of your subordinates."

"I know that."

"Then please don't treat me like one."

Jeff took a step, resting his hands on Kara's shoulders. "I saw some kids who were throwing rocks at the house running away. It may have been a childish prank, but pranks can turn deadly. What if you'd been standing in front of the window when they threw them?"

She closed her eyes against his intense stare. "I don't want to think about that."

"Neither do I." He kissed her forehead. "Take care of Oliver while I clean up the glass."

Kara opened her eyes. "You don't have to."

"Yes, I do. And I'm going to spend the night in case they decide to come back."

Twin emotions of anticipation and confusion twisted inside her. Jeff had appointed himself her protector. Though she appreciated all that he was doing, she wasn't certain she was ready for the sexy lawman to stay under her roof. "There's no need for you to spend the night because some kids decided to pitch rocks at the house."

"I'm staying."

Judging from his expression and his voice, Kara knew anything she said wouldn't get Jeff to change his mind. "I'll prepare one of the guest bedrooms for you."

"No," he said, shaking his head. "I'm not going to let you out of my sight."

"What aren't you telling me, Jeff? Please," she pleaded.

"Two words were painted on the rocks."

Kara felt as if her breath had solidified in her throat. "What are they?"

"*Leave, bitch.* I wish there was something I could do, but rocks can't be dusted for prints."

Her mood shifted from uncertainty to anger. Working as a child protection advocate had given her the tools needed to face down enraged parents once she recommended removal of their children, and becoming a social worker had fortified her resolve to fight for and protect those who couldn't defend themselves. Well, it was time for her to defend her own turf.

"I'm not going to leave."

"And I don't want you to leave," Jeff said.

Oliver squirmed to get out of her arms, and Kara placed him on the floor, watching his tiny black nose sniff her bare toes. "I'm going to have a security company install closed-circuit cameras in the house and around the property. Then I'm going to go through this house and try to find Taylor's gun. If I don't find it, then I'll buy one of my own."

Jeff cradled her face. "I don't want you carrying a gun."

"I'm not going to carry it. I'm just going to have it around in case I need it."

"You can't shoot kids for throwing rocks, Kara."

"Did I say I would shoot a child?" she asked him. "Some-one put those kids up to throwing rocks at my house. Weren't you the one who said that their so-called prank could've turned deadly?" She watched Jeff's chest rise and fall as if he'd run a grueling race. "You know and I know they're going to come back. Whoever put those kids up to stoning my house will try again. And I doubt they'll send a kid to do a man's job the next time."

"Baby, baby," he crooned. "Leave the police work to me and my deputies."

Rising on tiptoe, Kara brushed her lips against his. "Think of me as police auxiliary."

"No, Kara. I will not put you in the line of fire."

"But I'm the target, not you."

"They don't want to hurt you," he argued softly. "What

they want is to frighten you enough so you'll sell out and leave."

"I'm not selling."

"I don't want you to sell."

"And I'm not running," she insisted.

He smiled. "I don't want you to run, either." He kissed her again. "Take care of Oliver while I clean up the glass and tape something over the windows. I'll be up as soon as I'm finished."

"You can stay. But just for tonight."

Jeff gave her a withering stare that she was sure had intimidated men who'd dared to try him. "I'll stay tonight, tomorrow night, and the next night until the property is secured."

Kara couldn't help but become excited at the thought of having Jeff close by.

Chapter Thirteen

$\mathcal{L}$

Kara lay in bed, her face buried in a pillow. It wasn't until she'd stood in the bathroom, staring into the mirror while removing her makeup, that the enormity of what could've been hit her. She hadn't been able to stop the tears; however, by the time she'd finished with her shower, she was back in control.

Someone had gotten teenagers to throw rocks through her window to get her attention. Well, they had gotten it, and she heard their message loud and clear. Kara didn't want to think of what would've happened if Jeff hadn't come home with her. He said they were kids, but she'd known kids who'd killed their friends because they believed they'd disrespected them. Children so young they were tried as juveniles who'd turned on their parents, seriously injuring or killing them for an excuse as flimsy as not buying them a new pair of sneakers or a video game.

And she didn't want to think someone would want to do more than throw rocks to get her to leave Angels Landing.

She managed to drift off to sleep, but then something woke her. She lay there, listening to what sounded like moaning. Sitting up, she saw Jeff slumped in the armchair.

"Jeff?"

When he didn't answer, she turned on the bedside lamp, slipped out of bed, and walking on bare feet, approached him. His eyes were closed, chest rising and falling heavily, his breathing raspy.

Kara shook him gently. "Jeff, wake up."

"No, Briggs! Don't stand up! Medic! I need a medic over here."

A cold chill raced through Kara. She was witnessing PTSD firsthand. Jeff was having a flashback. Cradling his face, she held his head firmly. "Jeffrey. Baby, please wake up." He moaned, trying to escape her hold. "It's okay, baby. That's it, wake up."

His eyelids fluttered wildly until he managed to focus. "I'm sorry for waking you. Go back to bed, sweetheart," he whispered.

She stroked his handsome face. "No." Kara was afraid if she left him in the chair the nightmare would return. "Come to bed with me."

"I can't."

"Yes, you can." Reaching for his hands, she tried pulling him off the chair, but he weighed too much. "Work with me, Jeff. Stand up." She watched his expression change, as if he was seeing her for the first time. It was then Kara realized he'd finally emerged from a place where he'd relived the horrors of war in his dreams.

Jeff stood up, towering over Kara in her bare feet. "I can't sleep in the same bed with you."

"Yes, you can."

"Are you sure?"

She smiled. "Very sure. Come on. Take off your clothes and get into bed."

Walking back to the bed, she got in and turned her back to give him a modicum of privacy. The sounds of Jeff undressing were magnified in the quiet room. She and Jeff having sex wasn't a concern to her. His flashback was.

During family therapy, Kara had led groups where either the mother or father had served in Iraq or Afghanistan. Most of them had returned with a myriad of emotional problems ranging from insomnia, depression, and paranoia to having flashbacks. Their transition back into civilian life was slow and painful for the soldiers and for their families.

She felt the mattress dip, then the warmth from Jeff's body as he lay beside her.

Jeff couldn't believe Kara had asked him to sleep in her bed. When he'd entered the bedroom after the ordeal, Kara was sleeping soundly. When he'd told her that he wasn't going to let her out of his sight, he was true to his word. The armchair in her sitting area had become his bed, he stepping into the role of her bodyguard. But as he slept the disturbing images that always plagued his mind resurfaced. This time they weren't as vivid as the others, and when Kara woke him, he wasn't in combat mode, ready to go after anything that moved. He was getting better and for that he was thankful.

"Do they come often?"

Jeff knew she was talking about his nightmares. "Not as often as they used to. There was a time when I had them every night, sometimes two or three a night." He froze when she pressed her breasts to his back. She might as well have been wearing nothing because the fabric of her nightgown was not much of a barrier between her and his boxers and T-shirt.

"Have you talked to anyone about them?"

He nodded and then realized she couldn't see him in the darkened room. Shifting, he turned to face Kara. "Yes. I was seeing someone at the VA hospital. The psychiatrist wanted to put me on antianxiety medication, but I don't want to take anything."

"Do you feel anxious?" Kara asked.

"No. I don't think it has anything to do with anxiety. It's more like accepting that war is a game of odds and chances. When it's your time to die, nothing or no one can change that. But when it isn't, then you're coming home whole or maimed. I managed to come home whole, while others weren't so fortunate." He paused for a moment. "I'd lost count of the number of men who returned without arms, legs, or horribly scarred from IEDs."

"You can't feel guilty that you came home unscathed, Jeff. Have you thought that maybe you weren't injured because you had to take care of your grandmother and not the other way around?"

He smiled. "No. Thanks for reminding me."

"How often do you get to see your buddies?"

Jeff stared at Kara. "Are you going to bill me for this session?"

Kara looped her leg over Jeff's. "I didn't know you were a comedian."

He went completely still when her smooth leg touched his. He didn't want to believe she could be so trusting. They were in bed together, and only a cotton nightgown and his underwear kept them from being completely naked. And Kara was now well aware of how easily he'd become aroused whenever they were together.

"Well, you do ask a lot of questions."

"It comes with the profession. Speaking of professions. I repeat, how often do you see your buddies from the corps?"

Jeff rose on an elbow and rested his cheek on his fist. "Not as often as I would like to."

"My daddy has what he calls boys' week when he goes camping, fishing, or hunting with his friends from the corps. He had mild PTSD when he returned from the Gulf War, and adjusting to civilian life wasn't easy for him, so reconnecting with his buddies four or five times a year keeps him sane. Why don't you do something similar?"

"We usually meet in Charleston."

"And do what? Go to a bar and reminisce over drinks?"

"What's wrong with that?"

"Jeffrey, you can do that at the Happy Hour. What about inviting them to come here for a couple of days? Then hire a pleasure boat and go fishing. Sail down to Hilton Head or Savannah and spend some time soaking up the atmosphere before coming back."

"It sounds like a wonderful plan, but I wouldn't feel comfortable leaving my grandmother alone for that length of time. A night or two is okay but not a week."

"She doesn't have to be alone, Jeff. You could hire a certified home health aide to stay with her."

"Grams would never allow a stranger to stay in her home."

"Would she allow me to stay with her?"

Pushing into a sitting position, Jeff supported his back against the headboard, then turned on the lamp. Kara also sat up, and a shaft of golden light illuminated her face. Resting his hand on her cheek, he kissed her forehead. The warmth and sweet smell that he associated with Kara seeped into him. Never had he wanted to make love to a woman so badly. And he meant making love, not having sex. Sex was something he could have with any woman.

"I think she would love to have you stay with her."

Reaching for the sheet, Kara pulled it up to her chin. "How do you feel about it?" she asked him. "Are you comfortable with me staying in your home while you're not there?"

"Of course. Why wouldn't I be?"

"You're very protective of your grandmother."

He glanced away. "I have to be. She's all I have, and I'm all she has." Jeff's gaze shifted back to the woman whose very presence made him feel things he hadn't felt in a while. It wasn't her natural beauty or intelligence that drew him to her, but her empathy and compassion. "I never could've imagined sharing a bed with you for the first time without making love to you. I wanted it to be different."

Kara smiled up at him. "You wanted to date me first."

"How did you know?"

"You've been talking about taking me out ever since we met. But sometimes life works backward. I read a story in a magazine where this couple met, slept together on their first date, and then decided to get married because of their strict religious upbringing. They weren't in love when they married but learned to love each other."

Jeff covered her hand with his. "Are they still married?"

"They were celebrating their fortieth anniversary with

their four children and twelve grandchildren when the article was written."

"Is that how you see us, Kara? Making love, getting married, and settling down with children and then grandchildren?" She tried pulling her hand away, but Jeff tightened his hold on her slender fingers.

"No, Jeff. That's not how I see it at all. I'm not looking for a husband or children—at least not at this time in my life."

"What are you looking for?"

"If you would've asked me that question three weeks ago, I would've told you that I wanted my roommate to stop turning our apartment into a halfway house for the indigent. And instead of spending three weeks' vacation in Little Rock, I would've preferred spending at least two of those weeks in Paris. Everyone says springtime in Paris is magical."

"What's wrong with springtime on Cavanaugh Island?"

Kara rested her head on his shoulder. "There's nothing wrong with it. In fact, it's beautiful here. If it weren't for electricity and indoor plumbing, I would've thought that I'd stepped back in time. The swamps and marshes are primordial, the island's lifestyle is laid-back, and most people I've met are warm and friendly, but..."

"But what?" he asked when her words trailed off.

"I can't make plans for my future when I only plan to stay five years."

"If that's the case, then why stay at all?"

"Because of Taylor's will."

"Are you staying to spite your relatives?"

"No! The Pattons have nothing to do with my decision."

"You stay five years and go where, Kara? Are you going

back to New York and pick up where you left off? Or is
there a man in New York who promised to wait for you?"

She shook her head. "There's no man. And there hasn't
been one in two years."

"You're kidding, aren't you?"

"No, I'm not."

He stared at the woman who'd tugged at his heart within
minutes of meeting her. Kara coming to Angels Landing
had changed him. It was the first time, other than working the 8:00 p.m. to 8:00 a.m. shift that he hadn't slept in
his own bed. When he'd called his grandmother to let her
know he was spending the night with Kara, her response
had been, "It's about time." He knew Corrine liked Kara
because she was always asking about her.

Jeff let go of Kara's hand and smoothed her mussed
hair. "You're a young, beautiful, intelligent, educated woman.
Why wouldn't men be knocking down your door to take
you out?"

A wry smile parted Kara's lips as she stared at him.
"It's not that I couldn't get a date."

"Then what was it?"

"My job had taken over my life."

Jeff wanted to tell Kara it had been the same with
him. For twenty years his life centered around serving his
country. He'd known men who had addictions: drugs, alcohol, gambling, and women. For him it had been the military. And he knew if his grandmother hadn't had a heart
attack, he still would be on active duty.

"My hours were eight to four, but most times I didn't
leave the office until six, sometimes seven," Kara continued after a pregnant pause. "Updating case records had
become an uphill battle I had no chance of ever winning.

Whenever a social worker retired they were never replaced, so when the supervisors divided up their caseloads that meant a few more cases that I had to deal with."

"How many cases were you required to carry?"

"The ideal ratio is thirty to one, but there were times when I carried as many as fifty."

"It's a wonder you didn't burn out."

"Now, when I look back, I realize I was close to it." Kara smothered a yawn with her free hand.

He smiled. "Let's go to sleep, sleepyhead."

Kara yawned again. "I'm scheduled to meet with an engineer and a historic preservation specialist tomorrow."

He extinguished the light and eased Kara down beside him, pulling her close until her hips were pressed against his groin. "Good night, baby."

"How's Oliver?" Kara whispered.

He didn't want to believe she was worried about her dog when it should've been her own safety. "He's sleeping. Your baby's going to be a good watchdog because he reacts to every sound."

"I know," she said softly. "He's like an early warning system letting me know whenever Mrs. Todd comes and goes. I think she's a little put off with him being underfoot."

"Your baby is spoiled."

Kara laughed. "That's because he's so adorable."

"So is his mama. Go to sleep, Kara."

"Yes, Daddy."

Jeff left at dawn, warning Kara to keep the doors locked. He told her he would contact the security company the Cove used when they installed the cameras in the downtown business district.

Kara had taken care of Oliver's needs and then called a Haven Creek glazier, leaving a voice mail that she needed to replace broken windows at Angels Landing. The man had called her back an hour later, promising he would be there before noon.

She told Mrs. Todd about what had happened but not the rocks' message. "All of the doors to the house must remain locked at all times," she told the housekeeper.

"Miss Teddy and Mr. Taylor never locked the house until it was time to go to bed."

Kara gave the older woman a warm smile. "There will be a lot of workmen coming and going for months. Even though everything in the house is insured, I still need to take measures just in case something is stolen. I want to try and avoid having to have to deal with the insurance company."

Mrs. Todd sucked her teeth. "Ain't no one stealing from here."

She decided to take another route. "When was the last time you had someone working in the house?"

"I don't rememba."

"And because you don't remember that means it's been a long time. It's not going to be one or two people, Mrs. Todd, but a lot of people coming and going."

"What you havin' done?"

Resting her hands on the housekeeper's shoulders, Kara steered her over to the table in the corner of the kitchen. "Sit down, I'll bring you your coffee while we talk."

"No!"

"Please, Mrs. Todd, allow me."

Mrs. Todd narrowed her eyes behind her glasses. "Okay. If you say so."

"I say so. Every morning you get up to make breakfast for me. Today's my turn."

"You can cook?"

"Why does everyone believe I can't cook?"

"Who said you cain't?"

"Jeffrey Hamilton."

Mrs. Todd angled her head. "Corrine raised a fine young man. The gals all over the island were after him at one time. That ended when he went into the service. He came back in his uniform looking all handsome, and it started up again. But he paid them no mind."

Kara didn't want to talk about Jeff, not when she woke to find his erection pulsing against her hips. His soft snores and the gentle rise and fall of his chest verified he was asleep when another part of his body wasn't. She was still in bed when he got up, dressed, and leaned over to tell her to get up and lock the door behind him.

"I'm going to have people come in and strip all of the walls," she said, deftly switching the topic from Jeff to restoring the house.

"Are you going to put up more paper?"

Kara nodded. "Yes." She filled a cup with coffee, then added a generous splash of evaporated milk, handing the cup and saucer to the housekeeper. Mrs. Todd had admitted she'd grown up using canned rather than cows' milk because she was lactose intolerant.

Mrs. Todd took a sip. "It's jest the way I like it. What about the paper?"

"The paperhangers will probably have to repair the walls before they put up new wallpaper. Personally, I would leave the walls bare, but that wouldn't be in keeping with what this house looked like in 1862."

Kara busied herself filling a pot with water for grits, then opened the refrigerator and took out eggs, butter, and breakfast links. "Do you want biscuits, Mrs. Todd?"

"You make biscuits, baby?"

"I sure do."

"Who taught you to cook?"

"My mama, who learned from her mama." Jeannette's mother was actually her aunt. Kara's maternal grand-mother had died when Jeannette was two, and the aunt for whom she'd been named adopted her. Kara didn't remem-ber either of her grandfathers. By the time she was ready to go to elementary school, both had passed away.

Mrs. Todd touched the coronet of hair she braided every morning. "You're nothing like these young girls nowadays who cain't even boil water. They always eatin' out or orderin' in."

"I order in and eat out, but I prefer eating home-cooked meals." Kara removed the top to a large crock shaped like a chicken and scooped out enough flour to make at least a dozen biscuits.

If she'd been in New York, her breakfast would've been a hastily eaten bowl of cereal with a cup of coffee. Lunch was usually on the run, and when she worked late, dinner hardly figured into the equation of having three meals a day. If she didn't heat up leftovers in the microwave, she would pick up something from the corner deli. One time she'd brought enough to take for lunch the following day, she woke to find it half-eaten; it was the last time she'd done that.

Her cell phone rang, and Kara took it out of the back pocket of her jeans, staring at the display. She tapped a button. "Hi, Daddy."

"Did I wake you, baby girl?"

Kara glanced at the clock on the microwave. It wasn't quite eight o'clock. "No. I've been up for hours."

"This is supposed to be your vacation. Don't you know how to relax?"

"I am relaxing, Daddy. I'm making breakfast for the first time in what seems like ages."

"Good for you. Your mama told me everything about the will."

Kara turned her back when she saw Mrs. Todd staring at her. "What do you think?"

"I think you're getting what you deserve, Kara. What Taylor didn't do for you in life, he made up for in death. And I'm glad he never stepped up to be the father he should've been because then I never would've had my baby girl. I don't know why me and your mama didn't have any more children, but we were blessed to have had you."

"And you're the best father in the world, Daddy," she whispered into the phone. "I want you and Mama to come to Angels Landing and spend some time with me."

"You know I have all the time in the world, but it's your mama who has a problem getting off from work."

"Please, Daddy, try and talk her into taking some more time off. I can even introduce you to a few ex-marines."

"Didn't I teach you that there's no such thing as an ex-marine. Once a marine, always a marine."

Kara laughed. "Sorry about that."

"I know she's taking off Good Friday and Easter Monday, so maybe we'll come and see you then."

"Thank you, thank you, thank you, Daddy. When do you plan to leave Little Rock?"

She'd thought her father would view her accepting her

inheritance from Taylor as an act of betrayal, when Austin had been the one who'd married her mother and given her his name. Austin was her father in every way; the exception was sharing DNA.

"If we leave Thursday night, with the both of us driving, we should make it to Charleston early Friday morning."

"That'll work. After you rest up I'll take you around to show you the island. This year you and Mama are going to relax while I prepare Easter dinner."

"That'll work," Austin repeated.

"I'll see you guys at the end of next week...Daddy?"

"What is it, baby girl?"

"I love you."

There came a long pause before Austin said, "I love you, too, Kara."

She ended the call, staring at Mrs. Todd who'd watched her between furtive sips of coffee. "That was my father."

"Humph. Your father or your daddy?"

Kara went back to adding baking powder and salt to the flour, then sifted the dry ingredients into another bowl. "He's both," she replied, cutting pieces of cold butter into the mixture until it resembled fine meal. She added a small amount of milk until she'd achieved the right consistency.

Mrs. Todd set down the china cup Theodora had used for her special guests. She'd told Kara that had all changed once Teddy died and Taylor began using them every day until he too passed on. "It wasn't that Mr. Taylor didn't want to be your daddy."

Kara's hands stilled, and then she turned on the oven. "Why would you say that?"

Mrs. Todd stood up, walking over to join Kara at the cloth-covered oaken table. "It was Miss Teddy. She ruined every friendship he had with a woman. And when she found the letter your mother sent him 'bout carryin' his baby, she was like a crazy woman. She went on and on 'bout how could he be so irresponsible to make a baby out of wedlock. Miss Teddy didn't even know your mama, yet she claimed she was out to trick her boy into marrying her."

Picking up a baking sheet from a shelf under the table, Kara took a forkful of dough and rolled it between her floured hands, then placed it on the ungreased sheet. "If Taylor knew my mother was carrying his baby, why didn't he contact her?"

"Miss Teddy knew how to work her son. She nagged at him day in and day out until he finally gave into her. Out of all of her children, Taylor was the only one who couldn't stand up to her, and she knew it. Her daughters are jest like her. They have tongues like switches, and they raised they kids to be nasty, too. In the end Taylor wouldn't have nothin' to do with them."

And now they're angry with me because I'll have nothing to do with them, either, Kara thought. "Don't they know they can catch more flies with molasses than with vinegar?"

Mrs. Todd sucked her teeth again. "You cain't tell them nothin' because they are Pattons, and 'round here that means everything."

"What do they do besides being Pattons?"

"They are doctors, lawyers, and teachers. Supposedly respectable folk. But they sure can act like heathens when need be."

Kara finished rolling out a dozen biscuits. She wanted to tell Mrs. Todd that she'd witnessed the Pattons' behavior in living color. "I'm glad my name isn't Patton."

"It doesn't matter what your name is. You still a Patton."

She didn't want to tell Mrs. Todd that her so-called relatives had fired the first salvo by having rocks thrown at the windows painted with a message she would have to be a complete idiot not to understand. What would be their next move? Have someone shoot at her?

Kara would take Jeff's advice and keep the doors locked at all times. She would also stay close to the house until the security company set up cameras around the property.

"What do you want with your grits and biscuits, Mrs. Todd?" she asked.

"I seasoned some whitin' 'cause I was fixin' to have fish and grits this morning."

"Well, fish and grits it is. Would you mind if I make it in the oven instead of frying it on the stove?"

"Will it be crispy?" Mrs. Todd asked. "My Willie likes his fish real crispy."

"Yes, Mrs. Todd. It will be crispy." Kara was aware that Mrs. Todd was old school, frying everything from chicken to fish to spareribs. The ribs were delicious, cooking in hot oil two to three minutes when compared to more than an hour in the oven.

What Kara had found startling was that even with their diet of fried foods, the Todds were slender, and she attributed that to them being in constant motion. Mr. Todd spent all day walking around the property, pruning and weeding trees and shrubs or cleaning out the pond where a flock of ducks had taken up residence. The highlight of his day was when he sat on the riding mower.

Mrs. Todd sat on a stool, watching Kara as she sprayed the seasoned fillets with a cooking spray, dusted them in cornmeal, and then sprayed them again before placing them gently on a parchment-covered baking sheet. "Where are you going to stay when they start working inside the house?"

"I'm going to move into the other guesthouse."

"Let me know when you are ready to move in, and I'll air it out for you."

"Thank you."

She'd thanked Mrs. Todd when she wanted to tell the older woman that she didn't want or need a personal maid. She made her own bed, cleaned her bathroom, and did her own laundry, leaving the housekeeper to dust and vacuum. If she hadn't walked the beach or passed the time digging up dead roots and vines that had been Theodora's award-winning garden, Kara would've gone completely stir-crazy.

Her cell phone rang again, and Mrs. Todd moved off the stool to check on the biscuits and fish while Kara answered the call. It was Jeff, informing her to expect the security company technician within the hour. Her entire morning and afternoon would be filled with meetings with the engineer, glazier, and now the security company.

"I really appreciate your help. How can I repay you?"

"Go to the movies with me."

"When?" Kara asked.

"Tonight."

"What time are you picking me up?"

"Nine."

"I'll be ready."

Kara hung up, smiling. She had a date—the first one in more than two years.

Chapter Fourteen

Jeff's grin spoke volumes. Kara had chosen to wear black again, but this time it was a pair of stretch pants, high-heeled booties, and a long-sleeved T-shirt and a wide leather belt that showed off her narrow waist. She brushed her hair and secured it in a ponytail, and the light cover of makeup accentuated her lush mouth and shimmering eyes. Dipping his head, he pressed a kiss to the gold stud in her ear.

"You look incredible."

She gave him a demure smile. "Thank you." She opened the door wider. "I just have to get my bag and keys."

He stood in the entryway, staring up at the plasterwork around the hanging fixture. If the walls could talk in the three-story, twenty-room mansion, they would probably tell secrets known by only the people who'd lived there. His grandmother knew more about the Pattons than he had. His only interaction had been with Harlan who'd bullied him relentlessly until by virtue of Jeff's height and weight it had stopped.

Jeff had decided to ignore the animosity between him and Harlan until the mayor of Angels Landing opened his mouth to defame Kara. The man's twisted mind had him assuming they were sleeping together when nothing was further from the truth at that time.

Kara had come to Cavanaugh Island a month ago, and during that time Jeff was aware that his feelings for her had changed dramatically. What had begun as a favor to his cousin was now an all-encompassing need to take care of her, though he suspected she didn't care for him the way he was beginning to care for her.

As Taylor Patton's heir she'd become the largest single landowner on Cavanaugh Island, and if the rumors were true, then she was also quite wealthy. If she did need him, it would only be for protection. He could do that as sheriff of the island, but his protective instincts were deeper than his civic duty. Jeff wanted to love her and take care of her—something he hadn't done for any woman other than his grandmother.

"Come back here!"

He turned just in time to see Oliver scurrying away from Kara. Moving quickly, he scooped up the puppy. "Where are you running to?"

"I opened the crate to give him fresh water, and he escaped."

Cradling the dog as if he were a football, Jeff carried him back to his crate. "Personally, I'd let you have the run of the house, but it's apparent your mama wants to keep you on house arrest."

"I heard that, Jeffrey Hamilton," Kara said behind him.

"I intended for you to hear that, Kara Newell. Do you let him out during the day?"

"Of course, I let him out. I only put him in the crate whenever I go out. Right now, he's teething and gnawing on the baseboards. He hasn't attacked the legs of the furniture, so hopefully they'll be spared."

Jeff placed the terrier in the crate and slid the latch shut. "I thought you bought him some chew toys."

"He doesn't want his chew toys. The only time he's quiet is when we sit out on the porch together. I think he's more feline than canine because he loves the sun. He looks for a patch of sunlight, then settles down to sleep for hours."

Reaching for Kara's hand, Jeff brought it to his mouth, kissing the back of it. "I hope you aren't thinking of replacing me with Oliver as your companion."

Smiling up at him through her lashes, Kara nodded. "He's a nice little companion. He barked so much today that it's a wonder he isn't hoarse. Every time the doorbell rang he went ballistic. But...there's no way he can replace you."

Jeff waited for Kara to lock up the house, then led her to where he'd parked his car. During the short drive to the Cove, she told him the windows had been replaced and the security technician had recommended wiring the house with different zones. The guesthouses and garages would also be secured. Cameras would be installed along the path leading up to the house and in trees around the perimeter of the property as far as the slave village. Everything would be monitored from a central location with access to the local police and fire departments. He would install control panels on all three floors, with no delay signals at the back and rear entrances.

"If anyone were to come in the back door after I armed the system, then the alarm would go off immediately."

"And the call would come in to the station house," Jeff said. "We'll answer the call and alert the Charleston PD in case the perp tries to get off the island using the causeway."

"I hope it doesn't come to that."

"I feel the same way."

Jeff parked in the lot behind the courthouse. He knew parking was limited at the movie theater, and on the weekends it was similar to trying to find a space at the mall during Christmas shopping season. "We'll walk from here," he told Kara as he opened the door to come around and assist her.

The downtown area was illuminated with streetlamps and tiny white lights throughout the town square. Water spilling from the fountain was a sure sign that spring had come to the island. The benches surrounding the fountains were filled with teenagers and other townspeople taking advantage of the warm weather.

He tucked her hand into the bend of his elbow. "You can tell when it's springtime on the island. Everyone is out at night, especially on the weekends."

Kara sniffed the air. "It smells like spring. I've been trying to clear away the overgrowth of weeds that had been Theodora's garden. I had Mr. Todd cut back most of the brush because I didn't want to have to deal with snakes."

"Are you afraid of snakes?"

"No. I actually have a healthy respect for them. If they don't bother me, then I won't bother them."

"We have at least six poisonous snakes here on the island. There are the three Cs: copperhead, cottonmouth, and eastern coral. The rattlers are eastern diamondback, timber, and Carolina pigmy. The pigmy is the most dangerous because most of the time you can't hear the rattles until it's too late."

"Now you're scaring me."

Jeff tightened his hold on her hand, nodding and smiling to several permanent boarders at the Cove Inn. "I don't want to frighten you. I just want you to be careful."

"How's David?"

"Other than a pounding headache, he says he'll survive. He claims he's going to call you and thank you for looking out for him."

"I'm sorry he broke up with his girlfriend. How long were they together?"

"They must have dated off and on for about five years."

Kara stopped, forcing Jeff to stop with her. "He dated her for five years and only now was he ready to propose marriage?"

"What's wrong with that?"

"What's right with it, Jeff? If a man can't commit to a woman after two years, then he should get out of her life and let someone else willing to commit step in. It's no wonder she cheated on him."

Jeff started walking again, she keeping pace. "Would you cheat on a man who didn't commit?"

"We're not talking about me."

"I'm talking about you."

"No, because I'd leave him before I cheated. I don't know what men are afraid of," Kara continued. "They find a good woman, but for some asinine reason they're always looking for someone better. Most times there isn't anyone better than what they have. Look at some of these entertainers who father children with either one or different women. And because they don't marry them, they don't think of themselves as adulterers. Well, in my book they are lower than a snake's belly."

"Damn, baby! Calm down."

"I won't calm down, Jeff. Did David tell you before last night that he was going to propose to Petra?"

"I don't think so."

"I'm not judging him, but he had to have known his girlfriend was getting restless; otherwise he wouldn't have suddenly decided to propose."

"I don't know."

"He's your cousin. Don't you guys talk?"

"We talk, but David has always been a very private person."

Kara stopped again, her free hand going to the middle of Jeff's chest. "I like David, and it bothered me to see him hurting like that."

"Do you ever stop being a social worker?"

"You're impossible," Kara spat out.

Jeff cradled her face. "I had a long talk with my cousin. He's not as fragile as he appears. He realizes he should've asked Petra to marry him a long time ago, but she always gave him mixed signals."

"Did you like her?"

A hint of a smile played at the corners of his mouth. "I like her but not for David. She's a party girl, while David is a homebody. You talk about David when it would be no different with us."

Vertical lines appeared between her eyes when she frowned. "What are you talking about?"

"We date each other for five years; then one day you tell me you're going back to New York. Would you expect me to remain faithful to you if I know what we have isn't going to last?"

"It's not the same, Jeff," Kara argued softly.

"Because you say it isn't, darling, but actually it is. Can you stand here right now and tell me you'll commit to staying longer than five years?"

"You know I can't do that."

"If that's the case, then we'll drop the subject and head over to the theater before the movie begins." She opened her mouth to come back at him, but Jeff placed his thumb over her parted lips, shushing her. "We'll discuss this later."

Kara smiled as if she'd won a small victory. "Fine. Later. What's playing?"

"*The Help.*"

Her eyebrows lifted a fraction. "I've read the book but missed seeing the film."

They made it to the theater with time to spare. Jeff paid for the tickets, ignoring the stares of moviegoers looking at Kara. He knew they were curious about her and even more curious about them as a couple. Plus, it was the first time any of them had seen him with a woman.

He looped his arm around her waist. "Would you like popcorn?"

"Only if you'll share it with me."

Kara watched Jeff as he stood in the concession line. She noticed the sidelong glances directed his way by several women, who whispered to one another, and she wondered how often he came to movies. He'd admitted that he had never dated a woman from the island, so there was no doubt tonight would spark talk about him being seen with Taylor Patton's daughter.

She saw him turn around and speak to a man with Deborah Monroe, assuming the tall man with salt-and-pepper hair was Dr. Monroe, Deborah's husband. Kara smiled when Deborah waved to her, mouthing hello. Kara nodded, returning her smile. It was Saturday night, date night, and couples were filing into the movie theater.

The Cove Theater claimed a single screen, unlike the cineplex theaters in New York City and its suburbs where moviegoers could choose from up to a dozen films. And for someone who'd spent the past fifteen years of her life in the big city, small-town life was beginning to appeal to her. She'd become accustomed to smelling fresh air and damp earth rather than exhaust fumes from cars and buses. Sitting on the porch had become a luxury when she was serenaded by the sound of crickets rather than the sirens from first responders and other emergency vehicles.

Moving to Angels Landing had given Kara a chance to restart her life. She was still a social worker at heart, but she wasn't forced to get up every day and go into an office. She no longer had to share an apartment with a roommate because she couldn't afford to live alone. A twenty-room antebellum mansion went beyond anything she could've ever imagined.

When she listed all of the reasons why she'd been so amenable about leaving a lifestyle she'd become accustomed to, Kara knew Jeff had a lot to do with it. He hadn't done more than kiss her, yet she'd come to look for his kisses. They'd shared a bed, and he hadn't tried to coerce her into making love.

She was a normal woman with normal urges, urges she'd forgotten existed until she'd sat across the table from Jeff in Jack's Fish House. Though Jeff was a friend, the feelings she was beginning to have for him weren't very friendly.

Kara's gaze lingered on his strong, distinctive profile. A myriad of emotions assailed her, and she refused to acknowledge that she could be falling in love with him. She closed her eyes and shook her head as if banishing the notion. She couldn't and wouldn't, not when she could not commit to living in Angels Landing beyond the five-year mandate.

Jeff beckoned her, and she took a large tub of popcorn from him as he picked up two cups of soda. Kara rarely drank soda, but soda and popcorn at the movies was like peanut butter and jelly. They just went together.

"I hope there're still some seats in the balcony."

They made their way into the theater where the screen was filled with images of trailers for upcoming movies. Kara followed Jeff as he climbed the stairs to the balcony. There were two seats but not together. Jeff leaned down and whispered to a young man who nodded and moved to another seat.

"Thanks, Wes."

"No biggie, Sheriff," the teenager mumbled.

Kara sat down, smiling at Jeff when he dropped down beside her, anchoring the drinks in the cup holders. "Did you get napkins?" she whispered. He'd added butter to the popcorn.

Rising slightly, he took a handkerchief from the pocket of his slacks. "You can use this."

Seconds later the lights dimmed and the filled theater settled down to view the featured film.

Jeff cast a sidelong glance at Kara as she pressed her head to the car's headrest. "Did they do the book justice?"

"Yes. I can't tell you how many times I read a book, then go and see the movie only to be disappointed. This time I wasn't."

He downshifted as he approached the road connecting the Cove with the Landing. It was scheduled to be paved at the end of the month, and that couldn't come soon enough for Jeff. He never complained publicly because there was a time when the Landing was virtually inaccessible except on foot. And there weren't too many people brave or reckless enough to attempt to drive or walk through the swampy area with poisonous vipers, quicksand, and alligators.

"My parents are coming here for Easter, and if you and Miss Corrine aren't planning anything, I'd like for you to join us," Kara continued when he didn't respond. "I told my father that I'd introduce him to several marines."

Jeff gave her a quick glance. "How long are they staying?"

"Just for the weekend. They plan to arrive on Friday and leave Monday."

"I'll make certain to join you." He'd given Kara's suggestion about a corps' week a lot of thought. He'd even called one of his buddies and ran the idea past him, who promised to contact the others in their group for their feedback.

"What about Miss Corrine?"

"I'm certain she'll also come with me. I usually give my deputies Christmas and Thanksgiving off because they have families. Easter's the only family holiday I claim for myself. So if there's someplace your dad would like to see, let me know."

"I'll give Daddy your cell number, and the two of you can talk."

A deep chuckle filled the interior of the small car. "Are you saying you don't want anything to do with the corps?"

Kara's laughter joined his. "Just say I've heard enough corps stories to last several lifetimes. I don't know what it is about marines that make them—"

"Don't go there, baby," Jeff warned softly. "The corps is sacred."

"And that is sacrilegious," she countered with a laugh.

Jeff winked at her when she met his gaze. "We'll get along just fine as long as you don't dis the corps."

Fisting her hands at her waist, Kara gave him a "no you didn't" look. "Are you saying you like the corps more than me?"

Jeff didn't want to believe, couldn't believe Kara had just repeated what Pamela had asked him when she'd issued her ultimatum. Six months into their engagement, they'd begun making plans for their wedding, and without warning his fiancée revealed she wasn't cut out to become a military wife. When she'd asked if he'd loved the corps more than her, she took his slight hesitation as an affirmative and gave him back his ring. What Pamela failed to realize was that the military was all he knew. It'd been ingrained in him like involuntary breathing.

Before he'd left the Cove to attend college, Jeff wasn't certain what he wanted to do with his life. He'd always excelled in math and science and had thought of becoming a doctor. It was when he was approached by a recruiter to enroll in the NROTC that he realized the military suited his temperament.

He'd come to love all things military, the corps becoming his wife, mistress, and child, his fellow officers brothers and sisters, and the men under his command his extended family. But that all changed when he got the phone call that his grandmother had been hospitalized due to a heart attack. Twenty years of drills, parades, and two tours in a war zone were forgotten when he stood at his grandmother's bedside, holding her hand while promising to take care of her. And he had.

"No, Kara. I don't like the corps more than you. In fact, I like you much more than I'd planned to."

"Are you saying you didn't want to like me?"

"That's exactly what I'm saying. David asked me to check on you after the Pattons threatened you, but you and I know my checking on you has progressed beyond protection. One of the most difficult things I've ever had to do was *not* make love to you last night. For a few minutes I forgot that someone tried to frighten you into leaving. And I wanted to forget the images from my dreams...men being blown apart by explosive devices, some whose bodies and minds would never be whole again."

Kara rested her hand over Jeff's on the gearshift. "I don't want you to want me to chase away your demons, Jeff. I want you to want me for me because I know in my heart I want *you*, not the marine or the sheriff."

He drove along the allée of oaks, slowing and driving around to the rear of the house. Kara had left on lights on the first and second floors, giving the appearance that the house was occupied.

Jeff felt an indescribable emotion of rightness. It was the first time he'd become involved with a woman where he felt a gentle, soothing peace. The only other time he'd experienced a similar feeling was when he'd stepped off the ferry at the Sanctuary Cove landing as a civilian. His decision to resign his commission had become a no-brainer. Nothing, not even the corps, was more important to him than his grandmother. But unknowingly Kara had also become important to him, much more important than she could've imagined. There were times when he couldn't keep his hands off her, and he found any and every opportunity to kiss her when he'd wanted to do so much more.

The one thing that kept him from aggressively pursuing her was the disclosure that she hadn't planned to stay on the island. And Jeff had to ask himself whether he was willing to engage in a relationship with a woman with an expiration date. His grandmother had begun to nag him that he was getting older, not younger, and it was time he think about his future. Did he want their branch on the family tree to end with him? Was he really so selfish that he refused to share his life with a woman? He'd given her a lethal stare when she asked if perhaps he preferred men to women. Corrine knew he was heterosexual, but she admitted she was just repeating some of the gossip she'd heard from those in the Cove.

He parked the car, shut off the engine, and turned to look at Kara. "There will only be Jeffrey and Kara, not Captain Hamilton or Sheriff Hamilton."

Unbuckling her seat belt, Kara leaned into him. "And there will only be Kara, not the social worker who must analyze everyone and everything."

Laughing, Jeff held up his hand, pinkie extended. "Pinkie swear?"

Kara looped their pinkies together. "Pinkie swear," she repeated.

"Don't move. I'll come around and get you."

Reaching for the small automatic strapped to his ankle, Jeff pushed it into the small of his back as he got out of the car. He held Kara's hand in a firm grip as he helped her to stand. All of his senses were on full alert when he walked with her to the side entrance, waiting as she unlocked the door. Within seconds of walking into the house, they heard Oliver barking.

Kara glanced at Jeff over her shoulder. "What did I tell you about my early warning system?" Kneeling, she opened the crate and Oliver launched himself at her, wiggling and whining in his excitement to be let out of confinement. She kissed the top of his head as she cradled him to her chest. "Hi, baby. Mama's glad to see you, too."

Jeff knew Oliver was a dog, but he tried to imagine Kara with a child. She and the dog had bonded instantly, and it had taken a very short time for her to spoil her pet. Would it be the same if she had children? But then he remembered her statement that she wasn't ready for marriage and children, and he wondered if she would ever be ready for it. Some women were destined not to become wives or mothers. Maybe Kara was one of them.

"I'm going to check around to make certain there're no more broken windows."

"As soon as I change Oliver's pad, I'll be up."

Jeff started at the third floor, opening and closing doors to closets and looking under the beds in the bedrooms. He repeated the action on the second floor, knowing the action would be unnecessary once the security company wired the house and property.

He'd just set the automatic on the bedside table in Kara's bedroom when she walked in. He extended his arms and wasn't disappointed when she walked into his embrace. He held her, heart to heart, man to woman, silently communicating feelings he couldn't put into words. The scrappy, intuitive woman in his arms had captured a part of himself he'd withheld from every woman in his past, including Pamela.

Jeff hadn't stopped to ask himself whether it was because he was different, that his focus had changed when he'd become a civilian for the first time in two decades. Whatever it was, he didn't want to spend time trying to analyze himself or why he felt so strongly about Kara. Burying his face in her hair, he pressed a kiss to her scalp, when she anchored her arms under his shoulders.

She lifted her head, and he stared at the serene expression that had spread across her delicate features. "I want to make love to you. Will you allow me to do that?" The question had come from some place Jeff was totally unfamiliar with. In the past he'd never asked. It was something that just happened.

Kara's eyelids fluttered as she blinked back unshed tears. "Yes, Jeff," she whispered. "Make love to me."

One minute she was standing, and seconds later she was on the bed. He removed his shoes and socks, then lay over her, his body pressing hers down to the mattress. Time stood still, and the earth stopped spinning on its axis as Jeff slowly, methodically undressed Kara, his mouth charting a course over her silken flesh from the scented column of her neck to her slender feet. Her clothes had concealed a curvy, womanly body that had shocked him with its lushness. Her firm breasts were full, perched high above a narrow rib cage and flat belly. Her hips were rounded, thighs firm, legs shapely.

Her eyes were wide, trusting as he sat back on his knees and removed his own clothing: pullover sweater, belt, slacks, and underwear. He paused long enough to remove a condom from the pocket of his slacks and placed it on the table. They shared a smile when she held out her arms, and he sank into her perfumed embrace. Jeff lay between her outstretched legs.

"Do you know how long I've wanted to do this?" he confessed in her ear.

"No. How long?" she whispered.

"Since the first night I came here, and you opened the door wearing next to nothing."

She laughed softly. "That's what you get for making unannounced night calls."

"I find myself losing control whenever I'm around you."

"Since we're into true confessions, I have one to make."

"What is it?"

"Since meeting you I've had a few erotic dreams and—"

He stopped Kara's words when his mouth covered hers in a smoldering kiss that left him feeling light-headed. Jeff had thought he'd been the only one harboring erotic fantasies, but apparently he was wrong.

He realized he was falling in love with her. What he didn't want to think about was losing her like every other woman he'd lost in his life.

He didn't know his mother, but she had to love her unborn child to hold on long enough to give birth to him. Then there was Pamela—the only woman he'd confessed to loving and she'd left him. Jeff didn't want to think of his grandmother, who, at seventy-nine, had most of her life behind her. And now there was Kara.

Could he afford to walk into a situation where he was certain of the outcome? As much as he'd tried to stay away from the pull, it was too strong to resist because he discovered that he wanted her in and out of bed. And if she'd insisted they wait a year before making love, Jeff knew he would've waited. She'd come to mean that much to him. "Having you here with me is good," Kara admitted. A small gasp of surprise escaped her when Jeff fastened his mouth to her breast, suckling her like a starving infant, and her body responded, arching up to meet him.

Nothing was rushed. His kisses started at the base of her throat and trailed lower to her belly. His teeth grazed over her nipples, turning them into hard buds. But everything changed when he placed his hands against her inner thighs, spreading her legs, sending a rush of moisture between them. Then the sensual assault began.

Kara rose off the mattress as he searched for the tiny bud of flesh at the apex of her thighs, and once finding it, laved it with his tongue until he knew she was close to climax.

She gripped the sheets, swallowing the moans trapped in the back of her throat, gasping as if unable to take a breath.

Cupping her hips in both hands, Jeff plunged his tongue into Kara's quivering flesh over and over until he lost count of how many times he'd drank deeply. He felt her entire body trembling and heard her plea for him to stop, but he couldn't. He'd wanted to brand her as his possession like a permanent tattoo and make her forget all the other men who'd been in her life. And for a brief crazed moment, he wanted to be the last man in her bed and in her life.

He did heed her pleas to stop, but it was to open the packet, remove the condom, and roll it down his tumescence. Taking her hand, he stared at her and together they guided his erection inside her. She gasped, going still until he was fully sheathed inside her hot throbbing flesh.

Jeff made slow, deliberate love to Kara until he established a rhythm she followed as if they'd choreographed it in advance, their bodies keeping perfect tempo with each other. Even with the thin barrier of latex, he still could feel her heat as he quickened his thrusts. Soft moans filled the room, and she rose to meet his strong thrusts, their bodies in exquisite harmony with each other, hurtling him to a point of no return.

His scrotum tightened painfully, and the burning sensation at the base of his spine was an indication that he was going to ejaculate. Jeff tried concentrating on anything but the woman writhing underneath him. He closed his eyes, shutting out the sight of her thrashing head and the rush of color darkening her face and chest.

Burying his head between her neck and shoulder, he quickened his movements and then released the desire, lust, and passion that had been building since the first time he walked into the garden room to find Kara rising off the chair like an apparition in a dream.

He felt Kara's orgasm as her flesh squeezed his penis, released him, and then squeezed him again and again. It was his turn to plead with her to stop when her vaginal muscles held his semierect penis in a viselike grip.

"Oh, baby, baby, baby," he chanted over and over until her throbbing flesh stilled and he was able to pull out. Rolling off her body, Jeff lay on his back, arms above his head as he tried slowing down his runaway heartbeat. He let out an audible sigh when Kara climbed atop him.

"Are you all right," she whispered in his ear.

"I don't know yet."

Kara rested her cheek on his muscled chest. "Don't you dare pass out on me, Jeff."

He smiled. "I'm not going to pass out. I just need to catch my breath."

They lay together, he barely feeling the weight of the body molded to the length of his. Jeff wasn't certain when Kara had fallen asleep because he had also. When he did wake, it was hours later. Kara lay beside him, curled into the fetal position. He went to the bathroom to discard the condom.

He returned to the bed, got in next to the woman whose scent was stamped on his skin like a tattoo, and pulled a sheet and lightweight blanket over their bodies. He fell asleep again. His internal alarm clock woke him at six, and Jeff managed to get out of bed, dress, write a note explaining his absence, and leave the house through the rear door, the door locking behind him.

It wasn't the way he'd wanted to leave Kara, but he was scheduled to relieve Nelson Lambert at eight that morning. It was early Sunday morning, and the Cove had yet to stir when he maneuvered his car under the carport next to his grandmother's.

Jeff used the back staircase to his bedroom. He shaved, showered, and dressed, then went downstairs to the kitchen to prepare breakfast. His cooking skills weren't four star, but he was able to put together a more than passable breakfast.

He'd just finished flipping buckwheat pancakes, placing them on a plate next to a bowl of sliced strawberries and peaches, when his grandmother walked into the kitchen. She was dressed for church in a becoming shirtwaist dress and sensible pumps. The single strand of pearls around her neck matched the pair in her ears.

"Good morning, Gram."

Corrine smiled. "Good morning, Jeffrey. Slept out last night, did you?" She picked up her favorite coffeepot and filled it with water.

Jeff refused to look at her. "Why are you asking a question you already know the answer to?"

"I just needed to hear it for myself."

His hands stilled before he set the plate on the table. "Who told you?"

"Hannah Forsyth called last night, waking me out of a good sleep to tell me she saw you and Kara at the movies. And I figured when you didn't come home, you were with her."

Jeff shook his head. "Damn, Gram!"

"Jeffrey, you know I don't abide with cussin' in my house on Sunday."

"Sorry about that. What did she do? Put a GPS tracker on my car?"

"You haven't been away that long that you don't know how fast gossip spreads across the island. The next thing you know they'll have you and Kara married with a house full of kids."

"That's not going to happen, Gram."

"Why not?"

"Because she doesn't plan on living here past five years."

Corrine frowned. "That's nonsense. If she stays five, then why not ten or even thirty? That will doesn't mean anything. He could've said thirty years. And what would she have done? Live here for that length of time, then pick up and leave? I don't think so, Jeffrey. You know I've never been one to get into your personal business, but it's going to be up to you to change her mind. And you don't need five years to do that. My sister called and told me how David messed up his life stringing that girl along for so long. In my day no girl would wait around for a man to get up enough nerve to marry her. But you young folks hem and haw, and when the girl leaves you for another man, suddenly you realize what you've lost. My mama used to say, *'You don't miss your water 'til the well runs dry, and you don't miss your baby 'til she says good-bye.'* Don't be a fool, Jeffrey. If you want Kara to stay, then you better start now trying to change her mind."

"Kara's parents are coming for Easter, and she's inviting us to Angels Landing for dinner."

"Tell her we're coming and find out what she'd like me to bring. And don't try and change the subject, Jeffrey. If you let this girl get away, then I'm going to disown you."

Jeff pulled out a chair at the table. "Please sit down, Gram, and eat before your pancakes get cold." Leaning down, he kissed her soft, curly hair. "Love you."

Corrine waved him away. "Don't try and sweet-talk me, Jeffrey. I mean what I say."

Sitting opposite his grandmother, Jeff blew her a kiss. He knew she was angry with him, but there wasn't much he could do to get Kara to change her mind short of proposing marriage. He'd done that once, and one thing he'd learned was not to make the same mistake twice.

He would enjoy the time given them, and when Kara packed up and left Angels Landing, Jeff knew he wouldn't have any regrets.

Chapter Fifteen

Kara felt as if she was on a roller-coaster. At first she'd complained about not having anything to do but read and weed a garden, and now she couldn't find enough hours in the day to complete her to-do list. However, keeping busy was the perfect excuse to keep from thinking about Jeff. Whenever she did think of him, it was always thoughts of their lovemaking. The image of his hands searching between her thighs, his mouth on her breasts, and his hardness moving in and out of her body invaded her dreams, and she'd wake gasping, struggling to breathe until the throbbing and pulsing subsided. She'd curse her traitorous body; then she would lie motionless until sleep claimed her again while praying the erotic dream wouldn't return. But it did return—not every night, but often enough to remind Kara of what she'd had for one blissful night and wanted again. She couldn't wait to see Jeff again, but had so much to do in preparation for the upcoming holiday.

Not only were her parents, Jeff, and Corrine coming for Easter dinner, but Dawn had called to say she was closing her dance studio for a week and had decided she needed a change of scenery. Dawn, who didn't like flying, had decided to take the train into Charleston.

Sitting in her car at the Amtrak station, Kara closed her eyes. She'd ordered all the food she needed from the supermarket in the Cove. Back in New York, she would have traveled to the grocery store herself. But Mrs. Todd told her that she hardly ever went to the supermarket. She'd call in her order and had the groceries, meat, and produce delivered. The market would bill Taylor, and he would mail them a check. Now that she handled all the expenses for the household, Kara found herself doing the same, in addition to writing checks for electric, gas, and other household incidentals. Even though there was no mortgage on the house, there were still property taxes. The insurance premiums on the vintage cars, the house, and its contents were astronomical.

The engineer had sent his report, stating the foundation was sound, and the historic preservationist had sent her a copy of the estimated costs of restoring the interiors and re-creating the exterior buildings and gardens. Morgan had recommended him because he'd been one of her instructors at SCAD before he retired to go into business for himself while hiring a few of his interns. Now she knew why Taylor had bequeathed her so much money. A large portion of the inheritance would go to restoring Angels Landing.

It had taken the security company three full days to wire the house and property. They'd placed tiny cameras in trees that were barely visible at first glance. Kara now felt safer, especially once she armed the system before retiring for bed.

Jeff came to see her whenever he was off duty but had only slept over once since the system was installed. She wasn't certain whether he didn't want to leave his grandmother home alone too often or if he wanted to keep gossip to a minimum.

Mrs. Todd had warned Kara that folks were talking about the sheriff spending the night at Angels Landing. What Kara didn't understand was how anyone knew he'd spent the night when he'd parked his car where it wasn't visible from the path leading up to the house. The nearest residence was more than two acres away, so unless someone had a powerful telescope trained on her property, it would be impossible for them to monitor anyone coming and going. She decided to wait a week, then contact the security company to review surveillance footage to ascertain who was watching her home.

Kara heard the sound of the train pulling into the station and got out of the car and walked to the platform to wait for Dawn. Her former roommate was the last one off the train. Kara waved to get her attention. "Hey, Miss Dee."

Dawn turned when she heard her name. "Miss Kay!" Shouldering a large tapestry bag, she rushed over and hugged Kara.

Kara returned the hug, then pulled back to look at her friend. Dawn's pixie hairstyle suited her. With her natural blonde hair, peaches and cream complexion, and tiny round face, she could be the perfect Peter Pan.

"Welcome to the Lowcountry."

Dawn pulled her sweatshirt away from her chest. "I

can't believe this heat. We're still wearing winter coats in New York, and here you are in a T, shorts, and sandals."

Reaching for Dawn's bag, Kara slung it over her shoulder. "You probably want to shower and get into something lighter than sweats."

Dawn closed her sky-blue eyes. "You're singing my song." She gave Kara a long, lingering stare. "You look good, roomie."

"I feel good. Come on, let's go before we run into traffic. Of course, it's nothing like rush hour traffic in New York—"

"Please don't mention New York until it's time for me to go back."

Kara led the way to the parking lot where disembarking passengers were hugging friends and relatives and loading trunks of cars and taxis with luggage. She put Dawn's bag on the rear seat, slipped behind the wheel, and drove away from the train station.

Dawn slumped against the leather seat and closed her eyes. "I envy you, Kara."

"What for?"

"For being brave enough to change your life."

"I've only changed my lifestyle, Dawn."

"Life or lifestyle. Same difference. Look at me. I'm a professional dancer who suffers from occasional stage fright, so in order to make ends meet I open a dance studio and teach kids whose mothers believe they'll be the next Nureyev or Dame Margot Fonteyn. But my students couldn't care less about first, second, or third position. I don't want to teach, Kara. I just want to dance, dance, and dance some more."

Kara and Dawn had talked at length about her inability to perform in front of a live audience. The talented dancer had tried hypnosis and antianxiety medication, but she wasn't able to overcome the disorder that kept her from doing what she'd been trained to do.

"What other alternatives do you have?" she asked. "Think of Nureyev or Baryshnikov. What did they do after they stopped dancing?"

"They never really stop dancing. Most times they become mentors or teach."

"What about choreographing, Dawn? I know if I were in your class, I wouldn't want to come in once or twice a week and learn steps and positions. That's boring as hell."

Dawn opened her eyes, sat up straight, and stared at Kara's profile. "What would you want to see?"

"*The Nutcracker, Sleeping Beauty,* and *Swan Lake* with an urban spin. Bernstein and Robbins took *Romeo and Juliet* and turned it into *West Side Story*, and the rest is history. Give your students something they can relate to: street dancing."

"You're a genius!" Dawn said, punching her shoulder.

"Ouch! You don't know your own strength."

"My bad, Kara. Can you imagine my kids putting on an updated version of *The Nutcracker*? The mouse king has to be a real badass."

Kara smiled. "There you go."

Dawn kept up a steady stream of conversation during the drive to Cavanaugh Island, falling silent only when Kara drove along the allée of oaks draped in Spanish moss. Her mouth formed a perfect O when the house came into view.

"You *are* freaking Scarlett O'Hara."

"Scarlett lived at Tara. This is Angels Landing."

Dawn stuck her head out the open window, staring up

at the three-story structure. "I see why you decided not to come back. This place is awesome."

"It needs a lot of work," Kara explained when she parked her car near the garages.

"What are those?" Dawn asked, pointing to the two one-story structures several hundred feet from the main house.

"Guesthouses. The groundskeeper and his wife live in one. I plan to move into the other once the workmen begin their restoration. What's nice about the guesthouse is that it has two bedrooms, a full bath, utility kitchen and living/dining area." Kara opened the car door. "Let's go in and get you settled." She led Dawn to the second floor and opened the door to a bedroom in the west wing. "You'll have your own bathroom."

"Where's your room?" Dawn asked as she placed her bag on the bench at the foot of the queen-sized bed.

"I'm at the other end. Have you eaten?"

"I stopped and had something to eat before I got on the train. Once it pulled out of New York, I reclined my seat and went to sleep."

Kara stared at the petite woman who barely tipped the scales at one hundred pounds. "We'll go out for dinner."

"Fancy or casual?"

"It's casual." She decided she would take Dawn to Jack's Fish House. "By the way, my parents are coming in tomorrow for the weekend."

Dawn's face split into a smile. "I love your folks."

"I know they'll love seeing you again. I'm going to shower and change. Meet me in the kitchen."

"Where's the kitchen?"

Kara pointed to the nearest staircase. "Take the stairs and turn left. It's the second room off the hallway."

She left Dawn, retracing her steps until she entered her bedroom. She wondered how Theodora would've reacted if she knew her son's daughter had become mistress of Angels Landing and that the house would be filled with people she probably would've deemed beneath her.

It wasn't the first time Kara had tried to imagine meeting her paternal grandmother. Would the woman reject her outright, or would she embrace her because they looked so much alike?

What she found strange was that anyone who mentioned Theodora's name didn't have anything nice to say about her, and Kara shuddered to think of how she would've turned out if her mother had married Taylor instead of Austin.

Walking into the bathroom and stripping off her clothes, she covered her hair with a shower cap. It was easier to think about Teddy than Jeff. She missed seeing him every day, sleeping with him, and making love with him. He'd become a drug, a very addictive drug she didn't want to shake.

Kara and Dawn walked into Jack's, and the room suddenly quieted before conversations began again. Most of the muted televisions were tuned to the Atlanta Braves baseball game while others were tuned to ESPN. As usual the restaurant was crowded with regulars and out-of-towners.

Dawn, wearing a pair of black cropped pants with a white man-tailored shirt and four-inch heels, leaned close to Kara. "Does this happen every time you come here?" she whispered.

"No. Folks are curious because you're a stranger."

Bright blue eyes grew wider. "Please don't tell me everyone knows one another."

Kara smiled. "They do."

"How do you deal with that?"

"I just deal. Tuesday, we need a table for two," she said to the waitress that had approached them.

"Please follow me."

They were shown to a table in a secluded corner. It was only when she sat down that Kara noticed Jeff sitting at a table with another man. He turned his head and their eyes met. Her pulse quickened when he said something to the man, stood up, and came over to her table. Those close enough to watch the interchange had stopped eating while craning their necks.

Rising to her feet, Kara smiled up at him. "Hey," she said softly. He smiled, bringing her gaze to linger on the attractive cleft in his strong chin.

"Hey yourself. I didn't expect to see you here tonight."

"I brought my ex-roommate and houseguest for the next week. Jeff, this is Dawn Ramsey. Dawn, Jeffrey Hamilton."

Dawn, who was usually never at a loss for words, stared up at the tall man with a gun strapped to his waist. She recovered enough to offer him a limp wrist. "It's a pleasure to meet you."

Jeff's raven-black eyebrows lifted. "The pleasure is all mine." His gaze shifted back to Kara. "Call me when your folks come in."

She nodded. "I will."

"I'd join you, but Mayor White and I have rescheduled this meeting several times, and there are some things we need to discuss."

Kara nodded again. "That's okay."

"How's Oliver?"

"He's allowed out of his crate during the day, but I still cage him at night. Other than that, he's perfect."

"You tell him Daddy will be over to see him in a couple of days."

Kara smiled and stared numbly at the man who made her look forward to every moment spent with him. For the past week, she hoped to get just a glimpse of him even though he called her every night. She went to bed thinking of him and woke looking for him.

"What's going on between the two of you?" Dawn asked when Kara sat down again.

She blinked. "What are you talking about?"

Dawn leaned over the table. "Only a blind person wouldn't see the sparks between you and that delicious-looking lawman. You've never kept a secret from me, sister, so please don't start now."

Kara picked up the menu. "I'll tell you after we order."

Dawn studied her menu. "What are chitlins?"

"They are small intestines of the hog."

"Ewww," she said, wrinkling her nose.

"Don't 'ewww' until you taste them," Kara said. "I'll order a side dish so you can try them."

"What do you recommend?"

"Everything's good, but I'm partial to the red rice."

"I like Southern food, but there's too much to select from."

Kara had introduced her friend to Southern cuisine when she used to prepare elaborate Sunday dinners, but all that stopped when her caseload increased and she spent the weekends doing laundry and trying to catch up on her sleep.

"I'll order for the both of us; that way you'll be able to sample dishes you've never eaten."

As promised, Kara ordered for the both of them and

then quietly told her about Jeff, leaving out the fact that they had slept together. "I went to Haven Creek yesterday, and within seconds of walking into a gourmet shop, I overheard someone whisper that I was the sheriff's woman."

Leaning back in her chair, Dawn shook her head in disbelief. "It's like that?"

"I'm afraid it is."

"We don't even know our neighbors like that."

"Tell me about it, Miss Dee," Kara drawled.

"Doesn't the gossip bother you?"

"Not really."

"It would bother me. That's why I moved from upstate to New York City. Where I lived everyone knew everyone else's business. If they didn't gossip about you, then they made up crap."

Dawn stopped talking when the waitress set out a pitcher of sweet tea and a plate of hot, buttery biscuits on the table. "What saves me is that Angels Landing is somewhat isolated from the other houses in the town. I come to the Cove to do some banking, occasionally eat at Jack's, and visit the local bookstore. I prefer Haven Creek because it has a lot of craft shops and local farmers that sell fresh fruits and veggies."

"So you've really become a country girl," Dawn teased.

"I've always been a country girl. All I have to do is open my mouth and folks know I'm from the South. What I hadn't realized until I moved here is that I still have small-town sensibilities."

Dawn's pale eyebrows met in a frown. "Are you saying you never felt like a New Yorker?"

"Although I lived there for fifteen years, I still found myself feeling like an outsider. Aside from my accent, I could never get used to the fast pace of the city. It's different here because everyone is so laid-back. I don't know if you noticed, but there are no traffic lights or street signs. There's not that frantic rush to get somewhere. Life expectancy here is twelve years higher than it is for people who live in urban areas. Maybe it's because there's no industry polluting the air or that most of the food is locally grown."

"Does your change of heart have anything to do with your new boyfriend?"

"What are you trying to say?" Kara knew she sounded defensive, but it was too late to retract her words.

"You're in love with the man, Kara. Don't forget, I've seen you with different guys. Some you liked and some you didn't. Your face completely changed when Jeff came over here. And if the man can't see what's so obvious, then he's more obtuse than me when I play the airheaded blonde."

"I'll admit that I like him."

"That's BS, Kara. You more than like him."

"Will you please lower your voice," she said when diners at a nearby table turned to look at them. "Can we finish this conversation back at the house?"

"Sure. Here comes our order. Wow." Dawn gasped when dishes of catfish fritters, black-eyed peas, greens, red beans and rice, fried chicken, and chitlins were set out on the table. "There's no way we can eat all this food."

"What we don't eat we'll take home with us. You know I'd rather have dinner for breakfast."

"How do you not gain weight living down here?" Dawn asked as she spooned a portion of rice and beans onto her plate.

"I go for walks along the beach."

"I never saw the beach living upstate. The closest I got to water was a stream that ran along a farmer's land he used to irrigate his crops."

Kara picked up the dish with the chitlins. "Taste a little bit, and tell me whether or not you like them."

Dawn speared a small portion with her fork. She took her time chewing, then smiled. "They're delicious."

"Now, when you speak to your parents, you can tell them you ate chitlins."

"That's not all I'm going to eat. When I go back to New York, I know I'm going to have to work out extra hard to shed the weight I'll gain here."

Kara smiled. "There's worse things than being round and happy."

"No shi—" She put a hand over her mouth to cut off the expletive. "I forgot where I was. Back home no one pays attention to four-letter words."

That was one thing it'd taken Kara a long time to get used to. She wasn't a prude, but she wasn't used to hearing people curse as eloquently as New Yorkers. And unfortunately it was taxicab drivers who were usually on the receiving end of their vitriolic rants.

Kara and Dawn fell into the comfortable camaraderie that had been the hallmark of their longtime friendship. They talked about mutual friends, the men they'd dated, and those they never should've dated. Dawn disclosed she'd given her freeloading friends the boot and it felt good to have the apartment to herself once again.

"You have an admirer," Kara whispered when she noticed a well-dressed man seated at a table to their left staring at Dawn.

Dawn ran a hand over the nape of her neck. "Not interested."

"Weren't you just saying that you were looking for someone new?"

"Someone closer to home, Kara. I'm not cut out for long-distance relationships."

"What makes you think he's from here? I'm willing to bet half the people in this restaurant are tourists. Besides, he's a little too buttoned up to be a local."

Dabbing the corners of her mouth with a napkin, Dawn shifted on her chair and gave the gawking man a dazzling smile. Then she did something that shocked Kara. She stood up, approached him, and introduced herself. The interchange lasted a few minutes, the man handing Dawn his business card.

"Satisfied?" she crooned, grinning at Kara.

"I didn't tell you to roll up on him like that."

Dawn dropped the card into her drawstring bag. "You know me. I'll strike up a conversation with a flea. He's with a film company, and he's here researching locales for a movie. I told him I was on vacation and would call him after I return home. I didn't tell him home is New York."

"Where's his home base?"

"New York. He's with Tribeca Film Company."

The two women exchanged high-five handshakes. They finished eating, and their server brought containers and boxed up the leftovers. Kara settled the bill, leaving a generous tip, and she and Dawn headed back to Angels Landing.

She punched in the code to disarm the alarm system, waiting for the signal to turn from red to green, then opened the door leading into the rear of the house. "I'll show you the house and grounds tomorrow morning before my parents get here."

"How long are they staying?" Dawn asked, following Kara into the brick-walled kitchen.

"They're leaving Monday. After that I'll take you around the island, and one night we'll hang out in Charleston. I still haven't taken the Gullah tour, so that's something we can do together."

Dawn watched Kara store the food in the refrigerator. "You don't have to babysit me, Kara. I came down here just to kick back and veg out. And I'm certain you're going to want to see your boyfriend."

"Jeff and I have plenty of time to see each other."

"Are you sure?"

"Very sure. We—"

"Do you have a dog?" Dawn asked.

"Yes. Come meet Oliver."

Dawn sat on the floor, laughing hysterically when the tiny Yorkie jumped on and off her lap. "He's adorable, Kara. Where did you get him?"

"Jeff gave him to me."

Picking up the puppy, the dancer held him to her chest as he tried licking her chin. "You have the house, a beautiful classic car, and a dog. Now, all you need is a husband and a couple of kids. And I'd better be at the top of your list when you pick a maid of honor."

Kara sat on the floor next to Dawn as Oliver jumped from one lap to the other. "*If* I ever get married, then of course you'll be my maid of honor, but I'm willing to bet you'll get married before I do."

"I don't have the temperament to be a wife and mother. The only constant thing in my life is dance. You're the grounded one, Kara. Even though you had a very challenging and stressful job, you always kept your cool." She rested her head on Kara's shoulder. "I know I invaded your privacy when I allowed my friends to crash at the apartment, but I just didn't know how to say no. It wasn't until after you left that I realized how much you meant to me as a roommate, friend, and sister from another mother," she said.

Kara patted Dawn's flaxen head. "Don't you dare get maudlin on me, Dawn Renee Ramsey. You know where I am, and anytime you want some place to crash, you're always welcome to come here. It'll probably take a couple of years to restore every brick and stick of furniture in this house, but there's still the extra bedroom in the guesthouse."

"We can be roomies again. That is..."

"That is what, Dawn?"

"That is if you don't marry Jeffrey Hamilton."

"Please give it a rest. I'm not going to marry Jeff." Kara stood up. "I have to clean Oliver's crate."

The notion of marrying was not an option for Kara. He didn't believe in love, and she would never consider marrying a man who didn't love her. Kara had carefully mapped out her five-year plan in order to comply with Taylor's mandate. She would move into the remaining guesthouse and oversee the restoration of the property.

Dawn also stood up. "I think I'm going to turn in. I got up before the chickens to take the 6:00 a.m. train down here." She hugged Kara. "Thanks for dinner. I'll see you in the morning."

"Good night."

She cleaned her puppy's crate, but instead of putting

him in for the night, she took him with her to the front porch. A near-full moon silvered the countryside. Sitting on a cushioned rocker, Kara inhaled the scent she'd now come to associate with the Lowcountry.

Oliver turned around and around until he found a comfortable spot on her lap, tucking his muzzle against his side. Running her fingertips over his soft fur, Kara rocked back and forth in a measured rhythm until she found her eyelids closing. She wasn't certain how long she'd dozed off before the sound of an approaching car jerked her back to wakefulness. She sat up straight, smiling when the headlights flashed twice. Kara knew the driver.

Jeff unfolded his body out of the Miata and mounted the porch steps. Bending over, he kissed Kara, then sat down beside her. "I'm officially on vacation for the next ten days."

Kara placed her hand over his on the armrest. "Who's filling in for you?"

"The deputies are going to hold it down for me. They're both family men and could use the overtime pay."

She started rocking again. "What do you plan to do while on your vacation?"

Stretching out his legs, Jeff crossed them at the ankles. "My original plan had to be revised once I discovered my girlfriend has a houseguest."

"I didn't know that I was your girlfriend."

"And why not?"

"Because we never talked about us."

Jeff stared at her profile. "I didn't think we had to talk about it."

Kara closed her eyes for several seconds. "I think we do. Are we a couple?"

He smiled. "Of course we're a couple." He angled his head and brushed his mouth over hers, deepening the kiss until her lips parted. "What else do I have to do to prove to you that I want us to be together?"

She smiled. "I think you've made your point."

His eyebrows lifted a fraction. "And that is?"

"We're a couple."

Jeff pressed a kiss to her hair. "I'm glad we settled that. Now, back to your houseguest."

"I just found out yesterday that Dawn was coming down."

"It's all right, baby. I would never interfere with you being with your friends. Now if that friend had been a dude, I don't think I would be so magnanimous."

"Do I detect some jealousy, Jeff?"

"Hell yeah, you do."

"There's no need for that."

"And why is that?"

"The only man I'm involved with is you."

"You think I don't know that," Jeff countered. "If you were seeing someone else, I'd know it immediately."

"Like everyone knows about you coming to my house and spending the night?"

Moving off the rocker, Jeff sat down at her feet. "I've heard the gossip, too, but I don't care, Kara. I knew when I took you to the movies, folks would talk because they've never seen me out with a woman. We're both consenting adults, so whatever we do together is our business."

"How do they know you come here at night?"

Chuckling, he shrugged his shoulders. "It beats the hell

out of me. I've checked my car inside and out for a tracking device, but I couldn't find anything."

"I told Mrs. Todd that maybe someone has a powerful telescope trained on the house."

"Perhaps you're right, but there's no law against someone owning a telescope."

"But is it legal to spy on people, Jeff?"

"It would be if they were Peeping Toms. But we've never given anyone a show. The drapes are always drawn." He paused. "It could be they recognize my car because it's the only Miata on the island."

Kara trailed her fingertips over his head. "I'm not bothered that people see us together."

"If it's not that, then what's bothering you?"

"I just have this eerie feeling that I'm being watched."

Rising to his knees, Jeff held on to Kara's shoulders. He leaned closer, brushing his mouth over hers. "I think you're being just a little paranoid. You've secured your property, so if you feel something's wrong, then call the company and have them review the surveillance tapes. I think you're still spooked from the rock-throwing incident."

"I don't think I'll ever forget it."

"Kara, baby. Do you trust me to keep you safe?"

"Jeff—"

"Just answer the question. Do you?"

She nodded, then said, "Yes."

"Then let me take care of you."

Kara closed her eyes and pressed her forehead to Jeff's. "How are you planning on doing that?"

It was the first time since meeting Kara that Jeff felt her vulnerability. Even the rock-throwing incident hadn't appeared to unnerve her, and he wondered what had happened, which she wasn't telling him, to shake her resolve. She'd been so adamant about not running away, yet people talking about their relationship had her rattled. It just didn't add up.

"When are the workmen scheduled to begin working on the restoration?"

"A week from now. Why?"

"I want you to move in with me and my grandmother instead of you staying in the guesthouse."

Kara shook her head, her ponytail swaying with the motion. "I can't do that."

"Why not?"

"Because it wouldn't be right."

Jeff angled his head. "It's not what you think, baby. I would never disrespect Gram by sleeping with a woman under her roof. You'll have your own room."

"I can't give you an answer now. Please let me think about it."

The fact that she hadn't said no made Jeff feel a modicum of hope that Kara would eventually accept his offer. She'd told him of her plan to move into the guesthouse for the duration of the restoration. And when he'd informed his grandmother of Kara's intent, it was Corrine who'd offered to open her home to Kara.

Initially, Jeff had believed his grandmother was playing matchmaker but quickly changed his mind when she mentioned overhearing several churchgoers talk about how the Pattons were trying to prove that Kara was a fraud. Corrine normally eschewed gossip, but in this case what she'd heard had been helpful.

He kissed her again. "Don't worry, sweetheart. We'll find a way to make love."

Kara laughed, the sound disturbing Oliver who stood up and shook himself. "Your car is too small for a quickie."

"Wow, I haven't done that since I was a kid. I was thinking more along the lines of renting a bungalow on one of the other islands."

She smiled. "So you want to set up a love shack."

"I'll do whatever it takes to keep you safe."

"Safe and happy."

Jeff nodded. "Safe and very happy," he repeated. "How long are you going to sit out here?"

"Oliver's up, so I'm going in now."

"I'll wait here until you go in and activate the alarm."

He eased Kara up off the chair, kissing her again; he watched as she walked into the house and closed the door. He waited a full two minutes before returning to his car and driving back to the Cove.

Jeff hadn't wanted to believe that he'd managed to take vacation for the first time since becoming sheriff; he'd planned to surprise Kara and spend the time with her, but the unexpected arrival of her ex-roommate had ruined it, at least for him. But if Kara did accept his suggestion to come and live with him, then he would get to see her every day for the next fifty-nine months.

Chapter Sixteen

Jeannette walked into the formal dining room, stopping short. "The table looks spectacular."

Kara's head popped up. She'd just finished setting the table with the silver, crystal, and bone china that she and Dawn had spent hours polishing and cleaning.

"Thank you. Mama, please turn on the chandelier. Wow," she crooned when the prisms in the chandelier reflected off the faceted fully leaded stemware. "It does look nice." Looping her arm through her mother's, Kara led her back to the kitchen. Dawn sat at a small round table in a corner with Corrine while Jeff and Austin were perched on high stools talking about the corps.

Kara had gotten up early to season and stuff the turkey and score the ham she'd studded with cloves and topped with crushed pineapple. Her mother had joined her, and together they'd made potato salad, collard greens with smoked turkey, macaroni and cheese, and corn bread. She'd never perfected making gravy from pan drippings and enlisted her mother to make the giblet turkey gravy. Corrine had volunteered to bring dessert, and sweet potato pie, lemon coconut cake, and peach cobbler sat on a serving cart. And when she'd spoken to Corrine, Kara also invited her and Jeff to spend the night so everyone could be in one place, and much to her surprise the former schoolteacher had accepted because she wanted to spend more time with Jeannette.

The doorbell chimed, followed by Oliver's barking. Kara had locked him in the crate to keep him from being underfoot. He seemed to understand what she was saying when she told him she would let him out after dinner was over.

"Are you expecting anyone else?" Jeannette asked.

Kara shook her head. "No. Jeff, could you please get the door?"

"Sure, babe."

They shared a smile as he left the kitchen to answer the door. Her gaze shifted to her father who smiled and winked at her. Austin had put on a few pounds since she'd seen him at Christmas. Either he was eating too much of her mother's cooking or he was spending too much time sitting in front of the television in his newly converted mancave. Jeff had taken him into Charleston the night before to meet some of his buddies, and it was close to dawn when they returned to the island.

Austin came over and kissed her cheek. "You picked a fine young man," he whispered in her ear.

Kara patted her father's shoulder. He'd affected a short beard since his retirement, and the neatly barbered white hair gave his nut-brown face character. He'd begun losing his hair in his midthirties and now shaved his head like so many other men. Austin wasn't tall but appeared much taller because of his ramrod-straight posture. "I like him, Daddy."

"And he likes you, too, baby girl."

"Kara, someone would like to see you," Jeff said when he returned to the kitchen.

"Excuse me, Daddy." She walked out of the kitchen, Jeff following her. "Who is it?" she asked him.

"I don't know. He wouldn't tell me."

"I guess I'll find out soon enough." Jeff had left the front door half open, and when Kara opened it wider, she saw a tall, slender man with cropped light brown hair standing on the porch. He wore jeans, running shoes, and a College of Charleston sweatshirt. "May I help you?"

"Are you Kara Newell?"

She felt the heat from Jeff's body as he moved closer. "Yes, I am."

The young man reached under his sweatshirt and handed her a sheet of paper. "I was told to give this to you." That said, he loped off the porch and got into an updated Volkswagen Beetle and drove away.

Kara opened the sheet of paper, scanning it before she handed it to Jeff. "I don't believe it," she whispered. "They waited for Easter Sunday to serve me with a summons to submit to a DNA test."

Jeff shook his head as if in disbelief. "The Pattons just won't leave it alone."

Her eyes met his. "That's because they refuse to believe Taylor is my biological father." She let out a groan of exasperation. "Please don't say anything to my parents about this."

Jeff folded the single sheet of paper and handed it to Kara. "Don't you think they should know?"

"No, Jeff. I'll handle this by myself. I'll go to the lab and give them a sample along with something that has Taylor's DNA."

"Do you have anything?" he questioned.

"Yes. Mrs. Todd packed away all of his clothes and personal items in a closet on the third floor. There's an engraved silver-backed comb and brush set that belonged to him. I'm certain the technician will be able to lift some strands of hair from the brush."

"I'll go with you to the lab. I'll also call someone I know at the Charleston PD lab to conduct their own test just in case your relatives decided to bribe someone to say it's not a match. Meanwhile, you should call David and let him know what they're up to."

Wrapping her arms around Jeff's waist, Kara leaned into him. "Thanks. I don't know what I'd do without you."

He ran a hand over her hair. "You would do just fine. I don't think you realize how strong you are."

Leaning back, she smiled. "It takes a great deal of energy trying to stay strong. Promise me you won't mention any of this to my folks."

"I promise."

Kara left the summons under a hand-painted bowl on the fireplace mantelpiece where she would retrieve it later. When she'd gotten up earlier that morning, it was to look forward to sharing a festive dinner with her family and friends, not being served with a summons from a bunch of spiteful relatives with whom she shared blood ties. Mrs. Todd, who at first had been reluctant to talk about her former employers, now felt comfortable enough to reveal that

Theodora had raised her children to be as malicious as she was.

What the Pattons didn't know was that the more they pushed, the harder Kara would push back. If they wanted a fight, then they were going to get one. When she walked back into the kitchen, she saw four pairs of eyes looking at her.

"It was some college kid looking for work," Kara lied smoothly.

"On Easter Sunday?" Dawn asked.

"I guess he figured it was the best day to find folks at home," she replied. She affected a smile she didn't quite feel at that moment. "Daddy, could you and Jeff bring the turkey and ham into the dining room? Mama and I will bring the side dishes."

Dawn jumped up. "I'll help with something."

"So will I," Corrine volunteered.

Kara gave her a pointed look. "No, Miss Corrine. We've got everything covered here. You and Dawn please have a seat at the dining room table." Corrine mumbled something under her breath about not being an invalid as she left the kitchen. An hour later, Kara covered her wineglass with her hand when Jeff went to refill it. "No more."

Dawn extended her glass. "I'll take a little more, please."

"So will I," Jeannette said.

Kara had filled crystal decanters with red and white wine to accompany the meal, and after her second glass, she was beginning to feel the effects. Picking up her water goblet, she took a sip while peering at Jeff over the rim. She'd removed several leaves from the table that seated fourteen to accommodate six. Her parents were at either end, Jeff with his grandmother, and she and Dawn sitting

opposite them. Thankfully she hadn't lost any of her cooking skills. The turkey was moist, the ham tender, and the
side dishes savory.

"Not only do I miss my roomie," Dawn admitted, "but I
also miss our Sunday dinners."

"I told Dawn I'd teach her to cook, but she said why
should she learn when I did all of the cooking."

Corrine wagged a finger at Dawn. "How do you expect
to get a husband if you can't cook?"

Dawn blushed a bright red color as she lowered her gaze.
"I've dated men who didn't care if I could cook or not."

"Did any of them ask you to marry them?" Corrine asked.

"No, ma'am."

"Gram," Jeff warned in a quiet voice.

"Stay out of this, Jeffrey. I'm trying to school the young
woman so she can get a husband. You do want to get married don't you?"

Dawn gave Corrine a direct stare. "Yes, ma'am."

"You spend a couple of days and nights with me, and
I'll teach you how to make rice, bake a chicken so tender
that the meat will literally fall off the bone, and a few other
side dishes. I know you say you're a dancer, but you're
nothing but skin and bones. And no man wants a bone.
Don't look at Kara because she knows how to cook."

"Yes, ma'am."

"Yes, ma'am, what?" Corrine asked.

"Yes, I'll spend a couple of nights with you."

Corrine smiled as if she'd just negotiated a peace treaty.
"Jeannette, could you please pass me the collards?"

Kara stared across the table at Jeff, wondering if he was
thinking what she was thinking. His grandmother suggest-
ing Dawn spend several nights at her house would give her

and Jeff time alone together. She had to have known Jeff would never stay over at Angels Landing with someone else in the house. He smiled at her, and she returned it, glorying in the shared moment, knowing in a few days they would reunite in the most intimate way possible.

The conversations around the table turned to sports with Jeff and Austin debating who would make it to the World Series. It segued to a discussion about a young actress who purportedly had slept with her leading man *and* a supporting actor and didn't know which one had fathered her baby.

"That is so grimy," Kara stated.

"It's worse than grimy," Dawn quipped. "It's downright stink. And why did she have to make that public?"

Austin dabbed his mouth with a linen napkin. "The real question is how much did she sell the story for? It has to be about money."

The topic segued again, this time to reality television. Everyone agreed that even though exhibiting bad behavior translated into big bucks, it also sent the wrong message to young impressionable people. Dinner stretched into more than two hours, and no one seemed ready to leave the table to retreat to the parlor where Kara had planned to serve dessert and coffee.

"Are you all right?" Kara asked Corrine when Jeff stood up and pulled back her chair.

"I'm fine. I just need to get up and walk off some of this food. Jeannette, will you please walk with me?"

"Of course." Jeannette looked at her husband. "Honey, you need to get up and walk, too. You keep saying you have to exercise."

"She's right, Daddy," Kara agreed. "You're getting a little round in the middle."

Austin patted his belly. "I wouldn't be round if your mama's cooking wasn't so good." Pushing back his chair, he rose to his feet. "We'll be back later to help you clean up."

"I'll help with the cleanup," Jeff volunteered. "By the time you get back it'll be time for dessert."

Kara, Dawn, and Jeff made short work of clearing the table and putting away leftovers. Kara turned on the radio on a countertop, tuning in to a station with R & B and old school jams. Dawn rinsed while Kara stacked pots in the dishwasher. They alternated hand washing and drying china, crystal, and silver; they sang along with some of the songs made popular in the '90s.

"The downside of setting a formal table is that the good stuff has to be hand washed," Dawn said as she held up a water goblet checking it for water spots.

Drying her hands on a dish towel, Kara nodded in agreement. "We only had to wash place settings for six. Can you imagine hosting a dinner with twenty or thirty people?"

Dawn pushed out her lips. "That's lunacy. I can barely put together a meal for myself, and you're talking about thirty people."

"That's when you hire a chef and have him bring everything. That way they're responsible for cleaning up."

Dawn's eyes sparkled like polished blue topaz. "That's what I'm talking about."

"I hope you didn't let my grandmother intimidate you," Jeff said when he reentered the kitchen with the tablecloth.

"Of course not. She's right. I should know how to cook, but whenever my mother tried to teach me, I always found something else to do," Dawn admitted. "Eating out isn't always the healthiest because some of my friends have really put on weight. Their funds are limited, so they're forced to eat fast food."

Jeff nodded. "You hang out with Corrine for a couple of days, and she'll teach you enough so that you can put together a palatable meal that will cost no more than a few dollars a day. Even though she grew up during the Depression, the folks here never went hungry. They grew their own vegetables, owned milk cows, and raised their own hogs and chickens."

"Do you cook, Jeff?"

He smiled. "Just say I cook enough not to starve to death or give someone food poisoning."

Dawn waved a hand. "Well, it doesn't matter because you have Kara to cook for you."

"She can cook for me anytime," Jeff said with a smile. "Everything was delicious."

Kara opened her mouth to tell Dawn that she'd never cooked for Jeff before preparing Easter dinner, then held her tongue. She still hadn't revealed that she and Jeff were sleeping together. She took the tablecloth from him, folding it. "I'll take this to the dry cleaner next week."

"Do you think anyone is going to want dessert?" he asked.

"I don't know. We'll play it by ear. I'm going to let Oliver out so he can get some exercise." Forty-five minutes later Corrine, Jeannette and Austin returned from their walk, and Kara sat back with a satisfied grin on her face. She knew this Easter would remain with her always. Angels Landing was filled with the sound of laughter for the first time in years. After everyone had dessert and coffee in the parlor, Miss Corrine and Dawn sat out on the porch until midnight talking to each other. Her parents had bedded down in a third-floor suite, and Jeff had selected a room on the second floor that doubled as a study/bedroom with a connecting door to what had been Teddy's office. Once Dawn and Jeff's grandmother came in for the night, Miss Corrine retired to a first-floor room so she wouldn't have to climb the staircase.

The house was still quiet when Kara got up at seven to see after Oliver before making preparations for breakfast. Her parents had mentioned they wanted to be on the road before noon. She didn't find Oliver in his cage but found fresh food and clean water. When she did find Oliver, he was in bed, the puppy curled up against Jeff's back, asleep.

Kara was tempted to pummel Jeff with a pillow for doing what she'd told him she didn't want to do: have the dog sleep in the bed. She closed the door and went into the kitchen.

Mrs. Todd was already there. The woman and her husband had celebrated the holiday with his cousins in Haven Creek. "Good morning, Kara. I didn't expect you to be up this early."

"Good morning, Mrs. Todd. How was your Easter?" Kara didn't want her to know that she'd slept fitfully because she couldn't stop thinking about the summons requesting a sample of her DNA.

"It was nice, but Willie knows I only tolerate his family. After all these years I still can't get used to the folks in his family talking over one another. It's a wonder they hear what the other is saying. Enough about Willie's folks. How did your dinner turn out?"

"It was wonderful. Thanks to my mother and Miss Corrine's desserts."

Mrs. Todd smoothed down the front of her crisp gray uniform. "Miss Corrine's desserts are as good as those Mabel and Lester sell at the Muffin Corner."

"You may be right. I think I'm going to fix a buffet breakfast."

"I'll get the warming dishes," Mrs. Todd volunteered. "Where do you want me to set them up?"

Kara glanced around the kitchen. The oversized table in the middle of the kitchen doubled as a dining and preparation table. "Put them on the table. We'll eat in the breakfast nook." The table in the corner of the kitchen was hewn from the same oak as the larger one and bore initials and dates going as far back as 1886. She'd had the portraits of Shipley and Oakes Patton taken down from the wall, put into slipcases, and stored in a third-floor closet. The canvases would have to be cleaned before they could be restored to their original vibrancy.

"After breakfast I have to take Willie to the VA hospital," Mrs. Todd announced. "He's been complaining about headaches and pain in his legs, so the doctors want to keep him for a few days to give him some tests. He still has shrapnel in his head from when he was in Vietnam. I'm going to stay at a hotel, so I can be available to him if he wants me."

Kara patted the older woman's back. "Do whatever you need to take care of your husband."

She'd just finished chopping ingredients for omelets when Dawn walked into the kitchen. Her short hair was pasted to her scalp from her shower. "Good morning, Miss Dee."

Dawn smiled. "Morning, Miss Kay. Yesterday was awesome. I'm glad I decided to come down, but I don't want you to get mad at me."

"Get angry with you for what?"

"I told Miss Corrine that I would go home with her today for cooking lessons. It's not that I really need to cook to land a husband, but I need it for myself. I grew up with a lot of sisters and brothers, and after that I always had roommates. This is the first time I've really lived alone, and it's made me realize I have to take care of myself, and that includes cooking for myself. So I hope you don't mind if we don't see each other for a few days."

"Dawn, please. You're here on vacation. You can do whatever you like. And I'm going to expect you to cook for me when you get back here."

"That's a bet. And I promise not to give you food poisoning."

One by one everyone filed into the kitchen as Mrs. Todd and Kara flipped pancakes, grilled waffles, and broiled bacon and breakfast links. Someone mentioned grits, and Jeannette put up a pot of water for the Lowcountry staple. Breakfast was more subdued than dinner had been as Kara's parents prepared for the drive back to Little Rock. She packed food for their trip, storing the containers in an insulated bag with ice packs.

Kara and Jeff stood on the porch, waving to them until their car disappeared from sight. Her father had announced he was returning to Cavanaugh Island for the Memorial Day holiday weekend for a corps reunion with Jeff and six other marines.

Jeff moved closer, resting a hand at the small of Kara's back. "I'm going to drive Gram and Dawn back to the Cove; then I'll be back later."

She gave him a sly sidelong glance. "We're going to have the house to ourselves. Dawn is staying with your grandmother, and Mr. and Mrs. Todd will be in Charleston tonight."

"What do you want to do?" Jeff asked, when his hand slipped lower to her hips.

"I don't know. I'll leave that up to you."

He patted her behind. "I'll think of something before I get back."

Once everyone left, Kara had the house to herself. She'd put away food, rinsed and stacked dishes and flatware in the dishwasher, and was sweeping up the brick floor when the doorbell rang. "I hear it, Oliver," she said when the terrier raced into the kitchen. "Let's go see who's at the door."

Kara peered through the sidelight to see the figure of a woman. She opened the door, stunned to see one of the Pattons standing on the porch. "May I help you?"

The stylishly coiffed and dressed woman smiled. "May I come in, Kara?"

Kara peered down at Oliver who was barking furiously. She managed to close the door. "I still don't trust him not to bite. Please sit down." She waited for the woman in the tailored suit to sit, then sat down opposite her. "It's apparent you know who I am."

"I'm Eden Patton-Cox. Taylor was my uncle."

Crossing one denim-covered leg over the other, Kara met a pair of smoky-gray eyes. The diamond studs in Eden's ears and those in her wedding set must have set her husband back a pretty penny. Eden's smooth dark skin, chemically straightened black hair styled into a chignon at the nape of her neck, and subtly applied makeup made her a very attractive woman.

"How can I help you, Eden?"

"It should be how I can help *you*, Kara. My cousins

don't know I'm here. I wanted to warn you to be careful because there are people who don't want you in Angels Landing."

Kara's expression was impassive even though she couldn't stop her stomach muscles from contracting. "Who are these people you speak of?"

"I can't name names because I don't want to incriminate myself."

"You're an attorney." Eden nodded. "Are you telling me you've broken ranks with your family to come and warn me that my life may be in danger?"

"I'm just telling you to be prepared to fight to keep what you inherited from my uncle."

"Don't you mean my *father*?"

"That will be verified once the results of the DNA test are in."

"So you know about that?" Kara asked.

"I was present when the vote was taken." Eden stood up. "I must leave because I have to meet a client." She held out her hand. "Good-bye and good luck, Kara."

Kara rose and shook her cousin's hand. "Thank you, Eden. It's too bad this meeting couldn't have been for a different purpose."

Eden smiled. "I agree."

Leaning against a marble column, Kara watched the taillights of Eden's Cadillac CTS as she drove along the allée of oaks. First the summons and now a warning. She wondered if the Pattons would ever give up their quest to deny her her birthright. Kara knew it wouldn't stop until the DNA test proved conclusively that she was Taylor's daughter.

When Jeff returned, she was sitting in the rocker on the

porch while Oliver lounged on a chair with cornflower-blue seat cushions. The puppy got up, whining for Jeff to pick him up. Jeff scooped him off the chair, setting him down on the porch.

Kara raised her chin for Jeff's kiss. She held his wrist. "I don't want Oliver sleeping in the bed with you."

"Jealous, sweetheart?"

"Of a dog, baby?"

"It's a warm body," Jeff teased.

"I guess I'm not warm enough for you," she said, pouting.

"That's where you're wrong, Kara." Reaching down, he pulled her smoothly to her feet. "You're hot. Hotter than a ghost chili."

Her arms went under his shoulders. "That's the hottest chili in existence."

"That's you, baby."

Wrapping his arms around Kara's waist, Jeff lifted her off her feet. "Open the door," he whispered in her ear. She complied, and Oliver darted inside. Using his foot, he kicked the door shut and managed to lock it while still holding on to Kara who'd locked her legs around his waist.

She tightened her hold on his neck. "Where are you going?"

"I'm going back to bed, and you're going to join me."

The smell of his cologne still clung to the linen in the bed where Jeff had spent the night. She watched, transfixed, as he undressed seemingly in slow motion. Making love in daylight was different from when they'd come together in a darkened room. Her blood warmed and raced through her veins with a desire that resulted in a gush of wetness bathing her core. She couldn't believe the perfection of his toned body when he stood over her, fully aroused.

If she'd wanted to look away, Kara couldn't when he reached into an overnight bag and removed a length of condoms. Her gaze did not waver when he removed one and rolled it down the length of his erection. Their dance of desire began when Jeff got into bed with her and pulled her T-shirt over her head, then unhooked her bra. His hands were steady when he unsnapped her jeans and eased them and her panties down her hips in one, smooth motion. Like a sleek, large cat, he moved over her.

Kara gasped as his blood-engorged arousal brushed her inner thigh. Instinctively, her body arched toward him, she caressing the length of his spine, smiling when her fingernails raised goose bumps along his skin.

"Love me," she breathed out. Jeff answered her entreaty when he eased his swollen flesh into her, both moaning in satisfaction as their bodies melded as one.

Closing her eyes, Kara's heart rate skyrocketed along with the uneven rhythm of her breathing as Jeff's hardness slid in and out of her. She experienced extreme heat, then bone-chilling cold that made her teeth chatter.

Jeff had set a pace that quickened, slowed, then quickened again until she was mindless with an ecstasy that became a mind-altering trip, shattering her into millions of tiny particles before lulling her back to a euphoric state. What had begun as a groan escalated until it became a low growl when Jeff pumped his hips until he collapsed on top of her.

They lay joined together, waiting until their hearts resumed a normal rate. Kara issued a small cry of protest when he pulled out. She curled into a fetal position, still savoring the aftermath of a lovemaking that made her want more and more. Jeff came back to the bed, pressing his chest against her back.

"Don't tell me you're going to sleep on me," he whispered against the moistness of her nape.

"I am. I need to rest so when I wake up we can do this again."

A laugh came from his throat. "You want more?"

"How many more condoms do you have?"

"Five."

It was her turn to laugh. "Then I'm going to want five more courses. You should've asked before you took up with me. I like five- and six-course meals. Next time I'll be the one doing the eating." He sucked in a breath. "Did I shock you, baby?"

"A little."

"It's all right. I'll go easy on you."

Jeff cradled her hip. "Go to sleep, sweetheart. But let me warn you I've been known to overindulge."

"Consider me warned."

She lay in the protective cocoon of Jeff's strong arms as he pulled her closer. Within minutes Kara forgot everything, including Eden's warning and the summons for her to take the DNA test.

Chapter Seventeen

Kara opened her mouth and closed her eyes as the police department technician swabbed her inner cheek. She knew the drill because she'd gone through the procedure twenty minutes ago. As promised, Jeff drove her to the private lab where she left samples from Taylor's brush and razor, while allowing the technician to swab her cheek and take several strands of hair. She'd thought it overkill but wanted to put the issue of her paternity to rest. Forever.

Even though the ME claimed to be backlogged, she'd promised Jeff she would make the Taylor-Newell test a priority.

"Don't you need a sample of my hair?" Kara asked the police techie. They'd taken hair samples at the private lab.

"No. Your cheek cells are enough."

She slipped off the examining table. Jeff's ten-day vacation had come and gone much too quickly, and they tried to spend every day in bed making love. The only time they had left was to go to the Cove and spend time with Corrine. Although on duty, Jeff had taken the time to drive her into Charleston for the tests. "I'm ready," she told him when he approached her.

Cupping her elbow, Jeff escorted her to the parking lot where he'd parked his official vehicle. Kara hadn't mentioned Eden's visit to him because she felt once the results of the DNA tests were revealed the Pattons would end their character assassination.

Dawn called her every Sunday with an update on what new recipe she'd attempted. Corrine had given Dawn her prized gumbo recipe, and her former roomie could not stop talking about it once she'd duplicated the dish. When Kara asked her about taking in strays, Dawn had laughed, declaring she'd gotten over that phase and she liked having a clean and quiet apartment all to herself. She'd also begun teaching street dancing, and her young students took to the new routines like ducks to water.

Today Kara wouldn't return to Angels Landing to spend her days and nights, but to Sanctuary Cove where she would stay with Jeff and Corrine. The restoration staff had moved and covered all the furniture as they removed ceiling fixtures and began the arduous task of stripping wallpaper. Mrs. Todd had assumed the responsibility for deactivating the alarm for the foreman when he arrived in the morning, and she reset it at the end of their workday.

It was Corrine who'd convinced Kara to move in when she mentioned she'd always wanted to learn hand quilting. Living with Corrine was a win-win for both of them. They could keep each other company, and Kara would have the advantage of seeing Jeff every day. She'd brought Oliver to the Cove the day before so he could become acquainted with his new surroundings. Even when coaxed, the terrier refused to leave his crate.

"I have to stop at the house to pick up my car," she told Jeff as he reached the causeway.

"I thought you were going to use my grandmother's car."

"I have all my summer clothes in the trunk." It was May and daytime temperatures were in the mid-80s. Dawn had packed up her clothes and personal items and shipped them to Angels Landing.

"Do you want me to wait for you?"

"You don't have to. I've taken up enough of your time today." Jeff gave her a quick glance, glaring at her from under the worn bill of his baseball cap. Kara couldn't understand why he continued to wear it. The cap was falling apart.

"Let me judge whether you're taking up my time."

"Touchy, touchy, Jeff?"

"I'm not touchy. I merely stated a fact."

She looked out the side window. "Forget it," Kara mumbled under her breath and bit down on her lower lip to keep from smiling. She liked teasing Jeff because he was always so serious.

"Are you spoiling for a fight?"

"No!"

"Now who's touchy?"

"If this is the way it's going to be when we live under the same roof, then I'll just move in the guesthouse like I'd planned to."

"I doubt whether we'll even get to see that much of each other. I've switched my hours from 8:00 p.m. to 8:00 a.m. When you and Gram are out and about, I'll be sleeping.

And by the time you two are winding down for the night, I'll be going to work."

She may have promised Corrine she would move into her home, but the Hamiltons were also aware that she *did* have some place to live: the vacant guesthouse.

Having to deal with DNA testing and Eden Patton-Cox's warning was weighing heavily on Kara. It was obvious the people who didn't want her there were of Patton blood. Greed had turned them into ravenous beasts that would probably resort to more drastic measures to force her to leave the island.

She and Jeff slept together whenever he was able to come to Angels Landing and not once had he ever mentioned the word *love*, not even in the throes of passion. The endearments flowed freely: *baby, sweetheart, darling, babe,* but never *love*.

Kara had told herself it was futile to fall in love with Jeff, but she had. It was impossible to tell the heart what to do or how to feel.

She'd come to love the Lowcountry: the food, local shops, the unique language of the Gullah, the tradition of sitting on porches or residents gathering in groups under trees, vegetable stands and craftspeople selling their trademark baskets, seeing the brightly colored houses with their windows often trimmed in blue to keep out evil spirits. The blood of the Gullah ran in her veins, yet Kara still did not feel a sense of belonging, and she knew it had to do with Eden's warning.

They didn't want her, and she didn't want them. She'd promised Jeff that she wouldn't run, but Kara wondered how many more times she would be put to the test before they broke her spirit. Knowing Jeff loved her, truly loved her as much as she loved him, would help make her plight easier. Make her rethink her decision to leave after five years.

Kara was out of the Jeep as soon as it stopped. "I'll see you later."

Not waiting for his response, she reached into her bag for the key to Taylor's Mercedes-Benz. She didn't know why, but she couldn't think of the car as hers even though it was now registered in her name. It was Taylor's house, Taylor's land, Taylor's cars, and Taylor's money.

Taylor had left her all of his worldly possessions to make up for abandoning her mother when she needed him most, but it still wasn't enough. Those who resented and hated him resented and hated her, too. Kara had given David her word that she would fulfill the terms of the will, and she would. However, she would not stay on the island one day longer than required.

She put the key in the ignition and turned it, and the engine roared to life. Instead of heading east to the Cove, Kara drove west to the Haven. When Miss Corrine had asked what she wanted to quilt, her response had been a crib blanket. Blankets she would donate to needy families.

"Always the social worker, aren't you?" Jeff's words echoed in her head. She smiled. Yes, she would always be a social worker because that's who she was and always would be.

Kara sang along with the radio as she maneuvered the car along the narrow road. It'd taken her more than an hour to select the squares she wanted for her first quilting project. The soft pastel colors of blue, green, pink, and yellow in solids and prints would make a beautiful quilt for a baby.

A scream caught in her throat when large objects

appeared in the middle of the road. In the split second it took for her to identify them as hogs it was too late to slow down. She swerved at the last possible moment, the car crashing head-on into a tree. The impact of metal slamming into the tree sounded like an explosion as shards of glass littered the dash, passenger seat, and Kara's lap.

There was a burning sensation along the right side of her neck, and when Kara pressed her fingers to the area, it came away wet. Blinking, she stared at her trembling fingers covered with blood. She looked down at the front of her blouse and it was dotted with red.

Luckily her cell phone sat on the console next to her. It took two attempts, but she was finally able to grab it and punch the speed-dial button on the screen. Jeff answered after the second ring. "What's up, baby?"

"Jeff." His name was a trembling whisper.

"What's the matter?"

"I'm hurt." The blood was flowing faster.

"Where are you?"

Kara couldn't remember what she'd said, but she did remember Jeff telling her he was on his way.

Kara lay on an examining table, staring at Dr. Asa Monroe. He leaned closer. "I gave you an anesthetic that will make you a little groggy."

She blinked slowly. "Why does it hurt so much?"

"You have a piece of glass embedded in your neck. I stopped the bleeding, and in a few minutes I'm going to take it out."

"Where's Jeff?" She was slurring her words.

He moved into her line of vision. "I'm here, baby." He took her left hand, gently squeezing her fingers.

Her eyelids fluttered wildly. "I don't think I'll ever eat swine again."

"Why not, sweetheart?"

"There...there were hogs in the...the road. I...I..." Her words trailed off as she drifted off to sleep.

Jeff exchanged a look with the doctor. "Judging from where I found her car, I know who those hogs belong to."

"People have to be responsible for their livestock," Asa said as he sat on a stool at the head of the table. Reaching up, he adjusted a bright light, then swabbed the swollen area with a disinfecting solution.

"How bad is it, Doc?"

Asa's gloved fingers touched Kara's neck. "It looks worse than it is. One millimeter lower and you would have lost her. The shard is close to her carotid artery."

Jeff watched intently as Asa opened a package with a sterilized scalpel. The doctor adjusted the light again and seconds later deftly removed the glass, dropping it in a metal bowl.

Kara's chest rose and fell as she slept through the entire procedure. Quickly and neatly, the incision was closed with four tiny sutures.

Asa covered the wound with gauze and a waterproof bandage. "She needs to keep it dry for several days. Bring her back before the end of the week so I can change the dressing."

"What about the sutures?"

"They'll dissolve on their own. I'm going to give you some painkillers for her. If she complains about the pain, then give her one every six hours."

Waiting until the doctor discarded his gloves, Jeff shook his hand. "Thanks, Doc. Please send me the bill."

Chapter Eighteen

⌇

Corrine put on her half glasses and looked closely at the faint scar on Kara's neck. "Dr. Monroe did a real fine job. You have to look real close to see where he took out the glass."

It had been two weeks since the accident. The Mercedes was towed to a garage on the Cove where the insurance adjuster documented that the vintage car was totaled.

Jeff had hovered over Kara like a hen with a brood of chicks. He'd gone as far as to sleep with her for two nights until she threatened to lock the bedroom door, because whenever she moaned when turning her head or changing position, he'd ask if she was in pain. The result was he forced her to swallow a pill that made her lose track of time. For several days she didn't know where she was or whether it was day or night.

It didn't take long for news to spread across the island

that she was convalescing at the Hamiltons' house. Mrs. Todd and Morgan had come to visit, bringing flowers, get-well cards, and sweet breads from the Muffin Corner.

Eddie Wilkes, editor in chief of the *Sanctuary Chronicle*, also stopped by for an interview. He was forthcoming when he said it was the first time in nearly seventy years that hogs were responsible for a road accident. There had been a time when feral pigs were destroying the farms on Haven Creek, but farmers had concocted elaborate traps and hunting parties to capture them. What had been estimated to be more than one hundred pigs decreased dramatically over a three-month period until the numbers dwindled to single digits.

Eddie also interviewed her as the new owner of Angels Landing. When the article appeared in the *Chronicle* with news that she had no intention of selling the house or the land surrounding it, and that it was currently being restored to become a museum, the Pattons fired another salvo at her. This time they were contesting Taylor's will, stating he wasn't of sound mind and body when he had it drawn up.

Kara touched the spot where Dr. Monroe had made the small incision. "It's only slightly tender."

Corrine removed her glasses. "The Lord was watching over you that day because that glass could've struck you in the eye."

"You're right about that."

"You gave us quite a scare. Jeffrey in particular. You know that he's in love with you, don't you?"

"That's where you're wrong, Miss Corrine."

Corrine folded her arms across her chest. "When it comes to my grandson, I'm seldom wrong. Jeffrey is in love with you."

"Has he told you that he is?"

"He doesn't have to tell me, Kara. I see the way he looks at you. Even when he was engaged to that teacher, he never looked at her the way he looks at you."

Kara stared at the woman she'd begun to relate to as her own grandmother—tall and slender with soft, curly, silver hair; smooth skin that reminded her of dark brown velvet; and a sweet fragrance of gardenia. She and Jeff had talked about a lot of things, yet he'd neglected to mention that he'd been engaged. She managed to mask her surprise with a deceptive calmness.

"Why didn't he marry her?" she asked Corrine.

Corrine smoothed the crease in her cotton slacks. "It wasn't Jeffrey but Pamela who didn't want to marry him. She said she couldn't be a military wife."

"But didn't she know he was a career officer when she'd accepted his proposal?"

"She did."

"That is so wrong, Miss Corrine." A rush of relief replaced Kara's annoyance. Now she understood why Jeff had failed to mention his engagement. There was no doubt he was too embarrassed to tell her of his former fiancée's rejection.

Corrine smiled. "You're preaching to the choir, child." She stood up. "I'm going to put up water for tea. Would you like a cup?"

Kara pushed to her feet. "Please sit down. I'll make the tea."

"Okay. I'll set up the table in the sunroom."

Walking out of the parlor, Kara made her way to the kitchen. When she and Jeff had discussed David's inability to commit to his longtime girlfriend, he'd never mentioned that he'd been engaged. They'd talked about how men were reluctant to propose marriage, and not once had he taken himself out of that equation.

Kara didn't expect Jeff to profess his undying love for her after three months, but hearing the word would make it easier for her to consider changing her future plans to include possibly spending the rest of her life on Cavanaugh Island.

She'd come to appreciate the homey warmth of the Hamilton residence. Although the house was larger than those along Waccamaw Road, it was one-fourth the size of Angels Landing. Corrine had disclosed that her neighbors were quite curious when a contractor had begun knocking out walls to expand rooms, replacing old windows with those that would withstand the force of tropical storms and replacing the clapboard siding with maintenance-free vinyl that Jeff power washed twice a year. Not to be outdone, one by one the residents began updating and renovating their homes. The ongoing renaissance on Waccamaw Road had become a blueprint for many of the older homes in the Cove.

Filling a kettle with water, Kara placed it on a cook-top stove, then took down two cups and saucers from an overhead cabinet. She moved around the kitchen with the familiarity of someone who'd lived there for years instead of two weeks. Corrine had become her mentor when she instructed her in preparing traditional Lowcountry dishes. She'd taught her how to make and perfect old-fashioned brown gravy, crab cake sauce, and sweet potato pone.

Without warning Corrine would speak Gullah, and Kara would have to try and figure out what she'd said. One day when Corrine was going on and on about Jeff, she'd stopped and said, *"Ebry frog praise é own pond."* That she understood to mean that every frog praises his own pond.

She finished brewing the tea, pouring it into a hand-painted teapot. Tiny jars of locally made honey, a small pitcher of milk, the teapot, cups, and teaspoons were placed on a tray. Kara carried the tray into the sunroom.

Corrine sat in her favorite club chair, feet resting on a footstool. Oliver lay on the chair beside her. Her pet had quickly switched his allegiance from her to Corrine who'd permitted him the run of the house. No room was off-limits. Not even the kitchen. What she wouldn't permit him to do was beg for food. Kara also suspected the tiny dog slept in the bed with Corrine but loathed accusing her host of the infraction as she'd done Jeff.

She set the tray on the coffee table before filling a cup with the steaming fragrant blueberry tea. "Do you want honey?"

"Not today. But I could use a couple of those shortbread cookies you made yesterday."

Kara smiled. "Okay."

She'd just entered the kitchen when the doorbell rang and Oliver began his frenetic barking that echoed through the house. When she returned to the sunroom with the plate of cookies, Corrine handed her an envelope.

"A messenger just delivered this."

Sitting, Kara opened the mailing envelope with the return address from the lab that had conducted the DNA test. Her heart was pounding, hands shaking, as she broke the seal on the flap and opened the envelope. Slumping back in the chair, she smiled. The results of the test were irrefutable. The medical examiner had signed the letter, then covered her signature with the department's official seal. She handed the single sheet of paper to Corrine.

"Only a fool would doubt you were Taylor's baby girl."

Kara nodded. "If I know, they have to know. Maybe now they'll drop their crusade to challenge Taylor's will."

"Please don't tell me they're going to try and prove Taylor was crazy. He may have been a little strange, but he wasn't crazy." Corrine handed Kara back the paper. "Don't you worry yourself none 'bout those silly folks. I think we can go out and celebrate."

"Where do you want to go, Miss Corrine?"

"There's always Jack's, but Jeffrey told me that someone in the Creek opened a panini café last week. All of the bread is baked on the premises, and it's become very popular with the college students that come over from the mainland."

"It sounds good to me."

"Maybe we'll go after we finish our tea, so we can avoid the crowds."

Kara wanted to ask Corrine if they should invite Jeff to go along with them but quickly decided against it. Sleeping under the same roof had changed them and their relationship. She knew he'd been more shaken than he appeared about the car crash, but that didn't explain why he'd cleverly devised ways not to be around her.

The doorbell rang again, and Kara and Corrine exchanged a look. It wasn't often they had visitors, and to have two within the span of half an hour was indeed rare. Oliver, barking frantically, stood up, turning around and around to indicate he wanted to get down.

"Stay, Oliver," Kara said firmly. "Should I get the door, Miss Corrine?"

"Please."

The doorbell rang again before she opened it. "Eden."

Eden flashed a plastic smile. "I need to speak to you. May I come in?"

Opening the door wider, Kara shook her head. "We can talk out here." She stepped out onto the porch and pointed to a cushioned chair. "Please have a seat." Waiting until she sat on the chair, Kara sat opposite her on a matching love seat. "What do you want to talk about?"

Eden leaned forward. "I want to be honest with you, Kara."

"Honest about what?"

"What you need to ask yourself," Eden continued as if Kara hadn't spoken, "is do you really belong here. If you did, then you never would consider turning our ancestral home into a museum. You have no connection with the land or the people who've lived here for centuries. Folks will never accept you, so why would you want to live someplace where you'll always be thought of as an outsider?"

"That's enough out of you, missy." Kara and Eden turned to find Corrine standing a few feet away. "Please leave my home."

Eden stood up. "I have no quarrel with you, Miss Corrine."

"And I won't have one with you if you leave my home."

"I haven't had my say with Kara," Eden insisted.

Kara knew it was time to take charge of a situation that was quickly spiraling out of control. "You heard what she said, Eden. Get the hell out!"

Eden's eyes grew wide. "Who do you think you are to speak to me like that?"

"She is who she is," said a softly spoken deep voice. Jeff had walked out of the house without making a sound. He'd pulled on a pair of jeans but had left his chest and feet bare. He beckoned Eden. "Come. I'll see you to your car."

"You can't protect her forever, Jeff."

He shook his head. "I hope that's not a threat, Eden."

"Of course not." She nodded to Corrine, then Kara. "Good afternoon."

When Jeff returned, Kara shook her head. "She just won't give up."

"What are you talking about?" Jeff asked. He listened when Kara told him about Eden coming to Angels Landing. "Why didn't you tell me about this before?"

"There's no need to raise your voice, Jeffrey."

He glared at his grandmother. "Gram, this is between Kara and me."

"And this is my home, Jeffrey, and you know I don't tolerate folks raising their voices."

"Gram, you don't understand." He told his grandmother about the rock-throwing incident.

Corrine pressed a hand to her chest. "Oh, my word!"

"To answer your question, Jeff, I didn't tell you because Eden said she'd come to warn me that her family wasn't going to give up fighting for what they believe belongs to them."

"A dog that brings a bone will take a bone," Corrine mumbled under her breath.

Jeff approached Kara. "Gram is right. The Pattons sent Eden as a decoy. She wanted you to believe she was on your side, but she was really sent here to intimidate you."

She stared at the stubble on his lean jaw. "The DNA results say I'm Taylor's daughter."

He smiled. "I know. The ME called me the other day. She didn't want me to say anything until you got the official notification." He took a step and cradled her face. "Now you know why I wanted you to stay here."

"I thought it was to keep your grandmother company," she whispered.

"That's only half of it."

"What's the other half?"

"I'll have to show you."

Corrine grunted loudly. "I'll leave you two alone to *talk*."

"I'm off this weekend. If you're not doing anything, then I'd like you to come with me to Myrtle Beach."

"Should I bring a swimsuit?"

"Of course. But panties are optional."

Turning on his heels, he walked out of the parlor leaving Kara staring at the space where he'd been. As exasperated as she could be with Jeff, Kara never doubted her love for him.

Kara opened her eyes, peering at the clock on the nightstand. Even after three months on the island, she still woke up without an alarm clock. Knowing she wasn't going back to sleep, she slipped out of bed and went into the bathroom across the hall. The house was as quiet as a tomb.

She completed her morning ablutions in twenty minutes; slipped into a halter top, shorts, and flip-flops; and went downstairs to sit on the front porch. Corrine had unofficially adopted her dog. Oliver slept at the foot of Corrine's bed and sat in her lap whenever she read or watched television. He also claimed a spot beside her on her favorite chair whenever she did her needlework projects. Oliver was now Corrine's pet because she'd taken over the task of feeding him. Kara was tempted to rename him Traitor.

She'd discovered Waccamaw Road didn't begin to stir until six thirty when high school students piled into cars to drive into Charleston for classes. She returned the wave of a pretty coed who lived several houses away. The girl's older sister, a local college student, came twice a week to clean Corrine's house to earn extra money.

It was after seven when Kara stood up to go into the house. As soon as she opened the screen door, she heard breaking glass. Running into the house, she was met with smoke and the ringing of smoke alarms. The smoke burned her eyes and lungs as she raced frantically, maneuvering through the thick haze trying to find Corrine.

"Miss Corrine!" Gasping, she went in and out of rooms, looking for her. Holding a hand over her mouth to keep from choking, she found Jeff's grandmother on the kitchen floor. Oliver lay beside her, shaking uncontrollably.

Snatching a dish towel off the countertop, she wet it and placed it over her nose as she dialed 911. She gave the operator the address and told him to hurry because smoke had filled the entire house. Anchoring her hands under Corrine's shoulders, she managed to drag her out of the kitchen, through the living room, and onto the front porch. She returned to get Oliver, nearly panicking as he lay limply in her arms.

By the time she returned to the porch a small crowd had gathered. Kara had begun administering CPR when Jeff and Dr. Monroe arrived at the same time. Sitting on the floor, she pulled her knees to her chest, rested her head on her knees, breathing deeply to clear her lungs of the smoke. Then she cried. Tears blurred her vision as she watched the doctor give Corrine oxygen, waiting until she began to stir before he shifted his attention to Oliver.

I can't do this. It can't continue like this. The silent voice shouted what she couldn't form her mouth to say. Whoever wanted her gone had won.

Jeff hunkered down beside Kara. He was frightened. More frightened than he'd been when he and his men were pinned down by sniper fire. Cradling her in his arms, he rocked her back and forth.

"Baby," he whispered over and over, placing tiny kisses all over her face.

"How is she?" Kara asked hoarsely.

"Gram is going to be all right. Asa is calling the mainland for a chopper to have her airlifted to a mainland hospital."

Kara pulled back, her eyes wide with fear. "I thought you said she was going to be all right."

"She is. It's just a precaution because of her heart condition." He smoothed back her hair. "Oliver is also breathing on his own, but I'm going to take him to the vet just to make certain he's okay. Meanwhile, you're coming with me to the hospital so they can check your lungs."

"I'm okay, Jeff. I didn't inhale that much smoke."

"That wasn't smoke, Kara. It was pepper gas, the same gas used by the military." He kissed her mouth. "Don't get up. I'm going inside to open the windows. And when I come back, I'm taking you to Charleston."

Taking a handkerchief from his jeans, he covered his nose, entering the house and opening windows on the second and first floors. A light breeze coming in through the screens did little to dispel the acrid smell, and Jeff knew it would take hours before it dissipated completely. His foot hit an object on the kitchen floor. The moment his hand touched it Jeff experienced déjà vu. The message glued to the brick was different from the last but held the same meaning: "KN—Get out of town."

It was the second time someone had threatened Kara. And he planned for it to be the last. Whoever had tossed the pepper grenade cared little for who else was in the house with her. He'd lost every significant woman in his life, and he swore an oath that he would hold onto the last two until his final breath. He loved his grandmother and had fallen in love with Kara.

Chapter Nineteen

⌒

Kara sat on a gurney in the ER's examining room, waiting for Jeff. She was examined, her chest x-rayed, and medically cleared to be discharged. Home for her wasn't Sanctuary Cove or Angels Landing. It was nowhere on Cavanaugh Island. Home was Little Rock. She was going to forfeit her birthright. He walked into the room, and she didn't know how, but she'd managed to hide her love for him behind a façade of indifference. The strain of possibly losing his grandmother was apparent by the lines bracketing his firm mouth.

"How is she?"

"They're going to keep her for a couple of days."

Kara couldn't stem the tears filling her eyes. "She's in this hospital because of me."

"Stop it, Kara! I'm not going to let you blame yourself for something you couldn't control."

"But I could control it, Jeff. If I'd packed up and left the first time someone threw a brick through the window, your grandmother wouldn't be lying in a hospital fighting for her life."

"Gram is not fighting for her life. She has a little trouble breathing, so they have her on oxygen."

"Don't, Jeff."

"Don't what?"

"Don't try to minimize what happened. What if I hadn't been there when that smoke bomb came through the window? What if I'd gone for a walk instead of sitting on the porch? Your grandmother would've died, Jeff, because I'm too stiff-necked to accept the truth. Eden is right. I'm an outsider, and the people on the island will never accept me. And the fact that I'm Taylor's daughter is of no consequence to anyone. At least not to the Pattons."

Jeff moved closer. "I told you I would protect you."

"I know. But the truth is you can't. No one can." Kara couldn't stop her chin from trembling. "I'm trouble, Jeff. I've been trouble since the moment I discovered I was Taylor's daughter. It's like there's a bull's-eye on my back that says hit her with a brick. What's next? A bottle filled with gasoline and a lighted rag? I may be some crazy's target, but how many others will become collateral damage if they were to come after me again? I'm going to call David and let him know that I'm giving up the house and the two thousand acres. After that, I'm calling my mother and father to tell them I'm coming home."

A shudder shook Jeff as he met her eyes. "You can't leave."

"Why not?"

A beat passed. "Because I love you."

Kara couldn't stop the sob that began in her throat. "And I love you, Jeff. I love you so much my heart hurts. But our love isn't enough to protect those we love."

Bending slightly, Jeff scooped her off the gurney. "I didn't visit hell, not once but twice, while losing my soul when I did unspeakable acts all in the name of war, to let you walk away from me, Kara Newell."

"You can't stop me from leaving."

"Yes, I can. I'll lock you up and keep you in jail until I find out who's trying to run you out of town."

"You can't."

He gave her a lethal stare. "Do you want to test me? I thought not," he said when she didn't answer. "I'm going to hire someone to watch Angels Landing around the clock. Wherever you go, they go. Think of yourself as the first lady with a secret service detail."

"That's not funny," she countered.

"No, it's not. Now, we're going home where I'll pick up a change of clothes. I'm going to drop you off at the station house where you'll stay until I return. Then we're going to Angels Landing to stay in your guesthouse for the night. You will come with me tomorrow to bring my grandmother home before your house arrest begins."

"You're really going to lock me up?"

"You can stay in our break room. It's where we bed down while on duty."

"Will I be allowed one phone call to my lawyer?" she teased.

"You can call anyone you want."

Kara laid her head on Jeff's shoulder. *Why now?* she asked herself. Why did he wait until she was ready to walk out of his life to admit that he loved her? He'd promised to protect her from a phantom who struck without warning, not caring who stood in their way.

"Can I see Miss Corrine before we leave?"

"She's resting."

"What about Oliver?"

"I called my clerk and told her to take him to the vet. I'll stop by and check on him, too."

I can't believe I'm doing a bid. Kara tried to find a comfortable position as she lay on a cot with a too thin mattress in a room that looked directly into a cell. She may not have been behind bars, but she definitely was spending time in a police station. She and Jeff had returned to the Cove where she changed clothes and packed an overnight bag with enough clothes for two days.

Kenny peered at her through the half-open door. "Do you need anything, Kara?"

"No, thank you. I'm good here."

"I'll have you know the boss told me to change the linen."

"Thank you, Deputy Collins."

"Please call me Kenny."

"Okay, Kenny."

"You can turn on the TV if you want."

Kara just wanted to tell the deputy to go away and leave her alone so she could think. She'd called David, but his secretary told her he was out of the office and wouldn't return until the following day. She left a message for him to call her.

Everyone on the island was chatting about the incident at Corrine's house. There was talk that if and when they found the person, he or she would beg the police to get them before they meted out their own form of Cavanaugh Island justice.

Turning on her side, she closed her eyes and miraculously fell asleep.

Jeff walked into the Angels Landing town hall, heading for the mayor's office. He knocked on the open door, garnering Harlan's assistant's attention. "Good afternoon, Erin. Is Harlan in?" There was something about Erin that reminded him of Kara's friend Dawn.

"He is, but he's in a meeting with someone very important."

Bracing both hands on her desk, Jeff leaned closer. "Who is he?"

Her round blue eyes looked like marbles. "I can't tell you his name."

"Why not?"

"Because Harlan told me I was never to mention his name in or out of the office."

"Do you have his business card?"

She smiled. "Yes." Opening her desk drawer, Erin took out a card and slid it across her desk.

"Bingo." The man with Harlan was from the same company who'd sent Porter to soften up Kara. "Don't bother to announce me."

"Wait, Jeff. You don't have to go in to hear what they're saying." She handed him a tiny earpiece, then flipped a switch on a box in a drawer in her desk. "Sit over there and pretend you're waiting."

"Why are you doing this?" he asked.

"Because I hate the greedy bastard. If Harlan knew that I listen in on his meetings with these vultures, not only would he fire me, but he would also have me arrested."

Jeff winked at her. "I promise not to out you." He placed the listening device in his right ear, then sat on a wooden bench.

He recognized Harlan's voice immediately: "You can't come in here and threaten me."

"And why not, Mayor Patton? You told me the girl wouldn't stay. Not only is she staying, but she's turning the house into a museum."

"The house, Scott. The house isn't two thousand acres."

"Take your head out of your ass, Patton. If the house becomes a museum, what do you think is going to happen with the rest of the property? It will become a mini-Williamsburg. I want you to put more pressure on her."

"Eden tried talking to her."

"I'm not talking about lip service, Patton. I'm talking about action. I had my people send her a message by throwing a brick through her window, but apparently it didn't work. I'm certain this morning's brick with the pepper grenade got her attention. There won't be any more bricks. The next time there will be a bullet with her name on it."

"You're nothing but a piece of shit if you think I'm going to be a party to murdering my cousin or hurting anyone else on this island. We protect our people, not take them out. And the other woman in that house just happened to be the sheriff's grandmother. What do you think is going to happen when he finds out you were behind the latest bully scheme?"

"I'm not concerned about *your* sheriff. Let's get back to Miss Newell. I thought she wasn't your cousin."

"Of course, she's my cousin. We asked for the DNA test and said we were going to contest the will to intimidate her."

"Well, apparently intimidation doesn't work with your *cousin* because she's still here. And that means we now are going to do things my way."

"You're not going to hurt her, Scott."

"You're right. What we're going to do is eliminate her. I know people who can make her disappear just like Jimmy Hoffa."

"Get the hell out of here before I call the sheriff."

"Call him. She's still gone."

Jeff had heard enough. He stood up, walked past Erin, and pushed open the door to Harlan's office. "What's this I hear that you were looking for me, Harlan?" Both men stared at him as if they'd seen a ghost. "Scott Pierce," he crooned. "May I call you, Scott?"

The slightly built, deeply tanned man in what appeared to be a three thousand dollar suit and imported footwear, perfectly barbered black hair, and equally black eyes glared at him. "I'm sorry, but I don't know you."

"And you really don't want to know me, Mr. Pierce. I just happen to be the sheriff of this beautiful island you're looking to turn into your own personal playground. And the woman you plan to make disappear is someone I love very much." He rested his right hand on the butt of his gun. "How are we going to do this? The easy way or the hard way?"

"You can't arrest me."

"And why not?"

"You can't prove anything. Patton and I were discussing business."

"Business that included you threatening my cousin," Harlan said. He opened a desk drawer and pushed a button.

Jeff watched the natural color drain from the man's face

when he heard his words played back on the tape. "You can't tape me without my permission."

Harlan smiled. "That's where you're wrong. Legally I can tape every meeting in my office. Jeff, please get this garbage out of here."

Jeff took a pair of handcuffs off his gun belt, stood behind the dapper developer, and cuffed his wrists. "Scott Pierce, you're under arrest for conspiracy to commit murder. You have the right to remain silent. Anything you say or do can and will be held against you in a court of law. You have the right to speak to an attorney. If you cannot afford an attorney, one will be appointed for you. Do you understand these rights?" He turned to Harlan. "Please call Charleston PD and tell them to have a bus waiting at the causeway."

"It'll be my pleasure. I'm sorry I ever got involved with this pond scum, but I hope to make up for it when I get to testify against him in court." He offered Jeff his hand. "Thank you. And please let Kara know how sorry we are for the way we treated her. As you know, we can be a lethal bunch when we feel threatened. To make up for our behavior, I'd like to arrange a get-together so we can give her a proper welcome and apology."

Kara lay in bed with Jeff, her leg resting over his. The room was pitch-black. A thunderstorm had temporarily knocked out the power on the island. When she couldn't find any candles in the guesthouse, they'd decided to go to bed early.

"How long do you think we'll be in the dark?"

"It all depends."

"On what, Jeff?"

"If it's a blown transformer or if a line is down. The

one thing I know is there will be zero crime on the island tonight."

She laughed. "Cavanaugh Island is dark enough without a blackout."

Jeff shifted on his side, pulling Kara to his chest. "Thankfully it doesn't happen too often. After the last one most folks bought generators."

"What time are we leaving tomorrow to pick up your grandmother?"

"Any time after ten. We'll pick her up, then go to Haven Creek to get Oliver; then we're going home."

"Miss Corrine and her baby both had overnight stays in the hospital."

Jeff chuckled. "You know the first one she asked about was Oliver. I told her he was at an animal hospital in the Creek, and the vet wanted to keep him overnight for observation."

"Do you think I'll ever get my dog back?" Kara asked with a smile.

"That's something you're going to have to take up with Gram."

A beat passed. "I still can't believe Harlan knew who was behind the threats against me."

"He didn't know until this morning, Kara. Your cousin felt he could intimidate you by forcing you to take the DNA test and by contesting Taylor's will, but he had no idea Scott was resorting to violence."

"Did you suspect Harlan was behind the brick throwing?"

"I wasn't certain whether he was behind it, but I suspected he knew something. Instinct told me the Pattons were involved in some way because of Eden's visits."

"What about Porter?"

"I gave the DA his name, and he says he's going to subpoena Mr. Caldwell as a witness for the prosecution."

Kara didn't want to believe it was over, that she didn't have to leave the people she'd come to love. "Will I be called in to testify?"

"If the DA can convince Pierce to accept a plea, then you won't. It would be in his best interest to accept it because legally you could sue him and his company, and I don't think he'd want that."

"If he does take the plea, what will he get? A suspended sentence? Probation?"

"I don't know, baby. I'm not an attorney."

"But Eden is," Kara countered.

"What is it you want?"

"I want restitution. If Pierce accepts a plea, then I want Eden to sue the hell out of him and his company. I want them barred from doing business in South Carolina, and I want whatever money we get to go to charities dedicated to advocating for women and their children. And don't you dare say it, Jeff. Yes, I'm still a social worker. Now that I've decided to stay I'm going to apply for a part-time social work position with either the public schools or a municipal hospital."

"What other plans have you made, baby?"

"That's it," she said.

"What about us?"

She smiled. "What about us, Jeff?"

"How long do you think we're going to shack up together without getting married?"

Kara tried turning over, but Jeff's arm wouldn't permit her to move. "You were the one who invited me to live with you and your grandmother."

"That was before you were in jeopardy and before Gram

needed someone to keep her company. We've uncovered who was behind the threat to force you to leave, and Gram has bonded with Oliver, so there's no need for us to live together."

"Your grandmother can't take my dog!"

"You can fight with Corrine Hamilton if you want, but you'll wind up on the losing end." They both shared a laugh before Jeff cupped Kara's chin in his hands. "I love you, Kara, and I don't know how else to say it."

"Say what?"

"Marry me."

Kara felt her heart beating through her chest. Jeff had just uttered the two words that lay in her heart when she'd been too much of a coward to acknowledge that was what she'd wanted from the first time they'd slept together. She'd fallen in love with Jeff. He was someone who made her feel safe, someone she could envision growing old with. She knew living with him was fodder for gossip, and as sheriff his morality would be called into question when it was time for his reelection.

"I marry you and what happens after that?"

"That would depend on you, Kara. I want children, but if you don't, then I'll accept your decision. I want to spend the rest of my life here, but if you don't, then I'll follow you wherever you decide to go. And if I was still in the corps and you didn't want to become a military wife, I would resign my commission. I love you that much."

Tears of happiness pricked the backs of her eyelids. A man who'd told his cousin that he should've let his girlfriend love him more than he loved her had just flipped the script. Kara loved Jeff, and she suspected he loved her more. "Love is not about giving up what you want for the other person. It's about sharing what you have. I want to marry you and give you a baby, lots of babies before I get too old, and I want to spend the rest of my life on Cavanaugh Island. And when I die, I want to be buried in the cemetery with the Pattons who came before me. I'm home, Jeffrey Hamilton, because you've become my home."

Jeff moved over Kara, supporting his greater weight on his forearms. "You have just made me the happiest man in the entire world."

"Kiss me, babe. Kiss me and make love to me so I know this is real."

He nuzzled her neck. "I can kiss you, but I can't make love to you because I didn't bring protection with me."

Kara's fingertips trailed up and down Jeff's back. "I thought we'd get a jump on starting a family."

"I guess you don't want to have a long engagement."

"Of course not. I've always wanted to be a June bride, and that means we'll have to plan something quickly."

"Your father and my buddies are getting together over the Memorial Day weekend. We can use the occasion to get married and have a blowout of a reception on the beach."

"I love the idea of having a beachfront ceremony, but I'd like to hold the reception here at Angels Landing. A caterer can set up tents and tables, and we can invite the entire island to attend."

Jeff caressed the length of her leg and thigh. "Do you plan to invite the Pattons?"

"Of course. If they choose not to come, then it's okay. But if they do, then I'll know they're serious about extending the olive branch."

"You are a lot more forgiving than I would be."

"The animosity has to stop somewhere, darling. I was

raised by two people who loved me and were never shy about letting me know. We're not perfect, but I didn't grow up fighting with my relatives. It wasn't about who had more than the other or a parent favoring one child over the other. I may look like Theodora, but I hope and pray I'll never be like her."

"You won't, baby."

Kara gasped softly when she felt Jeff's growing erection against her thigh. Her hand found him, caressing the hardening flesh until it pulsed against her palm. She opened her legs, sighing when Jeff eased inside her.

She'd asked him to love her and he did. It was the slowest, sweetest love she'd ever experienced. Minutes before she fell asleep Kara thanked Taylor for doing in death what he hadn't been able to do in life—reuniting his family.

Chapter Twenty

Jeannette walked into the bedroom at the Hamilton residence and stopped when she saw her daughter in her wedding finery. "Oh, Kara, you look so beautiful. Does Jeff know how lucky he is?"

Kara nodded. "I think he knows, and I know how lucky I am to have fallen in love with him. Have you seen him, Mama?"

"I have. He looks so handsome in his dress uniform."

She and Jeff had discussed whether or not he would wear his dress uniform, and they'd decided he would for the ceremony, then change into a suit for the reception. She'd sent invitations to the Pattons, and much to her surprise they'd all accepted. As promised, Dawn was her maid of honor, and she'd come down the week before to select her dress from a local bridal boutique.

Kara had selected a stark white, strapless ballgown with a hand-sewn pearl-beaded bodice of matte satin and a tulle skirt. Dawn floated into the room in a cornflower-blue halter A-line gown that was an exact match for her eyes. Her headpiece was a coronet of fresh violets and tiny rose petals that made her look like a fairy-tale wood sprite.

"Oh, my!" she gasped. "You are truly a princess, Miss Kay."

Holding out the skirt to her gown, Kara inclined her head. The stylist at the Beauty Box had rolled her hair on narrow rods, turning her straight tresses into tiny ringlets that framed her face. In lieu of a veil, she'd opted for miniature roses and jeweled hairpins.

"Thank you. I'm so nervous my knees are shaking."

Dawn took her hand. "I saw the groom, and he looks good enough to eat. And his best man isn't too shabby, either. They were getting into the car to drive to the beach."

Kara had noticed that the man Jeff had selected to be his best man was also a retired marine captain who'd appeared totally enthralled with her ex-roommate. Never one to act as matchmaker, Kara hoped the two would become more than friends.

She picked up her all-white bouquet of roses, gardenia, and lily of the valley. "I'm ready."

Jeannette pressed her cheek to her daughter's. "Your father is waiting downstairs in the limo with Corrine."

Kara lifted the skirt of her gown as she walked down the staircase in the house that was to become her permanent home. She and Jeff had decided to live in the house where he'd been raised, and they would use the guesthouse at Angels Landing as their private getaway whenever he was off duty. Corrine and Oliver had become inseparable, and Kara had come to regard him as Gram's dog.

The permanent residents of Cavanaugh Island had

warmed to the idea that when restored, Angels Landing would be listed on the Lowcountry and Gullah tours because it would mean more tourists and additional revenue for the businesses on the island.

She and Jeff had delayed having a honeymoon until late fall. He'd wanted to wait until after the local elections were over because the Cove's incumbent mayor was being challenged by the first female mayoralty candidate in the island's history. Alice Parker, wife of US Representative Jason Parker, had announced that she wanted the town council to pass a law that would limit developers wishing to do business in Sanctuary Cove. Scott had posted bail, surrendered his passport, and was scheduled to return to court at the end of the summer, so Kara had the entire summer to concentrate on being a wife to a man she loved unconditionally.

They'd decided on a late-morning wedding before the temperatures made it prohibitive to remain on the beach for an appreciable amount of time. Austin stepped out of the limo to help his daughter into the vehicle. He repeated the action with his wife and Dawn before sliding in beside Corrine. Kara thought she saw tears in her father's eyes before he averted his head. He'd admitted he had gained too much weight to fit into his uniform and had purchased a tailored suit for the occasion.

Kara tightened her hold on her bouquet when she exited the limo and placed her hand on her father's arm when he led her along the path to the beach. She would never forget the expression on her groom's face when he saw her for the first time in her wedding finery. She saw the blood stripe on the leg of his dress blues and the Mameluke sword carried by all Marine Corps officers in the gloved hand of his best man.

"Daddy!" she whispered as her knees buckled slightly.

Austin caught her elbow, holding her until she regained her balance. "It's all right, baby girl. Take your time. If Jeffrey waited this long to marry, he'll wait a few more minutes for you to pull yourself together."

A string quartet played softly as she struggled to regain her composure. She nodded, smiling. "I'm ready, Daddy."

She smiled at those sitting on chairs under a large tent that had been erected for the ceremony. She recognized Dr. and Mrs. Monroe and their children, some of the women who quilted with Corrine, and when she glanced to her left, she recognized the faces of those she'd encountered when she walked into the law office for the reading of a will that forever changed her life. She smiled at Morgan, who sat on the side of the groom's family and friends with David. Turning her head, she nodded to Willie and Iris Todd.

Her smile was as dazzling as the sun when her father placed her hand on the outstretched one of the man who would become her husband. She met Jeff's gaze under the shiny bill of his cap. She lowered her eyes demurely when he mouthed the word *beautiful*.

Malcolm Crawford, the pastor of the Cove's interdenominational church, had been selected to officiate because it was where Jeff had been baptized and attended services as a child. It was the church where they planned to baptize and send their children.

They repeated their vows, and when Jeff slipped his grandmother's wedding ring on her finger, Kara knew it was for keeps. She was now Mrs. Jeffrey Malachi Hamilton. When the minister told Jeff he could now kiss his wife, she looped her arms around his neck and pressed her mouth to his.

"I love you, Gullah man," she whispered in his ear.

"Not as much as I love you my beautiful Gullah woman."

They were showered with rice, birdseed, and flower petals as they followed the procession to the beach to where they would pose for pictures before returning to Angels Landing for a reception that was rumored not to end until after sundown.

Kara had spared no expense when she hired three caterers to have enough food on hand for more than two thousand people. It would be the first time the entire island would come together en masse to celebrate a single event.

She kissed Corrine's gardenia-scented cheek. "Now that I'm married to your grandson do you think I can now call you Gram instead of Miss Corrine?"

Corrine touched her cheek in a loving gesture. "Of course. I've always wanted a granddaughter. But I didn't think I would get one as perfect as you."

Kara hugged her grandmother as she exchanged a loving smile with her new husband. Eden approached her, arm extended. "You look beautiful, Kara. I know my uncle is smiling down on you today."

Returning the hug, Kara looked at her cousin. "We have to get together one of these days."

Virgie joined them. "Let her get used to sleeping with her gorgeous husband before talking about getting together."

Kara smiled at her cousins. "That's something I don't ever want to get used to." The three women exchanged high-five handshakes, then dissolved into laughter.

Those standing around watching exchanged knowing looks. It had been Theodora who'd torn her family apart and her granddaughter who would bring them together again. Good things were happening for the folks in Cavanaugh Island, and those who lived there were looking for better days ahead.

About the Author

Bestselling author Rochelle Alers has nearly two million copies of her novels in print. She is also the recipient of numerous awards, including the Gold Pen Award, the Emma Award, the Vivian Stephens Award for Excellence in Romance Writing, the Romantic Times Career Achievement Award and the Zora Neale Hurston Literary Award.

Learn more at:
  RochelleAlers.org
  Twitter @RochelleAlers